SANT...

Spur watched. Now it was a waiting game. The rawhider would use what chips he had: the biggest was the boy's life. There would be no quick killing and then a shootout with the outlaw. He would hold the boy as his best chance for escape. Spur had to make sure he kept thinking that way.

"You out there," the heavy voice came from the wagon. "It's the same standoff as before. I have the boy, and I'm leaving with him. You bother us, and he dies."

"Fine with me," Spur called back. "The boy means nothing to me. You're in my jurisdiction now. Sheriff don't hold me down none. All I want is the posted reward on your dead carcass. Hell, I figured the kid would be dead by now and you'd want to shoot it out man to man. But I guess that's not your style."

Five more shots came toward Spur's location, but he had dropped behind the pine log just in time. Now he put a rifle round through the canvas, well over either of the occupants' heads.

"Not much protection in there against hot lead, Schmidke. I might as well use my dynamite and blow you both to hell."

LOUISIANA LASS

"Ma'am, a man and a woman just slipped in here. They're dangerous criminals and it's my job to catch them. Did you see them?"

She shook her head. "Out! Out of my shop or I'll call the sheriff. He knows what to do with men who burst into women's dressing rooms!"

"But, ma'am, I'm—"

The full-bodied shopkeeper grabbed a feather duster and pushed it into Spur's face, making him sputter and gag. "Get yer hide out of my store!" she yelled.

Spur sensed rather than heard movement behind him. A heavy object crashed onto his skull before he could whirl to face the danger. He momentarily blacked out, but quickly returned to a hazy consciousness as his cheek hit the slick floorboards.

"Kill him and let's get out of here!" It was a younger, softer woman's voice....

SPUR

SANTA FE FLOOZY
LOUISIANA LASS

Dirk Fletcher

LEISURE BOOKS **NEW YORK CITY**

A LEISURE BOOK®

August 1995

Published by

Dorchester Publishing Co., Inc.
276 Fifth Avenue
New York, NY 10001

Printed in the United States of America.

SPUR

SANTA FE FLOOZY

CHAPTER ONE

(The year was 1874. General Ulysses S. Grant was in his seventh year as President. A U.S. baseball team traveled to England for an exhibition game. Goal posts were used in football for the first time that year at Cambridge, Massachusetts. The Greenback political party was organized. The first recorded kidnapping for ransom was staged in Germantown, Pa. King David Kalakaua of Hawaii was the first reigning king to visit the U.S. Barbed wire, the development that would spell the eventual end to the wild west, was invented that year by J. F. Glidden in De Kalb, Illinois. The Cathedral of San Francisco de Assisi was over half completed in Sante Fe, New Mexico in 1874. Work began on it in 1869. Hamilton Fish continued as Secretary of State in the Grant administration.)

Spur McCoy lifted the Colt .45 and cocked the six-gun with his right thumb, then edged up to

5

the corner of the adobe block building on a side street in Santa Fe, New Mexico. Sweat furrowed down through dust on his forehead as he tensed against the bricks. With a sudden lunge, he charged around the corner.

Two shots blasted hot lead on him, but already Spur had dived forward into the dust, his .45 spitting flame as fast as he could pull the trigger.

The two men in the alley stared at McCoy for a second, then the first looked at the black hole in his leather vest and brought his hand up to touch his shirt that had blossomed with a red rose before he groaned and slid sideways into the alley. His nose plowed a line through the dust, the soft dirt building up a pile of dirt against his forehead, covering his eyes as the outlaw died.

The second man had no time to wonder. The .45 slug burrowed a straight hole through a rib, then his chest and his heart. It killed him instantly and he slammed backwards from the force of the big .45 lead messenger of death.

Spur McCoy nodded and sat up, then felt a stinging in his left arm. He looked down to find the upper sleeve of his light blue dress shirt stained red with his own blood.

"Damn!" he muttered.

Three men ran into the alley and stared at the dead outlaws. One of them ran back to Main Street.

"He done killed them bank robbers!" the young man screeched. "He gunned 'em down in the alley!"

Spur knew the sheriff would come, asking questions. And he would show them his credentials and fill out the necessary papers. But before that he wanted to look at his arm.

Spur holstered the .45 and grabbed his left upper arm with his right hand and winced. Annabelle Dare would look after it for him. She was better than a sawbones any day, and a damn sight prettier. He stood and walked back to Main Street. Half a dozen men hurried past him to look at the dead men. Two women chattered as they tied on sunbonnets and scurried toward the alley.

McCoy was tired. He had been chasing the two bank robbers for almost two weeks, all of it on horseback in the high desert. Now he wanted a hot bath and a bed, and he knew Annabelle could supply all three, including Annabelle herself in the bed. He tried to grin but he was too tired.

Annabelle stood on the porch of the Santa Fe Carriage House looking his way. When she saw him she lifted her long skirts and hurried down the steps to the dusty street. She met him halfway across the avenue which was an inch deep with powdered dust from the continual grinding of steel wagon wheel rims and horses' hooves.

She had never looked prettier. He swore she was no more than five feet tall, with a pile of blonde hair on top of her head to make her look taller. Her face was round and pixie-like, with darting brown eyes, high pink cheeks and a cupid's bow mouth. Now her pretty face wore a

7

frown.

"The idea, Spur McCoy, is to shoot the bad guys without letting them hit you. Gracious! You gone and got yourself wounded again. Don't you ever listen to what I tell you? Menfolk will be the death of me yet. Inside! Inside with you and let me get out my alcohol and scissors and bandages. I swear, Spur McCoy, I just don't know what I'm going to do with you!"

She was beside him then, holding his right arm, and "helping" him forward despite the fact that he was two inches over six feet tall and weighed twice her own ninety-eight pounds.

Spur laughed softly. "I bet you'll think of something to do with me," he said softly so only she could hear. He saw a trace of a blush color her neck and then she lifted her head and turned toward him.

"Yes, of course I can tie up a gunshot wound. I *am* a frontier woman, after all." She said it for the benefit of two ladies walking by. Both were of Mexican ancestry, and were leaders in the Spanish speaking section of town.

Quickly they went up the steps, through the lobby and into the door marked "Manager." As soon as the door closed behind them, Annabelle threw her arms around his neck and pulled his face down so she could kiss him.

When the kiss ended she sighed.

"Damnit, McCoy! You've been in town for two days, and haven't even stopped by to say hello."

"Hello, Annabelle Dare," Spur said and kissed her. He felt her press her delicious body against him and he moaned. "Hey, we have lots of time. First the arm?"

She kissed him again, then kissed his arm.

"Mommie kissed it and made it better."

"Mommie can do even better, though, can't she?"

Annabelle grinned and rolled up his sleeve, but the fabric was too tight.

"Awwwww. Have to take off your shirt," she said.

He unbuttoned the blue shirt and stripped it off. She admired his muscle-sculptured upper body for a moment, then looked at his arm.

"At least the round went on through." She was all business then, filling a pan with water and using a cloth and lye soap. She washed the blood off his arm and from around the wound. It had started to clot. She took a clean square of cloth and pushed it over the back of the wound which was the larger hole.

"Hold that there while I get some whiskey."

"Terrible waste of good booze."

"Hush up. The sheriff will be here soon." She brought a bottle of whiskey from the cabinet and uncorked it, then sloshed some across both wounds.

"Eeeeeeeeha!" Spur whooped as the alcohol hit raw nerve endings.

"Yeah, if it hurts, it works. Doctors finally found out what we were doing with the whiskey. Now they tell us the alcohol in the whiskey does something good for the wound. We been telling the sawbones that for years."

She poured more whiskey into the wounds, then used a clean roll of bandage made from a bed sheet and wrapped up Spur's arm so the clean compresses she had put on both sides of the wound would stay in place. When she came to the end of the bandage she tore the strip down the middle, put one end each way around his arm and tied the ends together with a hard knot.

"You should be a nurse," Spur said.

"I am. Now, the sheriff first, or a bath first?"

"The sheriff, and that bottle of rotgut." He took the whiskey bottle and tipped it up, gulped down a couple of swallows and lowered the firewater. He drank two more shots of the whiskey, put the cork back in and set the bottle on the desk.

"Now, let's go find the sheriff."

The lawman was coming into the hotel when they walked out of the office. It took only a few minutes. The other men had fired first, according to witnesses, so it was self defense. Period, end of report.

Spur relaxed. He would not have to prove who he was. Lately he had found things worked out much better for him if no one knew his official capacity until they had to. It made his job easier all the way around. Now he shook hands with the sheriff, and followed a small Mexican boy who said Spur's bath was ready.

When Spur got to the bathroom at the end of the hall on the second floor, he found a steaming tub of water. It was one of the new long tubs you could sit down in and stretch out your legs.

Beside it were two pails filled with cold water. On a chair were two large, fluffy towels, a bar of lye soap, and on another chair, his saddle bags and the carpet bag from his mount.

Spur dug into his pocket, found a liberty seated quarter and tossed it to the boy. The young Mexican-American's eyes widened.

"Gracias, senor!" he said and hurried out. It was probably more hard money than he had seen in weeks. A grown man worked all day to earn a dollar these days.

McCoy locked the door after the boy left and stripped, then he heard a noise behind him. A door at the far side of the small bathroom opened and Annabelle stepped in. She wore a white robe and carried a bath brush.

"I heard, sir, that you wanted someone to scrub your back," she said and smiled.

Spur stood there naked yet totally at ease, and stared at her. "Only if you'll have a bath with me," he said.

She let the robe fall open and then pushed it off her shoulders so it slid to the floor. She was all white and pink naked flesh under it and a swatch of soft blonde crotch hair.

"I *love* to take baths. And if you hadn't asked me, I was going to volunteer." She walked toward him, swaying her hips, her small round pink-tipped breasts thrust forward, bouncing and jiggling with her movements.

Spur caught her shoulders, then bent and kissed each blooming breast, making her suck in a breath of surprise and appreciation.

"How long has it been, beautiful-man Spur?"

11

"I was here about a year ago."

"And then I was in St. Louis and missed you at Christmas."

"We'll make this our Christmas," Spur said and kissed her lips gently. Her mouth was open and her tongue darting at his closed lips until he opened them. He pushed her away a minute later and tested the water.

Boiling. He added a bucket of the cold water. Still too hot. After the second bucket of cold water he stepped in, and held out his hand to her.

"I remember we got into all sorts of contortions the last time we tried this," she said.

"First, we wash off my two week's worth of trail grime, then we think about weird positions."

She nodded, grabbed the soap, brush and a washcloth, sat down in the water and began washing his back. He told her what he had been doing since he had seen her, and she said not much had been happening in Santa Fe until now.

When the washing was over, she turned and leaned her back against his chest and drew his hands in front of her to hold her breasts.

"That's nice," she said.

He petted her breasts and kissed her neck. "It gets better."

"I've heard it can't be done underwater."

"Have you tried?" he asked.

"No."

"How about now?"

"Anything," she said.

12

Spur had her move forward, then he soaped his erect phallus thoroughly and, staying out of the water, eased her back to him. Still facing her away, he lowered her slowly and his sabre slid easily into her ready scabbard.

"Oh, my God!" Annabelle yelped. "You did it!"

Spur eased back into the water and they both giggled. A minute later they had sloshed a bucketful of water out of the tub.

"So that's why they say you can't do it in the tub!" Annabelle said. She eased away from his hard shaft, then stood and stepped from the tub, holding out a towel. Spur dried her, taking pains that her breasts and crotch received special attention. She motioned him into the next room and he found it to be a second bedroom joined to her suite below by a spiral staircase. The bed was the largest he had ever seen.

Annabelle turned back, put her arms around him and held Spur tightly.

"Hold me close," she whispered. His arms came around her and she pushed against him.

"Spur McCoy, I'm feeling shy. I . . . I don't want you to think I'm a loose woman. I mean, I don't jump into bed with every man I see. You're a special person, do you know that? I tried to trick you into marrying me once, remember? The trick almost worked, but you said no. I know you're not going to marry me, but I can still dream. And now, right now, Spur, I want to dream again. I want to pretend that this is my wedding night. Would you let me do that?

13

The ceremony is all over and we're home and you have just undressed me and now I hope that I can please you so you'll take me to bed."

He could feel the heat of her loins soaking into him. Her breath was hot on his chest as he tilted her head to kiss her. Annabelle's breasts were twin cones of fire burning into his chest.

Their lips met.

Never had he felt lips so alive, so burning with anticipation and desire. He kissed her again, then nibbled at her lips as she moaned in joyful expectation. He felt her hips pressing against him. Then they began a soft movement that soon turned into a slow grinding against him. She parted her legs and moved slightly so his leg came between hers, and the soft hair caressed him. Then he felt the thatch parting and a soft wetness pressing hard on his leg. One of her hands slid between them and grasped his turgid shaft.

She moaned again, and chewed at his lips, then moved her mouth lower and licked his nipples. Her breath came quickly now and her eyes closed as she sucked.

Spur bent and picked her up. He reached down and kissed both her breasts and she climaxed in his arms. Her small body shook, jolted, and trembled and she gasped for breath as the spasms rolled through her again and again.

He lay her on the bed and she caught his shoulders and pulled him down on top of her. Again the tremors flashed through her and he saw that her legs were spread and her pubis thrusting upward against his legs.

"Now, darling! Now, please now! Come inside me and make the whole world perfect!"

A moment later they had joined and her arms were around him, her legs locked over his back and she purred throatily like a tigress as tears slid down her cheeks.

"I always cry when I'm the most happy," she said, then closed her eyes and thrust against him as Spur lay there suspended over her, barely touching her small form.

"Lie down on me hard, with all your weight," Annabelle said. "It feels good when you're crushing me."

Slowly they both built to a gentle, soft kind of lovemaking that Spur found most rewarding. It built and built until she gave a soft cry and her whole body spasmed under him, triggering his own response and they both cried out softly and moaned and panted for breath as the physical release came and he settled down gently against her again.

"Oh, yes!" she said, holding him tightly with her hands locked around his back. "I'm never going to let you get away from me again!"

Spur was still sucking in air from wherever he could find it to replenish his drained system. His breath came like a volcano for another two or three minutes before he could begin to think straight.

He eased most of his weight to one side on a pillow and she nodded a quick thanks.

It was ten minutes before either of them moved again, or said a word. Then she looked at him.

"I hope you won't be leaving, now that you caught the bank robbers."

"I'm a working man, Annabelle li'l darling. I go where the boss sends me."

"Uh-huh. But the boss doesn't have to know you're done. Don't you deserve a few days vacation? When did you have your last little bit of time off?"

"Don't remember."

"Then stay a few days. I can't promise it will always be as sweet as it was this time. Lordy! But you do get me wound up tight! I just want to stay in bed all day and all night with you!"

"It was great."

"Then stay a while."

"We'll see. Depends how good the cook is here at your hotel. I've been eating trail food for almost two weeks."

She pushed him to one side and sat up, her breasts bouncing. He captured one with his hand.

"Anything you want to eat tonight! You just name it and we'll kill the goose or go find the fish or hunt a pheasant! Anything you want! I mean it. Give me an order right now so I can go get our cook started!" Her eyes were flashing, darting brown beacons. Her face was so alive and vivacious he was amazed. She was a remarkable little lady.

"Ready? You have a pencil and paper? You won't be able to remember all of this." Spur waited until she had the paper, then he began reeling off exactly what he wanted to eat for supper.

CHAPTER TWO

THE MAN WHO called himself Zack White sent a stream of brown tobacco juice past the ponderosa pine he lay behind and stared more intently at a small ranch just below in the valley. He was only fifty yards from the cabin, but he saw no one moving. Zack rested easily, chewing on the wad in his mouth, and then spitting at insects that crawled on the high pine country forest floor. He had time. Nothing else to do but sit and wait. They would come out sooner or later.

It was an hour later, almost noontime, when the cabin door opened and a teenage girl walked out carrying a bucket. She took it to the well pump twenty yards from the house. The girl had pretty, ripe-wheat-straw blonde hair and good tits. Zack rubbed his fly and grinned.

"Keep yer damn shirt on, big stick," Zack said staring down at the bulge in his dirt-stiffened brown pants. Things were starting to move; it would happen soon.

A woman with the same color hair and not much over thirty came out and stared at the girl who hurried her pumping and lugged the heavy pail of water back to the cabin.

Ten minutes later a man rode into the clearing on a plow horse, dismounted and tied the heavy animal to a post. Then he pulled off his shirt and scrubbed his hands, face and torso at an outdoor washstand.

Zack put his hands to his mouth and made the call of a hoot owl. Hoot owls never out this time of day, and if they were, they wouldn't advertise it by calling. He gave the call a second time and with it came the sharp report of a rifle from across the clearing.

The rancher below spun around, a Spencer .56 caliber slug through his shoulder.

Zack pulled his six-gun and ran down the slope screaming at the top of his voice. He heard his two sons, Birch and Piney, screaming the same way. The boys got to the wounded man first and were about to put a knife into his throat when Zack stopped them.

"Boys, ain't I never done taught you no manners? Feller here ain't harmed us one little satchel full. I reckon his missus can patch up his shoulder. Fetch her and the girl, too."

Piney nodded and ran for the cabin door.

A shotgun boomed into the mountain stillness outside Santa Fe, and the three men dove behind any cover they could find. The two boys thundered pistol rounds into the one window, then Zack bent low and raced for the side of the cabin. The rancher packed no gun, Zack had made sure of that before he left. He slammed against the log wall and edged around so he could kick the door open. As he did, a blast of buckshot lanced out the opening.

When the thundering roar of the ten gauge scattergun faded, Zack listened intently.

A woman cried softly.

A younger voice whined in protest.

They didn't know how to load the shotgun. He risked a look around the doorframe, and saw both women at a table trying to open the double-barreled weapon.

Zack jumped through the door and, holding his pistol ready, walked toward the women.

The older one was pretty, softly blonde, not weathered and wrinkled yet by the tough, harsh pioneer life. She looked up with deep blue eyes that showed anger and fear.

"Please, don't hurt us!" she said.

"Now why would I hurt you folks?" Zack asked. "Just move away from the shotgun."

They did and he walked toward them. The girl was a beauty, maybe seventeen, better tits than he'd guessed. He stopped in front of the women and reached out. The older woman was shivering, but she held still when he touched her chin.

"Pretty lady," Zack said. He moved on to the girl. Her face turned when he tried to touch her chin. Angrily his hand caught the neckline of her calico dress and he jerked downward, hard. The seams held for a moment, pulling her head lower, then the threads broke and her dress and chemise ripped to her waist. Both breasts swung into view and Zack grinned.

"Nice tits, little filly. Knew you had good ones." His hand fondled them, and the girl turned her head away and burst into tears. The woman leaped at him, clawing at his face. Zack backhanded her with his closed fist. The blow caught her on the side of the face, scraped off skin and drove her to the hard packed earth floor.

"No reason to get hurt. Just do what we say, and don't go clawing us. Understand?"

The old woman nodded. The girl would not look at him.

A moment later he caught each woman by a hand and pulled them out the door. They stumbled after him, the girl trying to keep herself covered. Zack led them to the washstand and dropped their hands.

"My turn first, Paw, you promised!" It was the wheedling voice of his youngest, Piney. The young man's long fingers stroked the fly of his britches. He was shorter than his brother, and his shoulders were narrower, but he was the best man with horses Zack had ever seen.

"Well, hail, Piney. Why not? We get to watch. How about over there in that patch of shady grass under that golden cottonwood?"

Piney already had his pants open. He yelped in delight, sprang forward and grabbed the girl by both hands and tossed her over his shoulder. The girl screamed in terror.

"No! By God, no! Leave my little girl be!"

The roar of fury came from Willard Bukowski as he surged to a sitting position, holding his bleeding shoulder.

Zackery White sent a squirt of tobacco juice at Bukowski, then kicked him in the face with his heavy boot, dislocating his jaw, tearing his nose half off and gashing a three-inch wound in the thin flesh over his eye. Bukowski dropped to the ground and lay there.

"Asshole! You keep quiet or you're dead in five seconds. Savvy?" Zack's eyes narrowed, his face worked with sudden hatred.

Bukowski lay in the dust and weeds. His eyes couldn't focus yet, but he looked where the voice seemed to be coming from and nodded. Mrs. Bukowski whimpered as she saw the man wearing grease-stiffened, filthy clothes drop her daughter to the ground and kneel beside her.

"Sir! Have mercy on my daughter. She knows . . . she knows nothing about men."

"Shit! And her that big? Reckon she's gonna find out damn quick. You want to get closer to watch?"

Murial Bukowski turned away and stared at the house.

"Tie him," Zack said to Birch. Zack's oldest son was twenty-three, and his father figured he was slow witted. But Birch jumped to the task with rawhide strips he drew from his pocket. He tied Bukowski's hands behind his back, then reached for the man's ankles.

Bukowski slammed one boot into Birch's

stomach before the younger man fell on his legs and tied his ankles.

"Now look at that!" Zack said.

Piney had stripped down the girl's dress and was licking and sucking on her breasts. The girl was on her knees, her hands tied behind her back. She was not trying to get away.

Zack turned to the woman. "Your turn," he said.

She watched him. A long sigh came from her and her shoulders sagged.

"If . . . If I let you do . . . do what you . . . you want to do, then will you leave us alone and move on down the trail?"

"Fucking right! Won't hurt you none at all. Girl over there will be smarter, and you can patch up your gun-shot husband."

Zack reached for her breasts. She pulled back.

"Don't play games, bitch!"

"How . . . how do I know you'll keep your word?"

"Trust me."

Bukowski roared in protest where he lay near the washstand. Birch dumped the washpan full of water over his head and cackled with laughter.

Slowly the woman began to unbutton the front of her dress. Zack's rough hands pushed hers away and he ripped the front of the dress apart, popping buttons and tearing the fabric. A chemise covered her breasts.

"Soak some," Zack said to Birch. The oldest

son grinned and grabbed a bucket of water.

"Take the rest of them off," Zack said to the blonde woman.

The girl under the tree screamed. Zack saw Piney holding her down on her back. He lay between her spread, kicking, creamy white legs, as he jammed his hips at her crotch.

"Dear God, tell him to be gentle with Cynthia!" Mrs. Bukowski wailed.

"Him? You worry about me, cunt!" He tore the dress off her, then the chemise. Zack grinned at the size of her breasts, full and with heavy brown circles and thick, thumb-sized nipples already rising.

He pulled down her cotton petticoats and looked with delight at her lush V of blond crotch hair. Zack grabbed her by one breast and pulled her forward until they were four feet from her husband, then pushed her down on the dirt.

"Makes it better when your man over there can watch. Bet he's never seen anybody else fuck you."

Murial screamed and tried to crawl away. He hit her in the face and she screeched in pain, but fell on her back. He spread her legs and unbuttoned his fly, spit on his hand and coated his penis before he jammed it into her vagina hard and fast, searing the unlubricated flesh, bringing a howl of pain from both the woman and her husband.

"Bastard!" Willard Bukowski screamed. But then he could scream no more as Birch tied wet rawhide around his throat. It was tight enough so talking was uncomfortable. The sun gleamed down with noontime heat on the scene, and even as Bukowski thought about it, the wet rawhide began to dry and shrink back to its former size before it had been wet and stretched.

"Now, Paw?" Birch asked, a whine in his voice.

"Christ, go ahead."

Zack looked away. He had always known something was strange about his firstborn, but he had never expected this.

Birch used his sharp knife, cut the front of the pants off Bukowski until his genitals were exposed, then gently, lovingly, Birch began arousing the furious man who lay bound, and half throttled by the rawhide.

Zack was nearing his own satisfaction. He always liked women with big tits and a tight cunt. He gave one final series of long, hard thrusts and grunted with his climax, then rested on her soft body.

Birch was busy behind him. Zack usually never watched, but this time he turned just as the rancher's extended phallus vanished into Birch's mouth.

Under the golden cottonwood tree, Piney had finished the first time and was playing with the pretty girl's young, soft body. Zack could hear him talking to her, promising that he would be careful and gentle if she helped. Soon Piney was after her again.

Zack heard the horse coming and didn't look up. He knew the sound—it was Zelda's nag. The horse stopped and a scream of delight and madness greeted him as he looked up.

"Jesus, husband! Don't you know how to control your issue!"

Zelda slid down from the horse, pulled off the doeskin squaw dress she wore and ran to Bukowski. She backhanded Birch along the side of the head, spinning him away from the prostrate, excited man on the ground. Zelda looked at Bukowski a minute, then squatted over him, lifted his still turgid tool and lowered herself on it. As it slid into her vagina she squealed in delight and moved back and forth gently. She talked quietly to Bukowski all the time. A minute later she rested some of her weight on her hands and began riding his phallus like she was a jockey at a horse race. She grinned at Zack and every thirty seconds let out a scream of lustful satisfaction.

Zack looked back at the woman under him. Her face had been turned away. He was excited again. He came out of her and pushed upward until he sat on her cushiony breasts and thrust his erection at her mouth. Her eyes flared and she screamed at him.

Zack knew she never would take him in her mouth, and his big hands slapped her twice. Then his fingers closed around her throat and he lay on top of her again as his fingers tightened more and more. Her eyes were wide, then rolled upward until only the whites showed. They came back and she tried to scream but couldn't. Her fists beat on him but the force became less and less until at last her hands fell to her sides. He held tightly until the last shiver and twitch had left her body. Then he stood, buttoned up his pants and went into the house.

The fun was over. Now it was time to go to work. A family like this would have cash money hidden here somewhere, all he had to do was find it. Zack began by tearing the cupboard apart, then he systematically destroyed the inside of the house.

Outside under the tree, Piney talked soothingly to the girl. She told him her name was Cynthia.

"You liked it, didn't you, the fucking?"

Cynthia was still crying. She blinked. "Some of it was good, but it hurt so. Does it always hurt?"

"Next time will be better."

"I couldn't!"

"You can if I say so," Birch thundered, saying it just the way his pa would.

She let him play with her breasts. There was nothing else she could do. His knees held down her hands by her sides and he sat on her stomach. His . . . his . . . *thing* hung there limp and shrunken. It was ugly, horrible! She rose up a little and looked at the well where she saw her mother lying naked on the ground. Oh, no!

"I want to get up now," she said.

"Well, ain't that dandy. I want to fuck you again."

"No."

He slapped her hard.

"Woman, you do what I tell you to do!" For a moment he was furious. He wanted to hit her again and again. Then he took a breath and he got control again. His anger cooled, and he smiled. "You sure as hell are pretty, and you got beautiful, big tits. You want to come travel with us, be my woman?"

"No, I can't leave my parents."

"Hell, you'll change your mind."

"*No!*"

He reached for his pistol and put the muzzle in her mouth. "I say you come, little pussy, you come or I blow your brains out. You understand?"

Eyes wide, terror in complete control of her now, she nodded. He took the gun away.

"You want to come away with me? I'll be good to you. We got money, plenty to eat. Clothes even, you want. We get lots of clothes. You come with me?"

"Yes," she said softly.

Piney brightened. "Good, let's go tell Ma. You can do the cookin' and dishes and keep the fire. Ma will like that."

He stood and lifted her up.

"But I don't have on my clothes."

"Don't matter, Ma probably don't neither by now." He laughed and his voice went high and wild.

He took her hand, pushed his privates back in his pants and buttoned them, then led her toward the well.

They were twenty feet away when Piney looked up and saw Birch glaring at him. Birch pulled up his big handgun and fired three times. All three slugs hit Cynthia in the chest. She was dead before her body slammed backwards three feet to the ground.

Piney stared at his brother, then at Cynthia. He knew she was dead. He charged ahead, jammed into Birch and knocked him to the ground.

"Why the hell you do that? Why you kill her? She was coming with us!"

"Sure, and you get all the fun. Pa said no, last time. Right, Pa?"

Zack had just come out of the cabin. He knew what had happened the minute he heard the pistol shots. A look at the girl confirmed it.

"Done is done. Don't do no good to jawbone 'bout it now. We travel light, you done been told, Piney. Now, help me, you two. We got work to do. Piney, run fetch the wagon. Somebody might stop by. We got to move smart."

The three White men looted the Bukowski cabin of everything of any value that could be sold. As they worked, Zelda White sat beside Willard Bukowski. The sun was rapidly shrinking the rawhide now. It cinched tighter and tighter around his throat. Only a wheezing gasp could bring air into his lungs now.

Zelda sat in the dust, rocking gently back and forth as she watched the man beside her. She knew he was dying. It was simply part of the ritual. She was not going to let him die alone. She rocked and sang a little lullaby. She used a different one each time. The tune went on and Bukowski gasped and wheezed as his eyes pleaded with her to cut the thongs.

Zelda shook her head. He should know that

she couldn't do that. It wasn't fair, there were rules that had to be obeyed. Besides, Zack would slit her throat if she even tried to save one. He had been good, though, long and thick, best she could remember in the past six months. Zelda sighed. His hands were still behind him, but his arms were twitching, then his legs jerked and for a moment she thought he was dead.

A rasping, keening kind of sound came from deep in his throat, then his eyes stared at her without moving. She saw a jet of urine stain the pantsleg that had been cut away. She made the sign of the cross over him, stood and walked toward the house.

Zelda wondered if this lonely cabin would have anything that would sell in Santa Fe.

A half hour later the covered wagon was loaded with everything of value in the house. The two horses in the corral had been tied behind the wagon and the one cow had been slaughtered and half the carcass tied to the side of the wagon. They would eat well tonight and for two days until the meat spoiled.

Zack headed the wagon down the faint trail toward Santa Fe, still two days' drive away. He would meet with his two brothers before they came to the New Mexico Territorial capital. Zack wondered how his medicine man brother and the outlandish fake itinerant preacher were doing. It was a kind of contest, to see who could steal the most between the larger towns where they would arrange to meet, stay a few days and enjoy the fruits of their hard work.

Zack slapped the reins on the two sturdy mules. The blonde rancher woman had been good. Someday he would push Zelda over a cliff and claim himself a younger wife. Someday soon. He turned to look at Zelda who leaned on a pillow against the side of the wagon and slept. She was snoring and her mouth was open.

Zack nodded. Someday soon, bye, bye Zelda.

CHAPTER THREE

SPUR MCCOY LINKED Annabelle Dare's arm through his as they strolled down the boardwalk in Santa Fe's more "proper" district. That was the stretch from the Santa Fe Carriage House to the McGill Drygoods Emporium, a distance of more than fifty yards with some twelve to fourteen retail establishments involved. Along this respectable area of old Santa Fe, there was not a bawdy house, bar nor gambling den.

"Mr. McCoy, it's been a delightful evening. I especially enjoyed the roast quail and dove under glass, then the wine and now a walk in the twilight. How romantic!"

Spur held her arm tighter. He could learn to get used to talk like that, and a woman like this, and a town like Santa Fe. What was he thinking? Even if the "quail" and "dove" were chicken, it had been a delightful meal.

"Miss Dare." He stopped. She looked at him

out the corner of her eye and he began again.

"*Mrs.* Dare. Respected hotel owner and widow of the late and lameted Douglas Dare. It has been an honor and a privilege . . ." He stopped and they both broke up laughing.

She tugged at his arm and he felt a small lift as she pulled him firmly and intentionally against her breast.

"McCoy, you've simply got to stay for a week at least. There must be something else around here that needs to be checked out by a federal lawman . . . The post office! Yes, that's it! Our mail delivery is terrible. Do an investigation for me about the post office. That should take you at least a week!"

He held her arm tighter and angled across the street toward a medicine wagon that had lanterns out. Someone had let down the side of the wagon which formed a platform where the medicine hawker evidently gave his pitch. There were half a dozen men and women standing there waiting for the show to start.

"Now here is something I could investigate," Spur said.

Annabelle laughed. "Silly. You know these medicine shows are harmless. So they sell a little colored water mixed with fifty percent whiskey. Who knows, maybe it will cure everything from rheumatism to old age."

"Maybe it will," Spur said. "I've also heard of some of these guys who sell worthless railroad stock on the side, and seduce young girls under the guise of treating them. Why do you suppose they move around so much?"

"Get run out of town?"

"At least half of them. Most sheriffs watch the roving medicine man like he had the plague."

"Then you don't have to."

A trumpet fanfare blasted into the gathering dusk, and a man wearing a flowing black robe and a top hat pranced onto the small platform. To him it was a stage. He had a dramatic flair that caused Spur to frown.

"Ladies and gentlemen of Santa Fe! Greetings. I come to you all the way from Boston, in the great commonwealth of Massachusetts, far across this great country of ours on the Atlantic Ocean. I bring you some of the latest in medical discoveries, some suggestions how you can live a happy and a longer life, and I have a few surprises for you along the way.

"For instance, do you know that sometimes when you get sick it's because of little bugs that are so small the human eye can't see them except through a magnifying microscope? A Frenchman is starting to call them bacteria. And bacteria probably cause almost all of our diseases. When we figure out how to control and kill these bacteria, we'll put an end to sickness and perhaps even death itself!

"And now for another amazing product—Dr. White's fantastic Lifeline Tonic, absolutely guaranteed to perk you up, to help with rheumatism, neurology of the extremities, the common cold, and those strange women's ailments that come every so often. This amazing elixir is scientifically blended and balanced by some of the top medical experts in their respect-

34

ive fields, and combined into a practical and in-expensive home remedy that today is used by millions of good Americans just like you."

"Hey, Doc. How much it cost?" a man's voice asked from the rear.

"That's the good doctor's shill," Spur whispered to Annabelle. "He buys a bottle and gets things moving."

"My good man, this elixir is not for sale. No, not at any price. However I have been franchised to make it available to you on a long term lease arrangement, at one dollar a bottle. Only one dollar for more than a pint of this magical medicine that has had the blessing of the thousands it has cured, from the Atlantic coast all the way to California."

"I'll take a bottle," Spur said, holding up a greenback one dollar bill. He moved to the front of the wagon.

"Sir, would you happen to have a gold piece?" Doc White asked.

"Afraid not, Doc. Isn't a greenback good enough for you?"

"It's better than a Continental! Certainly a greenback is fine with me, sir, and here is your bottle. Tell your friends. Now, ladies and gentlemen, I am sorry that I have only a limited supply. However I have a few bottles left, and will be more than happy to return here tomorrow night with a fresh supply straight from Boston. Now who will be next?"

Spur and Annabelle moved down the block, then turned and walked back past the wagon. As they crossed the street again, Spur saw a small boy slip into the back of the medicine wagon. A moment later a second boy, about twelve, went under the dark canvas and into the wagon.

Spur shrugged. No reason the fast talking medicine man couldn't have a family with him, which could include two boys. Spur tightened his grip on the lovely Annabelle and marched back toward the hotel.

"I have some paintings in my downstairs living room I want to show you," Annabelle said smiling seductively.

"And some etchings in your bedroom?" Spur asked.

"One or two, if you insist on looking."

Behind them, Dr. Rusty White found his crowd was fading quickly. A down-and-outer probably without a nickel to his name was the last one standing near the wagon.

"My good sir, I'm sorry but the last bottle of Dr. White's amazing Lifeline Tonic has been snapped up by a thankful public. However, if you'll come back tomorrow night . . ."

The bleary-eyed man shook his head. "Hell, I ain't buying none of that stuff. Got a bottle in Cheyenne once, same poison. Almost killed me."

"Get out of here, you miserable drunk, before I call the sheriff!" White snapped.

The drunk held up both hands, shook his head and wandered down the darkening street.

Dr. White closed up his wagon and stepped inside. He looked at the four young boys in front

36

of him and smiled. Santa Fe might turn out to be a good place to do business after all. He motioned for Luke and the thirteen-year-old jumped up and stepped to the front of the wagon.

"Now, what have we here, only three?" White whispered.

Luke bobbed his head. "Honest, I looked hard all afternoon and three was all I could find. I had to give them each a quarter to get them to come."

"They know what they are to do?"

"Sure. I told them, convinced them they could make more money than they ever seed."

"Good." He turned to the boys. "Have you had supper, yet?"

All three shook their heads.

"Well, we can't have that, can we? Luke, go to the cafe across the street and bring back eight big sandwiches and a gallon of milk. That should fill up your bellies." He gave Luke a greenback and the boy scooted from the wagon.

Dr. White turned to the boys, his expression grim.

"Young men, don't think that you are getting a free supper, or that you won't have to earn the quarters you already have. You'll earn it all. First some questions. From what Luke says, none of you have mothers or fathers who will be worried about you, correct?"

Two nodded. The third scowled.

"My paw went on a trip and I been staying with some friends. But they don't worry I'm gone a few days."

"Good. Now, how old are you lads?"

Two were ten, one was eleven.

"And you're good at climbing trees and buildings, I'm told."

They all nodded.

"You'll have supper, and then a nap. Later tonight, I'll wake you for your final instructions. You all know what you're going to do?"

One boy shook his head.

"Luke should have told you. I'm going to train you to be the best little thieves in the world. And you are going to eat better than you ever have before. You will be shown certain houses and you will slip in and steal any valuables you can find. We want jewelry, money, stocks and bonds. Nothing else. You'll be aimed at the best houses in town which have no live in servants. Nobody locks their doors in Santa Fe, so it will be easy."

By midnight the boys had eaten their supper and had had four hours sleep. White roused them and told them again exactly what to do, where to look for valuables in the houses and how to get away if they were discovered.

"Remember, you will go in, take the money and jewels and come back to the alley behind the church. Do *not* come back to the wagon. If any of you are caught, you do not know me. Tell them you were just playing a trick on the owners. If you say I sent you, I will find you, and cut off both your feet! Do you understand me?"

Dr. White had raised his voice to a shrill

shout, and the boys all jumped in surprise and alarm. The medicine man recovered his composure.

"But I'm sure you won't have any trouble. You'll work in teams, and each of you have four houses to search."

He gave them each a sack two foot square with a shoulder strap that went over the head and under one arm. It gave them a place to put the loot and leave their hands free.

"Now, off you go, and good hunting!"

Dr. White sat back in his chair in the wagon, lit a cigar and poured himself a glass of brandy. He had been in town two days and had selected the houses carefully. There would be only two nights to work the houses; then word would spread and the population would hide their money and valuables better and in the well-off owner's houses, they would leave a servant up all night.

Tonight the targets included the territorial governor's house, that of a judge, and several wealthy merchants. All he needed was to hit a big haul in one house, and the whole operation would be dramatically profitable.

He wondered how his brother Zack and Erick were doing. Rusty had no idea what last names they were using now. They changed theirs about as often as he did his. With any kind of luck he would win the contest again. He snorted. How much money would you expect to raise by selling household goods stolen from some poor dirt farmer or rancher? And a preacher took months to set up his flock to be plucked clean. Yes, he was the best of the three operations. He had told them that a year ago.

And there were always the side benefits. He thought of Luke. He was so young and pure and unspoiled. Absently, Rusty White let his hand reach for his crotch and rubbed. They should be back by about four in the morning. If the boys did well, they would have a real celebration!

Luke walked down the dark alley with his partner, Rufus.

"Nothing to be afraid of. We go in the houses, and most of the people leave money laying around. We just pick it up, look in all the places I told you to look for money and jewelry and walk out of the house. We got to be quiet, and if anyone wakes up, we stay still and hide until they go back to sleep."

"I'm still scared," Rufus said. "Never done this before."

"I have—fifty, sixty houses. It's easy." Luke paused and looked across at the first house. It belonged to the territorial governor, and held the best chances. "Come on, this is it. We'll go down the alley and in the back door."

It was a warm July night. Doors of many of the houses they had passed had been left open to catch the cooling breezes. They found the back door of the governor's house and crept up three steps of the porch. No lights were on inside. Luke tried the screen door. It was held by a hook. He took out his knife and pushed it through the crack between the door and jamb and lifted off the hook.

Inside, they went up the open staircase to a long hall. Four doors stood open. The first room was empty. In the second one a young girl slept. She wore only a thin nightgown and it had been pulled down to reveal one pink breast. Luke looked at her for several seconds, then went to the next room.

A woman slept on her side beneath a light blanket. Luke saw a necklace lying on a dresser. He put it in his sack. A jewel box with two drawers sat beside it. He pushed the whole box into his sack and went through a reticule next to it. In the coin purse he found ten double gold eagles and a wad of paper money. He took the coin purse and then silently opened the dresser drawers. In one, under some women's clothes, he found a flat box. Inside was a strand of pearls. He took them from the box and dropped them into his shoulder sack.

Rufus had stood at the door, watching, listening. Nothing moved in the house.

They crept to the next room, where they saw the governor laying naked on top of the sheets. His wallet and gold watch lay on a night stand beside the bed. Rufus picked them up and lowered them into his sack. Then he and Luke looked in two drawers.

The governor suddenly sat up in bed.

"I won't sign the damn bills!" he said loudly. Both boys froze where they were. The governor coughed, lay down and continued sleeping. They found nothing more.

Quietly then went down the steps and out the back door. A block down the dark alley, Luke stopped, opened the jewelry box and dumped everything in it into his sack, then pushed the box itself deep inside a garbage can that still glowed with the remnants of a fire. The small box would be burned to ashes before morning.

Luke did not stop to look over their loot. He put the contents of Rufus's bag into his own and they went on to the next house on their list.

By three A.M. Luke and Rufus were back at the alley meeting place. In a sheltered spot between two buildings, Rusty White examined the take in the light of a small lantern he had brought from the wagon. He smiled as he opened the governor's wallet. Inside were more than two hundred dollars in paper money, as well as a snap pocket with four double eagles. The jewelry from the governor's mansion alone had been a bonanza. He was sure of four diamond rings, and the necklace had three diamonds in it as well as two rubies! The other team had found much less, but they had the secondary houses. When it was all put together, Rusty White figured his small friends had produced over a thousand dollars' worth of goods, including over four hundred in cash!

He gave each of the three boys three green-back dollar bills and showed them where they could sleep the rest of the night. He warned them again sternly about not telling anyone what they had done.

"Lads, if you so much as sneeze about this, I'll cut off your feet sure as I'm standing here. We work together, we keep our mouths shut, and we all make money. Now off with you."

Luke and Rusty walked back to the closed, dark medicine wagon where it sat just off the main street near the edge of town. They stepped into the wagon and Rusty lit a lamp.

"I'm tired," Luke said.

"Yes, so am I. We'll help each other go to sleep." Rusty was a slender, tall man, with a clean shaven face and straight black hair. He stripped out of his clothes and sat naked on the edge of the bed built into the side of the wagon.

Then he undressed Luke, who was four and a half feet tall and starkly white under his clothes.

"I'm real tired," Luke said.

"I know, I know, and we'll sleep. But first we have to celebrate. You did fine tonight, Luke." Rusty kissed his cheek, then lightly kissed Luke's lips and pulled him into the bed on the soft quilts. Slowly the man's hands began to caress the boy.

"I know you're tired, Luke, but I want to show you how much I appreciate your help. Then both of us will go to sleep just real easy."

Luke swallowed hard and tried to relax.

The man's hand drifted down to Luke's crotch and played with his genitals. Luke gritted his teeth, but he couldn't stop his penis from reacting, enlarging.

Rusty moaned softly and Luke rubbed wetness from his eyes. He had to remember to relax . . .

CHAPTER FOUR

ANNABELLE'S PRIVATE SUITE at the Santa Fe
Carriage House was delightful. She had ripped
out a few walls, had some new ones built and
turned four hotel rooms into a comfortable,
impressively decorated apartment. She and
Spur sat on an antique love seat she said had
come across on an early English colonist ship.
Annabelle wore a thin silk gown that hid
absolutely none of her charms.

The bed was mussed from recent use and now
both sipped at a wine she said came from
California, a smooth port.

"I don't know enough about you, Spur
McCoy. I know that you are a United States
Secret Service Agent, and you keep that a secret
most of the time. Your office is in St. Louis, and
you do a lost of traveling with the whole West as
your responsibility. But that's about all I know.
You blow into and out of my life like a New
Mexican tornado."

She reached over and kissed him, then turned and leaned against his bare chest and brought his arms around her. "Now, while we're resting up, tell me your entire life's story."

"It's boring as hell."

"That's for me to decide."

Spur sighed. He wasn't close to many people, especially during the last few years with this wild West assignment. He sipped the wine, let his hand curl around Annabelle's delightful right breast, and began.

"What I didn't tell you before is that I grew up in New York City where my father was a merchant. I graduated from Harvard in 1858 and worked in some of my father's firms for two years. For the next couple of years I was in the army making it to Captain in the infantry before an old family friend called me out of the army to Washington, D.C. He could do that—he was a United States Senator, and he wanted me as his aide. Had enough?"

She shook her head and brought his other hand around to cover her left breast.

"So when the U.S. Secret Service Act was passed in 1865 I applied and was accepted. I took some training and then went to work. We were the only federal law enforcement agency at the time. Nobody else had jurisdiction across state or territorial lines, so we did a lot of work on wide-ranging problems. They set up our group originally with the sole task of preventing currency counterfeiting."

Spur reached down and kissed her neck and Annabelle purred. "Then what happened?" she asked.

"I had served six months in the main office in Washington, D.C. when they decided they needed a man out West. That meant everything west of the Mississippi. Since I had won the service marksmanship contest and was the best rider in the bunch, they sent me to St. Louis to open an office. And here I am."

She turned around and kissed him.

"You forgot the important stuff. You're six-feet two and must weigh about two hundred pounds. You're about thirty-two years old now and your hair is a little on the brownish-red side, and I *love* your thick moustache."

"You have any other complaints?" he asked.

"Yes, you're naughty, just *naughty* in bed!"

"Only twice, so far today." He stood and reached for his shirt. "The sheriff is due back in town. I need to talk to him."

"Now?"

"Right now. He went on a ride north to meet some of his men he sent out this morning to check on a ranch fire somebody thought must be a log house burned out back in the hills."

"Damn." She pouted.

"And I'll be back as soon as I get a couple of things straightened out with the lawman."

"Does he know who you are?"

"Not yet."

He pulled on his boots and tucked in his shirt, then bent and kissed her softly on the lips.

"You stay put until I get back." He touched her breasts through the filmy material. "I wouldn't want you to catch a chest cold in that thing."

Five minutes later, Spur sat in a chair across from Sheriff George James.

"Rawhiders, Sheriff? You sure?"

Sheriff James was a small man, who wore a black suit and a white shirt and black string tie, because his wife thought he should. He stood barely five feet four inches, but he ran a tight and honest political organization that was the envy of the rest of the state. Now he slicked back his thinning black hair and preened a heavy moustache.

"Had all the signs. Family of three wiped out, women raped, one strangled, the young one shot. Both naked. The livestock run off, a cow slaughtered and half taken away, five or six horses trailed behind the wagon. The cabin had been looted and then burned to the ground. Same for the barns. Nothing left."

"Indians, maybe?"

"No. Not from what my men report. The clincher was the way the man died. Had wet rawhide wrapped tight around his throat, then they let it dry in the hot sun. The poor bastard slowly strangled to death as that stretched rawhide shrank."

"Now that sounds familiar to me. We had some reports six, eight months ago about a gang of rawhiders in Oklahoma and Texas. Always killed at least one in the family with rawhide around the throat. The name White mean anything, Sheriff?"

"Seen some posters on them. The White Brothers. I seem to remember there were two of them."

"Three. And all about as dirty and treacherous killers as you'll ever meet. But their real name isn't White—it's Schmidke. A woman in the bunch seemed to be the worst."

"You think we got the White brothers—I mean, the Schmidke brothers around here?"

"Might even be in town already."

"We have over five thousand people here. I can't know all of them."

"They will be trying to sell the goods they stole. You can have your men watch for that. Especially selling off a wagon. I take it your men lost the tracks of the rawhiders?"

"Dozens of tracks, leading off in twenty directions. I've heard of false trails, but my men said they had never seen so many. I only sent two deputies, and they had to give up when it got dark."

Spur reset his low-crowned brown hat on his head. "Now that is sounding more and more like the Schmidke brothers."

The sheriff looked up. "Mister, you said your name was McCoy, but nothing else. You some kind of U.S. Marshal or something?"

Spur took out a wallet he carried, pried apart two tintype pictures and took out a thin printed card. It carried President Grant's signature and proved that he was a U.S. Secret Service Agent. It asked local authorities to give him cooperation in anything he asked.

"Right, figures. I heard about you guys once. Not many of you out here in the West. What can I do for you?"

"You know I came to town hunting those bank robbers. But that case is closed now. I was getting ready to head out of town, but with a trail of the Schmidke brothers, I think I better stick around for a while."

"Want to look at the massacre site?"

"Seen enough, Sheriff. I hear the group splits up and goes separate ways, then comes together in some town to live it up. Wonder if Santa Fe is the site of their next meeting?"

"You have descriptions on them, McCoy?"

"Not much. Just ages, as I remember. Look through your wanteds, we might get lucky. As I recall they are from thirty-six to about forty-five. Only one of them was married."

"Sounds damn near impossible to find them."

Spur stood and grinned. "Yeah, and I like impossible. Let me help you with those wanted posters."

They looked through the posters for almost an hour and at last found what they were looking for. The brothers were wanted for twelve murders in Kansas, six in Colorado, and fourteen in Texas.

"And that wanted is most a year old," the sheriff said.

"I just got my next assignment. Changed my mind about going out to that burned-out ranch. Tell me how to get there. I want to light out first thing in the morning."

The sheriff drew Spur a rough map. The place

was about eighteen miles out and a thousand feet higher than the elevation of Santa Fe, which sat in a valley at 7,000 feet.

Sheriff James shook his head and watched Spur. "Hell, McCoy. How we going to find these yahoos once they get into town? The wanted says they usually clean up and act halfway civilized while they're in town. How the hell we gonna spot them?"

"Maybe watch for some strangers spending lots of money," Spur said.

The older man laughed. "McCoy, this is special session time for the new legislature. Half the folks in town are strangers, and most of them are spending the taxpayer's money. We got to do better than that."

"True, most true. That's why I'm riding forty miles tomorrow so I can try to find some little clue we can use against them."

"Good luck. I'll tell the livery man to put your mount on my bill. You will want a fresh horse?"

Spur said that would be fine and made a round of the saloons. He lost track after the first dozen. Nowhere did he find an example of a rawhider with grease and dirt stiffened clothes, unkempt beards and long hair, coupled with a nasty disposition.

Back at the hotel, he used the key Annabelle had given him and found her waiting for him, wearing the same transparent gown and reading a book. She put the book down and came to meet him.

"Where's the bed?" he asked.

"I like a man who's direct."

He told her he had to be in the saddle at four A.M. For a moment she pouted, then he told her he would be staying in town on another case, and she kissed him.

"Marvelous! Then I'll let you go to bed and sleep tonight. But tomorrow night I have a surprise for you."

"I'm not sure there are any surprises left," Spur said.

Annabelle laughed. "There are quite a few, and this one you're going to love!"

Spur barely got undressed down to his briefs before he fell into bed and went to sleep at once.

Annabelle sighed, kissed him on the cheek and cuddled close against his back. Then she slept too. It was good to have a man in her bed again.

By daylight, Spur had ridden up more than five hundred feet and could see Santa Fe far below in the valley. He was working into the Sangre de Cristos mountains, and could see several snow-capped peaks. He was on a trail of sorts. It headed almost due east toward the settlement of Las Vegas, and then on into Texas.

He left the trail and turned north at a lightning shattered pine tree. The jagged stump still stood eighty feet high and served as a landmark for travelers. He found the small stream he was to follow and let his mare drink. Then he pushed on. He figured it would take him five hours to find the ranch. The uphill climb was taking a toll on the mare and he rested her frequently.

Two and a half hours after sunrise, Spur found the ruins of the ranchita. The three fresh graves had not been molested. He found blood on the ground and was glad he had not witnessed the slaughter.

For half an hour he scoured the remains of the house and barn. Nothing. The rawhiders knew their work well. He drank from the stream, ate a pair of sandwiches he had talked the hotel into fixing for him, and then began to circle to find the wagon tracks. The tracks led in three directions, and despite attempts to cover the wheel marks, he found where two of the trails wound back over rocky stretches and came to the ranch again. One set of wheel prints did not backtrack.

He followed that one for a mile, then found a jumble of new wagon and horse tracks. In the army, Spur had worked through dozens of puzzles like this one. The winner was the one with the most patience. After an hour of tracking and backtracking and marking trails he had followed, he came to the one true track that led away from the mess, and angled downhill toward Santa Fe. He circled, found two tracks that later melted into one and then got down from his horse at a sandy area near a stream and studied the wagon wheel prints and those of the horses.

At once he decided the wagon pullers were mules. They seemed to be heavy and short gaited. There was nothing distinctive about their hooves, and only one was shod.

The wagon wheels were easier to read. An old Johnson freight wagon, if he figured it correctly. More than likely with bows and a cover on it to hide the stolen property and give some privacy. The front wheels on a Johnson were offset six inches inside of the rear wheels. No one had ever told him why, but it made the wagon easy to track and pick out of a crowd. Most freight wagons had axles the same width, and their steel-rimmed, wooden-spoked wheels tracked one on top of the other.

Twice he found where the wagon had to backtrack to find a safe route down the mountain; then it hit a gentle valley and a stream that paved the way toward the city below.

Spur left the tracking then, picked the quickest route and rode for town. He was looking for a Johnson freight wagon, maybe with bowed, covered top and loaded to the sideboards with stolen household goods. Should be simple.

He tried to remember where he had seen such a wagon before. Before he got to town he thought of one. The medicine man used a Johnson, a big heavy duty rig, and it had built-on sides and a top. But the medicine man's rig had been parked on the street three days before the sheriff said the attack on the ranch took place.

Clear one Johnson wagon owner of suspicion.

Spur came into town trail-weary just before dusk. He had been in the saddle for sixteen hours. He was hot, bone weary, and so hungry he could eat a side of raw beef.

Annabelle delighted in playing nurse and hostess. She fixed his bath and ordered dinner for him and picked at her food as she watched him. Spur almost went to sleep as he ate fresh strawberries and cream for dessert. He got through the cherry tarts and then staggered to the bedroom.

Annabelle whooped in delight as she jumped on the bed beside him, only to find Spur McCoy already sleeping, one arm thrown over his face, and his other hand resting on his genitals.

She sighed as she pulled off his boots and then his pants and spread a sheet over him.

Tomorrow night, she thought as she lay down beside him. It was nice just having him there. Tomorrow night for sure they would make wild, passionate love.

She gazed at his relaxed face for a moment, then reached over and kissed his cheek. She had a problem. How was she going to convince Spur McCoy he should quit the Secret Service and settle down here in Santa Fe with her? The hotel made plenty of money, and he could manage it if he wanted to. Or he could raise a few cattle on a little ranch she owned outside of town. It was a problem, but one she was going to enjoy working on!

CHAPTER FIVE

"Oh, yes! Sisters and brothers in Christ, I say Amen. Amen to the love of our heavenly father!"

"Amen!" someone in the small group gathered outside the covered wagon said. The side of the wagon held a small platform with a pulpit on it, and behind it stood a man of thirty-six, dressed all in black, with a beneficent smile on his face.

It was just dusk in Santa Fe, and Spur McCoy had passed the preacher as he rode in from the massacre site. Lanterns were hung ready to light when it grew dark.

"My sisters and brothers in Christ, the theme for my talk tonight is love. The good book is full of love. No man hath greather love . . . Love thy father and thy mother. Love God. I say unto you, love one another. God loves a cheerful giver."

Eric Thompson checked his gathering as he spoke. He had arrived in town three days before and put up broadsides on as many buildings as he could advertising the rally and revival tonight. Maybe twenty people out there. Ten who might give. Damn, but this was a hard way to make a living! If there wasn't a wealthy widow in this town who had a soft spot for itinerant preachers, he just might have to go back to more direct ways of becoming rich.

He droned on, describing the delights of the "place my father prepares for me, my house of many mansions." The preaching was no problem—he could do that in his sleep. He could be a spellbinder, but how could you wring gold pieces out of empty wallets? Mostly he drew lower class worshippers, and they were nearly as broke as he was. Just one youngish widow lady who was a staunch believer, was that too much to ask?

"And so, my new friends, tonight you have seen just a brief glimpse of the glory of Jesus Christ. Just a hint of the marvels that wait for you on the other side. But can we sit and hope for that day? Never!

"Never! We must work here and now for the glory of the Lord! Amen to that! We must improve our lives, be more loving and charitable. We must do the work of the Lord. And how better to do that than to support worthy projects with our prayers, our works and our gifts?

"Brothers and sisters, I am a humble servant of the Lord. But even I and my horses must eat a crust of bread or a fork full of hay. I have taken a vow of poverty, and all of your gifts and offerings go directly, I say *directly*, to the work of the Lord. Praise his name!"

"Amen!" A big husky man standing near the platform said.

Erick took two offering plates from the pulpit and handed them to the big man.

"Brother, would you be so kind as to pass these among the fine folks here and allow them to contribute to the Lord's work? I thank you, Brother. I thank you for the Lord, through our spokesman and our saviour, Christ Jesus."

There was a rustle of clothing as reticules were opened, as wallets and purses came out of pockets. He reached for a glass of water and drank slowly, watching the flock. It was so new to them, this first day. He needed time. In time he could extract plenty from them, perhaps even make a living. But it was that one big mark he was searching for.

His gaze traveled over the group, now numbering about twenty-five, he figured. Average. No one dressed well. His eyes held on a woman near the far side. She was better dressed than the others. She stood tall and straight, and while perhaps forty still had a remarkable figure. She was watching him, and he nodded to her, then looked on. The plate came to her and she emptied a handful of coins in the plate. He prayed they were double eagles!

A moment later the burly man returned the two plates to Erick which he held high.

"O, Lord of all men! Oh, Jesus Christ our

Savior! We do thank thee for these offerings, bless those who gave of their treasure, bless them in every way. We dedicate this bit of thy abundance to the work of bringing Jesus to every man, woman and child in Santa Fe! In Jesus's name we pay . . . Amen."

Erick held the plates high a moment more. A dozen "Amens" came from the audience. Then he put the plates onto the shelf in the small pulpit. With one hand he collected the bills and coins and pushed then into his pocket out of sight of the congregation. Before he ended his next few sentences he had emptied the plates. Yes, he felt gold coins!

"My new friends in Christ, I thank you for coming. If any among you need spiritual aid or counseling, my door is always open. Think of this as a rolling church wagon, dedicated to Christ and his way of life. And remember, do unto others as you would have them do unto you. We will have another meeting here tomorrow afternoon, and again in the evening. I pray that all of you can return and bring two or three families with you. This is a family Christian Revival, and I pray I will see you again. If any of you have burdens you wish to let me help you with, please come to the front immediately after the service. Now for the closing benediction. Would you all please bow your heads in prayer.

"May the Lord bless you and keep you, may the Lord make his face to shine upon you and be gracious unto you. May the Lord lift up his countenance upon you and give you peace. Amen."

Erick stood as the flock slowly moved away from the wagon. One young man held back, then changed his mind and walked away. To Erick's surprise the nicely dressed woman he had noticed before stood beside the back of his wagon, waiting. He stepped to the ground and walked to her.

"Pastor Thompson," she began, then hesitated. "I . . . I don't know how to say this."

He could see her plainly now. She had a handsome, somewhat stern face, high cheekbones that lent a note of arrogance to her features, and deep blue eyes that told of many mysteries. Most of her soft brown hair was covered by a small hat.

"Please, do you wish to step inside? Others might be curious."

"Yes, of course."

He preceded her, going up the three steps to the back of the wagon, lifting the canvas door so she could step inside.

She looked around, saw the lit lantern and nodded.

"Oh, my, it is so homey, almost like a living room. I've never been inside a covered wagon before."

"Thank you, ma'am. It is my living room, and my kitchen, and where I retire as well. Do you wish to sit down?"

He pointed to a rocking chair with a soft cushion he had won from his brother in a poker game. It was a beautifully carved chair. She murmured something and sat, knees together, on the edge of the seat. Now she turned her concerned eyes toward him.

"Pastor, I'm not catholic as most of Santa Fe is because of its Spanish origins. There's no Protestant church here and I feel left out. This is the first real service I've been to in almost a year. I'm deeply indebted to you for your kindness."

"My great joy in serving the Lord is seeing how quietly and gloriously he works in mysterious ways. Perhaps there is some higher plan that directed my path here tonight." He let her think about that for a moment, then he went on.

"I'm sorry I don't know your name."

"Oh, how stupid of me. I'm Hillery Gregson, Mrs. Hillery Gregson. I'm pleased to meet you." She held out her hand and Erick held it, then bent and kissed it.

"Always a pleasure to meet a beautiful woman, especially when she is so dedicated and consecrated to our Lord Jesus Christ."

"I was hoping I could talk to you about staying on in Santa Fe. I would be more than willing to help a fund-raising campaign to build a Protestant church. I'm not sure which persuasion you are. My own background is Methodist."

"Well, Sister Gregson, I am honored and flattered. Up to now I have refused all such offers, but I truly like this town. I think we could find enough dedicated Protestants here to form a church, and I will certainly consider the matter carefully. Since I have taken a vow to poverty, there is little I could contribute, except my enthusiasm, my calling to be a preacher, and my dedication. I'm not an old man yet—I think it would be a great challenge to build a church here. But I will think more, and of course, the most important part—I will pray about it."

Hillary Gregson smiled. "I am so pleased, Pastor Thompson. I'll do some more thinking about it too. I did some planning a year ago concerning a church. I'll find those notes and think it through again. I am so thrilled that you're considering it!"

Her face lit up as she talked and she became almost pretty.

She watched him closely for a moment. "Yes, yes, Pastor Thompson. I think you're exactly the man we need to start our church." She went to the door, then turned. "Would you consider coming to my house tomorrow night so we could discuss the project with some others in town who are also interested?"

"I think that would be a fine idea, ma'am."

"Good! I'll be at both your services, then drive you to my home in my carriage. Until tomorrow."

He helped her down the steps and walked with her to her buggy just down the street. A sleeping driver came awake and helped her into the rig, then wheeled it away down the street.

Erick Thompson grinned broadly as he

returned to his wagon. He had a fat fish on his line! Now all he had to do was play her carefully. His retirement from the "ministry" might be just around the corner! Quickly he took down the lanterns, closed up the pulpit and platform, and stepped into his wagon.

A girl sat on the bed built onto the front of the rig. She definitely was not Mrs. Gregson. The dress she wore left her shoulders bare, her lips and cheeks were red and pink, her hair piled high on her head, and the top of the dress had been pulled down so it came across her breasts just below large brown nipples.

"You! I told you not until the service was over!" Thompson hissed at her in a stage whisper. "You trying to ruin me?"

"The fucking service *was* over, and I got a good look at Mrs. Gregson, the rich bitch. Not much of a looker, but she's really got a yen for you, I can tell. You can flip up her dress any time you want to, Pastor, and bite her pussy."

Quickly Thompson snapped the canvas door shut and put two security boards across the back of the soft canvas of the wagon. Then he advanced on the girl who now pulled her skirt up so he could see a swatch of black crotch hair.

He sat beside her and fondled her breasts. "June, you are a total whore. But the next time you get here so early, you get half the pay. And if you breathe one word about me to anyone . . . you hear, to *anyone*, I'll slice your pretty tits off and let you bleed to death. Is that clear? Can that pea-sized brain of yours understand that?"

"Yeah, yeah." She caught his hand and

pushed it between her legs. "Talk about pussy, it's more fun!"

She pulled his head down to her breasts and his mouth covered one of her delightful mounds.

Pastor Erick Thompson sighed. "Glorious! Now get that dress off. You've got a mountain sized heat built up in me. And that Hillery Gregson! She would be something to upset in a bed, just to see what it did to that smug expression."

"I tell you, you can get her into bed anytime you try. Still, a couple of weeks of warmup never hurts with a frozen biddy like her. Now, let's talk about me. What are you going to do to me tonight that is delightful? You can't fuck me any way you did last night."

Erick let her undress him, turned down the lamp so their shadows wouldn't show on the canvas, then slapped her round bottom until it turned red and she moaned with rapture. He pulled her up on her hands and knees and she giggled, pushing her bottom at him.

"Oh, God! I like it this way. Which hole?"

"Both of them, you silly little whore. First one and then the other all night long until I've fucked your brains out."

"Cost you ten dollars."

"All night is *five*, you fucking whore!" He lunged forward, penetrating and driving in until his pelvic bones hit the soft cushions of her buttocks. He moaned in pure animal pleasure and pumped into her fast. Then he slowed. There was no rush, he had all night to

63

introduce this little slut into the marvels of being a temple whore. It didn't really matter what the temple was, or who it was dedicated to, just so the little priestess was willing and able. This one was both.

Erick smiled. All this fucking and a rich widow on the line to boot! It was a fine day! He was sure she was a widow. He would find out first thing in the morning. Either way, he was determined to bed her and rob her, one way or the other.

CHAPTER SIX

IT HAD TO be a dream. The giant grizzly bear licked his face again, but the beast's breath was sweet. Spur tried to get away but he was trapped under a heavy log. The bear moved to Spur's ear and repeated the licking and Spur began to giggle and laugh and try to get the grizzly bear to stop tickling him that way.

Something soft and scented touched his face and then his face and he knew it couldn't be the grizzly. He tried to roll over, to get rid of the dream, but something held him pinned to the rough forest floor.

The eight foot tall grizzly roared, but the sound came out as a tinkling bell-like laugh.

"You must be awake now," a feminine voice said.

Spur started to answer but when his mouth opened, something soft and sweet smelling surged into it and he sputtered and his eyes snapped open.

No grizzly bear.

No log pinning him down.

Rather a naked Annabelle lay on top of him on the big bed, and one of her generous breasts dangled half in his mouth. He grinned, moaned in contentment and chewed on the delicate mammery morsel.

"I think you finally woke up," she said. "I wanted to seduce you in your sleep, but you didn't cooperate."

She moved her other breast into his mouth as he began to talk.

"Even things up or she'll be jealous."

Spur chewed on the other breast for a minute, then eased away from her, rolled her to one side and sat up beside her.

"I hear some people think it's evil and wicked to make love in the morning," Annabelle asked. "Do you?"

Before he could answer she kissed him. He caught her and rolled her on her back, spread her legs and eased down on top of her.

"I think it's monstrous and pagan, especially if it happens to me when I'm sleeping so I can't enjoy it."

"You are a little crazy, but I love you all the more for it." She watched him closely as she said the words, but he didn't react. At least he didn't yell and scream at her.

"Aren't you supposed to be getting me all sexy feeling?" she asked.

"It's your party. I thought you were seducing *me*."

Annabelle frowned. "Did I tell you about my

husband, Donald? He was twenty-one years older than me. And he died. His heart gave out, and I never told anybody, but we were making love that night when it happened. He just yelled and grabbed his chest and fell on top of me. Talk about dead weight!"

"Now this is erotic talk. I'm really getting excited," said Spur dryly.

"Naturally I didn't tell anybody. You know what the gossip would have been in this town? So I just didn't tell a soul. I got dressed and put Donald under the covers and ran for old Doc Cunningham. I wanted you to know."

"Thanks."

"Kiss me, McCoy."

"No more story of your life?"

"No."

Spur kissed her and worked his tongue into her mouth, and soon he felt her temperature rising. Her hand wriggled between them to his crotch and found what she was seeking. Her breath came quickly and he moved his mouth to pink flowering buds on her breasts. Her slender body writhed under him.

"Lordy, that feels wonderful!" she said.

His hand moved up between her quivering flanks and caressed the soft pubic hair.

"Now, darling. Please right now! Come inside me, quickly!"

They joined smoothly, perfectly and for long moments Annabelle couldn't speak. She brimmed with surges of delicious feelings that left her shaken and spent, and fulfilled all at the same time.

Later they lay in each other's arms.

"Darling, I wish it could be this way forever. Not just once a year, but every morning of the year. Wouldn't that be heaven?"

"I'd be used up by the time I was forty!"

"You would not! Donald used to say, 'use it so you don't lose it.' "

"And look what happened to Donald!"

"Don't remind me!"

He slid away from her. "I am supposed to be working. A quick breakfast in the dining room while you get the rest of your beauty sleep, and I'll see you later."

Spur dressed in some old jeans and a blue shirt.

"They don't match your brown eyes," Annabelle said drowsily.

Spur threw a pillow at her and let himself out the door.

All morning he worked the trail he figured the wagon would take into town. It was the closest to the mountain where the bushwackings took place. Then he figured what he would do if he were in the Schmidke brothers' place: he'd go around and hit the town from the other side. He had saddled up his horse for the search, and now rode to the far side of the small town and began questioning people in the houses closest to what he figured would be the rawhider's route.

At the fourth house, an old man came to the door. He said he had seen the prairie schooner sail in day before yesterday, but he wasn't sure where it landed.

"One of them big wagons with bows and a canvas cover. Looked loaded down heavy. Pair of mules had all they could do to drag her along. I used to have one like that back in sixty-two."

Spur thanked the old man and moved on. Two houses later, a woman said her little boy had called her out to take a look at the wagon. There weren't many like it around in that area. She knew that it had gone down a ways, then turned left, toward the outskirts of town again. Spur thanked her and moved on.

He stopped his horse where the woman figured the rig had turned left and looked. There were ten or twelve houses out there, half of them with barns and outbuildings that could hide a wagon. That's what Spur would do with the rig if he wanted to come in town and not be noticed—put the rig undercover and rent or take over a house for a while.

They were here, somewhere. Spur could feel it. He knew they were in Santa Fe. Now all he had to do was flush them out. It would be the older of the trio, with his family. Nobody knew what they looked like. He had to find them, with the wagon. He would do some after-dark scouting and see what he could find. He didn't want to scare them off, not now that he was this close.

But even if he did spot the older brother, how would he recognize the other two in the family who some said were just as bad, but operated in different ways from their brother? It was all one big poker game and he was drawing to an inside straight flush, a sucker draw no matter what the size of the pot.

Spur rode back downtown and checked out the twelve biggest bars and gambling halls. The sheriff was in one of them, but Spur passed him by without a flicker of recognition. He had a beer and made it last. He could find nobody who looked like a rawhider.

He was in the tenth bar in his quest when he stumbled into the middle of a gunfight. It was a Texas Tenderfoot Can't Miss challenge.

The two men stood five feet apart. There was no way either man could miss the other. The first one who could draw, cock the hammer and fire would live.

Spur wished the sheriff was there. Nobody was trying to stop the slaughter. There was no cause for a killing like this.

McCoy walked into the bar and cut lose with a rebel yell he had heard so often for those bloody six months he had been on line fighting the Rebs. Every man in the place looked away from the duelists and watched him. He had out his .45 Colt and kept walking toward the two in the center of the big room.

"It's over, men," Spur said. "I don't know what the argument is, but this is no way to settle it. Both of you take your six-guns out by thumb and finger and lay them gently on the floor."

"No way, Mister," the younger of the men said. Spur guessed he was maybe twenty-one. "He called me names and I don't take that off nobody!"

"Instead of being called a name, you'd rather be dead?" Spur asked.

"What if we don't shuck our guns?" asked the other one, who was probably a year or two older.

"You stand there that way another fifteen seconds and I put a .45 slug in one kneecap for both of you. Neither one of you will ever walk normal again. You want that?"

"What cause you got, Mister? Do I know you?"

"Not up to now."

"Then back off and mind your own business!"

"You got five seconds left."

The older one took his weapon out. The younger one did too, holding it by thumb and finger on the handle. A moment later the guns were on the floor and a man wearing an apron around his stomach ran up and grabbed the irons.

With the excitement over, the rest of the bar patrons went back to their gambling and drinking. The two fighters followed the barkeep, asking when they could have their guns back. He said when they were ready to leave. The two turned and with a death-anger in their eyes looked around for the man who had broken up their party, but Spur had left the bar as soon as the guns hit the floor. He wasn't interested in their problem, or their anger.

At the next bar Spur found a likely candidate. The man was in his forties. The pants and shirt he wore were so dirt stained and stiffened they looked like they would stand up by themselves. The man was wearing a misshappen, dirty hat, and had an unkempt beard that was half gray, half black, and all tobacco stained. He growled and glarerd at everyone who came near him.

Spur asked the barkeep about the man.

"You mean Old Ned," the apron said. "Never have known his last name. He's kind of the town character. He goes from bar to bar and gets two free beers a day just to be himself. Seems like he musta been around Santa Fe since it was founded back in 1610."

Spur thanked the barkeep, then glanced up. "Did you say this town was started in sixteen hundred and ten?"

"True. It was part of the Spanish colony over here, this was the province of New Mexico and Santa Fe was its capital. Only they called it *La Villa Real de la Santa Fe de San Francisco de Assisi*, whatever all that means. They sent in mule trains every three years from Mexico City with supplies."

"Two hundred and sixty four years ago!" Spur said with surprise. "I thought the only thing out here then was pine trees and sagebrush."

Spur thanked the barkeep and moved down where he could watch the customers. He couldn't find a good prospect. The wagon was his only good lead so far, and he couldn't find that, either.

He checked with the sheriff, but the lawman had found nothing to indicate the Schmidke brothers were in town, though there had been a

72

rash of burglaries—four houses broken into last night and money and jewelry stolen.

"Doesn't sound like the Schmidke brothers' style," Spur said. "Never have heard of them being cat burglars. Still, you never can tell. Let's see what happens tonight." Spur didn't tell the sheriff about the Johnson wagon clue. He would wait and see what he discovered.

Spur found a hardware store and bought a box of rounds for his .45 Colt and went back to the hotel. He had to come up with a new angle.

Rusty White sat on the edge of the bed and watched Luke eating the rest of the meal he had brought in from the restaurant. Rusty felt a strange attachment to the boy. He felt like a father to him as well as like a lover. It was all mixed up. He had never let this happen before and he knew why. Luke had been with him now for over six months. There was a real and deep sense of attachment. The others had been quick relationships, spur of the moment things, but with Luke it had been much more.

"Good meal?" Rusty asked.

Luke nodded. "Yep." He looked up. "I got to thinking. I take all the chances, you keep all the money."

"We've talked about that, Luke. I give you ten dollars for every good night we have. You must have over a hundred by now stashed away in your saving place."

"Yeah, but we bring back a thousand, and I get ten. That's not fair."

Rusty sighed. "Didn't I pick you up in

Cheyenne just a jump ahead of the sheriff? Didn't I lie for you and hide you when we left town? Luke, ain't I been good to you? You got money, and a safe place to live, and I'll teach you the patter and the trade of being a medicine man, if you want."

Luke pushed the tin plate away and stood up.

Rusty realized the boy was growing up. He was a good three inches taller now than when he had first been rescued. And he was starting to look at women. Maybe Rusty should take him over to one of the fancy lady houses. No, not yet.

"Luke, let's have a little nap and talk about this. I bet we can work it out."

Luke stood where he was and stared down at Rusty White. "First, I want to know how much we took in last night, cash and jewelry. You said over a thousand. How much?"

"Well, I didn't figure it out for sure, maybe fifteen hundred or so."

"Fine. I want half! From now on, I take all the risk, we pay the boys ten dollars each and I get half!"

"Luke, that's crazy! What would you do with that much money?"

"What do you do with it?"

"Luke, let's talk about it. Come over here."

"No. I ain't gonna let you mess around with my privates no more. It's wicked."

"Luke, you better think over carefully what you're saying. You could be out on your ear, sitting on the street, asking strangers for a nickel."

The young man stood taller, then reached down and rubbed Rusty's crotch. "No, you won't do that. You like the way I let you asshole me. You love it! You're a damn queer, and you're trying to make me into one. But you won't throw me out. You like to suck on my prick too much!"

"Luke, I'll give you more money, a hundred dollars every night that you work the houses! A hundred! But let's not rule out being—good friends. I need you, Luke!"

The young boy grinned. "Damn right you need me. Make it two hundred a working night, and we'll leave the rest of it the way it is, agreed?"

Rusty White scowled. The boy had him in a bind. Just then he felt Luke unbuttoning his fly and the young hands crept inside his pants and did wonderful things. Rusty moaned and jerked down his pants, turned on his back and pulled Luke's face over his crotch. He gasped in pleasure as the boy's mouth closed around his erection.

Luke did what the older man wanted him to. He tolerated it, but all the while he was working out a plan of his own. He had seen last night where Rusty kept his money and the jewels he hadn't sold. There had to be five or six thousand dollars there in cash! And enough diamonds to set Luke up in business somewhere.

No more would he have to put up with the vile, ugly things that Rusty did to him, and demanded that Luke do for Rusty. At last he would be free! He would be out from under this weird man, and he would have enough money to last him a lifetime.

Luke knew that he might have to kill the man to get away. That didn't bother Luke. He was practical. His knife had drawn blood before when he was trapped and hungry. It could kill again. Tonight would be a good time, after they got back from the midnight burglaries. Yes, tonight! Then he would be free, and he would be rich!

CHAPTER SEVEN

THE PALE HALF moon disappeared behind a cloud and Spur ran quickly from the side of the house to the small barn behind it. This was his first real chance to find the covered wagon he figured the rawhiders used. The other house and barn had been too close to the street, and the barn not constructed correctly. This one had a large door in the center for a drive-through, probably with cribs and bins inside on the ground floor.

The tall Secret Service agent moved like a shadow to the back of the barn and went through the regular door built into the larger one. Inside it was darker than outside. He pulled a stinker match out of his pocket and scratched it on the rough wood of the barn door.

The match flared into light and the sulphur odor was unmistakable. That's why they called them stinkers, Spur decided.

Holding the match high, he looked as far into the gloom as he could see.

Nothing.

He walked forward slowly so the match wouldn't blow out. It began to burn down and he lit another from it and reached the front side of the barn. No wagon.

"Who the hell's that down there?" An angry voice sounded from above in the darkness.

Spur extinguished the match and crept silently toward the rear door in the darkness.

He heard cursing from above, and the unmistakable sound of a six-gun's hammer cocking.

The shot boomed in the dark stillness. Spur bolted for the back door, sliding through it just as a second shot blasted and a bullet lug dug into the wood beside the door. Then he was outside and running toward the next barn two hundred yards south. The moon had double-crossed him and was shining brightly again. He tried to forget the target he made as he ran.

But no more shots followed him. He got to an outhouse and leaned against it, panting. There was no pursuit. Maybe he had disturbed a hired hand who was sleeping in the haymow.

Spur shrugged and looked at the next barn. Not so promising. A square box with a lean-to on one side. Lamps glowed in the house which was only twenty rods from the house. He moved cautiously, found a rear door on the barn and slid inside. His eyes were more used to the faint light now and he moved slowly, but saw that there was no room here for a big wagon. He went out the back door and tried the lean-to. A canvas draped the front of the opening. He pushed it aside.

A Johnson covered wagon. The tongue had been removed and stored under the rig. He froze, listening. Nothing moved. He slipped under the canvas and looked at the inside of the structure. It was tightly built and would let no light show through.

His match flared and he looked in the front of the rig. It was a rolling home, and stuffed with household goods. It even had the smell of a rawhider's outfit. He blew out the match as he heard the screen door of the house slam shut. Spur crawled under the wagon and waited. Chances were someone was only paying a call on the outhouse. Then he saw the glow of a lantern under the canvas as it was flapped back.

". . . Come get her own damn stuff after this," a voice grumbled. The lantern vanished as the man climbed into the wagon. A moment later the figure jumped down, mumbling to himself and he and the lantern moved away in the night. When the screen door slammed again, Spur came out of the lean-to, and walked quickly toward the next house to the right of this one.

He knocked on the small frame home's front door. It was early and there were still lamps lit in the residence.

A man opened the door cautiously.

"Yep?"

"Good evening, sir. Sorry to be calling so late, but I'm a special deputy for Sheriff James. I need to ask you some questions."

"Never seen you before," the man said.

"I'm new in town. Do you know the people who live next door?"

"Yep."

"Have you seen them in the past two or three days?"

The man frowned. "Can't say as I have. Not hide nor hair of them, come to think of it."

"Who lives there?"

"Older gentleman and his wife. Both must be about sixty. He's got a bad limp." The man looked up quickly. "Something happen to them?"

"I hope not. Did you see a covered wagon rig around here in the last two or three days?"

"Sure did. About dusk one day, came right past the house."

"Notice where it went?"

"Nope."

"What are the people's names next door?"

"Galloway, Frank and Betty."

"Thank you." He started to turn. "Oh, it might be best if you don't go calling at the Galloway's for a spell. There is a chance that something has happened to them, and there may be dangerous people living there now. Just go on as you usually do."

"Outlaws?"

"Could be. But you shouldn't be in any danger unless you go over there."

The man nodded. "Damn! I should have kept better track of the Galloways."

"No fault of yours, sir. Thank you."

Spur left the house and walked back to his horse. There were lights showing through half the windows in the Galloway house. He wanted to kick open the door and start blasting them straight into hell. He would have, a couple of years ago. But now he had grown more cautious, and he played it more by regulations. As far as evidence went, he had none. There was no way yet that he could connect the owners of the Johnson covered wagon with the killings of the family on the mountain.

But he would find some. And he would find out what had happened to the Galloways. He had a strong feeling that the Galloways were both dead. Someone had ridden into town, scouted out the best barn and the best family to take over. Then they did it quietly and came in as close to dark as they could. The Galloways by now were probably in shallow graves behind the barn.

Spur rode to talk to the sheriff. The two lawmen agreed: there was nothing they could do right then.

"We could ride up with a posse and scare the hell out of them and chances are they would panic and start shooting," the sheriff said.

"And the town would lose three or four good men. No, Sheriff. There has to be a better way. I think tomorrow I'll go out there in my best shirt and tie and be a traveling salesman with a fine display of hunting and throwing knives."

"I'll be right behind you."

"No, Sheriff. I have to do this alone. They see anybody else, I'm dead where I stand. I know these kind of people—they kill first and ask questions later."

"In the morning?"

"Soon as I can get some good knives in a kit and ready to go. Maybe about ten. I'll let you know what happens. Any more burglaries reported tonight?"

"Not yet. I got two extra men out walking the better neighborhoods."

The lawmen said goodbye and parted. Spur headed for the Carriage House and that surprise Annabelle had promised him.

It was just after one in the morning when the four boys came back to the alley where they met Rusty White, the medicine show man. Two had come back quickly after they were sent out.

"No sir, we went into only one house, then Joey got scared and wouldn't go with me no more. I wasn't gonna do it alone." He passed over his shoulder bag. Inside was a fine set of sterling silverware, some silver goblets, a fat purse and a small leather bag filled with coins.

White glared at the offending boy, then back-handed him across the face, knocking him into the alley dirt. The ten-year-old wailed for a minute until he saw the gleaming knife at his throat.

"One more sound, laddie, and your throat gets slit!" White hit the boy again with a fist on the side of his head. Tears poured from the boy's eyes but he made no sound. "Lucky you're alive! You get no pay tonight, and you say one word to anyone about this, I'll track you down and slice your fingers off one by one and stuff them down your throat until you choke to death!"

Rusty White wiped beads of sweat off his forehead. He knew he was breathing hard, that his temper was raging again, but sometimes he couldn't stop it. He opened the leather bag, saw the gold coins and smiled. It might not be such a bad night after all.

Luke and his partner had worked all four of their houses and had found little cash, but did bring back two dueling pistols that should be worth something.

Rusty said they'd done good work, even though the take was small. He paid off the two boys and sent all three on their way. "We're through here," he told them. "You be good lads and keep your little mouths shut about this." He gave the two an extra dollar apiece and turned with Luke toward the wagon several blocks over.

"Do I get my two hundred?" Luke asked.

Rusty was furious in a flash. "You get what I give you!"

They walked another block. "A deal is a deal," Luke said. "You promised me two hundred."

"All right! Just be civil about it. Don't cause me trouble, Luke. I don't want to get angry with you."

Luke knew then that tonight had to be the

time. He had seen Rusty "get angry" at one of the boys in another town. Rusty had cut him into pieces with his knife. Luke had thrown up when he saw it and he knew he should have run away right then, but somehow he couldn't. Tonight he would. And his own knife would taste blood.

Inside the medicine wagon, they counted the money. Luke watched sharply. In the wallet there were one hundred twenty three dollars in greenbacks. In the leather pouch were twenty double gold eagles, four hundred dollars! Luke checked the bag again and found a large diamond ring. He set the value of the ring at a hundred dollars.

"I'll take ten of the double gold eagles," Luke said.

Rusty White glared at him for a moment, then shrugged and relaxed. "I'm not used to the new, more outspoken Luke yet," he said. "But as long as the rest of the bargain holds . . ."

"I said a deal was a deal."

"And I want to collect on it right now." Rusty caught Luke by the shoulders and pushed him to his knees, then pulled his face into the medicine man's throbbing crotch. "Right now, I want you to eat me. Then later on we'll use your other tender hole. Right now, you little whore!"

Luke knew this had to be the time. He had taken enough. He turned his head a little to get his breath, then his hand snaked into his pocket and he opened the snap-closed folding pocket knife with its four-inch blade. He always kept a razor-like edge on the steel blade.

He bent back suddenly and slashed upward with the knife, aiming for White's crotch. The blade missed, but bit a half inch into the medicine man's right leg, and he shrilled in pain, surprise and then fury.

Luke was in an impossible fighting position. Before he could jump to his feet, White kicked him in the chest, slamming him backward against the folding table. White fell on him, his one hundred and eighty pounds pinning the thin boy to the floor of the wagon. His hand slapped Luke's face from side to side a dozen times.

"What the hell you trying to do—castrate me, you little shit? You'll have to use a knife a lot better than that to hurt me." He had one knee on Luke's right bicep, crushing it, making the knife in his right hand useless. Luke tried to kick White but he could not touch him.

"Time you got a lesson, little whore. You're a male whore and a burglar and that's all you'll ever be. So don't get no more fancy ideas. You probably thought you were gonna kill me and take all my money and light out of town. Been tried a few times before, Luke. Didn't work them times neither. We gonna have a long, slow talk about that. Boy like you shouldn't never hurt a man who helps him, especially when you let him fuck your little ass."

White took a knife from his belt, sliding it from a hidden sheath. He brought the sharp five-inch blade across Luke's right palm. Luke dropped his knife and cried out in fear and pain.

"Don't hurt you much at all, Luke, not the way you gonna be hurting in a few minutes!"

Before Luke could scream again, White had pushed a handkerchief into the boy's mouth and tied another securely around his head to hold the gag in place. He ripped Luke's shirt open and drew three blood lines with his knife across the puny white chest.

"Such a shame, Luke. You were the best lover I've ever had, and that includes half a dozen women. You were the best!" He slapped Luke again, then caught both his hands and tied them together in front of him. White opened Luke's pants and slid them down, taking the short underwear with them.

Sparse, light colored pubic hair glistened in the lamp light over Luke's erection. The sudden fear had excited him, to his surprise and anger.

"No!" Luke shouted soundlessly, staring at his crotch.

"Oh, yes!" White roared. "You're just a little whore and you always will be!" White rubbed the swelling behind his fly, then shook his head.

"You like the knife, Luke? We'll see how well you like it." The blade flashed and a line sprang blood red down Luke's arm. It went deep and Luke screamed but no sound came out. His eyes were wide with terror.

Luke shook his head, eyes pleading.

Rusty White looked at the blood surging down Luke's arm. He rubbed his crotch again. Thoughts and emotions and yearnings slammed around in his head. Christ, but he was high! He was so excited he hardly knew what to do next. He slashed the outer arm now, and then quickly found a towel and covered up Luke's face where he lay on the floor.

Yes, better! Now there was no problem remembering the thing here as Luke. Forget the name, it wasn't important any more. Forget it!

The blade lowered again, slashed down one of the pure white, hairless legs, and blood gushed out. White stared at Luke's hard, twitching penis. Slowly he bent and kissed it, then took it in his mouth. A moment later he came away and shook his head.

Not this time, by God!

He cut Luke's other leg and watched the blood run.

Fantastic!

Exhilarating!

Tremendous!

He hadn't felt this way since that time nearly five years ago when he came west with his Uncle Zack on the wagon, and they found this little farm house that had a pretty mother and three daughters. Old Zack polished off the man of the house quick with his wet rawhide around the balls and the throat. Damn, what a day and a night that had been! They had taken turns and used up the women one at a time, then he personally had the fun of dispatching each one after the women slowly turned into raging lunatics.

He looked back at the thing on the floor.

Bastard! He had tried to kill Rusty White! There ws no doubt about it now, Rusty knew what had to be done. But there could be wonderment and marvels and joy even in difficult jobs.

"Boy, you picked the wrong man to run up against. You know that now. Shoulda been happy with that two hundred split. No, you got damn greedy! I warned you not to do that."

White opened his fly and pulled out his erection. He fisted it and pumped a few times, then grinned at the boy. White dropped to his knees beside him, grabbed the youth's still erect penis and cut a quarter inch slice from root to head.

Luke's screams came through the gag. He lunged upward, throwing off the towel. Fury and hatred seared through the air as Luke vented his agony, his frustration and his disbelief against Rusty White, then he passed out and fell back to the floor.

White hardly noticed. He knelt there, one hand busy at his crotch in his autoerotic flurry, and his other with the knife making small incision like cuts all over the unconscious form in front of him. None of the cuts alone would cause much harm, but they would bleed severely.

As his surging sexual heat increased, the knife dug deeper and deeper. White was panting now, his eyes glazed, his hands pumping rapidly. As the white hot surge came in his turgid phallus he moaned and the knife in his hand slashed at the untouched throat, again and again the knife descended until the whiteness of the neck bones showed through.

White gave one last moaning grunt of pleasure and fell backwards in the wagon, the knife dropping from his hand, a smile of total ecstasy on his face.

CHAPTER EIGHT

EARLY THAT SAME evening, the gathering at Mrs. Hillery Gregson's beautiful Spanish hacienda had begun promptly at nine. It was fashionably late, and she escorted Pastor Thompson from the revival to her courtyard.

The hacienda had belonged to a wealthy Spanish don during the early days of Santa Fe and had been built nearly two hundred years before. She had rebuilt part of it, added on to one wing with the same type of adobe construction, and regenerated the gardens in the courtyard that was fifty feet wide, and had an entrance and exit for buggies and riders.

"My, this is impressive," Pastor Thompson said, alighting from the buggy and helping Mrs. Gregson down. "Such a fine example of an old Spanish home. You must preserve it this way for posterity."

"I hope to do just that," Hillery said, pleased

at his comments. So many visitors thought the home quaint, but terribly out of date.

Three guests were already in the large living room, with its double fireplaces at each end, and furniture ranged around the other sides. A pair of musicians playing mandolin and guitar came strolling in with fast paced Mexican music.

She introduced the pastor to the early arrivals, and then to the others as they came.

Ten minutes later there were twelve people in the room. Half of them were dressed as if they had money. Interesting. But Erick Thompson was not at all interested in starting a church in Santa Fe. He was there only to make an impression on the lady. He had discovered that morning that she was indeed a widow. Her husband had been killed in a runaway carriage a year ago. He had been one of the wealthiest men in town, and now she controlled everything.

Erick's second purpose was to show his pleasure that she was heading the drive for a church. In the process he would be seeing her daily, and soon he would let slip his interest in her as a person and as a woman.

It might take a few days, a week at the most. This was the kind of lady you did not try to kiss after only a brief acquaintance. But he had the time.

The meeting was like those he had set up in other towns, and all for the same purpose, to select a target. An hour later it was over. They had elected Mrs. Gregson chairman. She would meet with the pastor the next morning, since there was no morning service, and they would lay out some additional plans. Then actual canvassing of prospective members would begin, an announcement in the paper would be made, and they would be on their way.

"Please come here for our meeting tomorrow, Pastor Thompson," she said at the door. The others had left, and Erick wanted to take the lady in his arms and kiss her a dozen times, then get his hands on her breasts . . .

"Pastor Thompson, I suggested meeting here tomorrow. Would that be all right?"

"Yes, of course. I was just thinking how lovely you look. I hope I'm not being too forward. My wife passed away a few years ago, in the big St. Louis flood. You may have heard of it." He turned away and brushed his eyes with his hand, then continued, "Well, I will certainly be here tomorrow. Did we set a time?"

"Ten o'clock, then we could have tea." She watched him closely. "Are you all right, Pastor? You look a little shaken."

"I'm fine. I just should not let myself get to thinking about Helen. I'm sorry. Yes, ten o'clock will be fine." He smiled at her, saw the hint of a smile in return and stepped into the cool summer night air. At the seven-thousand-foot level of the town, the nights were always pleasant, no matter how warm the summer days had been.

The fake pastor whistled as he walked the few blocks back to his wagon-church parked on the street. He had put his two horses in the livery stable for the night. He hummed softly to himself as he thought of the large amount of money he would get from Hillery Gregson, and how delicious she would be, naked and lying on her own bed.

He was sure there would be time. He had noticed the Medicine Wagon on the other side of town near the tenderloin district. That would be his brother Rusty. So he was in town and doing business as usual, Erick figured. That afternoon he had heard about a fight but it was all over by the time he got there. Two young hellions were about to shoot each other to pieces, but some stranger drew down on them and made them stop.

Erick had spotted the two gunmen; they were Birch and Piney, his nephews. That meant brother Zack was also in town somewhere. If he followed his usual pattern, Zack would lay low until both his brothers had time to finish their respective businesses. Sometimes Zack got itchy feet. If he did this time, one of the boys would make a late night call at one or both of the wagons and they would have a reunion in whatever house Zack had taken over. He was good at picking the places.

Lately the three men had been taking pains not to be seen together, to help avoid the lawmen who were looking for the Schmidke brothers. Erick laughed softly as he thought how many names he had used during the past two years. Schmidke had not been one of them.

He picked a new name for each town, which made it extremely hard for anyone chasing him. A man of the cloth had a lot of automatic defenses working for him, too. Everyone believed whatever he said. No one would suspect a preacher of anything bad, evil or illegal. And a pastor's title gave him immediate entrance to all the best homes in the city. It was the best diguise he had ever worked out to cover up his more profitable activities.

Pastor Thompson went up the steps and into his wagon. He never locked the door. Who would steal from a minister?

When Spur got back to the Santa Fe Carriage House and used the key in Annabelle's door, he remembered that she said she would have a surprise for him tonight. But there was little about the woman that he did not know intimately by now.

He closed the door and looked around the beautiful room. No one was there.

"Spur? In here."

It was Annabelle calling from the bedroom. That was a good place for a surprise. He tossed his hat on the love seat and went to the door. It was partway open. He walked in quickly, pushing the door aside.

On the bed was a scene that stopped him.

"I said I'd have a surprise for you," Annabelle said. She sat naked on her big bed holding a hand of cards. Across from her on the bed sat a dark-haired Mexican girl, also naked. The slightly brown-skinned girl had the biggest breasts Spur had ever seen.

"My God!" Spur said.

"I thought you would like Conchita. She works for me here at the hotel in various ways, and tonight she, and I, together, are all yours. Now don't tell me that you have ever enjoyed two beautiful women at the same time."

Spur stood there watching them.

Conchita turned toward him, got up on her knees and shook her big breasts, making them bounce and roll. She put her hands under them lifting them up so there was no sag. She laughed and looked at Annabelle.

"I think the big gringo is afraid of us poor little naked virgins," Conchita said.

Spur made a dive and landed on the bed between them, turned over on his back and pulled the girls on top of him, one with each arm.

"At a time like this, a man's got to be brave and face the music, even if he is petrified with fear."

"Honey, I don't care if you're petrified, as long as you're hard," Conchita said, and broke up laughing.

Spur reached up and nibbled on Conchita's breasts and she made soft little humming sounds. He looked at Annabelle.

"I don't understand. Don't you mind that Conchita is here? Aren't you jealous?"

"Jealous? Why? I figured out a long time ago that you're not going to stand still for a wedding ring, so why the hell not have a little fun while you're here? Conchita and I are best friends. Best friends share the good things they have. For a while I have you, so we share."

"What if I go for her big tits and kick you out of bed?"

"I'll punch you in the crotch and jump right back in. It's my bed!"

Both women broke up with laughter. Spur sat up and stared at the two naked women, the starkly white, slender Annabelle and the soft brown, heavier Conchita with the big boobs.

"Can you take care of both of us at once, Big Spur?" Conchita asked, smiling enticingly.

"I'll think of a way," Spur growled.

Conchita winked at Annabelle and rolled on top of Spur where he lay on his back. She pushed up and fed her big breasts one at a time into his mouth. As he sucked he felt hands at his crotch and knew it was Annabelle working up his head of steam.

The realization that he had two naked, sexy women working over him came slowly, and when it did he felt his blood begin to bubble and boil with desire. Conchita moved and her mouth covered his and the steam built higher. He could feel the heat of her body as she writhed and wiggled on top of him.

Then before he was entirely sure what was happening, Conchita moved lower over him, lifted his erection upward, and slowly backed her crotch down on it. He felt the slight resistance, then he plunged into her fully as she settled downward against him and growled deep in her throat.

Her black eyes sparkled as she looked down at him.

"Now we play cowboy, no?" she said and began to lift and lower herself, riding him like a calico pony. Each lunge brought a new surge of pleasure and desire to Spur.

When he looked up, he found Annabelle hovering over him. She kissed him and it was sweet, powerful.

"Now you're going to get your surprise," she said grinning strangely. She moved forward then, her body at right angles to his and gently lowered her crotch toward his face.

"Darling Spur, use your tongue inside me." She spread her legs and he saw swaying over him her pink love lips. They came lower and lower until he no longer could see them, only feel them on his cheek. He turned his head and darted his tongue out.

He heard her gasp in pleasure, and her voice was muted.

"Sweet Spur! Yes! I'm exploding. Please, yes, oh, God, yes!"

His tongue probed and probed, passing the nether lips, touching the soft bud of her clitoris, now risen and sensitive. He twanged it half a dozen times with his tongue and Annabelle began quivering and shaking in a climax. The vibrations rattled through her form and left her gasping for breath as she rolled away.

Spur looked down at Conchita, who had been

watching. She grinned and he saw sweat on her forehead. Conchita's breath came in gasps now; sweat dripped on him. He reached down and caught her swaying, bouncing breasts and she smiled at him, then he felt her surging in a powerful spasm.

"Oh, God! Oh, God! I'm going to die! I can't live through this. Sweet Jesus! So beautiful! I no can talk more . . ." Her eyes closed and her pretty face took on a look of ecstasy as her hips beat at his, countering his movements, pounding with steady hard thrusts.

Then she squealed and mumbled something in Spanish as her head began bobbing in rhythm to her hip thrusts. Spur felt his own floodgates open and now he joined in her thrusting, humping her into the air with each punching. She wailed, shouted in Spanish again, then screeched for fifteen seconds as she jolted and threshed and pounded at him again and again until her face was wet with sweat and she fell on him exhausted and unable to move.

Spur humped upward one more time and the whole world dissolved as he blasted his seed into the woman and then sucked in air through his mouth and nose and every pore of his body to replenish his oxygen-starved cells.

McCoy gave one final lunge and put his arms around the woman over him and closed his eyes. He could die happy now.

Five minutes later, Annabelle roused them and they sat up and took cold bottles of beer she offered. She nodded at Spur.

"Yeah, yeah, big city man. Of course we have

ice, and cold beer. You think we're out in the sticks? This is the capital of New Mexico, don't forget. Anyway, every hotel in town and about half the houses have their own ice house. We're at seven thousand feet, remember and we get all the ice we want in winter. We just cut it up into blocks with saws, and pack it in straw in an ice house that is dug halfway into the ground. We have ice all summer."

"Thanks for the guided tour." He reached over and petted one of Conchita's breasts. "How did you grow them so big?"

"I got up every morning and stretched them out, how you think?"

"I never grew any of my own," Spur said.

"I get from Mama. You should see *mi madre!*" She pushed his hand away. "Sometimes I wish I was tiny tits. Men all the time like big tits. Get all excited fast. I wear my clothes loose to hide them."

"Yeah, men are terrible. Sex crazy. Like two women who seduce one poor cowboy."

They hit him with pillows. The beer bottles fell to the floor and a wrestling match was in full swing on the bed. Conchita sat on Spur's head until he gently bit her bottom, then she jumped off and Spur rolled over and pinned Annabelle, who had fallen on her back.

In a heartbeat the wrestling was over and Spur bent and kissed Annabelle. "Thanks for the surprise," he said.

"You don't think it's over, do you? This is an all-night party. Conchita and I have a bet. I say five times, and she says you for sure can make love six times. So we have to test you out to see. Right now I'm going for number two. Do you think you can stand up under the testing?"

"It's a rough job to give a guy, but somebody's got to do it. But remember to be gentle with me."

She swung a pillow at him which he blocked then he kissed her gently, and Conchita sat on the side of the bed and cheered.

It turned out to be the longest, most exhausting night Spur McCoy could remember. But when the sun came up the next morning, he was still smiling.

CHAPTER NINE

ANNABELLE STARED AT Spur who sat on the edge of the bed in the morning light and put on his clothes. She was half asleep but shook her head in astonishment.

"Eight times! I still don't believe it. We must have lost track. I'm completely exhausted." She blinked and stared at him from drowsy eyes. "Where are you going?"

"It's morning. A man has to put in a good day's work, no matter what happened the night before." He bent and kissed her lips and lay her down on the big bed. She closed her eyes and had fallen alseep by the time he let go of her.

Conchita lay on her side, her big breasts billowing over one another toward the sheet. Spur reached in and petted the beauties and the girl smiled in her sleep and reached for him. He pulled back.

He had to get some kind of cover set up so he could go unnoticed on a door-to-door trip past the house where he suspected the rawhiders were hiding.

As Spur ate breakfast in the Carriage House dining room, a man tapped him on the shoulder.

"Mr. McCoy?"

Spur nodded.

"Sheriff wants to see you right away."

Spur stood, left the rest of his meal and followed the deputy toward the courthouse office of Sheriff James.

The sheriff looked worried.

"You must be right about them rawhiders being in town. All hell is breaking loose around here. We had five more reports of burglaries last night, with a lot of money, jewelry and silver stolen. Early last night there was a wild gunfight out in the north residential section of town and two horses were killed. The hardware was broken into last night and six long guns and all the ammunition for those stolen rifles was taken."

Spur scowled as the sheriff went on.

"Then this morning we found the body of a young boy. The poor kid had been tortured to death. Now how can you account for all of this?"

"Can't," Spur said. "Unless it *is* the rawhiders. Could I see the boy?"

"Ain't pretty."

"I've seen corpses before."

"Hope not too many of them looked like this."

Five minutes later at the undertaker's Spur pulled back a sheet and winced. It was a torture murder. Looked like some he had seen by the Apaches when the Indians had lots of time, and a good hate built up against another Indian or a white. But there weren't any Indians on the warpath close around there, and none in town.

Spur looked away, then glanced back at the boy's face and turned his head so he had only a glimpse of the face. He did it twice more and then set his jaw.

"Anybody know who he is?" Spur asked.

"Don't think he's local. Nobody who's seen him so far knows him."

"I might," Spur said. "I saw him first night I was in town. He and another boy were slipping into the wagon the Medicine Show man is driving. It seemed like he belonged there by the way he moved."

"Doc White and his Medicine Show." The sheriff stroked his jaw. "Could be some connection."

"A lot of blood went somewhere, Sheriff. If we could find some in that wagon it would be a strong piece of evidence."

Sheriff James reached for his gunbelt, strapped it on and spoke quietly to one of his deputies. The man brought him a shotgun with a special short barrel. Sheriff James pushed two rounds of double ought buck into the tubes, and snapped the barrels shut.

"Let's go pay a visit to this snake-oil man," he said.

When they got there, the door canvas was open. There seemed to be no activity. Sheriff

James positioned deputies at forty-five degree angles to the near side of the rig so the men wouldn't shoot each other through the canvas. Then he and Spur walked up to the wagon and knocked on the wood bow.

There was no response. Spur saw that the flap was untied. He flicked one side of it up with his drawn .45. Then he lifted it fully.

No one was home.

The sheriff went through the opening with Spur right behind him. It looked much like other prairie schooners Spur had seen set up for travel and living. He smelled something, then he realized it was lye soap. Strong soap. He bent and looked at the wooden floor. It was made of one-inch boards glued together on the side, to make a four-inch thick floor, stronger than a framed floor.

Dark stains showed on the polished wood. Spur bent to sniff them but came up only with the smell of lye. A braided rug had been pushed to one side. The edge showed a dark stain. Spur sniffed.

Blood.

"Look at this," the sheriff said. He held a ripped-apart shirt and a pair of pants. "Looks about the size to fit that dead boy. Too small for a grown man."

Spur found a bucket pushed under the built-in bed. He opened the seal on top and squinted to be sure he saw right. The bucket was half filled with rags all stained a deep red. The lye smell was there but so was that of blood.

"Look at this, Sheriff," Spur said.

The sheriff touched the blood stains. Some of them were not dry yet. Red came away on his fingers. He smelled it.

"Let's find this medicine man," the sheriff said grimly. Outside, he sent his deputies fanning out through the town. They were concentrating on the cafes and restaurants that were open that time of day.

"I'll check the livery," Spur said. "Our Medicine man might have gone for his team with plans to move on."

"See that he doesn't move too far, but don't kill him if he draws down on you. I want him alive. I want him to hang high for this dastardly crime, if he's found guilty. We should be able to dig up someone else who saw the boy here. Let's move!"

Spur walked quickly toward the livery. He was only halfway there when he saw a man walking behind a team of harnessed horses driving them up the street. It was the Medicine Man, all right.

But he wasn't alone. The man had a stable boy with him, and a big .44 with hammer cocked was held by the boy's head as they walked along behind the team. Spur watched closely. There was no way he could shoot down the killer without the rawhider's gun going off, and it would kill the innocent boy.

Spur drew his .45 and waited behind a balcony support four-by-four as the team came up to him. He fired a shot into the air, then came down on the "doc."

"Give it up, Schmidke, this is the end of the line," Spur bellowed.

The man jumped in surprise, looked at Spur but kept the gun against the boy's head.

"Not true. This boy's life says it's not true. Put down your gun or I kill the boy."

"No you won't, Schmidke. Then your shield would be gone. You'll bluff it as long as you can, then kill the boy. I know how you think."

They kept walking, the team's harness jangling, trailing the pair of singletrees in the dirt street. Schmidke slapped the reins against the pair of blacks.

"You fire at me, the kid dies. Make up your mind."

"I'll check my bet. I want to see you hitch up the wagon and still keep the gun on the boy."

"Easy, you'll see."

Spur knew at once how he would do it. The boy worked in the stable. He could probably hitch up the big wagon better than the man could, and all the time the .44 would be against the lad's head.

Spur followed, watching the rawhider's second hand. He had given the reins to the boy now and walked directly beside him, the gun still in place. The rawhider would have a hide-out gun somewhere. Spur hoped he couldn't reach it without being obvious. If he got the hide-out there would be lots of gunplay.

Ahead, Spur saw the sheriff standing in the street. Spur ran to him and told him the situation.

"Hostage? The Bennett kid from the livery? Damn!"

"It'll take a miracle to save the boy," Spur said. "If we start shooting, Schmidke kills him. If we don't shoot, Schmidke gets away and will probably kill the boy as soon as he's free." Spur decided in a flash.

"Sheriff, let Schmidke hitch up and drive out of town. Follow him but don't attack. Keep a little pressure on him. I'm going to get a horse and keep up with him. Somewhere out there he's going to make a mistake. Have one of your men get me the best sighted-in rifle you've got, a long range one, one of the new Army Springfield rifles if you have one. Have your men stay with him until he gets out of town, then I'll take over."

"Should have a posse. Whole county is my jurisdiction."

"We don't want to spook him, just let him know he's still being followed so he won't kill the boy. I can handle it."

"From the way he's acting, there's no doubt in my mind that he killed the other boy."

"I'll bring him back alive if I can, but he's a rawhider. Keep other folks off the road so he can't get more hostages. Clear the streets if you can, now!"

Spur ran for the livery stable. He got the strongest, longest-lasting mount he could find, saddled him up and got back to the street just as the big wagon pulled out. A deputy tossed him a new army Springfield, the model with plenty of range. It came with a box of twenty five rounds. Spur wished he had more.

The boy sat in front, driving. Schmidke was inside somewhere out of sight, but, Spur was sure, with various peep holes so he could see what the sheriff was doing.

Two mounted men stormed into the street ahead of the wagon, turned and rode ahead of it, warning everyone on the street or driving a rig to get out of sight or to drive down a side street.

A half hour later the situation was exactly the same. The boy sat on the front seat driving the Medicine Wagon. The outskirts of Santa Fe were behind them as they began to wind toward the Jemez mountains.

Spur had held back, showing himself now and then so the rawhider knew he was there, but not long enough to offer a good target. He guessed Schmidke had rifles and pistols in the wagon.

A plan had formed in his mind before they left town, but he hesitated to use it. Now there seemed no other way. The boy's life was most important now. Spur would put down two good horses any day to save an innocent life. He found cover to his left and rode through pines and brush until he was a quarter of a mile ahead of the wagon, then worked back toward the trail, staying well concealed. He dismounted, took the Springfield long gun and found a log to sight over.

When the wagon came five minutes later, it was one hundred fifty yards from Spur's position. He lifted up, sighted in carefully and fired. The horse on the near side took the heavy .45 round in the head, and went down at once, front legs buckling, then rear legs as the momentum of the rig tangled the dying horse with the live one, which stumbled and pranced but slowed and stopped within five feet with her dead harness mate on the ground.

A scream of anger and fury came from the wagon. Then a dozen rounds blasted from the canvas top aimed in Spur's general direction. Schmidke jerked the boy off the front seat into the back of the wagon.

Spur watched. Now it was a waiting game. The rawhider would use what chips he had: the biggest was the boy's life. There would be no quick killing and then a shootout with the outlaw. He would hold the life of the boy as his best chance for escape. Spur had to make sure he kept thinking that way.

It would be a long time before anything happened, Spur was sure. The rawhider would try to figure out a way to escape. He would check all the possibilities first. The horse in the harness would be one chance, but a plow horse could not outrun the mount Spur had.

Spur tried to figure out what the man would do. Schmidke's answer came before Spur thought it would.

"You out there," the heavy voice came from the wagon. "It's the same standoff as before. I have the boy, and I'm leaving with him. You bother us, and he dies."

"Fine with me, Schmidke. The boy means nothing to me. You're in my jurisdiction now. Sheriff don't hold me down none. All I want is the posted reward on your dead carcass. Hell, I figured the kid would be dead by now and you'd want to shoot it out man to man. But I guess that's not your style."

Five more shots came toward Spur's location, but he had dropped behind the big pine log in time.

Now he lifted and put a rifle round through the top of the canvas well over either of the occupants' heads.

"Not much protection in there against hot lead, Schmidke. I might as well just use my dynamite and blow you both to hell."

"Bluff," Schmidke said and fired again. "You want the kid alive, otherwise you'd have drawn down on me a long time ago. So we compromise with the only real thing, what we're both more interested in than anything else . . . money. I put three thousand dollars in cash outside the tailgate, and the kid and I cut loose the dead horse and drive away. You get what you want—the reward money. Only you get it from me. And I get away to fight another day."

"Not a chance, Schmidke. I kill you, and I take your whole bank in there of over six thousand, and I get the reward money too." He put two rifle shots through the canvas, low and to the rear.

"Bastard! You killed the boy!" Schmidke shouted.

"Bluff, Schmidke! If I did you would never tell me—you think he's your shield. But he isn't. I figure I better just burn you out. Remember all that hoarded paper money of yours is going to burn too."

Spur had been working on a long shaft he had cut from a sapling. He fashioned it into an elementary spear. On the tip of it he bound dry grasses, and tied them on with tough wild vines. When he was through, he had a serviceable spear.

Quickly he made three more. One he left the grass off. That one was to establish the range.

Now he worked through the brush with the rifle and four spears getting as close as he could to the wagon. There was a chance that the desperado would cut a hole in the canvas on the far side, jump down and run to escape, but Spur didn't think he would. The fruits of a year or two of the rawhider's efforts were all in the wagon. He would leave it only when he was dead.

Spur checked his location. Now he was less than thirty yards from the wagon. He was sure he could throw the spear that far. He looked at the spears and changed the design. He sharpened the point, and tied the grass a foot in back of the tip. That would allow the point to pierce the canvas and hold the burning grass there long enough to set the heavy material on fire.

Spur used one of his stinker matches and lit the first bundle of grass, then lifted and threw the spear. It sailed well, nosed down but hit short. At least the fire kept burning all the way to the target. He tried again. This time the spear slanted to the side and missed.

The fourth spear he threw punctured the top of the canvas and clung there. The fire burned brightly for a moment, then seemed to slow. A moment later the canvas caught on fire and Spur put two more rifle shots through the top of the rig.

Over the sound of the flames Spur heard the call.

"Don't shoot! Don't shoot! We're coming out."

CHAPTER TEN

THE TOP OF the big covered wagon began burning fiercely where it sat in the middle of the trail out of Santa Fe.

"Did you hear me out there, goddamnit? I said to hold your fire, we're coming out."

"Come ahead, Schmidke, and bring the boy."

A small metal chest sailed out of the back of the wagon, then a wooden box, and a suitcase. Next the boy backed out, the pistol in Schmidke's hand again aimed at the youth's head.

Spur was in the same situation as before; if he shot the rawhider the boy would probably also die.

The two stood on the ground a dozen feet in back of the wagon.

"You want that horse to burn up, bounty hunter? Or can we go around front and cut her loose?"

"Cut her loose," Spur said. He ran from his

hiding spot into the open so he could follow the movements of the outlaw. There might be a chance he would take his eyes off the boy for a minute. All Spur needed was one free shot.

He had no chance. The boy cut the traces and then the connecting harness between the live horse and the dead one and slapped the back flank of the mare. She ran twenty feet down the road, then began grazing on the fringes of summer grass. The gun had never moved an inch from the youth's neck.

Spur checked the wagon horse. She would not be much of a saddle horse, but would work in a pinch. When he looked back, the place where the outlaw had been was empty. The boy lay in the grass where he had been pushed down, and the rawhider was gone. Spur now realized that cover grew considerably closer to the far side of the trail than it did on his side.

The boy was free—dead or alive, Spur didn't know. It was done, and now he had to think of the rawhider. What would he do? Where would he go? Spur lifted the rifle and shot the grazing wagon horse in the head. Even a draft horse like that one would provide transportation for the man. He winced as the mare screamed in her death throes.

At once Spur turned and ran for his own mount. The rawhider would try for it, then he could come back later for anything that was left in the wagon. Spur brushed past small trees and shrubs, darted through a ravine and saw his horse grazing where he had left her.

A shot smashed through the quiet mountain air and Spur dove behind a tree. Pistol. Ahead and to the left. Spur was closer to the horse than the rawhider. He fired twice into the brush where he figured the shot had originated and ran ahead to a big pine tree.

There was no response. He fired and ran again, coming to within fifteen feet of the horse. Another shot came from the brush to the left and Spur answered with three more rounds, emptying his six-gun. He was closer. Schmidke could not get to the mount. Spur had won the battle.

"Reckon as how you killed the other horse," the rawhider called.

Spur figured he was behind a big Ponderosa about twenty feet away.

"Right," Spur called back.

"Then that makes us even." Four shots came in rapid succession and the bay Spur was moving toward screamed a high shrill cry and went down. One last shot caught it in the head and it was still.

"I'll kill you before we're through with this, bounty hunter," Schmidke said, then all was silent.

Spur ran back toward the wagon, figuring the outlaw had gone in the opposite direction. Quickly Spur checked the boy. He had been pistol-whipped, with a bloody gash down his forehead, but he would live.

Spur hustled him into the brush and behind a big log.

"What's your name, son?"

"Terry Bennett."

"Can you find you way back to town?"

"Sure. I've lived around here all my life."

"You got most of the day, and it's only eight or nine o'clock. You stay here for half an hour or so, then start walking back. Tell the sheriff what happened. I'm going to get that rawhider."

The boy nodded. "He's a bad one. Pistol-whipped the night man at the livery, then grabbed me."

They looked at the wagon. The canvas had burned away, leaving the ribs of the top, but the fire had not caught anything else except one blanket that smoldered. Spur pulled it out of the wagon and let it burn itself out on the ground. He picked up the metal chest and the wooden box. Both were surprisingly heavy. Spur put them in the edge of the woods, covering them with leaves and some branches.

The boy watched him.

"What's in the boxes?"

"I don't know, Terry. But it was something that Schmidke must have wanted pretty badly. We'll save it so he can't find it. Now, you stay here for a half hour, then start for home."

Terry nodded and sat down under a tree.

Spur ran back into the woods where his horse lay and picked up the trail the outlaw made as he charged through the brush and woods. Every fifty feet, Spur stopped and listened. His guess was that the rawhider would run back to his brothers for help. There was plenty of firepower back in Santa Fe on his side.

116

The trail angled in that direction after two false starts. An hour later the trail came out on the track of a road. Spur sat down to rest a moment and think through his strategy. The easiest way and the quickest would be to stay on the road. Spur decided he could catch Schmidke faster that way as well.

He held the rifle at port arms and ran down the road at an Indian trot he had learned from a friendly Navajo. If he did it right, he could use up very little of his energy and move across the ground at twice the usual walking speed of about three miles an hour. A horse walks at four miles per hour. With his trot he should be able to cover six miles in an hour. He guessed they were not more than eight or nine miles out of town.

The first mile went well. He broke into a sweat and felt better, then he got into the rhythm of it and it came easier. After the second mile, he began watching for the other man's bootprints in the soft dirt. They were still there, and moving forward. Schmidke was not running—there was no digging in of the toe as a runner's footprint shows in soft dirt.

He would catch up with him during the next mile.

Spur came to a slight rise and slowed. Just over the rise he moved to the side of the trail and stood behind a ponderosa. Ahead he could see for two miles down a slight incline. There, four hundred yards ahead, he saw his quarry.

Schmidke sat by the side of the road under a tree. He had one boot off. Spur looked at the country. Sparse growth here, thinning out into a grassy valley that led down to the river. If he worked his way through the fringes of trees along the trail, he could make good time and stay out of sight. He did it.

When he got within two hundred yards, he would settle for one sure shot and rid the world once and for all of a Schmidke rawhider. Spur figured he had another fifty yards to go. He brushed past some brush and found only one opening ahead. Just as he stepped into it, he heard a swishing sound. He looked up in time to see a young pine tree slamming toward him. The pine had been bent back and held in place with some kind of trip device.

He fell to the ground and the sapling blasted past two feet over his head. It could easily have killed him, or broken both his legs.

Spur groaned and let out a feeble cry. If Schmidke was around close by, he would want to come in and finish off his victim.

For a moment, sounds came from directly ahead, but then they faded. Spur had crawled away from the trap site, and crouched behind a tree. It all had been a ruse, Schmidke showing himself in the trail with his boot off. And it had almost worked. Spur would be more respectful of his foe from now on.

More noise to the side, and Spur swung his .45 that way. The rifle was useless here in the brush—it took too long to lift and aim. The noise faded.

Spur looked around. There was a two-hundred-foot sharp cliff behind him. It rose upward steeply, and had a few trees on it. Ahead he could see the road and the mountain meadow that expanded into a wide valley through which the river flowed.

He should get back to the road. Schmidke must be well away from the area now.

The first sound was so slight he missed it. The next ones came so quickly he had little time to react. Then a boulder the size of a milk pail bounced past him. He looked toward the cliff. Dozens of boulders of all sizes were raining down, smashing forward over the downslope, tearing dirt and bushes with them. In a minute it would develop into a full scale landslide.

Spur leaped up and ran back the way he had come. There was a thick stand of three-foot ponderosa pines there. They might shield him, maybe divert the flow of rocks and dirt. A large rock bounced past Spur, then he charged the last twenty feet to the three big trees almost side by side and slid behind the largest.

Half a dozen times he felt the big tree vibrate as rocks and dirt and smaller trees slammed into the ponderosas. But all three held. The flow was reducing, it would be over soon.

Then a head-sized rock bounced high off one of the pines to his left, angling toward Spur. Only a lunge to his right saved him from being smashed by the rock. It hit the ground where he had been standing.

Far too late, Spur thought of the rife. The new army Springfield lay where it had been, but the rock had crushed it, broken the stock, bent the barrel at a weird angle and mangled the bolt and breech.

Now his weapons advantage was gone. No longer could he hope to stay well away and pick off the rawhider. The last boulders went rolling past, and he left his haven, running straight toward the trail. Many of the larger boulders were strewn over the roadway. He hit the trail and continued his Indian trot toward town. Wherever Schmidke was, Spur wanted to get ahead of him. He would plan his own ambush. It was time he went on the offensive.

After he had covered what he figured was two miles, Spur went to his side of the trail and began looking for a good spot to confront the outlaw. He wanted a narrow canyon, but there were none along here. He settled for a stretch with absolutely no cover. A house-sized rock near the trail was the only hiding place for half a mile each way.

This would be the spot. He sat down behind the rock to wait and rest a minute, reloaded his six-gun and looked at the remaining rounds in his belt. He had fifteen on each side. Not much of an ammo supply. If he were lucky, he would need only the five in his Colt .45.

Every two minutes, Spur edged to the side of the rock so he could see both ways down the trail. Schmidke would still be moving toward Santa Fe, where his reinforcements and resupply point was.

Spur's job was to stop him from getting there.

Spur had wished for some settlers, or farmers, or ranchers out this way, but he had seen no human habitation since crossing the river near Santa Fe that morning. It was afternoon now, maybe two o'clock. He set up a small sundial with three sticks and marked in the sand where the shadow of the long stick was. He would check to see how the shadow moved with the sun.

The small makeshift sundial had moved two finger-widths when Spur saw movement on the trail behind him. He watched closely and soon could make out Schmidke hobbling along using a cane. The trapper must have been trapped by his own avalanche, or one of his other booby traps.

Spur sat back and waited. In another five minutes he could tell if the rawhider still had his six-gun. There was a chance he had lost it. Should he take Schmidke in alive or dead? Usually the question never came up, there was no time to make a decision. In this case, there was time. Spur knew the sheriff wanted this man alive so he could stand trial.

On the other hand, how could Spur be sure that he could keep him prisoner all the way back to town? Many things could happen. Perhaps he should enact justice now while he had the chance. The more he considered it, the more he leaned toward gunsmoke justice this time.

He stared at the man coming down the road. He was a hundred yards off yet, and Spur could tell the man carried no gun. His holster flapped empty at his thigh, no gun was in his hand, and he doubted he would put it in his belt with a good holster. Spur smiled. He looked down the road the other way, as he had been doing regularly, and this time saw a trail of dust.

Someone was coming. A few minutes later he saw a buggy. The rawhider stopped where he was, still fifty yards from the rock. The rig came faster then. Someone stood up in it and let out a Rebel yell. The rawhider answered and did a little jig, bad leg and all.

"Where the hell you boys been?" Schmidke screeched.

The buggy rolled past the big rocks and Spur kept low and out of sight. Were these some more of the Schmidke clan? The buggy stopped and two young men jumped down. Spur looked in surprise at the men not more than twenty yards away. They were the same two he had stopped from shooting each other in the bar.

On the trail the three held a pow-wow. The older man the boys called Uncle Rusty insisted they go back to the site of the burned wagon to get what they could salvage. The boys insisted their pa had told them to grab him and get him right back to the house, if they could find him.

Rusty Schmidke kept arguing, but he was in no condition to win. The boys simply picked him up, put him in the buggy seat and turned the rig around. A moment later they sent up a trail of dust into the clear summer mountain air, as they hurried back toward Santa Fe.

When they were well clear, Spur stood and

stared after them, then holstered his gun. There was a time he might have tried to gun down all three of them, but he had no proof, damnit! The two young men might be clean as Sunday School teachers on a Sunday morning. Then on the other hand, they were Schmidkes. It was hard to believe that any of that clan could have clean hands.

Spur looked at the sun, checked back down the road and saw a figure coming toward him. It was the boy, Terry. He waited. They could walk back to Santa Fe together.

CHAPTER ELEVEN

"PASTOR" ERICK THOMPSON arrived at Hillery Gregson's hacienda promptly at ten that morning. He had spent an hour in the Third Street public baths, scrubbing his body within a shadow of its life, shaving carefully, and using a small bit of lotion on his hair. He had liberally slapped on bay rum and rose water after shave and put on his best black suit and cravat.

A small Mexican woman answered the door, and without saying a word showed him into a library.

"Señora Gregson be here soon," the woman said in heavily accented English, then vanished out the door.

He looked at the books. Few of them he recognized. His formal education had been brief and uninspired. He had used the Good Book to put a foundation under his preaching, and to obtain the needed polish and flair, but what his followers admired in his sermons was the total extent of his culture and education. His flock never knew it.

He could read well, but just never had the inclination. Now he took a book from a shelf, admiring the beautiful leather binding, and had just opened it when Hillery hurried in.

She wore a simple white dress that molded her upper body nicely. The dress had puffed sleeves and flared from the waist to the floor. He saw it was made of lace with an undergarment of some kind. For the first time he saw the swell of her breasts and he wondered if she had put on the dress to impress him. He hoped so. Maybe that whore was right about Hillery.

"Mrs. Gregson! Simply dazzling. That dress is so beautiful, and it sets off your hair and your eyes perfectly."

She showed a touch of blush at her long white neck, then her soft blue eyes gained control.

"Pastor Thompson, good morning. And thank you for your thoughtful words. I see now how you have been so successful in starting new churches. It's a gift." She smiled a moment. He took her hand and she led him to a patio where dozens of flowers bloomed and birds chirped and ate at feeders while two ruffled their feathers in a round bird bath.

"What a delightful spot!" he said. "I would love to have a place like this where I could meditate, and write my sermons. Somehow the outdoors seems the best place for me to compose."

"I like it here, too," Hillery said. "Many days I take my lunch here. Would you stay for lunch with me? I would be pleased."

"I would be honored!" He paused. "Now to work. How is your list of potential parishioners coming along?"

"Mrs. Darlow and I are working on it. As you can see, so far it's only from memory, but we have quite a group, about thirty families. One of us will be at each of your services, to ask people we don't have on the list about their interest."

"Yes, excellent, Mrs. Gregson."

"Pastor Thompson, I do wish you would call me Hillery."

He smiled, and bowed. "Mrs.—Hillery, nothing would give me more pleasure. And I ask that you call me Erick."

"I will. Erick, I will. Except when there are others around, when we should be more formal, don't you think?"

"I do."

The planning went on. They set another meeting for the next day. Lunch was a joy. They had tiny sandwiches, two kinds of tea and apple tarts for dessert.

Twice he saw her watching him when he was talking. He thought she seemed embarrassed, but he thought nothing about it when their lunch was over, he said it was time for him to leave.

"Oh, Erick, if you have nothing pressing, I would like to show you through the hacienda. I'm quite proud of the restoration."

He said he would be delighted. She led him through a dozen rooms, into the south wing, and then the west which was yet to be converted and restored. They were in a room that had once been a master bedroom. Only a bed was there now. The room was thirty feet long and twenty wide, more like a ballroom than a bedroom.

She started to go toward the door but tripped and fell against him. Erick's hands came out quickly and caught her and as he did, one hand brushed her breast and lingered until she found her balance. He started to move his hand, but her own came up and held his tightly on her bosom.

"Oh, my!" she said softly. "Oh, my!" She looked at him with the wide-eyed innocence of a virgin. Slowly he bent his face toward hers. Her eyes met his and for just a moment she hesitated. Then their lips met. The kiss was chaste and quick, but so important.

"Oh, my goodness!" she said softly. "That was so very sweet! I know that you are a man of the cloth, but you *were* married."

She moved her hand from his and eased it away from her breast.

"Hillery, I have been madly in love with you from the moment I saw you at the meeting. Did you know that?"

"Oh, my!"

"I knew you were a lady of quality, and that I would never in the world be worthy even to tell you of my devotion."

"Oh, Erick! Those are the sweetest words! When you told me about your wife, I wanted to take you in my arms and comfort you."

"It's not too late," he said softly.

"Oh, my!" She opened her arms and he put his around her, drawing her body firmly against his, crushing her breasts to him.

He kissed her again, and then again.

"My, I'm getting so dizzy—I should sit down."

"The bed," he said. She looked at him for a moment seriously, then he nodded. She smiled and he led her to the bed.

"The door . . ." she said. He walked to it and closed it and threw the bolt, then walked back to where she sat.

She patted the place beside her and he sat down, his arm around her. She lifted her face to be kissed again and then she sighed.

"Darling, sweet Erick. This is all so new, like a whirlwind. I had no idea you felt . . ." She kissed him again and he felt her lips part slightly.

"Erick, I want you to hold me and to kiss me, but we must go slowly. Today I want you to kiss me and touch me and to dream of how it might be . . . someday."

This time when he kissed her her lips parted. He darted his tongue between them and she sent her tongue in return. His hand moved down and caressed one of her breasts and she moaned in pleasure. He massaged first one, than the other gently, tenderly.

Before the kiss ended he had moved his hand

again, edging it past an open button and pushing aside her chemise. He touched her bare breast.

She shivered.

"Oh, darling Erick!" She shivered again, then kissed him with more force and desire than she had previously shown.

He started to lie down with her, but she resisted.

"No, no, Erick. Darling, I know what you want to do, but this is too sudden, too quick. I need time to sort things out." But she did not take his hand away. He unbuttoned the top of her dress and pushed it back, lifting the chemise. Her breasts were larger than he figured, pink tipped with upthrust nipples throbbing with excitement.

He bent and kissed one, and Hillery gasped, then quivered and wailed in delight as spasm after spasm of joy pulsed through her body. She caught his head and held it to her breast as she trembled in one climax after another.

At last she lifted his head and kissed his lips. There were tears in her eyes.

"Darling, it's been so long since I've even thought of making love with a man. And now— I'm so thrilled I can hardly talk!"

She hugged him, unmindful of her state of undress. He found her breasts with his hands again and petted them, then put his hand on her legs and began lifting her skirt.

"No!" she said sharply. Then she kissed him. "Tomorrow morning we'll have another meeting, here. I'll give you the rest of the guided tour and we'll end at my bedroom." She moved her hand over his crotch and rubbed the hardness. "Save this for me, until then!"

She stood, straightened her clothes and buttoned the dress.

"Now, Pastor Thompson, I have a lot of wonderful things to think about. Until tomorrow?"

He reached out and touched one breast through the fabric, then bent and kissed her.

"Until tomorrow. Oh, I would feel more secure if you give your servants the day off."

She lifted her brows. "I could get lunch for you myself! Yes, that would be fun. I'll see to it." She smiled radiantly, stood on tiptoe and kissed him again, then held his hand as they walked to the front door.

Their goodbyes held a special meaning. He turned and walked down the street.

Tomorrow morning. The clan reunion might have to be in a different location. He heard that Rusty left town in a hurry this morning with the sheriff chasing him. He'd found out what had happened. Tomorrow might be his last day in town as well, if it all worked out with the rich widow. He wondered how much cash and jewels she would have in the house. Erick grinned. He was damn well going to find out! Would it be too much to ask her for a twenty thousand dollar gift in cash to get the church donation drive started? he wondered.

He was moving quicker than he thought. The whore had certainly been right about Hillery. She had a hot little bottom and she wanted him. It would take her until tomorrow to convince herself that it was all right, and that they probably would get married.

Erick Thompson Schmidke laughed. What a surprise she was going to have tomorrow afternoon!

Zack White screamed at his two sons, Birch and Piney. They had been back with the buggy and Rusty only ten minutes and their pa was furious.

"You come back and left his wagon setting right there on the trail? How stupid are you guys? He said he's got three or four thousand dollars hidden around the wagon body!"

He whacked Piney on the shoulder. "Get those two wagon horses out in the barn and ride one, and get back out to that wagon. Hitch up the rig and drive it into the woods and then rub out the tracks so nobody can tell. You can do that 'fore it gets dark if you hurry. Take Birch along with you. Now scat!"

He went into the next room where Zelda was working on Rusty's right leg. The pants leg was slit to the crotch and she had the knee packed in steaming towels.

"Sprain," she said when Zack looked at her. She put her hand down the top of her dress and scratched one breast. "Stove up some, good as new in a week."

"Ain't got a week," Rusty said. "Got to get back to my wagon."

"Lucky you're alive, you fucked up bastard," Zack said. "Boys went out to hide the wagon. We'll go out tomorrow and get everything worth anything. You ride with us for a spell."

"You don't get to keep my goods, Zack. You tried that before."

"We're family, Rusty. Hell, I ever cheated you?"

"Damn right, every chance you get!"

"So don't give me no chances."

Rusty snorted. "Seen Erick? What's he up to?"

"Playing preacher still. Right now he's probably pussy-poking some rich widow lady. He told the boys he's got one on the string right now."

"About time," Rusty said. "Damnit, no, bitch!" Rusty said. He backhanded Zelda, spinning her away from the hot towels on his knee. "Look at that! It's swelling up more, not going down. I need some ice, you crazy bitch. Get me some ice!"

Zelda stuck her tongue out at him, turned around and farted, cracked a laugh and walked into the other room. "Fix your own damn knee, you weird little-boy lover! I got no time for bastards like you."

Zack laughed.

Rusty snorted. "Same old Zelda. Her pussy that good that you keep her around?"

"You should know, Rusty, you fucked her

enough."

"Hell, that was when she was young and pretty."

Zack nodded. "Christ, I should dump her, but she cooks good."

Rusty stared at his swollen knee. "Big Brother, bring me a bucket of cool water from the well. Could you do that for me? Got to have this knee fixed by morning so I can go out to my wagon."

Zack swore but went for the water.

An hour later the cold water started the swelling to go down.

"You had enough of city life, Zack?"

"Hell yes, no fun here. Too many people watching. Maybe tomorrow we'll pull out."

"First, Zack, you got to get me some new canvas for the wagon top from the hardware store, and then a team. I'm gonna fix up my rig again. Just burned off the top, I'd guess. Need some horses."

"Hell, we'll steal the horses. You pay for the canvas, I'll buy it. Goes against my grain, paying for stuff. What the hell, maybe just one more time." Zack stared at his brother.

"Rusty, same rules. You keep it in your pants around here. You start fucking around with Birch and I'll blow your head off. That boy's got troubles enough, you hear?"

"Yeah, I hear. Right now I just want to get this knee working again and get out of this town. Still don't know where that damned boulder came from. I was fifty feet away from the rock slide."

"Lucky it didn't hit you in the head. When in hell are them two boys getting back?"

CHAPTER TWELVE

Spur and Terry Bennett were friends by the time they had walked the rest of the way back to Santa Fe. A rancher with a wagon stopped for them about a mile out and they were glad for the lift. Terry wanted to be a cowboy when he grew up—that was why he was working in the livery stable. Already he was a good rider.

Terry's parents were at the courthouse when they arrived for a tearful reunion. They thanked Spur a dozen times. The sheriff had told them it would be a miracle of Terry survived his abduction.

After the Bennetts had left, Sheriff James picked up a shotgun.

"It's time we go out there to the Galloway place and find out who those people are and what's going on. Bet you a lop-horned steer that the Medicine Show man rushed right back to that house, to his kin."

"We go in there now and we lose half your

135

deputies. You want to do that, Sheriff?" Spur asked. "We've got to wait until we have some real proof. Of course, it's your town."

"Hell, I don't want any of my men killed."

"Then let's wait a while. I'm out on my feet right now. In the morning I'll go out there on a delivery of some groceries. Reasonable that the emporium would send somebody to do that. I can get to the house and talk with somebody without any shooting. Worth a try."

Grudgingly the sheriff agreed.

Spur got up from the chair and groaned. "Never knew a body could be so tired in so many places. See you in the morning, Sheriff."

He limped a few paces, then got the kinks out of this tired legs and walked back to the Carriage House. The door of Annabelle's suite was unlocked. He walked in and slumped on the first chair he saw.

"Spur! What in the world happened to you?"

"Just a little tired. Two wenches kept me up all night last night."

"Wonder who the lucky girls were?" Annabelle teased. She wore a loose top and four petticoats but no skirt.

"You getting dressed or undressed?" Spur asked.

"Whichever you want," she said totally honest, no defense, no joking.

"Thanks. Make it dressed. I want a hot tub to soak my bones, a big dinner and ten hours of sleep."

"No fucking?"

He laughed. It bothered him when women used that word, but he nodded. "Yeah—no fucking tonight."

Conchita came in the hall door, saw Spur and waltzed up to him, pushing her breasts an inch from his mouth.

"Hey, *gringo*, you want to eat *mucho* titties?"

Spur chuckled and grabbed one, then let go. "Marvelous, but not tonight, I have a headache."

She laughed at him. "Still tired out from last night?"

"Right. I was the one who didn't get any sleep then or today."

Annabelle had Conchita arrange for the bath, and she went to the kitchen to bring up his dinner.

Both turned out to be hit performances. The women scrubbed Spur and he was so tired that their topless washing costumes never even caused his limp phallus to stir.

He had dinner of steak and four vegetables, chicken and heaps of mashed potatoes and gravy, coffee and thick slabs of rye bread and a big slice of chocolate cake.

Five minutes after the meal he crawled into bed. Spur never knew it, but that night a naked, interested, frustrated woman slept on each side of him.

"And so, my brethren and sisters in Christ, it is by His love that we are saved. It is nothing we do ourselves. It is by the grace of our savior

Jesus Christ, who died for our sins, that we have the opportunity to be saved... Yes, you're right, sister. There are a great many things that each of us must do to *keep* ourselves saved.

"Yes, there are the ten commandments, there is 'love thy neighbor,' there are dozens of codes of conduct that we must strive to follow, if we are to be true believers and children of God, who are saved in the Lord."

Erick looked down in the front row and found Hillery. He gave a small nod.

"And so we close our meeting tonight with the one abiding fact: Christians must live their faith, or it is a sham, a mockery, mere cant and a blasphemy unto the Lord!"

"Amen!" someone called.

They sang one of the old hymns that everyone knew.

"Brethren, there will be no offering tonight. You have been more than generous in the past." He held up his right hand.

"Shall we bow our heads for the benediction?" He recited a shorter one he had learned, and stood below the platform to shake hands with those who cared to.

Hillery was the last in line. When prying eyes had left, they went to the rear of the wagon in the shadows. He pecked a kiss on her lips and she melted against him. The touch of her body against his warmed his blood.

She shivered as she looked up.

"Darling, I want you so much it scares me! This morning was just... Well, I never dreamed that I could feel that way about any man, ever again. But you . . . It was simply wonderful! I can't wait for you to come tomorrow."

"I could stop by later tonight."

He left it hanging there.

"I'd love you to, but you can't. I . . . I just need a little more time to think about everything."

His lips brushed her cheek. "Tomorrow. I can hardly wait." He frowned slightly. "We must remember that we have a higher purpose too—the new church. We should launch the fund drive as soon as possible. I think now is the time."

She watched him. "Darling, I was going to save it as a surprise for you, but some stock paid a dividend this week and I want it to go to our church! It's ten thousand dollars. Should I give it to you now?"

He nodded. "The whole idea behind a drive like this is to get as much money as quickly as we can, so people say 'Oh, it's going so nicely, I want to be a part of it.' Then they jump on the bandwagon. If you could have it tomorrow it would get us off to a bangup start!"

"Yes! Yes, of course, I can have it tomorrow. It's in the bank. We'll have a ceremony the next day maybe, and get the drive started officially!"

He kissed her lips softly and she sighed.

"Hillery, I could never have dreamed of establishing a church here without you. Whatever would I have done?"

"Oh, Erick, you would have managed. It might have been harder, but you are so dedicated, so industrious. I love to watch you preach. You are so committed to your faith."

"Saving endangered souls is a serious business," he intoned sanctimoniously.

She hugged him again, then stepped back. "I must get to my rig. You be on time tomorrow, dear Erick."

"Hillery, I most certainly will."

"Goodnight." She turned and walked down the street twenty feet to where her driver was waiting. A moment later she was gone. He closed up the church wagon quickly, put away the lanterns and the portable pulpit, then set off walking quickly, following directions he had received that afternoon.

In fifteen minutes he was a mile across the spread-out town to a white clapboard house with two young pine trees in the front yard and two dormer windows. It had to be the right house. He went to the back door and knocked. It came open slowly but no one was there.

"It must be the Schmidke ghost," Erick joked.

A hoot went up from behind the door and Zelda jumped out where she could see him. She wore one of the clean dresses they had taken at the last house. It was too big for her, and bagged on her skinny frame.

"Erick, you sonofabitch, how are you?" Zelda screeched, ran and gave him a quick hug, then backed away as Zack came out of the living room into the kitchen.

He hadn't seen his youngest brother for almost three months.

"Hotter'n, Hell, if it ain't little buddy!"

"Howdy, Zack. Look like you're eatin' well."

"Tolerable." He grinned. "How's the soul-saving, church-raising game?"

"Tolerable. Might get even better tomorrow."

"Got a big fish on your line?"

"Seems to be. How did Rusty do? He get away?"

"No so the Hell you could notice," Rusty said hobbling into the room. He stared at Erick. "You still got those high and mighty ways?"

"Rusty, you want to catch a big fish, you got to know fish, you got to talk like fish, you got to think and act like fish. Same way you get the suckers to buy that snake oil of yours."

"Yeah, if it works."

"It's working. Least I ain't been run out of town. One of your cunt boys get out of line? The one at the undertaker's?"

"I don't talk about it."

"But you came running back here for help. You're putting us all out on a limb, Rusty."

"I asked him to come back," Zack said harshly. "I sent the boys out to help. And I still run what's left of this clan. You got objections, Erick, you draw a blade and we'll settle it." Zack stared at him.

Erick had forgotten how tough Zack could be. He wore a shirt with the buttons ripped off, his hairy chest and belly showing. He was sweating. His beard was matted, his face dirty and pimpled. A gash on his left cheek had not healed properly and oozed puss.

Erick shook his head. "I ain't challenging you,

Zack, but fact is fact. The sheriff finds him here, we're all in trouble. I got too much riding on this town right now."

"Then get your high faluttin' ass outa here," Rusty said, hobbling to a chair and easing into it. "'Less you know how to make this god-damned leg better."

Zack got up and walked to the window and back. He looked at Rusty, then Erick.

"How much longer your little swindle gonna keep you here, Erick?"

"Fund drive to start a church takes a spell."

"How long? I don't aim to be here more'n a day or so. Too many folks asking questions about the old folks who used to live here."

Piney and Birch came into the room, bobbed their heads at their uncle and sat on the floor.

"You boys damn well better've hid that wagon good or I'll cane your butts till they bleed," Rusty said.

"We drove it into the woods a far spell, Uncle Rusty," Piney said.

"Nobody find it 'less they look real hard," Birch said.

"Nobody gonna find it 'fore we do. We'll drive out there 'bout noon tomorrow. This damn leg should be feeling better by then."

They looked at each other. Erick realized it had never been a closely knit family, not even when they ran two wagons together. Now they were further part than ever. In a way, he was relieved. He had managed to lift himself a little above the others.

"It could take me several days, even a week or

two, to get this fund raiser to a point where it's worth while," Erick said.

Zack scowled. "Hell, we got to move on, a day or two at the most. Get Rusty's wagon fixed up and he can come with us for a few weeks till he gets well."

"You sell here in town, Zack?" Erick asked.

"Hell no! Dumb ass! Can't you remember nothing I taught you? Get it on one side of town, and sell it in the next town a hundred miles down the road. Hell, you'll never learn. I'm going to bed. Got to get up early and get ready to move." He stood and looked at Erick. "Hell, little brother. You'll probably outdo all of us again. We'll be heading on toward Denver. You get there in August, we'll find you."

Erick waved at his two brothers, and went outside into the cool evening. He shook his head. The air seemed pure and clean out here. Had he been away from rawhiding that long?

As he walked back toward his wagon, he kept thinking about the next day. Ten o'clock. It would be a great day! By noon he could be ten thousand dollars richer! These days a man worked all year to make five hundred dollars as a clerk or laborer. Ten thousand dollars was what most men would earn in twenty years!

The thought bounced around in his head until he went to sleep.

CHAPTER THIRTEEN

A LITTLE BEFORE nine the next morning, Spur
McCoy had a cardboard box filled with
groceries. He had made a stop at the general
store and stocked up on some items he figured
the Galloways might want: oatmeal, bacon,
sugar, flour, and some tins of beans and
peaches. Spur bought a billed cap and a pair of
eye glasses with heavy black rims. He wanted a
false beard, but had no idea where he could find
one.

The poor disguise would have to do. He rode
his horse, balancing the foot-square box on his
leg. When he came in sight of the Galloway
place he acted as natural as he could. He was
coming on a visit to a friend.

Spur dismounted and left his horse tied to
one of the trees in the yard and walked to the
front door. The door looked like it didn't get
much use. He knocked and waited. After a

respectful time he knocked again. He heard movement inside and some whispers.

Soon the door edged open and he saw a thin-faced woman with dark, stringy hair. She looked out a three-inch crack in the door with a frown on her dirt smeared face.

"Hello. I was expecting Betty Galloway. Is she home?"

The woman opened the door more and he saw the dress was too fancy for her. It was much too large for her, too. "Course Betty's here. I'm her kin from Missouri."

"Betty told me to bring the grocery order over as usual. I come every week or so, knowing how they can't get around too good. Betty isn't sick, is she?"

"Nope. Nope, just resting this morning. Had a bad cough last night, wore the dear out. They both sleeping right now. I'll tell her you was here."

"Wanted to talk to her." Spur shrugged. "Guess I'll have to wait."

" 'Pears so."

Spur handed her the box of groceries. "Oh, she always pays me. Cost two dollars and ten cents this week."

"Two dollars!"

"Well, Betty said she wanted some sliced peaches."

"Just a minute." The woman vanished into the house and pushed the door closed but not latched. Spur heard more whispering, then the woman came back with two one-dollar gold pieces. Spur didn't like them, they were so small he often lost them.

"Much obliged. You tell Betty to get well quick." Spur turned and walked back to his horse. He knew there were two or three guns trained on his back. He hoped they believed him. If not, he was as dead as the Galloways must be.

But no weapon fired. He mounted up without looking at the house and rode away smartly toward town.

When he was out of sight, he gave a long sigh. The woman must be one of the rawhiders. She looked tough enough, and the dress obviously wasn't bought to fit her. Stolen. Spur knew it was down to the short hairs now. He was going to have to decide whether or not to go into that house the next time with his six-gun blazing.

The Galloways. If he could find their grave he would have all the proof he needed. That meant wait until evening. He hoped that everyone concerned would lay low today.

Inside the Galloway house, Zack watched Spur walk toward his horse. The double barreled shotgun was trained on him all the way. The other three men had guns on his back as well. When the horse hoofbeats faded, the men gathered in the kitchen where Zelda had been frying eggs.

"Cocksucker!" Rusty Schmidke roared. "I wanted to blast that sonofabitch right out of his socks! Told you he was about the size of the guy who bushwhacked me yesterday. Then when I heard the voice, I figured it had to be him. But by then he was moving out to the road and the neighbor couple came out their damn house."

Piney snorted. "That was the Jasper who stopped me and Birch from fighting down in that saloon. Hardnosed bastard. That was him!"

"You assholes are slow," Zack said snorting. "Shoulda figured it was him and invited him in for some lead breakfast. Now what the hell do we do? He must know we're here and who we are. He didn't buy that nap story about the oldsters."

"We bushwhack him!" Rusty said. "We send Piney to follow the fucker and see where he goes. Then we find out where he stays and we watch for him and gun him down."

Zack looked at Piney. "Yeah, go follow him. Now! Fast, damnit, before you lose him!" The younger of the two boys jumped up, grabbed his gunbelt and ran out the back door.

"Rusty, you can't go. Sheriff is watching for you, and too many in town know you. Me and the boys'll do it. Birch, go get us two rifles and twenty rounds for each one."

An hour later Zack and Birch lay on the roof of the Fancy Cat Saloon across from the Santa Fe Carriage House hotel. Piney had spotted the big rider going into the hotel. He was bound to come out sooner or later, and when he did he would be a perfect target for the old .56-50 Spencer that was Zack's favorite. He could pick the legs off a fly at a hundred yards with the weapon. He'd knocked over rabbits with the long gun at six hundred yards.

Birch was on the other end of the roof facing the street. It had a fancy grillwork they would shoot through and no one could see them. It was perfect. After the damn meddler was dead, they could go down a ladder on the back of the saloon and nobody would be able to tie them to the killing.

Piney was in the street, three doors down, leaning against the hardware store in a tilted back chair. He had his six-gun and he was good with it. Just in case this big man got away from the rifles, Piney could get him in the back as he ran into the street.

Zack grinned. No way this big hombre wasn't gonna be dead a minute after he came out the hotel door.

Spur looked over his gear in Annabelle's rooms. There was little he could do now until it got dark. His next best move was to ride back out to where that burned-out wagon was and see what Schmidke was trying to save in those boxes. He could take his time going through the wagon as well looking for more evidence. He'd take a deputy along with him to make it all legal and proper.

Spur cleaned his Colt .45 and then the Winchester repeating rifle, took out a supply of rounds for the pistol and an extra box of shells for the Winchester. He got his high crowned brown hat with the Mexican coins around the band and looked for Annabelle. She was in the hotel someplace.

He gave up looking for her and went toward

the front door. He had the rifle over his shoulder and the six-gun in his holster. The mount he had used that morning was still at the rail outside. He could get out to the wagon in about an hour, maybe a little more.

The stage pulled up in front of the hotel as he came out and a dozen people crowded around, greeting people and getting baggage down. Santa Fe had no railroad yet and the arrival of the stage was the biggest event of the day. He stepped around a pretty blonde lady who won a hug from her husband who got off the stage.

A rifle shot blasted into the morning air, and Spur felt something nick his thigh. He ran two steps and dove behind a six-foot-long horse trough and scanned the area. The shot had sounded as if it came from across the street. There were dozens of places over there a gunman could hide, between buildings, and on top of three of them. There had been only one shot. Most of the passengers and greeters huddled behind the stage.

"Get the sheriff!" somebody yelled.

"Shot came from the roof!" another man called.

"On top of the saloon! I saw the smoke," another voice called.

"Get somebody around there fast!" Spur yelled.

A pistol shot barked into the conversation as someone put a shot into the framework over the saloon.

Spur looked down the sidewalk along the businesses next to the hotel. He saw another man with a gun out, but he was not looking across the street. The young man was staring at Spur. In an instant Spur recognized the gunman, one of the two he had stopped from shooting it out in that saloon.

Spur's .45 was out—he had drawn it as he dove behind the water trough. Now he saw the young man run closer. He stopped at thirty feet and stepped behind a post holding up the second floor of the store that extended out over the sidewalk.

Spur stayed where he was, lying on his stomach, propped up on his elbows. The rifleman could still be sighting in on the area. He was trapped for the moment.

Before Spur could reason it out, the man ahead left his protection of the post and ran forward, straight at Spur, his six-gun bucking in his hand.

Spur felt the first slug whizz past him, then another hit the front of the trough. The Secret Agent fired twice. The first slug tore through Piney Schmidke's hand and dumped the gun from his grip. The second round caught him in the throat and tore a chunk out of his spinal cord as the big .45 lead missile ripped on through. Piney stumbled once, then dove off the boardwalk into the dust of the street. His eyes turned glassy as he stared up at the blue sky for a moment and screamed. Then his eyes shifted and stared directly at the sun, but he could see nothing.

"Look, that man is dead!" someone said on

the boardwalk. A woman leaned against the milinery shop, suddenly faint.

Someone shouted from the roof of the bar across the street.

"Hey, nobody up here, but I found an empty shell."

Spur was up now, caught his horse from the rail, mounted and rode hard for the alley across the street. He knew who he was looking for now. The kid was maybe twenty-two or three. Both had a strong family resemblance, he realized now. They must have been brothers. It had to be the same pair he had stopped from fighting.

The alley in back of the saloon produced nothing. They were on foot, but must have had horses close by. Spur rode a square around four blocks, looking for anyone riding hard. On the second block he saw two riders whipping their mounts north. He gave chase. For fifteen minutes they drove their mounts forward. Spur gained a little ground on them, but they were still almost a quarter of a mile ahead of him.

They came to a ravine and split up, going in opposite directions. Spur chose the smaller of the two men since it looked as if he had the slower horse.

But before he had gone twenty yards, the second horseman had stopped and began firing a rifle at Spur. The agent grabbed his own rifle, jumped off his horse and rolled behind some rocks.

Three more shots spanged off the rocks; then

there was only the silence of the New Mexico mountain air. Spur took a look and saw that the gunman had mounted up and ridden away toward a heavy patch of timber. He had gained five minutes' head start and at this distance, Spur knew he would never catch him in the brush. The first rider was out of sight heading back for town.

Spur gave up the chase and angled back to Santa Fe. He rode directly to the sheriff's office. The youth's body lay on top of a cheap wooden casket outside the door. A deputy asked everyone who passed if they knew the young man.

"No identification?" Spur asked the deputy.

"No sir. Nobody knows him. There was nothing on the body."

In the office the sheriff looked at him.

"You're bleeding."

Spur looked down at his thigh. "Just a scratch. That rifleman who was on the saloon roof. He missed. So did I. Chased two of them, but they got away."

"One didn't. Any idea who he is?"

"No. I broke up a fight between him and another kid I think might be his brother. They didn't like it. But don't seem like they would try to bushwhack me." Spur frowned and rubbed the back of his neck. "If that stage hadn't come in just when I left the hotel, that rifleman would have had me dead center. Stage shielded me most of the time. I was lucky."

"Maybe damn lucky." The sheriff handed him a wanted poster. It was newer than the other one they had found and was for a family of raw-hiders with the father called Zack. It said there were two sons aged twenty and twenty-two and a woman about forty.

"That corpse out there could be twenty to twenty-three. He could be one of the rawhiders."

Spur read the flyer again. Then he told the sheriff about his trip to the Galloway house that morning.

"Not possible, McCoy. That woman you saw couldn't have been a relative to the Galloways. The Galloways don't have no kin. They told me about six months ago. She was worried about what was going to happen to them if they got sick."

"The woman I talked to was about forty or so." Spur slapped his holster. "Sheriff, I'm going out there right now. I have to find some evidence we can work with. I think I can find a grave around the back yard somewhere. I want you to create some kind of a disturbance out front for them to watch. Arrest somebody, or stage a fake watch on a house, or something. And I want you to make up some special sticks of dynamite for me, with six inch fuses and caps. One way or the other, we're going to find out what happened to the Galloways!"

CHAPTER FOURTEEN

"PASTOR" ERICK THOMPSON Schmidke had left Main Street ten minutes before the shootout took place, and he was unaware of it. He was blocks away ringing the bell at the hacienda owned by Hillery Gregson.

She met him at the door. Today she wore a low cut dress that showed a hint of cleavage. Her hair had been brushed and combed a hundred times, and her eyes misted with joy when she saw him.

As soon as the door closed she ran into his arms, pushing her breasts hard against his chest, her lips reaching for his.

When the kiss ended she stared up at him, still holding him close.

"Darling, where have you been? You're thirty-seven seconds late! I didn't sleep a wink all night thinking about you."

He kissed her again, hard, demanding. His hand came away from her back and caught her breasts and he kneaded them. He broke off the kiss, picked her up and smiled.

"Your servants are gone, right?"

She nodded.

"Where is your bedroom?"

"But first . . ."

"The only thing we're going to do first is tear each other's clothes off!"

She pointed the way, snuggling against him as he carried her, humming to herself, watching his face, then reaching up and kissing his cheek and his lips as he went up the stairs, through a hall and into her bedroom. It was almost as large as the one in the other wing. He lay her down on the bed and moved his mouth over her breast, sucking one into his mouth, and licking the fabric until he felt her shivering.

He leaned up and tore the thin fabric of her dress that went over her shoulder.

Hillery looked up in surprise, then wonder and desire flooded her face.

"Yes! Yes, tear it all off me. No one has ever torn my clothes off before!"

He ripped the bodice open and stripped off the chemise, revealing her breasts. He lifted her to a sitting position so he could play with her tits. She tugged at the buttons on his shirt, working her hand in to his naked chest.

Erick backed away and slid out of his shirt, then his shoes and stockings, and pulled his pants and underwear down together.

He stood over her where she sat on the bed.

Impulsively she caught his hard penis and stroked it. He pulled away and tore her dress

155

down over her hips. Her petticoats went the same way and her silk drawers; then she writhed on the bed, nude and entranced.

Erick bathed her in kisses, starting at her forehead, then her eyes, and her ears, her lips, her chin and neck, then both her throbbing breasts. She shuddered in anticipation, shivering and moaning softly.

His mouth moved down across her stomach and her flat belly to the fringes of her pubic hair and she gasped.

"Oh, you don't have to!" she said.

But he continued, through the forest of soft brown hair until her legs spread apart in invitation and demand.

Erick licked the soft nether lips of her wet crotch and she jolted into a climax. Again and again she quivered, letting out a keening wail as her body vibrated.

"Oh, so beautiful! Darling, so wonderful. Oh! Oh! *Oh!* Darling, no one has ever touched me that way! Fabulous. Again, do it again! I can't move until you do it again!"

"Beg me," he said, lifting up. She kissed his lips, writhed against him, pushed him on his back on the big bed, and kissed his breasts, bit his nipples.

He caught her head and gently moved it lower.

"Sweetheart . . . ?" she asked.

"Beg me," he said again and brought her face to his erect, purple, pulsating penis.

"It's so beautiful!"

"Kiss it."

"Oh . . . Yes! Anything, darling. Anything you want me to do!"

She kissed his erection, held it tenderly, then experimentally let the purple-reddish head slip into her mouth. Erick watched.

"Yes, Hillery, beg me that way!"

She knelt there, her mouth working up and down on his swollen phallus. Erick moaned in pleasure, his hands reaching down and holding her breasts as she worked on him.

Once she stopped and looked at him.

Now his hips were grinding slowly, humping upward to meet her mouth. "Just a little more, Hillery. Just a little more."

She went back to work and he humped harder. She caught his rhythm. He groaned and then, with gentle hip thrusts, he shot burst after burst into her mouth. She gagged, then swallowed and stayed with him until he sighed and gasped for air.

She came away and wiped her mouth, then lay beside him on the bed. "I've never . . ." She began, but he kissed her and nodded, still breathing hard. As he recovered, she crawled off the bed and brought a small varnished jewel box about ten inches long with fancy copper hinges and fittings. She put it down between them on the bed and sat back cross-legged, watching him.

Erick looked at it, lifted up on one elbow and watched her.

"Pretty. What's inside?"

"Take a look." Her smile was filled with secrets and pleasure.

He undid the clasp and lifted the lid. Inside was more money than he had ever seen before. It was a stack of bills, with a hundred dollars on top, all tied with a pink ribbon and a small card. He opened the card.

"For my darling Erick and his favorite project." It was signed "Yours forever, Hillery."

He reached over and kissed her.

"I don't want you to be angry, and I know we talked about ten thousand, but I decided it would be better if I put in fifteen thousand. Is that all right?"

He set the box aside, touched the bills, then took Hillery in his arms and kissed her. He lay her down gently and lay on top of her and the kiss lasted and lasted. He could feel himself becoming excited again.

When their lips parted he watched her.

"Hillery, that is wonderful. You are amazing, beautiful, marvelous as a lover, and devoted. I don't know what to say."

"You don't have to say anything." She reached and caught his erection and guided it toward her moist crotch. "Just love me, Erick Thompson! I don't care what you are or who you are, or what you do or what you want to do, just make love to me all day and all night! And then all day and all night again, for years and years and years!"

It was past noon when they came apart for the third time. They nibbled on grapes and sipped brandy she had provided.

This morning Erick had actually been considering giving up his life of crime and settling down. What a woman to do it with! Not beautiful, but devoted and sexy, and most important of all, *rich!* He would never have to work again in his life. But would that mean he would have to follow through with starting a church and stay in his role as a preacher? That would be too much.

They made love twice more that afternoon and twice they talked about marriage. He brought it up first and she was surprised.

"Darling Erick! I'm thrilled and delighted that you are considering settling down. But you've been an itinerant for so long. Would you miss it? Would you be happy in one place?"

"Hillery, the wear and tear of constantly moving is starting to become tiresome. Frankly, I've been looking for some place to stay. Perhaps this is it."

She rolled on top of him, her breasts pressing against him as she hugged him.

"Sweet Erick! I don't care what you do or where you go, just so I can go with you! You don't even have to be a preacher. I have plenty of money for both of us to live on the rest of our lives. We could even move to Denver, or New York City! A big city would be exciting. Yes! Let's talk about that."

They did for a while. Then she soberred. "I want you to know that I am serious. Come along." She caught his hand and took him down the hall to the library on the second floor.

There, behind a set of books, she showed him a safe. She turned the combination and pulled open the door. Inside was a cache of money. There were stacks of bills, even a small stack of Confederate money, and sacks filled with gold coins, all double eagles.

"This is some of the money I keep on hand. The bank has lots more drawing interest, and I have accounts in Denver and New York—stocks and bonds, even some railroad stocks that are going up in value every day. My late husband taught me about business. I'm making more money every day then I can possibly spend."

"You have a tremendous dowry," Mrs. Gregson.

"See that painting? It's quite valuable. It was painted by Rembrandt. It's worth thousands of dollars." She smiled, standing there naked. "As you can see, I am a woman of means. I just wanted you to know that if sometimes I seem to get too demanding, it's because I have been used to having my own way for so long."

He caught her hand. "Lets go back to your bedroom. I need to find exactly the right way to propose to you."

Her eyes widened and she caught her breath, pressing herself against him, hugging him tightly. They walked close together to the bedroom where they made love again.

About three that afternoon, they dressed and went to the kitchen where she made sandwiches and coffee for them. He insisted that she leave her blouse off so he could watch her bare breasts. She laughed and was self-conscious for a few minutes, but then after a while it seemed natural.

Erick had decided. He would marry this rich woman. They would go to Denver, he would "give up" the ministry and become a rich man for the rest of his life. No one could prove he was one of the rawhider Schmidke Brothers. He was in the clear. All he had to do was play it very carefully with his brothers for the next few hours.

They decided they would be married the next day by the judge in the courthouse. Then they would leave for Denver on their honeymoon, and find a house to buy there. Soon she would sell this place or they could keep it as a second house, and transfer all her accounts from here to Denver.

She watched him eat the sandwich of ham and slabs of fresh baked bread, and drink his coffee. "Darling Erick, I've never been more happy! I have missed making love this last year, but I never knew how much. I am enraptured—you have totally captured me!"

"You be careful or I'll rip that skirt off you and make love to you right here on the kitchen floor."

She giggled. "That would be fun, but I don't believe you can again so soon. Poor peter, I've worn him out. He needs a rest. And I'm going to be sore tomorrow. But what a glorious way to hurt!"

She kissed him and poured him more coffee.

"I'm delighted you suggested that the servants take the day off. It's been the most wonderful day of my life!"

"And mine!" He covered her hand with his. "We'll be married in the morning and get the afternoon stage for Denver. Then we'll begin our new life in the mile high city. Denver is getting to be quite a large town now."

She kissed his hand. "Darling, have I begged you enough yet?"

"What?"

"You asked me to beg you so you would do . . . do me with your tongue again."

Erick laughed. "My tongue still works." He stood and picked her up and sat her down on the edge of the kitchen table. Erick spread her legs and lifted her skirts around her waist, exposing the soft brown swatch of fur.

"Right here?" she asked. "On the *table?*"

"I always eat off a table."

He knelt in front of her and kissed around her pubic area, then used his fingers to arouse her, massaging her mound and her outer labia.

Then he moved forward, and nestled against her soft white flank with his cheek. His tongue darted out and she moaned. He touched her again and she wailed. When his tongue found her clit it was surging upward eager for combat and he twanged it from side to side with his tongue as Hillery wailed and climaxed again and again. She bent and grasped his shoulders and then held his head, forcing it harder against her crotch.

At last she sighed and lifted his head. She

kissed his wet lips and tasted some of her own juices.

"Now," she said with satisfaction. "*Now* I think that we're ready to get married."

CHAPTER FIFTEEN

SPUR MCCOY CARRIED a cloth sack with him as he pushed around a fence directly behind the Galloway target house. He had his six-gun and a short shovel. It had been five minutes since he had left the sheriff. He and his men had worked up a fake raid on a house about fifty yards down from the Galloway place. They would be on the little dirt street that went between the houses, in full sight of those in the Galloway place.

It was supposed to keep the rawhiders inside the house looking toward the front. It had to work.

Spur crouched out of sight thirty yards from the back of the Galloway barn.

Four pistol shots hammered into the Santa Fe morning. It was still an hour from midday. Spur listened and heard men shouting, then more shots. After another two minutes he got the barn between himself and the house and ran forward across a pasture area, watching for

164

fresh earth. He had seen none as he waited. Now he scanned the ground closer for twenty yards on each side of him.

Nothing.

He got to the barn and looked around the outside of it. Two horses shied away from him. They were on long tethers so they could graze. The ground near them had been beaten bare of grass. Could be. Like burying someone in the middle of a trail drive route so the Indians couldn't desecrate the body. He pushed the shovel into sections of the barren, dusty section every three feet, but found it to be solid.

Inside the barn he looked in the stalls and straw covered areas, anywhere there was dirt underfoot. He was almost through checking the spots when he came to the last stall near the back. There had been a horse there, and the straw was matted down. He clawed it back with the shovel and pushed.

Soft!

He moved the spade and put his foot on it, it sank into the ground a foot deep. Carefully he began to dig. He had taken out only a dozen spadefuls of dirt when he hit something. He moved the shovel and lifted. A man's hand and arm came out of the dirt.

There would be two bodies in the shallow grave, he was sure.

He put the dirt back, spread the straw over the area, and walked to the front of the barn. Through a knothole he watched the rear of the house. Nobody moved. He heard more shots coming from down the road. The ruse was still working.

Spur ran out the back of the barn, taking the cloth sack with him. He left the short shovel and hurried to his horse. Before he mounted he opened the cloth sack and took out three of the sticks of dynamite. It was twenty percent, but all he could get. The blasting caps had been inserted into holes in the middle of the sticks, and six-inch fuses pushed in the hollow end of the metal cap.

The fuse had burned at a minute a foot when he tested it. He had about thirty seconds on each fuse. Too long. But sometimes the fuse burned faster. He took his knife and cut each of the eight fuses in half. Now he had eight small bombs that would burn for fifteen seconds before they exploded.

He mounted up and kept three of the sticks of dynamite in his left hand, and the stinker matches in his right. Spur rode up to the back of the barn using it as a shield, then readied the bombs and his matches and walked the horse toward the house. If the Schmidkes looked out the back, it would mean trouble.

A fresh burst of pistol and rifle fire came from the diversion down the road. Spur wanted to kick the bay and race her toward the house, but that could cause enough noise to attract attention. He gritted it out and a minute later he was near the back window. He had planned on using one stick in the kitchen, one in the side window and the third in the front bay window.

He struck the match and lit two fuses at once, immediately throwing one hard through the small kitchen window. Then he spurred the bay forward to the side window and threw the sputtering bomb in that opening. He charged forward to the front edge of the house, and started to light the third bomb just as the first one went off in the kitchen.

The blast belched smoke, fire and glass out the kitchen window. He heard screams from inside the house; then the second blast shattered the structure. He struck the match and lit the third bomb, raced around the corner and threw the dynamite through the bay window in front of the house and kicked the bay twice to keep her going flat out for the road fifty yards away.

The firing stopped down the road, and when Spur looked that way, he saw three of the sheriff's men.

The third blast behind him caused him to pull up the bay and wheel her around. The front half of the house had sagged. One man came running out, firing a pistol. An immediate response came from the lawmen who had been firing at the diversion house. The man Spur figured must be a Schmidke darted back into the smoking structure.

Flames licked out a window on the near side.

The horses!

The back of the house was not covered. The rawhiders could go out the back, get the horses and ride away. Spur rode fast around the burning house and saw with relief that the horses were still staked out behind the barn.

Then where were the Schmidkes?

The sheriff and his men rode around the barn just then and Spur waved them over.

"Didn't see them out there, Sheriff. They might still be in the house or the barn."

The sheriff pointed at two of his men who rode to the house, dismounted and charged inside the burning building. They came out a minute later, one of them carrying someone. Spur rode up and saw the woman he had talked to at the front door the day before. The back of her head was blood red and pulpy.

"Dead," one of the deputies said. "Don't see how there could be nobody else in there alive."

The sheriff dismounted and all four of them stormed into the barn. It was empty of humans.

The lawmen came out of the barn and began looking around. In back of the barn about two hundred yards was a barn of the place across the field. As they looked that way, they heard a woman's scream followed by a pistol shot.

Spur jumped into his saddle and kicked the bay into a gallop. He put the barn across the field between himself and the other house. The rawhiders would go for the house to get weapons and maybe take hostages.

The agent leaped off his horse and sprinted the last five yards to the barn, worked his way around the near side and fell prone in the grass beside the front edge of the structure. He looked across thirty yards to the back door of the house. The screen door hung open, the spring broken. Smoke came from the kitchen chimney. A bucket hung on a rope over a well near the back door. Two golden cottonwoods spread across the front yard, towering over the house.

Spur heard noise behind him and turned as the sheriff bellied down into the grass beside him, a new army Springfield in his right hand.

"Got two men on the other edge of the barn to cover that side of the house," the sheriff said. "Seen anybody?"

Spur shook his head. "Woman screamed. Who lives here?"

"The Funkhowsers. They have five kids. He has a saddle shop in town. Best saddle maker in the state."

"So a woman and four kids inside."

"And some rawhiders."

"At least two, if we figure those Jaspers who bushwhacked me this morning are part of the bunch. Then the Medicine Man is somewhere. Call it three."

"Got to get them out," the sheriff said. He leveled the Springfield and put a .45 round through the kitchen window that faced the barn. For a moment there was no sound. Then a rifle barked from the house. The upstairs window shattered and the sheriff yelped.

"I'm hit!"

Spur had been moving as soon as the rifle fired. He pulled the sheriff back with him until they were out of line of fire of the upstairs window. The round had smashed the sheriff's shoulder.

"Sheriff. Sheriff!" a voice called from the

house. "There's no way you can touch us. You pull your men back and we won't kill any more of the kids. You understand?"

Spur looked at the sheriff; it was his decision.

"Tell the bastard he's bluffing. He has two minutes to come out or we'll dynamite the place into rubble."

Spur crawled up another six feet and shouted the response. Two more rifle shots ripped from the house. One missed Spur by an inch, and he moved back two more feet.

The back kitchen door swung open and something hurtled through it. The object was a child, three or four years old. The small form hit the dust and crumpled, not moving. Spur could see the child's head was a mass of crushed bones and blood.

The voice from the house came again.

"We don't bluff, Sheriff. Now pull back!"

Spur told the sheriff about the child.

"Christ! Animals!" The sheriff shook his head. "We can't risk the rest of the hostages. We pull back. Tell him."

Spur crawled forward and relayed the message. Two more shots slammed into the ground near his shoulder.

"Just target practicing," the voice from the house said. "I want all your men back to the other barn, two hundred yards over there. I'll have a rifle following you, so move it now. You don't move, we shoot the kids!"

Spur helped the sheriff to pull out. He told the lawman about the grave he had found in the barn. Both old people were probably in the same grave. The sheriff nodded grimly, the wound in his upper shoulder paining him. Spur got the man on his horse and had one of the deputies lead him back to the nearest doctor.

At the lean-to, Spur put one of the sticks of dynamite on the front wheel of the rawhider's prairie schooner and blew it off. The killers wouldn't be able to come back and get the rig.

He told the sheriff's men to fan out along the road, and make sure the rawhiders didn't work back into town. Spur then rode around the end of his picket line and studied the hostage house. They had weapons and horses. What would they do? He wasn't even sure how many of them there were.

As he thought about it the number came up three: Zack the leader of the clan, his brother the "Uncle Rusty" who must be the medicine man, and one of the younger boys.

Spur rode into the open about five hundred yards from the house and a rifle slug whistled past him. He jerked the mount around and got out of sight. Spur rode back to the barn. He sent one deputy out on each flank until they could see the front of the house. It was possible the rawhiders would try to leave that way. After that precaution, it was a wait and see situation. There were no more demands from the rawhiders.

An hour later they heard a scream and the woman was forced out the rear door. She was naked and had a rope around her neck. A booming voice cut through the silence.

"Sheriff, you've got five minutes to pull your

men back. If you don't we start shooting this bitch, first in the hands, then the elbows, then the feet and the knees. She'll be screaming to be killed long before she dies. Now get your men out of there!"

The senior deputy nodded at Spur.

"Sheriff would do it," the deputy said.

Spur agreed. "Pull everyone out. I'll stay in the barn. Make it a show so he thinks you're all gone. Best to form a rough square around the house, big enough so they can't see any of your men. My guess is they'll head out of town." The deputy nodded and moved his men away.

Spur sat by a knothole in the back of the barn watching the other barn two hundred yards away. He could see only two horses in the pasture behind the structure. They would need horses and supplies.

Then it was waiting time again.

An hour slid by, then another. It was mid-afternoon and nothing had happened. They were waiting for darkness. The woman had been pulled back inside. Spur heard a scream, then nothing more.

It was a long afternoon.

A half hour before dusk, Spur saw a young man race into the pasture and pull both horses into the barn. Shortly after that, three riders burst from the back door of the barn and rode away. All had sacks of provisions tied to saddles, and rifles in boots. Spur picked the largest man and fired four times with his rifle, but missed the moving, bouncing target. He jumped on his horse and went after him. The man fired once over his shoulder, then concentrated on riding. He headed past two more houses, then towards the towering mountains toward the north of town.

Spur soon realized the man was an excellent horseman, and his mount was built for speed and stamina. It was going to be a long ride.

The trail left the scattering of houses at the edge of town and swung due north across fields of sparse grass and a few young pines, then turned west toward a long valley that angled upward and north into the mountains. The rawhider was a quarter of a mile ahead now, and Spur concentrated on keeping him at that distance as the two worked upward into the hills. There was no wagon road, no trail. They were cutting across virgin country.

Spur frowned at the gathering darkness. He would lose sight of his foe in another half hour, and then the outlaw would have all the advantages. He would keep moving, putting as much distance as he could between them. Spur would not be able to move, with no trail to follow. He would have to wait for daylight and then pick up the trail. The man was in his element. He would be twice as hard to capture out here as in town, and Spur McCoy was sure that he knew it.

CHAPTER SIXTEEN

SPUR MCCOY SAT on the horse and stared out into
the darkness. He had reached the 8,000 foot
level, a climb of about a thousand feet from
Santa Fe, but still not at the end of the long
gradual valley moving northward. The rawhider was somewhere in front of him. Spur had
lost sight of him more than fifteen minutes ago
when the man's sorrel vanished into a thick
stand of ponderosa pine.

It was getting close to decision time. Surely
the fugitive would keep running. He would not
stop to camp and build a fire like some tenderfoot. A wild idea sparked in Spur's mind and he
let it build and flesh out. Possible, yes, just
possible. The rawhider was used to calling the
shots, doing what he wanted to, taking over the
problem and solving it his way. He might just
try it.

Spur pulled into a thicket stand of young
pines, and made camp. Quickly he built a small

fire and let the smoke trail through the tall trees. Then he moved his horse two hundred yards into a deep thicket of brush where it should be well hidden. He went back to the fire, and made a dummy figure of blankets, with its head resting on the saddle. For a final touch, he put his hat over the place where the face of the man sleeping would be. As a final bit of bait, he lay his six-gun at the side of the blanket in quick reaching distance of the dummy. Spur built up the fire, using some heavy pieces of wood that would burn for two or three hours, then moved back from the site.

It took him ten minutes to find the spot he wanted. The position was a little higher than his fake camp, and gave him a field of fire of almost three quarters of the area in front of him. Anyone trying to sneak up on the camp would come from somewhere ahead of him. In the process, the attacker would become a perfect target.

That was the theory. Spur had decided that this rawhider would not keep on running. He would turn and fight, and he would do it the first chance he had when he would have the advantage. That meant darkness. He would hope that Spur would make a camp, and the best of all would be if his pursuer would build a fire. Spur would give him both.

He waited. Even from his position Spur could smell the smoke from his campfire. It drifted through the pine forest like a beacon, a foreign element that any woodsman would pick up in a minute. If the rawhider was coming back to find him, the fire would be a perfect lure, a highway of smell.

There was no way Spur could see the stars from where he lay beside a big pine tree and a flat rock. He guessed about two hours had passed when he picked up the first sign of company. An owl which had been giving out regular calls to the west of the fire suddenly went silent, then came winging through the trees on its nocturnal flight. Something had disturbed it.

Spur watched the area closely. For five minutes nothing moved. Then through the dusty gloom of the moonlight, Spur saw a shadow move suddenly from one tree to another.

Spur smiled. He was taking the bait! The rawhider was attacking the way a white man would, quick, sudden movements followed by periods of immobility. An Indian would use the opposite method. An open space that had to be crossed would be covered with infinite slowness. His shadow would merge with those around him and move so slowly that it would not attract attention to itself. The scout might look directly at the shadow of an Indian on the open spot and move on past it. Then inch by inch the Indian would be across the open area, and the unwary scout would have a knife in his back.

Again the shadow darted to the next cover.

There was no target, not yet. Spur lifted the rifle and held it ready. His fire had burned down to glowing coals, yet would give some light. Enough for a target was all he needed.

The secret agent admitted that the rawhider was taking his time, making sure. There had been no noise other than the usual night creatures—a night hawk, an owl or two, and far off, the screech of a mountain lion.

The shadow moved closer to the fire. Spur could see the glint of light off a blade. He lifted the Remington and zeroed in on the dark shape of the figure below.

In a sudden lunge, the form lifted the knife and thrust it into the blankets pretending to be a body.

Spur fired the Remington repeater. Four times he blasted shots into his target below. There was no cry of pain, no new motion.

Far off the echoing of the shots made their last feeble sounds and then were gone forever. Spur watched the area intently, but could see no movement.

Either he had killed the rawhider or missed him entirely. For another half hour Spur watched the spot intently, but saw nothing move. The rawhider could not be more patient than that. Spur moved away from his firing location silently, wormed into a bramble patch of thorny brush and nestled down for a nap. He had to have some sleep. The rawhider was either asleep or dead. He would find out in the morning. But if he didn't get some sleep now he would be in no condition to track anyone tomorrow.

Twice he awoke with brambles digging into his flesh. At least he was still alive. With the dawn, he was up and moving, silently, cautiously, toward his firing site. He saw his camp below, but no body. Using his best silent movement techniques, he circled the campsite twice, but could find no one lying in wait for him. That cleared up, he got his horse, rode to the camp and found where the blankets had been stabbed three or four times, and bullet holes in the nearby tree, but no body, and no blood.

Spur moved out on the trail, found the marks left by the horseman moving in the same general direction and followed them north into the mountains. He knew there was a stage coach road through to Denver, but the rawhider was not using it. A horse could move by a much more direct route then the stage, and quicker.

All morning he trailed the man he assumed was a Schmidke up the mountain through the thinning timber, until they came to an area where sheets of rock gave poor footing and a few signs of passage. But Spur was a good enough tracker to find the nicks and scratches on the rock to keep on the trail.

Now the route led up a narrow gully that would end in a high pass between tall peaks. There was only one way to go here. Spur kept watching the route ahead, always wary of an ambush. The trail narrowed again and up ahead passed between two giant boulders which had been loosened by the eternal erosion and freeze-thaw cycle perhaps hundreds of years ago and crashed down to the valley.

He moved cautiously around the first boulder and was just ready to kick the sorrel's flanks to urge her up the foot-high step when he saw a sunflash ahead off metal and dove off the side of his mount, hitting the rocks on his hands and rolling behind the boulder.

A second after his dive, the sound of the rifle shot came and the angry report of a lead bullet glancing off the rock and whining away into space. His mount had shied backward at the sound of the rifle. Spur grabbed his rifle from the boot and crawled ahead so he could see the spot where the rifleman had been. There was nothing there now.

Spur ran around the rock on the far side out of sight of the sniper's spot, and scurried a hundred feet along the trail where he was shielded from view ahead.

He paused at the last bit of cover, then brought up the rifle and charged the last twenty feet to the shelf of rock where the rifleman had fired.

There was no one there.

The trail took a slight down-slope here for a hundred feet and at the end of that Spur saw a horseman. Automatically Spur's rifle came up and he slammed four shots at the target.

Almost in slow motion the man in the saddle reared up. His voice screamed out an oath and he pivoted out of the leather and fell hard against the side of the canyon wall, then tumbled to the trail where he sat up holding his shoulder.

Spur put another rifle round into the dirt beside him, then ran forward.

"Don't try for the iron or you're dead for

certain," Spur called.

Zack Schmidke roared in pain and anger. Never before had he been in such a position. He darted his hand to the pistol on his hip, only to hear the rifle fire again. The lead slammed into his right wrist, breaking the bones, slamming it backward, leaving his .44 deep in his leather.

"Bastard!" he roared. He glared at Spur who walked forward, the Remington held at hip level aimed at the rawhider. Zack's left hand pawed at the Colt .44, got it half way out of leather before the rifle cracked again. The round bored into his left shoulder, jolting his arm and hand away from the gun, pitching him backward until he lay in the dust looking up at the mountain tops and the morning sun.

Spur stood over him, the Remington aimed at his forehead.

"Zack Schmidke?"

"Who the hell is that? My name is Phil Jones."

"That's as good a name as any other to hang by. You kill that child yesterday afternoon?"

"Wouldn't stop bawling. I told him to stop."

Spur had out his .45 Colt now and he shot Zack in the right knee. Zack screeched in agony, then in stark fear. At last his screams scaled down to sobbing and he looked up at Spur.

"Go ahead, kill me. I'm no good this way. Finish me off, damn you!"

"Not a chance. You're going to stand trial and hang. You want to walk back to town or ride your horse?" Before the outlaw could get out his reply Spur held up his hand. "Remember,

Zack, you've still got one more knee and two elbows I can shoot up. And right now I'd damn well enjoy the target practice on a cold-blooded killing machine like you!"

It was over six hours later that Spur came riding into Santa Fe with Zack tied to the saddle of the second horse. His wounds had been patched up the best Spur could do, using the rawhider's shirt for bandages.

Sheriff James met them at the edge of town, told Zack he was under arrest for seven murders, and that the trial would start the next day. The sheriff had his shoulder bandaged up but grinned through the pain.

"At least we got one of them. The other two got away." He shook his head. "They killed that whole family before they left. Just no way we could have stopped them. At least this one will pay."

Spur sighed. The bad ones just got worse. "This kind tend to stick together. The other two may be back to try to get this one out of jail. Better put on extra protection."

Sheriff James said he had already ordered it. "We found that old couple in the grave you told me about. We won't have much trouble getting a jury to convict this one. Wish we had the other two."

"Anybody checked through their gear in the wagon?" Spur asked.

The sheriff said nobody had. He sent a deputy with Spur and they rode out to the house where the wagon had been parked. First they used a pry bar and got a block under the front axle where the wheel had been blown off.

The inside of the wagon was a storehouse of merchandise, all of it stolen and all for sale. There was everything from silverware to fancy dueling pistols, envelopes of stocks and bonds and several metal boxes filled with gold coins and tied bundles of paper money.

"This whole thing should be taken down to the courthouse and put under official custody, so as much of it as possible can be returned," Spur said. The deputy went into town to bring out a wheelwright with a new front wheel. Spur kept examining. He found family Bibles, fancy sets of books, expensive china all packed in papers, and some paintings that looked as if they could be valuable.

Something kept bothering him. There were three Schmidke brothers. They had found two, and the two sons, evidently of Zack. Where was the third brother of the clan? Now that he had a start on cleaning out the rattlesnake nest of killers, he wanted to get them all. Maybe the third brother hadn't come to town yet. Or he might be here and they didn't know who he was. None of them were using their real names, which made it a lot harder.

The wheelright came and they worked together getting the new wheel in place and axle repaired, then hitched up a team and hauled the heavy wagon down to the courthouse where it was put under guard in one of the stables in back of the jail. The cash boxes, the paintings and the silver were taken inside, where the cash was counted, the silver inventoried and the stocks and bonds duly registered and put in the safe.

The sheriff looked at the names they had found and a few addresses.

"It's going to be next to impossible to find out who most of this belongs to," he said. "The cash will simply revert to the county treasury. Some of the registered stocks and bonds can be returned to estates or heirs. The negotiable ones are almost like cash."

He threw up his hands. "We'll have the county attorney take over the whole matter. The other goods will probably be sold at a sheriff's auction one of these days."

Spur realized he hadn't had a good meal in a day and a half, and no real sleep to speak of. He thought of the hotel, and a hot bath and a meal. Then he thought of something else.

"There's another wagon we haven't brought in, the one that the medicine man left town in. Tomorrow morning I think I'll ride out and see if I can find it. It could have something in it that might tell us who the third brother is."

Sheriff James waved him off. "Help yourself. One rawhider wagon at a time is enough for me to worry about."

Spur was more interested in the metal chest and the box that the medicine man had tossed out of the wagon. What was he trying to save from the fire?

First a fine hot bath, then some dinner, and then he would think about those boxes. Or would Annabelle have something to say about what they did next? Spur smiled, thinking about it. He had worked hard for two days. It was time he had some food and some relaxation. The government couldn't expect him to work all day and all night forever without some time off. Yes, that's what he needed, a little rest and relaxation.

CHAPTER SEVENTEEN

SPUR AWOKE THE following morning with Annabelle's head nestled against his shoulder and a sweet smile on her face. When he reached down and kissed her lips softly, she wrinkled her nose and giggled.

"Do it again," she said in her sleep and turned so her arm fell across his chest.

Spur carefully slid away from her and dressed. It was 5:30 and he had work to do.

At the sheriff's office he arranged for a deputy to drive two wagon horses out the road where the medicine wagon had been left. Spur would ride on ahead and find the wagon if it had been moved, and get it ready to be brought back to town.

He picked a new horse from the livery, a young black mare who seemed eager to get on the road. Her ears stood up and she kept pawing the dirt with her right front hoof.

Spur urged her gently on and got to the spot

185

in a little under two hours where the wagon had burned. He found charred remnants of canvas but no wagon. His first concern was the boxes he had hidden near the trail. He looked over the area, then walked to the spot and pulled the boxes from under the leaves and branches where he had concealed them.

The first was a metal box a foot wide and eighteen inches long. A hasp held a small padlock. Spur shot it off with one round from his .45 and lifted the lid. A two-inch deep tray in the top of the box held gold coins, packets of paper money, stocks and bond certificates. There was enough here to launch a good sized fortune. Under the tray were leather and felt pouches filled with jewelry, mostly unmounted precious gems: diamonds, rubies, and a few emeralds. Another fortune in the making. Jewelry that had been stolen locally could be returned, and maybe some of the cash.

But the rest was loot from probably hundreds of robberies around the country. The county coffers would get another bonanza.

The other box was wooden, the top secured with a strap with a buckle on it. Spur undid the binding and opened it. What else would the rawhider value as highly as his cash and jewels?

The first item Spur saw was a family Bible, listing births and deaths in the Schmidke family for the past fifty years. Under it was a stack of newspaper clippings showing the early exploits of a gang called the Smith Boys. Later papers identified the gang as the Schmidke Brothers, and traced their degeneration from train robbers and bank robbers into rawhiders who killed for the sport of it.

There were wanted posters, warning letters, notices and one picture of one of the boys. The Medicine Man must have been the historian of the family. It all would be helpful in prosecution of the family members.

Spur put the two boxes back where they had been concealed, then began his search for the wagon. It was possible that the Schmidke's had sent someone back to hide it when they saw the man the boys called Uncle Rusty was so badly hurt.

It took him two hours to find the rig. At last his series of searching circles had come across the trail of the heavy rig as it had passed through a soft spot near a small stream. The wagon had been hidden in a tiny ravine, with bushes and branches cut from trees to conceal it even further. Spur checked it quickly and saw that only the canvas had burned off the wagon. The ribs were still in place and most of the contents had not be damaged.

Back at the trail he met the deputy with the wagon horses and led him to the rig.

It took them two hours to get the heavy wagon out of the ravine, through the soft areas and back to the trail. Spur lifted the two boxes into the back of the wagon from their hiding place and tied his horse to the back of the rig. He rode in the wagon sorting through some of the items on board. Most of it was day-to-day living items, but he was sure there would be more money hidden around the wagon once they began to search it in earnest.

He looked at the metal box. Money had never been terribly important to him. He had always had all he needed. His father was well on his way to being a multi-millionaire and it all would be Spur's someday. Still he wished he had more expense money to do his job, even to help some of the people who needed it.

He opened the case and sorted through the bills. Each stack seemed to contain a thousand dollars, the equivalent of three or four years' salary for a working man in that year of 1874. It was more than two years of his own annual pay.

One of the bundles had big bills in it and he saw it was marked with a slip of paper indicating that it contained ten thousand dollars. That would be a good expense fund for him. He slid the packet of bills into his inside shirt pocket behind his brown vest. He would find a better spot for it later. The county would be somewhat less rich, but they would never miss it, and Spur would be able to help a lot of people who needed assistance.

Spur got back on his horse and rode shotgun the rest of the trip back to town. There were still some of the rawhiders on the loose and he didn't want them hijacking this wagon.

Back at the court house he carried the two boxes in and put them on the sheriff's desk.

"Another small problem for you, Sheriff. Cash, jewelry, more stocks and bonds and a history of the Schmidke clan. Some of the stolen jewelry reports might match some of the goods here. Anything new on the other two Schmidkes?"

"Not a whisper, but I'll bet they'll be showing up again. The kid and the other brother are both without funds or supplies. They'll need both before they strike out again. I've got my men watching for both of them."

"Anything on the third brother, the one we haven't seen yet?"

"Not a thing. We're watching." The sheriff looked at the cash in the box and shook his head. "A lot of good folks died giving up all this. I just wish there was some way we could get it back to their kin."

Spur went back to the Carriage House Hotel and slid the packets of greenbacks into his small leather case, just in back of the outer lining. It fit perfectly. Then he found Annabelle and took her to a late lunch in the dining room. But he was still worried about the other two rawhider brothers who were on the loose.

Rusty White was wishing he had some of his own magic elixir that he had sold to the suckers. Anything with alcohol in it right now would taste good. He lay on a grassy bank beside a tiny stream somewhere above Santa Fe. It had taken him most of the afternoon to lose the posse that had been chasing him.

By that time his leg had swollen so that he could hardly ride. He had spent the night in another small valley, moving for fear the posse would be back after him. Now it was clear they had lost him, and he could decide what to do. He had a rifle and pistol and a horse. Zack's planning had meant that they had each packed a pillowcase full of food before they left the house.

At least he wouldn't starve for a few days.

Revenge!

Zelda was dead!

Piney was dead!

From what he had seen on the trail, Rusty figured Zack had got himself caught by that wild man called Spur.

First things first. He had to get Zack out of jail before they hung him. Today, somehow he had to get Zack out of there. If he had two good legs he'd ride into town, shoot his way into the jail and give Zack a pair of six-guns, and they would blast their way out.

But he didn't, so he needed a plan. What? That new fangled dynamite they used on the house, the stuff that killed Zelda—he'd get some of it and blow a hole in the jail and get Zack out! Yeah! He had money. He'd hire some bum to buy the powder and fuse the caps. A guy had showed him how to use it one time. Yeah!

His leg had swollen again. But an hour or so in the cold water would make it feel numb enough to ride. He'd steal some different clothes, a hat and shirt off a clothes line somewhere and nobody would recognize him, especially not with his three day's growth of black beard.

Rusty's leg hurt worse than he figured it would when he tried to get on his horse, but he made it. Then he was farther from town than he had thought. It was almost supper time when he rode into Santa Fe and called a drifter over to him. He arranged for the man to buy six sticks of dynamite, two caps, and two foot of fuse.

The drifter looked at the two dollars with a glint in his eye.

"If you're not back here in five minutes, I'm gonna come dig you out of whatever bar you're in and shoot your balls off! You hear me, drifter?" Rusty snarled.

"Sure, sure. I warn't thinkin' about that. I'll get the dynamite. Hell. If I can earn a quarter that easy I'll sure as hell do it right!"

"Better, by damn!" Rusty said and waved him toward the hard goods store.

Rusty watched from the alley. The drifter came out with a package and walked straight to where Rusty still sat on his horse. He was halfway sure that once he got off, he wouldn't be able to mount up again.

Rusty checked the goods in the sack, the dynamite and the caps and fuse, then gave the drifter a quarter and an extra dime from the change.

"Now get out of here!" Rusty said, and wheeled his horse back into the alley.

He rode to the alley behind the courthouse and turned in. He had seen two deputies but they were not concerned with him on his horse. The jail was in the back part of the courthouse. It was on the ground floor, and there were bars on the windows. He lifted up in the saddle to look in the window, but his leg hurt him so much he dropped back down at once.

Tears of pain filled his eyes. The leg had to be looked at by a doctor. That would be next.

Quickly he pushed the detonating cap into one of the dynamite sticks, and fit the fuse into its hollow end. Then he wrapped the six sticks of powder together with the paper from the sack. Where to put it? There was a rear door. That would be the best spot. He rode up to the door. He could lean down in the saddle and drop the dynamite against the heavy wooden door.

The decision made, Rusty struck a sulphur match and lit the fuse. He bent low in the saddle and tossed the dynamite bundle a foot to the ground beside the door. Then he pulled the horse around and rode out of the alley toward the closest street.

He had left a foot of fuse on the bomb. That should burn for about a minute. The time seemed much longer. He turned his horse and moved partway back down the alley, sheltering against the wall of a building fifty feet from the jail.

A brilliant flash daylighted the alley ahead of him in the dusk of almost dark. The sound of the explosion shredded his eardrums as it roared down the alley. A hot gush of air slapped him in the face as it rushed by. Then he kicked the startled horse into motion and rode toward the jail. There was no wreckage in the alley; it had all blown into the jail. The door was gone. A section of the rear wall eight feet high and half that long lay in crumbled adobe rubble.

A deputy struggled over the pile of adobe. Blood streamed down his face, one arm hung useless at his side, and he was screaming for someone to help him.

Two more deputies rushed out, and helped the injured man to sit down next to the wall. A dozen men ran in from the alley. One of them was a doctor who attended the wounded deputy.

Now Rusty saw the sheriff stumbling through the wreckage.

"Dynamite—had to be a bomb back here by the door. Damn fool thing to do! Most of the damn door hit Pete. Killed him instantly. And there isn't much we can do for that rawhider. Zack's cell was just beyond the door and caught most of the blast. At least it saved the county a trial and the cost of hanging him."

The sheriff stood there by the wreckage as the men began to clear it away. He motioned to another deputy. "Get over to the hard goods store and see who bought dynamite the last few days. Not much sale on it yet around here."

The sheriff turned and stared at Rusty for a minute, then looked at the others in the alley who had come to watch the aftermath of the explosion. Rusty turned his horse and walked out the alley.

Zack was hurt by the blast? Zack was almost dead? It couldn't be. Not possible! He was trying to get Zack out of there, not hurt him! Rusty rode around to the street near one of the saloons where there was a boardwalk set up a foot above the dirt street. He slid off his mount, touching down on the boardwalk, favoring his leg. He tied his horse to the rail and stood on the boardwalk watching the courthouse.

People on the street buzzed with talk about the explosion.

A man in a black suit, black string tie and white shirt came by, talking to another man.

"Well, I just heard that rawhider is dead. The blast killed him sure as shooting. But the bad part is the deputy got killed, too. Wonder who tried to blow up the jail?"

Rusty felt tears rolling down his cheeks. Zack dead? That wasn't supposed to happen! He gritted his teeth, reached for his gun, and almost shot the man who'd told the lie. Then he held back. No, he had to get on his horse first. Then he would take out as many of these city folks as he could. *They* had killed Zack!

He stood on the boardwalk and looked at the saddle. It seemed higher than usual. With the help of the roof post he lifted his boot up and, working the horse around, finally got the foot of his good leg in the stirrup.

He was sweating, and still crying. Rusty felt a wave of nausea sweep over him. His leg burned like it was on fire. He'd have to get to a doc soon.

Rusty wiped the sweat off his face, then with both hands on the saddle horn, he lifted and kicked his bad leg over the mount. But his leg didn't make it. It hit the front side and slide halfway, then stuck on top.

The pain made Rusty groan. He bit his lip

until he tasted blood, then reached out with his left hand, lifted his pants leg and pushed the useless leg over the horse. He never did get that leg in the stirrup.

But he was in the saddle! He lifted his six-gun out of his holster and rode slowly down the street. A man came out of a saloon to his right, silhouetted in the light from the doorway.

Rusty shot him in the belly and watched him fall.

He kept moving slowly down the street.

Somebody screamed behind him. Rusty ignored it.

Another man came from a small cafe, and Rusty shot him in the chest at twenty feet. The man slammed backward and went down. Another man beside him drew his gun, but Rusty shot him twice before he could fire.

There was nothing frantic or fast-paced about Rusty. He rode slowly forward. The next man he shot came from the court house. He was a deputy and he returned fire. Rusty's shot had hit the deputy in the shoulder.

Now there was shouting up and down the street. The deputy fired twice more as Rusty reached for his rifle.

Spur McCoy ran out of the sheriff's office and saw the man fire his last pistol round at the deputy. Spur drew his Colt .45 and before the gunman on the horse could bring his rifle up, Spur put two heavy lead slugs into his chest, blasting him backwards off his horse, killing him before he hit the dirt of the street.

Spur ran up and stared down at the man in the fading light.

He recognized the man he had chased out of town.

"He's Rusty Schmidke," Spur said. "One more of the Schmidke brothers. He must have been the one who dynamited the jail."

The sheriff ran up, saw Rusty and nodded. "Four down, and two more to go."

CHAPTER EIGHTEEN

ERICK THOMPSON SCHMIDKE rolled over in the big bed and caught Hillery Gregson's breasts where they hung in front of him. She gazed at him and smiled as he fondled her.

Erick had never been able to resist a woman's breasts. There was something so pure and delightful and primal about them. The essence of a woman . . . and so enticingly beautiful.

They had put off the wedding a day. The judge was out of town hearing cases, but would be back tomorrow. Erick had moved his gear into the big bedroom. They told the servants that the marriage was set and there was a holiday atmosphere within the big house.

Erick had heard about the deadly shootout on the other side of town the day before from a deliveryman who brought ice to the house.

"From what I hear, the sheriff had some outlaws surrounded in a house, but the killers held some hostages and then got away. My brother-in-law is a deputy sheriff and he said it was a couple of wild killer rawhiders!"

Erick had discovered later downtown that indeed Zack and the rest of the clan had been chased out of town. He was betting they would all get away.

Then this afternoon he had found out that Zack had been captured and jailed. Erick sat and sipped a whiskey from a fancy goblet as he thought about it. Should he swoop down on the court house and try to rescue his brother? Or had he broken the family ties? Had he put all that behind him when he had asked Hillery to marry him?

Before he had satisfied himself with an answer, he heard the explosion downtown and knew it had to be either Zack or Rusty. He heard the news that both rawhiders were dead soon after it happened. Erick had finished his glass of whiskey, marched into the bedroom and made love to Hillery, realizing that he had made the decision before it had been made for him. All that family crime and killing were behind him.

Hillery traced his mouth with a finger.

"You look so sad, so worried. Darling, is anything bothering you?"

"All this killing! It grieves me that so many have died in this small town in the past two days. How can a loving God let this happen?"

She pulled his face to her breasts and stroked his hair.

"My soon-to-be husband, you must not worry yourself about that. You must learn to leave all that kind of religious worry to those who are active in the ministry. Since as of today you have retired as a minister, we have only to concern ourselves with our own interests."

She pulled his mouth to cover one breast and smiled when he kissed it.

"There, now, isn't that better?"

They both were still naked, lying on the big bed. He sat up and stared down at her womanly form. Handful-sized breasts, pinkly tipped; narrow shoulders, and a long neck. Her face was kind and soft, but not beautiful. Her waist had thickened over the years but her legs were still slender and graceful.

He stroked the softness of the fur at her crotch and then kissed her.

"Sweet Hillery, you are right. I must learn to concern myself with my new wife, and what is important to both of us."

"You will have certain responsibilities. You'll want to keep an eye on my business agents in Denver, to be sure that they are managing my . . . *our* affairs correctly. You'll be in charge, of course. Whatever you say will go."

"Well, it will take me some time to learn about everything . . ."

She smiled. "Not long. You are a smart man, you catch on quickly. You'll do fine."

Hillery stood and stretched. "Making love with you gives me tremendous appetite. Let's dress specially nicely tonight!"

He agreed and sat there still dazed, watching her begin to dress.

Slowly he realized that his life really was

changing. Zelda, Zack, Rusty and even Piney were dead. The only one who could tie Erick to the clan was Birch and the way things were going he couldn't last long. It was like a new birth for Erick.

He stood and went to the closet, put on his finest "preaching suit" and best shirt. It was going to be a night to remember, a night that would mark his final transformation from raw-hider and phoney preacher, to a man deserving of respect . . . and a damn *rich man* at that!

The same night, Spur McCoy looked at the flyer the sheriff handed him in the lawman's office.

"This came in today on the stage," the sheriff said. "'Pears as how our third Schmidke brother has been right here in town all the time."

Spur glanced at the broadside. It had a line drawing of a man that looked somewhat like the other Schmidke brothers. He read the type.

"A man believed to be Erick Schmidke, one of the notorious Schmidke Brothers who are wanted for murder in six states, is believed to be posing as a itinerant preacher, moving out of Texas into the west with a 'church wagon.' He stops at towns, holds revival meetings, and at times pretends to settle down and start to raise money to start a new church. When sufficient funds have been raised, Schmidke vanishes out of town on a stage or train and is not seen again.

"Anyone with information concerning his whereabouts is advised to wire the nearest U.S.

Marshal or the following city police departments . . ." It then listed twenty southwest towns.

"Haven't had time to more than make a few inquiries so far," Sheriff James said. "From what I've found out, the preacher has left his wagon, given up the ministry and moved in with the widow Hillery Gregson, the richest lady in town. She's worth at least a million dollars, mostly in Denver banks."

"So the preacher made a good convert?"

"My sources say they tried to get married yesterday, but the judge was out on his circuit. He comes back tomorrow."

"Then it's time we pay the couple a call. With a rich widow on the string, he won't do anything stupid. He'll deny who he is, and we'll have a hard time proving it."

"The drawing will help," the sheriff said.

"But not enough. If he denies who he is, I don't think we'll have enough evidence to arrest him. And with the widow Gregson backing him, they'll be in Denver before we can get any evidence from one of those towns."

"So what can we do?"

"We smoke him out, get him so scared that he tries to cut and run."

The sheriff frowned. "Gonna take a lot of scare to get him to run away from a million dollars. This is the big strike he's been looking for."

"I know. That's why I'm going to visit the Gregson mansion tonight as Brother McCoy, a fellow preacher in Christ, for some spiritual sustenance."

"I hope it works. I'll have a dozen deputies outside the house covering every door."

A half hour later, Spur walked up the steps of the Gregson house and rang the bell. He had made a quick visit to the Carriage House and changed into a dark suit, white shirt and black tie. He left his six-guns in his room, and carried only a small Derringer in his boot as a hide-out gun. He had been digging back into his Presbyterian roots for some old-fashioned religion. He was going to need it.

The door opened and a Mexican girl smiled at him.

"Brother McCoy to see Mrs. Gregson," he said and stepped into the entranceway.

A striking woman of about forty came at once from the doorway. She was not plain, but not really pretty either. A kind of glow emanated from her. She was, Spur decided, handsome.

"Yes, I'm Mrs. Gregson."

"Praise the Lord! I was told that I could find you here and that you are a true believer and one who could help a newly dedicated servant of the Lord!"

She frowned. "I am a Christian, Brother McCoy, but I don't remember hearing about you in Santa Fe."

"True, I have recently arrived, and am looking for a base of operations so I can open a new church."

A man came through the door behind the widow. He was taller than she, well dressed in a brown suit, cream-colored shirt and flowered cravat.

"Mrs. Gregson is not feeling up to talking about her religious activities tonight," the man said.

He was Erick Schmidke, Spur knew at a glance. He matched the drawing on the poster.

"Pastor Thompson! This is a surprise, and a pleasure. I've been at some of your revivals. You are truly inspired by our Lord Jesus Christ! I am in awe of your way with words, how well you serve the Lord. It's an honor to meet you!" Spur enthused.

The rawhider showed surprise and anger for a moment, then covered it and held out his hand.

"Brother McCoy, it is good to meet you, but I'm afraid you've caught us at a rather bad time. You see, Mrs. Gregson and I are to be married tomorrow, and we will be going to Denver on our honeymoon. So as you can understand, we have a thousand small things to get done. If we could postpone our talk until we get back late next month, both of us would appreciate it."

McCoy shook his head. "No. Absolutely not! The Devil waits for no man! Do the Lord's work today! Thrift, obedience and labor in the vineyard of the Lord are my daily tasks! I can't shirk my duties as a Christian and a preacher of the gospel, Pastor Thompson. I respect your views, but I must ask for time to talk with you about my call to the ministry and a problem I've been having."

Schmidke frowned. He looked at Mrs. Gregson, then shrugged.

"All right. We can give you a half hour, but no more. There simply are too many details to take care of here before our important day."

"Brother, I understand. And may the joy of the Lord go with you in your new life of wedded bliss."

They led the way into a sitting room where all took seats in finely upholstered chairs.

"Now, first, let me assure you that I am absolutely certain of my vocation," Spur said intensely. "I have heard the clarion call and accepted it and am committed to preach the gospel of our loving Lord Jesus Christ for as long as I live."

Spur saw Schmidke move uncomfortably on the chair. Good.

"Pastor Thompson, would you tell me about *your* call to preach the gospel?"

"I really don't think we have time for that right now, Brother McCoy. Do you have any other questions I could help you with?"

"Yes, that problem I mentioned. It's a matter of the vow of chastity I have taken. In my last parish, a young lady was appealing to me. I longed for her. I lusted after her! How can ministers like us maintain our chastity and stay pure for the good of the church?"

Spur saw the widow turn her head and hide her face behind her hand. He figured she was laughing.

"Are you criticizing me, Brother McCoy?"

Schmidke's voice had taken on a sober, angry tone.

"Oh, because you are to be married? Not at all, not at all. I know most pastors are married. It just isn't for me. And I thought that perhaps you could give me some help . . ."

Spur stood and walked to the window. "Could we speak alone for a few minutes, Pastor Thompson?"

"Mrs. Gregson and I have no secrets from one another, we . . ." He paused. "Very well, come into the hall."

When the door was closed Spur's attitude changed.

"Hey, Thompson, or whatever your name is, I caught your act in one of them Texas towns. Figured I could string along and learn the trade. Got it down now, and all I need is a stake. I mean, if you're getting out of the business, I'd be willing to take your church wagon." He chuckled softly. "Looks like you've caught yourself a live one here."

"I really don't know what you're talking about! I . . ."

McCoy waved his hand at the other man. "Come off it, Thompson! I've been in three towns where you worked your church-starting racket. It's a beauty, and I want to do the same damn thing. You've been my teacher for the past two months!"

"I don't know what you're talking about," Schmidke grated.

"Don't admit it. I don't care! I just want your

wagon, if you're getting out of the business. You can do that much for me."

"Yes, take the wagon, and the horses, I won't be needing them. Now, will you leave?"

"I have to see your lady first. Thank her properly."

Spur went back into the room where Mrs. Gregson still sat. He took the folded wanted poster from his pocket and handed it to her. She glanced at it, then looked up, startled.

"Yes, I'm afraid it's true," said Spur. "We got word just today. As you can see, the resemblance is exact. There can be no mistake. We've been tracking this man down for three months now. Let me introduce you to the wanted killer whose real name is Erick Schmidke."

The rawhider turned as Spur said his name. For a moment hatred flared on his face; then his better judgment prevailed and he laughed.

"My name is Thompson, and I can prove it. I don't know what paper you have there, but it doesn't concern me."

The widow was frowning now. "Erick, all those scars on your body—where did you get them?"

"In the war."

"But so many?"

"The war, I told you."

"Then sometimes you talk in your sleep. You say some of the strangest things."

"Hillery, darling, you can't believe those lies this man is telling you. I am Erick Thompson, preacher of the gospel. I don't know who this man is, but he's obviously a fraud. I'll put him out of the house and we'll forget all about it."

"Erick, I wish it were that easy. Since we've met, I've been checking upon you and I can't find any trace of an Erick Thompson in St. Louis."

"You don't believe me?" For a second he almost exploded. Then Erick gathered his senses and suppressed his anger. "Hillery, I'll put this imposter out and then we'll talk about it."

"No, Erick. We'd better talk now. My lawyer in Denver wired me yesterday that he had no record of you or any Pastor Thompson. He suggested we postpone the wedding. I was going to ignore him. Come here and look at the drawing of you, Erick. It's quite a good likeness."

Erick walked to where she sat, took the wanted poster from her hands and stared at it. He read the words, looked again at the picture, then lifted Hillery from where she sat.

In a move so swift Spur had no chance to counter it, Erick pulled a Derringer from his inside pocket and held it to Hillery Gregson's head.

"You make one false move, *Brother* McCoy, and I blow this lady's brains all over the sitting room!"

CHAPTER NINETEEN

ERICK SCHMIDKE PUSHED Hillery toward the window and looked past the heavy drapes. He saw a man two houses down talking to someone in a buggy. In the opposite direction he saw another man examining the shoe of his horse's front hoof.

Spur McCoy nodded.

"You'll never find them all, Erick. But they're out there. This place is surrounded and there's no way for you to get out alive."

"The hell there isn't! A hostage is always worth at least a million dollars." He caught Hillery by the hair and pushed her toward the door, then looked back at Spur. "Don't make the mistake of thinking that I might not hurt the lady. She would have been worth a million to me alive and in Denver. Right now she's worth more than that; she's worth my life."

He twisted Hillery around so she protected his body.

208

"There isn't one chance in hell that you or the sheriff are going to shoot down the town's richest lady just so you can get to me. We'll meet again, McCoy, and I won't have to conserve my shots the next time. I want you cold, slab-dead!"

The pair vanished out the doorway and Spur moved cautiously to it so he could see them. He followed them toward the front door where he saw Erick pick up another weapon, a six-gun from the closet. Now Spur was more careful.

"You'll never get out of town," Spur called. He had drawn the Derringer but had no chance to use it.

"I'll get away, and take plenty of cash with me. This little lady will warm my bed and also be my ticket to freedom. You just watch me!"

Erick used the next five minutes productively. He kept the Derringer against Hillery's head as she opened the safe, took out all the cash and put it in a small carpetbag. He then moved her to the kitchen where he told one of the servants to saddle up two horses and bring them to the back door.

By this time the sheriff would know something had gone wrong, Spur hoped. He followed the pair but had no opportunity of stopping them.

Hillery had hardly changed expression during her ordeal. Spur decided she was frightened and angry, but holding up well. If they worked it right they might rescue her yet.

The argument came through clearly. Hillery was arguing about something. Spur edged toward a door in the hallway so he could see.

"I simply must have a divided skirt if I am to ride that horse," Hillery said. "It's been months since I've ridden, and in a skirt like this I'll only hold you up. It's just common sense to let me dress properly for the trip. You are usually more intelligent than this, Erick."

He scowled, motioned to her to move and she led the way to the stairway, the Derringer still pressed against her head.

Spur decided it was time to make his move. When they were out of sight, he ran for the kitchen, slipped out the door and caught the reins of the horses. He leaped aboard one, grabbed the lead of the other and rode fast down the alley and away from the house.

The sheriff rode up to meet him.

"He panicked, wants to run. But now he's lost his horses."

The sheriff nodded. "What will he do now, do you think?"

"Hostage demands. A carriage, I would guess. Might take another person from the house."

An hour later Spur's worst fears came true. Erick had come out of the house with the six-gun against Hillery's head, and two women servants tied to her. He demanded that a buggy for the four of them be harnessed up and brought around. They had a box of food and he had a rifle and three six-guns.

"Just stay back and don't try to follow us. If you follow us, I'll kill one of the women and dump her on the trail. Believe me, Sheriff, I'll do it. Now clear out! I don't want to see any of you by the time the buggy gets here."

They had all faded back out of sight. Sheriff James and Spur talked it over.

"He'll definitely kill both the girls if he thinks it will help him get away," Spur said.

"We can't have that."

"We'll let him go, let him think he's getting away clean," Spur said. "Only I'll be tracking him all the way. He'll never see me. When it gets dark, I'll move in and take him. The women won't be hurt."

"Be sure."

"I'll be sure or I won't do it the first night."

"I can't figure out anything better," the sheriff said. "Can I send a man or two along with you?"

"No, but you can send a man down to the store and get me a day's worth of traveling food. I can't remember if I had breakfast or not."

Erick and his buggy left about a half-hour later. There was no sign of the posse, but Erick knew the sheriff's men were around. He would have some surprises for them if they showed up. He had tied the Derringer against the side of Hillery's neck, and put a cord around the trigger. He would grab the cord and jerk it and the rich widow lady would die quickly. The two servants were tied together and roped in to the buggy. Both were scared to death and he knew would give him no trouble. If the sheriff or Spur McCoy followed him, he would kill one or the other without a second thought.

Erick grinned as he cleared the last of the houses in town and headed along the trail north toward Denver. Once a Schmidke, always a Schmidke, he reckoned. It would be a long trip, but there were some stops along the way. He planned on holding the servants for not more than three days. By then he could tell if there was any pursuit, and he should also be able to eliminate McCoy or any deputies who were on his trail and be on his own at last. He hadn't decided yet what to do with Hillery.

Marriage would have been ideal, but that was impossible now. Too bad—he'd really been getting fond of her. He had about twenty thousand dollars from the safe and that would have to do. Yes, she would be eliminated when she was no longer of any use to him.

That problem solved, Erick laid the whip to the black pulling the buggy and moved up the road faster. He had seen no one following them yet, but he knew there was someone there, probably the man McCoy. He must be a U.S. Marshal, Erick figured.

Several hours later, Spur settled down three hundred yards from the hostages, watching. It was dusk and fast becoming dark. The tenor of the hostage situation had been established early on. Erick had stripped all three women to the waist, and forced them to stay that way. It was part of his plan to humiliate them and prove that he held their very lives in his hand. They must do whatever he said.

Spur figured the outlaw knew he was being

followed, knew someone was out there watching for a chance to blow him away with a rifle. Consequently, Schmidke had made every move with one of the three women clasped to his chest. There had not been a single chance to pick him off safely with a well-placed shot.

The sleeping arrangements were as Spur had suspected. Two women lay on one side of Erick and one on the other side, and a blanket covered them all. While Spur wondered what Erick was doing under the blankets, there was no chance he could draw a head on the man with the women so close to him.

That night when he figured everyone would be sleeping, Spur made his first move. He worked his way silently to the spot where the black had been picketed, studied the tie down rope for several minutes, then unwrapped a six-gun from the hookup, and let the hammer down softly. It had been rigged to fire if the rope was moved beyond a certain limit and had to be moved by a human hand to make it go off. After that, Spur led the black away into the trees, came out on the trail a half mile down and slapped the mare on the flank, sending her home to her stable in Santa Fe.

When daylight came, Spur heard Erick swearing before he saw him lift up between the three women.

Spur had been awake for an hour, and the new Springfield 1873 army rifle had been loaded and ready.

Now he moved his sighting slightly, refined his aim, and squeezed the trigger.

For a brief moment, it was as though time stood still.

The rifle cracked in the thin mountain air. Erick Schmidke sitting up between the still sleeping women had made a fatal mistake. He seemed to nod, then his whole body slammed forward from the force of the big .45 rifle slug that had bored into the back of his head, dissipating most of its force as it tore through his brain, pulverizing vital motor centers, and then exited through his forehead, tearing away a chunk of skull.

Two of the women screamed.

Another female voice spoke quietly, soothing, telling them that it was all right, that they were safe now.

"Mrs. Gregson," Spur called. "Are you all right down there?"

Hillery turned, and he saw that she was sitting up, still bare to the waist. She nodded.

"Yes, Mr. McCoy, we are all fine. Erick is dead, as you know." Her voice was remarkably self-possessed.

"I'm coming down," Spur said.

When he had moved the three hundred yards to the campsite, he found little change. The two servants sat numbly in the same spot. All three women were still topless. Spur noticed with interest the differences in the women's breasts. After all, he was something of a connoisseur. Mrs. Gregson's were pinkly nippled. The older Mexican girl's soft brown breasts were large with dark nipples and almost no noticeable aerolas. The younger Mexican servant girl's breasts were still forming with small nipples.

"Mr. McCoy, I hoped you were following us," Hillery Gregson said, standing to meet him and graciously holding out her hand as if they were at a formal reception. "I thank you for your heroic rescue."

He took her hand and smiled.

"Any time for a trio of beautiful ladies. But I won't demand that you continue to dress in this fashion."

The Mexican girls giggled and turned away. Hillery smiled.

"There is a certain innocent freedom this way, Mr. McCoy. But if the sight offends you . . ." She smiled again, making no move to cover herself.

"Not in the least! Perhaps we could talk about it at a later time," Spur said. "Now we should be getting ready to move back to town."

It took them all morning to make the trip. Spur's saddle mount was unhappy pulling the buggy, but at last Spur talked her into the task. The ladies had dressed once more and were chattering away as if nothing had happened by the time they met the sheriff's men who had followed them at a half day's distance.

News of the rescue spread around town quickly, and a crowd had gathered at the sheriff's office to gawk at the body of the third of the famous Schmidke brothers rawhide gang. Spur had then turned off with the buggy, taking the women back to the Gregson mansion.

As he handed her down from the buggy, Hillery Gregson held Spur's hand longer than was absolutely necessary. She looked up at him.

"Mr. McCoy, I would appreciate it if you could call on me this afternoon. I realize you're some sort of law officer, but I must insist on a reward for your work in saving my life, as well as that of my two servants. I'll expect you at three p.m. sharp." She turned and walked into her house with the air of a person who is used to being obeyed.

Spur tipped his hat and unhitched his mount, then rode back to the sheriff's office where they talked for a moment. Spur would send a wire to the home office reporting the demise of the last of the Schmidke brothers, and his work here would be done.

But there was still Mrs. Gregson. He had saved twenty thousand dollars that Schmidke had stolen from her, but somehow he had a feeling she would show him more personal appreciation than a reward of money.

It was almost three o'clock before Spur realized it. He was still in his trail clothes, but it was too late to change. When he knocked on the door at the Gregson mansion it opened at once and Hillery smiled up at him.

"Welcome, Mr. McCoy! I am delighted to see you. Won't you come inside?"

She was dressed in the shearest of silk fabrics, the material showing every voluptuous curve of her body as if the material wasn't there at all. It was slightly pinkish and lent an added touch of color to the scene.

He stepped inside and she smiled.

"I hope you like my new negligee. I've never worn it before this afternoon. Come into the sitting room for a glass of wine."

Spur nodded and dropped his brown hat on a settee. She led the way and Spur appreciated every sensual movement revealed by the negligee.

Inside the sitting room he saw the two Mexican serving girls. Now both were scrubbed until they shone, black hair pulled back and braided, and to Spur's surprise and delight, they both were naked to the waist, with only the wispiest of streamers of gauzy material draping from their waists, half covering the blackness of their pubic hair.

The girls served each of them wine, pouring it from a newly opened bottle into long stemmed crystal glasses.

Spur and Hillery Gregson sat on a small settee, just the right size for two.

"Mr. McCoy, this afternoon the girls and I are three women who owe our lives to you. We are now your slaves to do with as you wish, one, two or all of us. There is no greater gift one person can give another than the gift of pleasure. Any small thing we can do for you in return for saving our lives will be done with joy, excitement and total delight. What *is* your pleasure?"

The three women moved in front of Spur,

knelt and then bowed down before him.

Spur lifted his brows, then one by one lifted them to a standing position. He kissed each woman softly on the mouth, then kissed their breasts. He moved the two servant girls to one side.

"Ladies, I am honored by your gratitude, and your offer, but you have given me the pleasure of being able to continue your lives. That is reward enough for me." He motioned them out of the room.

As he did, Hillery caught his hand, pushed it firmly over one of her breasts and led him down the hall to her bedroom.

"That was sweet, what you told the girls. Both are still virgins. But don't think you're going to get off that easy with me!" In the bedroom she closed the door, pulled off part of the flimsy material so her breasts were bare and pressed herself tightly against him.

"Today you killed my fiance. I'm holding you responsible for taking his place this afternoon and all night. This was to be my wedding night. Can you fill the bill?"

"Hillery, I think I can fill any opening that one might have to offer."

She squealed in delight and fell backwards on the bed.

Spur shucked out of his trail clothes and tore off the wisps of silk still clinging to Hillery, then lay heavily on top of her. Hillery moaned in delight.

"Oh, yes! Before Erick, I had nearly forgotten what a good hard man's body felt like crushing me into the mattress! Marvelous!" Her hands worked between them, found his already erect phallus and massaged it.

"It's difficult for a widow to have any kind of normal sex life," she continued. "Most men respect you too much, and there is seldom a chance for a romantic involvement. So sometimes a widow has to take matters into her own hands." She giggled. "And I certainly like this matter that is in my hands right now!"

Spur bent and licked and then kissed and sucked on her breasts and brought a quick, hard climax racing through her. She shivered and moaned, then shut her eyes and wailed a dozen times before she relaxed under him.

"Glorious! And you aren't even inside me yet! This is going to be a beautiful and a *long* afternoon!"

Spur felt his own temperature rising. Ever since he had come into the house and been greeted by the frank display of female nudity, he had been growing more and more excited. Now he pushed her legs apart and settled between them. She murmured in encouragement. Then he reached down and lifted her legs, moving them high over her head and resting them on his shoulders.

"Like this?" she asked.

He nodded, probed, found her moist slot and drove inward, bringing a low scream of rapture from her. She adjusted her position and then began to move against him, looking up in surprise.

"I never knew I could bend this far!" she said

and giggled.

Spur leaned on his elbows and charged into her steaming center, feeling her gripping him inside with a regularity that drove him higher and higher and before he wanted to, he exploded with an eruption of white-hot lava that scalded them both. He let her legs down and fell against her in his own mini-death as they both gasped for air.

As they rested, the younger servant girl came into the room. She was naked now, and carried bowls of freshly frozen ice cream, made with a little hand-cranked ice cream freezer and ice from the ice house. The delicious confection had been sprinkled with chocolate drops and fresh cherries.

They ate the delicacy before it melted.

Hillery smiled at Spur.

"I hope you like it, that you like *me*. This doesn't have to be a one time celebration, Spur McCoy. I get to Denver often. We could meet there. I have enough contacts so we could enjoy ourselves in almost any manner you chose."

"I do have certain responsibilities."

"Your job? Pooh! You could resign and live with me. I have more money than both of us could ever spend."

"I enjoy my work. I want to continue doing it."

"But don't you enjoy this—me—just a little?"

"More than a little! This is the kind of life that can become intoxicating, addictive. But for a man there must be something more to life, something of substance, of value, some feeling of accomplishment and worth. Like today, I saved three lives. Every time I get nightmares about killing a man, I'll try to balance them against the satisfaction of saving a life or two."

"Men—I'll never understand them! Most men work all their lives so they can take it easy in their old age, so they will have enough money to relax and slow down. I'm offering you all that now, while you're young and vibrant and can enjoy it all, with me."

He lay on his back and she slid over him, dipping one breast after the other into his mouth for his willing ministrations.

"Do you like that?" she asked.

He nodded, not able to talk at the moment.

"Good. I'm going to show you other wonders which you'll enjoy even more."

She turned and found his limp sabre and began to revive it. Spur gave little cries of delight as her tongue entranced him and soon he was eager to invade her flesh once again.

Hillery got on her hands and knees and looked at Spur.

"Big Man, I have an opening you haven't tried yet. I think you should see if you can fill it as you promised."

Spur chuckled and found that he was up to the task as he mounted her again from the back and she yelped in sudden pleasure, then quickly cautioned him to be gentle.

This time they climaxed together and both wailed and roared with a total lack of inhibition. Afterward, they sprawled on the big bed in exhaustion and wonder and a new regard for each other.

A short time later she leaned over him and kissed her lips.

"Spur McCoy, I want you for my husband. Will you marry me, today?"

He watched her green flecked eyes, then slowly shook his head.

"Hey, the man is supposed to ask the woman. Are you trying to upset the whole set of mores, our code of social conduct?" he teased.

"Fine. Will you ask me to marry you?"

He watched her eyes, then leaned up and kissed her soft, quivering lips.

"No, because you would say yes, and I'm not ready to get married, not with the job I have. The whole western half of this nation is my responsibility. I travel all the time."

"Marry me and you won't have to work."

"We covered that."

"It's worth another try. My husband right before he died said he was worth four million dollars. There must be more than that by now. Are you turning down four million dollars, or me?"

He kissed her. "Both."

"Ingrate!"

"But remember I saved your life. You could be dead by now."

She stopped, wrinkled her brow, then kissed him. "Yes, I had almost forgotten. I owe you everything. So if you won't marry me, I can still offer you my body and my wealth on an anytime-you-come basis. Then I can give you gifts, and establish an endowment for you. Yes, there are many ways I can continue to thank you for saving my life."

She kissed him and rolled on top of him. "Promise me that you will give me the satisfaction of making love to you for twenty-four hours."

"Twenty-four. . . . Do we get to sleep any at all in between?"

"Sure."

"Done. We fuck for twenty-four hours!"

She blushed when he said the taboo word. He laughed and said it again, then made her say it out loud and they both laughed. It was going to be an interesting twenty-four hours.

CHAPTER TWENTY

THE YOUNG MAN in trail-stained clothes sat at the
last table against the wall in the Silver Dollar
saloon, one of the worst establishments on
Santa Fe's main street. He nursed a beer and
stared at the men around him through glazed
eyes.

He had made his way back to town
cautiously, and even now kept one hand near
his six-gun, but there had been no hue and cry.
No one was looking for a lone rider. There
seemed no interest in him at all.

Not like the day they had chased him out of
town when his mother had been killed.

The damn dynamite bomb!

He looked at his hands, flexed them, and then
let them go limp. He would never strangle the
man who had killed her as he had promised her.
He stared at the men around him, drinking,
gambling, grabbing at the round bottoms and
breasts of the dance hall girls.

It wasn't fair!

Of course it wasn't fair, he had learned that years ago. It wasn't fair, but that was just the way it was.

Now his paw was dead. His Uncle Rusty had been shot down in the street, and less than an hour ago he had heard that his Uncle Erick had been killed while trying to get out of town.

Gone.

All of his family gone!

He wanted to lash out at someone.

He wanted to make love to someone.

It always happened. Every serious problem in his life, every crisis had always come down to this. To kill or to make love. He fingered his six-gun. He could kill four or five before someone put a bullet in his head. That would be the best way. Yes!

Then he thought of a soft body next to his, of his own sexual gratification rising to fever pitch.

He stood up quickly and went out the saloon door, his hands well away from his gun. The dry goods store. He was sure the small youth in the dry goods store had been watching him that day.

Birch walked directly to the store and opened the door. Two women were buying cloth. They finished their transaction and left. He was now the only customer in the store.

The clerk came from the far side and watched him.

"Can I help you?" the youth said. He wasn't more than sixteen.

Birch heard a catch in his voice. He stared at the boy's face. Then he knew.

"Yes, you can help me," Birch said. "And you know exactly how you can help me." Birch reached toward him but the boy backed up slowly, moving behind a screen that shielded the front of the store from the supply room.

They stood and watched each other. "What's your name?" Birch asked, his voice husky.

"Lester."

"Good. Lester, you know how you can help me, don't you?"

Lester nodded. He fell to his knees and leaned against Birch's waist, then his arms went around Birch and Lester kissed the fly of his pants.

"Oh, yes, Lester, I knew you understood!" Birch said. Quickly he opened the buttons of his pants and pulled out his erection. "Do it, Lester! Birch said softly, and the young man bent and took the phallus into his mouth. Birch erupted almost at once, holding Lester's head firmly against him. Then his hips began to move and he patted Lester gently on the back of the head.

"Again, Lester, once more."

The front door bell rang as a customer came in and Birch cursed. He helped Lester to get up.

"Get rid of them fast!" Birch commanded.

Lester went to help the man with some canvas, and when he came back several minutes later, Birch was furious.

"What took you so long? I said get rid of him, not wait on him. Did you lock the front door?"

"No—can't. Mr. Norton would kill me."

Birch fumed. "All right, take down your pants and turn around."

"We can't right here. It's too risky. Somebody might come in."

Birch thumbed back the hammer of his six-gun and put the muzzle against Lester's mouth. "Take them down and bend over, or you're dead."

Three minutes later Andrew Norton came silently in the back door with the change from his usual walk to the bank. He put down the bank bag on the counter and looked for his clerk. Lester was the best he had ever had work for him. Norton had made almost no noise coming in, and now he was curious, not seeing Lester immediately. Curious, he checked behind the front screen.

What he saw enraged him. Lester was bent over a straight-backed chair, his pants around his ankles, and some stranger was behind him snorting and wheezing and humping him in the ass!

Norton pulled from his pocket the pistol that he carried to the bank every day. He was a good shot. He fired just once. The bullet tore through the tall man's head and slammed his body to the floor on one side of Lester.

Lester jumped up and turned, stunned, protesting.

"Mr. Norton! I . . ."

"Lester, don't worry. He was raping you. I know how it can happen. Don't fret about a

227

thing. Pull up your pants and get your clothes fixed. Then run and bring the sheriff. You tell him this man was trying to rob the store and I got back just in time."

When Lester ran out the front door, Norton put a wad of bills in the dead man's pocket and then waited for the sheriff.

He wasn't sure who he had killed, but whoever he was he deserved it. Lester was his! Nobody could love Lester but him! A few others in town understood that. This stranger didn't know, so he was dead. Too damn bad!

The sheriff arrived moments later. He looked at the man's face, and then nodded.

"Can't be sure, Mr. Norton, but I'd swear that was the third man we chased out of town a few days ago, one of the Schmidke rawhider bunch. You were lucky he didn't just kill both you and then take what he wanted. Tell me how it happened again."

Norton went through the story he'd concocted once more, feeling more than a little lucky that the rawhider had been looking for sex, rather than for money or supplies.

Sheriff James nodded. "Sure as hell matches up. He's a dead ringer for that other Schmidke boy who got himself killed. The county owes you a debt of thanks, Mr. Norton."

When the sheriff was gone and the last customer had left for the day, Lester and Mr. Norton went back to the cot in the small office as they did every Thursday.

"He made me do it, Mr. Norton," Lester whined, his face white with nervous fear.

228

"I know he did, Lester, don't worry about it. It will be another one of our little secrets."

"Yes, Mr. Norton," Lester said, and watched his employer lock the door. Then Lester began to undress just as he did every Thursday.

CHAPTER TWENTY-ONE

LATE THE FOLLOWING afternoon, Spur McCoy walked somewhat unsteadily down the boardwalk toward the Santa Fe Carriage House. He knew he had some luggage there, but his state of mind was not clear enough for him to be exactly sure just where it was or what his room number might be.

The quantity and quality of the wine at Mrs. Gregson's mansion had progressed during the evening, as one bottle after another was emptied. Most of the daylight and dark hours at the big house had blended into a fuzzy, sexy, wonderful blur.

Spur ran into the post holding up the overhand portion of the General Store, and one of the three old-timers loafing in a tipped-back chair leaning againt the store front guffawed. Spur turned to glare at him, but never quite located the offender.

Once he reached the Carriage House he felt

more secure. He walked across the lobby, down the first floor hallway and turned in at the owner's room. He finally found the door, but there appeared to be bodies standing in front of it.

On closer inspection they turned out to be pretty ladies. On closer inspection, they merged into one pretty lady—Annabelle.

"Annabelle!" Spur said, surprised and pleased that he remembered her name. He reached for her but she batted his arms down.

"Can you tell me exactly where you have been for the past twenty-four hours, Mister McCoy?" Annabelle asked icily.

"Where? Certainly. Fighting desperados, criminals and rawhiders. I cracked the famous Schmidke brothers rawhider case. Ya know that?"

"Yes, I know that!"

She was mad but she was weakening.

"And I did it so I could come back and spend a week with you." Spur grinned. He knew it was a drunk, silly grin.

She frowned. "You're lying. You'll be heading for Denver and the train just as soon as the next stage comes through!"

"Honest . . . honestinjun."

"And you're stinking drunk!"

"No, not drunk. A gentleman . . . a gentleman does not get drunk on good wine. He gets a glow!"

"Drunk as a stinking skunk!" She sighed. "Oh, hell, come on in. I might as well sober you up and see what's left of you. That damn Widow

231

Gregson certainly has changed."

"Th . . . tha . . . thank you."

"Congratulations, you put two words together!"

Annabelle scowled at him, then led him to her couch, aimed him at it and pushed. Spur toppled on target and relaxed. He was snoring almost at once.

"Damn that rich bitch!" Annabelle said softly. She snorted and put a pillow under Spur's head. But she had him now, and she would keep him! But how would she work it? Spur had seen all the tricks. She had used a lot of them on him herself. By the time he woke up she would have some plan.

But four hours later she had nothing worked out. She sat with a cup of coffee and watched him sleep. He was restless, stirring. She guessed he would wake up in a few minutes.

When Spur came back to the conscious world half an hour later, his head was clear. He was rested and ready to do battle.

"That's not fair," Annabelle wailed. "You should at least have a massive hangover."

"Sorry," Spur said. "I never do. Too much clean living, I guess. Did I get any mail from the stage?"

"You weren't supposed to ask," Annabelle said. "Mail or telegrams always mean you have to leave."

"Not always."

She took three envelopes from under the doily on the end table.

"They came yesterday, but I couldn't find you."

Spur looked at two of the envelopes. They were from the Denver Chief of Police. Inside he found two wires. Both telegrams had been sent to the Chief, who was instructed to send them on the stage to Spur in Santa Fe. The wires had come from Washington, D.C. in a matter of seconds, then had taken three days to get from Denver to Santa Fe.

Spur opened the first one.

"Good work closing out Bank Robbery job. Are you sure about the White brothers? Last report on them was that they were in Georgia."

The second wire must have arrived the same day. It said:

"Schmidke brothers also known as White, reported in Texas, heading West. Make them your first priority. Report progress weekly."

Spur handed them both to Annabelle.

"See. These don't always mean I have to leave."

Spur read the next wire and frowned.

"Frank and Jesse James still giving local authorities trouble in Missouri, Kansas and Texas. Suggest a conference with you in St. Louis next month to offer Federal help to the states regarding these interstate outlaws."

Spur put that one deep in his pocket. It was the first time his superiors had mentioned any of the outlaw gangs that had developed from wild raiders such as Quantrill during the Civil War.

"What's that one about?" Annabelle asked.

"Nothing you can see. When's dinner? I'm starved!"

"The kitchen closed an hour ago! You expect me to keep it open just so you can eat whenever you want to?"

"Fine—I'll find something."

She flew at him, her hands like claws reaching for his face. He caught her and stopped the threat and held her firmly. Then the anger faded from her face and she reached up and kissed him.

"Spur McCoy, you make me furious, and then you make me turn to jelly. What am I going to do with you?"

"Put up with me as long as you can, then kick me out of your bed and tell me to get lost."

"Not in a million years, Spur McCoy. Not ever!" She unbuttoned the front of her dress, caught his hand and towed him toward the bedroom.

"I imagine the widow has worn you out, but I'm going to check and see. Then I'll let you rest up a little before we see if we can beat your eight-times-in-a-night record. Or was it seven? I've forgotten. Spur McCoy, while I have you captured in my bedroom, I'm going to love you like I've never loved you, because one of these days, you'll leave and you won't ever come back. That will be the time my heart breaks."

Spur picked her up and carried her into the bedroom.

The Schmidke brothers case was closed.

There would be another one all too quickly, perhaps even some work with local authorities on the Jesse James gang. But until then, he was going to take a few days to rest up and relax and eat and sleep and make love and pretend he was just an ordinary man.

Too soon, he would be back in the saddle as a Secret Service Agent.

Annabelle pushed one breast upward toward his mouth. Spur couldn't pass up the offer. He bent and kissed the warm, vibrant flesh and felt it pulsating with excitement and desire . . .

LOUISIANA LASS

CHAPTER ONE

Lambert G. Hanover bent his six-foot frame to check his appearance in the mirror. The suit had travelled well. He looked every bit a gentleman, which was what he was counting on.

He heard Teresa's laughter from downstairs where she was distracting the sweet-faced farm woman. It was almost noon, judging from the thin slice of shadow that the sun cast through the window. It was time.

Lambert walked quietly from the guestroom and paced along the hallway. The door stood open, inviting him inside, inviting him to help himself.

The gambler held back a smile as he walked into the woman's bedroom. He wasn't expecting to find riches but most farmers had money stashed away in case of emergencies. If he didn't find anything it wasn't a real problem. They had plenty to live on for some time.

Hanover quickly went through the plain wooden

dresser. Finding nothing, he searched the footed, heavy closet, rifling through tiny drawers of women's underthings, gloves, stockings and handkerchiefs. Again, nothing.

But he felt money in the room. He smelled it.

Lambert Hanover stood in the center of the room beside the quilt-tossed bed. He put his hands on his hips and circled.

An old Bible caught his eye. He went to it and flipped back the leather cover. An envelope fell out. He opened it and pulled out two $100 bills.

He smiled at the money. So the widow's husband had left her some cash. Lambert G. Hanover pocketed the easy earnings, replaced the Bible on the table near the bed and returned the room to its normal appearance.

"Ah, really, Mrs. Johnson, you don't have to—"

Teresa's voice was far louder than usual. A warning. Lambert slipped from the room. Shadows moved up along the staircase. They were coming.

"No, it's nothing at all."

Hanover silently returned to the guestroom, took off his jacket and held it as he walked back into the hall.

"Hello, Mr. Overland!" Betty Johnson said as she reached the landing. "I was just about to show your dear wife some of my things—heirlooms that my late husband brought here from Norway. They're all I have left of him."

"That would be splendid, but I'm afraid that Penelope and I do have to be going. We'd hate to miss that marriage." Hanover smiled at the attractive woman who stood behind Mrs. Johnson on the stairs. "Perhaps upon our return."

"That would be fine! I hope you've enjoyed my hospitality," the vibrant, blonde-haired widow said. "Such as it is."

"More than you know, dear lady. More than you know."

Lambert G. Hanover and Teresa Salvare were back in their buggy within five minutes. As soon as they'd turned onto the rutted road leading south and were some distance from the farmhouse, Teresa grabbed Hanover's right knee.

"Well?" she demanded, excitement puffing her high cheekbones and making her blue eyes glow.

"Well what, dear wife?"

"Stop joking! What did you get? Did the old biddy have anything worthwhile?"

Hanover straightened his back. "How can you doubt me? Reach into my vest pocket. There's a surprise for you, Tessa."

The thirty-year-old woman squealed and pushed her hand inside Lambert's coat. The two bills crackled between her fingers.

"Not much, but it'll do." she tucked the money into the front of her gray striped travelling dress, loding it firmly between her breasts. "I thought that old crow'd never stop talking. Yak yak yak. 'Norway this. Norway that. My dear husband.' I would've tossed my cookies if she'd mentioned him again!"

"I'm glad you approve," Lambert said as the buggy rolled between endless white picket fences. "So why didn't you stop her from coming upstairs? She nearly caught me, Tessa! Besides, I'm sure she had more money salted away up there. You didn't give me enough time!"

She removed her bonnet and flipped a lock of hair from her eyes. "I did warn you, you big oaf!" Teresa patted her chest and shook her head. "That woman was absolutely uncontrollable."

Lambert Hanover shrugged. "That's never been a problem with you before. How many jobs have you done so far? Thirty? Fifty? Not to mention that great week in Kansas City. We should just relax until we get to New Orleans. No more work for a while. Promise?"

Teresa Salvare blinked her big eyes and pouted. "Work? Why whatever do you mean, sir?"

He tightened the reins, urging the horses to move faster. "You know exactly what I mean. I don't want to catch you taking any more women's purses like you did two towns ago. It's too dangerous! Do you have any idea how much we have so far? At least two-hundred-fifty thousand dollars in cash, jewelry and bearer bonds and stocks!"

She flashed her white teeth at him. "Are you saying we should retire? Give all this up?"

"No, no. Not until after we do the big one."

"Good. You had me worried there, Lambert." Teresa readjusted her breasts in the tight confines of her dress and smiled at him. "Although I wouldn't be sorry to stop eating dust for a while."

"All in due time, Tessa. All in due time."

They rode in silence for two hours until the single horse that pulled their buggy balked at going any faster.

"Come on, girl," Lambert said in a soothing voice. "Water and oats up ahead." He eyed the distant spire of a church that showed a town almost hidden in the trees. "You can do it."

The roan whinneyed, tossed her head and plodded on.

"If only you were that manageable," Lambert G.

Hanover said as he glanced at the woman beside him.

"My dear Lamb, you wouldn't like me half as much if I was."

They stopped at a small town minutes later. Hanover rubbed his horse's neck as it drank at a trough.

"I'll be right back," Teresa said as she replaced her bonnet.

"Where are you going?" he asked suspiciously.

"Just you never mind. I'm going to say a prayer in that cute little church across the street."

He guffawed.

"I'll have you know that I was a good Christian before I met you. Not great—just good. I'll be right back."

She snapped shut her purse and strode across the broad street, holding up her skirts and avoiding stepping into the steaming horse droppings.

Lambert shook his head and let the horse nuzzle the bucket of oats he'd purchases at the livery stable. Tessa could be a bit of a bother at times but she'd been a fine partner. With her help he'd been able to more than double his take at every town they'd visited.

But the woman was too volatile, ready to use a pistol or rifle to settle things. Her style clashed with his own smooth, polished manner. Teresa was liable to get them both locked up if she didn't rein in her temper.

Still, she was an asset.

He turned to watch his partner step into the white church. The roan munched and drank, munched and drank.

Five minutes later Teresa walked quickly across

the street.

"I feel so spiritually refreshed," she said, fanning her forehead. "Let's leave now. On to New Orleans!"

"Okay, okay. No hurry."

She grabbed his arm. "Let's go, dear!" Teresa looked back at the church. "Right now!"

Lambert frowned. "Fine."

Ready for the road again after her break, the roan didn't argue as Hanover switched her along Main Street heading south out of town.

"Teresa, you didn't—"

"Come on now, Lambert!" The blonde gasped as she felt the bodice of her dress. "All that money sitting there and no one in sight. Why, what kind of a woman do you think I am?" Teresa said. She dramatially fanned her face. "I guess it must have been a month's collection, or the church building fund or something."

"Did anyone see you?"

"No, silly. I told you, no one was in sight. I sat down and pretended to pray, but that silver dish on the altar filled with money was too tempting to pass up." She reached under her skirts and produced the collection plate. One dollar bill still laid within it. "Those pockets I had sewn into my petticoats sure do come in handy, don't they?" Teresa admired the dish as it shone in the sunlight.

Lambert growled. "Yes. Put that away!"

A breeze caught the dollar bill, sending it fluttering into the air. "Okay. You sound just like my father!" She stuffed the gleaming plate into one of the bags that sat in the buggy behind her, straightened up in the seat and stretched. "It sure will be great to get to New Orleans, won't it?"

"That's a fact," Lambert G. Hanover grinned. He

had to admire the girl's daring. "How much did you get?" Transferring the reins to his left hand, he reached inside the woman's dress.

"Well, ah, ah—don't reach."

Hanover's smile vanished as he pulled a short knife from the woman's bodice. It was still sticky with traces of blood. He threw the weapon into the brush that lined the trail and raised his hand to slap her. "You stupid girl!"

Teresa flinched. "I thought you were a gentleman! I thought you detested violence!"

Lambert controlled his sudden anger and grabbed the reins with both hands.

The thirty-year-old woman lifted her chin. "So I lied. I didn't see the preacher walking up behind me. He surprised me, so I gave him his fondest wish. To see his Lord."

"I don't believe you. Did you really kill him?"

The woman sighed and played with her bonnet. "I don't think so. He was such a girlish man. He darn near fainted when I turned toward him with the knife. I just slashed his arm. He dropped the second the blade touched him. I didn't wait around. I got the hell out of there!"

Lambert G. Hanover shook his head. "What am I going to do with you?" He looked up at the cloud-scattered sky. "You just promised, Tessa. No more jobs!"

"Well, I'm sorry." She tossed her head. "Maybe I have some kind of disease. I'm sure if you were there, and saw all that money just waiting to be taken, lying in plain sight with no one around, you would have turned and walked out without touching it. Right, Lambert?"

"Well, I'd—" Lambert laughed. "I may be a

gentleman, but I'm not that much of one. Okay, Tessa. You're right. You just did what I've trained you to do. But it won't do either of us any good if you keep taking dangerous chances like that. Do you understand?"

Teresa Salvare lifted her pretty shoulders and shrugged. "I guess. Say, can't you make that old nag go any faster? We're still days away from New Orleans and all the riches that are waiting for us there!"

"And on the steamer *Natchez*. That money isn't going anywhere, Tessa. Pass the time like you always do—thinking up ways to spend it."

She sank against him. "That's always fun for a while. And I know exactly what I'm gonna do."

Lambert G. Hanover smiled. "What is it today? Open a saloon? Or a string of fancy women's apparel shops?"

She made a face. "No, that was last week. I'm going to buy myself a ship and sail around the world. London. Paris. Venice. Alexandria—not the one in Louisiana, either. Then on to India and China and—and everywhere!"

"Who's gonna be your captain?"

Teresa smiled. "I don't know. A tall, dark, handsome man who knows how to sail and also knows just what to do to pleasure a lady."

Hanover bit back a laugh. She wasn't a lady, but she sure was pleasant to look at.

CHAPTER TWO

Midnight.

Insects still buzzed in the air. The slow-moving river ten yards to the left slapped at rocks and spoke as fish breached its muddy surface and dove back into their watery homes.

A full moon cast yellow light on the dense growth that fed on the river's nourishment and the frequent squalls that dumped gallons of water onto the area.

Louisiana was muggy, wet and uncomfortable.

Spur McCoy brushed a hungry mosquito from his chin, tilted his Stetson lower on his head and rested the butt of the Spencer Carbine on the log. He hunched forward into a less painful position and stared into the greenery.

Thirty yards ahead the brush quivered in the moonlight. It quited a second later. A woman softly laughed from the hidden clearing. A man cleared his throat. Boots ground against dirt, dead twigs and leaves.

They seemed to be making camp, Spur McCoy
thought as he watched the darkened trees. He'd
been waiting two weeks to be this close to them, and
he didn't intend to let them slip away from him
again.

In the darkness before him, the dun horse that
had pulled the couple's buggy talked softly to itself.
The clanking of the rings and leathers that soon
followed made Spur assume that the animal was
being unhitched from the front of the rig.

From his position all he could see was the black
back of the side spring, two-person buggy. They had
driven it so deeply into the heavy brush that the
contraption was almost concealed by the lush
Louisiana growth.

Spur McCoy didn't like the terrain. The strange
trees, the stench of the sluggish river beside him,
the silver moss hanging from overhead branches
were foreign to him. Where was the high pine
country, or the open prairies of the plains states?
He knew who he was out there and what was
happening. Here, in this wet, rainy state, he was far
from home.

Spur held his breath and listened. The faint
sounds of people making camp issued from the
dense bushes. The crack of the kindling for the fire.
The scrape of a coffee pot. The rustle of a blanket.

McCoy fought the urge to rush into the camp.
They were probably both armed, he knew, and that
made it imperative that he surprise them. He'd been
instructed to capture both of the suspects alive.
This order put dangerous and difficult parameters
on the whole mission. General Halleck's insistence
on not killing them hadn't made Spur's day. His

boss in Washington hadn't explained in his cryptically encoded telegram, but Spur figured that it had something to do with the fact that one of the fugitives was a woman.

McCoy had worked for the United States Government's Secret Service since its establishment in 1859 by a special act of Congress. It was originally set up to stop counterfeiting and to protect the integrity of American currency. Later, as the only interstate law enforcement agency, its agents took on any type of crime where state borders were crossed. Now McCoy was permanently assigned to investigate any federal law breaking west of the Mississippi.

Light suddenly blushed from the bushes—they'd lit a camp fire. The pair of thieves were having all the comforts of a train.

The telegram had come to him when he was in Denver. A couple of con artists and thieves had swept through Kansas City's best families and left with an estimated $100,000 in cash and at least that much in bearer bonds and corporate stocks which could easily be converted into cash. No one at Secret Service headquarters seemed to know much about the pair.

As he watched, smoke billowed from the camp fire. Spur frowned. It was the first fire they had used in three days on the trail coming down from Shrevesport. They must feel secure being so blantant about their whereabouts.

He'd wait for two hours until they were both in their bedrolls and then rush the campsite to take them while they were sleeping.

It wasn't dramatic or colorful, but all Spur McCoy wanted now after two weeks of tracking them down was to capture the pair and be off to a better, more interesting assignment.

He brushed away a biting insect.

And a more comfortable assignment.

His reports had stated that the suspects were a man and a woman. She was about thirty-years old from most reports, tall for a woman at 5 feet 8 inches, slender and supposedly beautiful. She had long blonde hair that she wore in a variety of fashions. One report said she was an actress who was good with makeup and disguises. She was from New York where she was wanted on a theft charge.

The telegram said her name might be Teresa, though she often used the shorter form Tessa, and sometimes Penelope. His sources had not known the last name for her; she usually used her companion's last name. They travelled as husband and wife.

The man had been described as an ex-gambler. Down on his luck, he'd become a con artist and thief, which he found much more profitable. Lambert G. Hanover was distinguished looking with a Van Dyke beard and moustache, fairly short sideburns and piercing blue eyes. He had dark black hair, sometimes wore a monocle in his right eye, and dressed extremely well.

He was at ease in high society. He fit in at lavish parties and in the homes of the wealthy. It was there that he did his best work, pretending to be a friend of a friend and gaining access to exclusive homes, clubs and parties. The telegram had said that he was from a poor family from Philadelphia. Mother and father both deceased. He was a shade under under six feet tall, strongly built and about 185 pounds.

As Spur recalled the information he'd received about the two people, the campfire behind the brush flared up, lighting the mist that had crept into the air from the river. He heard some low voices and the creak and slap of leather. Were they pulling the harness from the horse? If so, why?

Spur sighed and eased back on the log that he'd chosen to keep his butt out of the damp leaves that littered the ground. He had left his horse back 200 yards and worked up silently on foot. It had been a tough two weeks riding out from Kansas City, trying to find their trail. It was only known that they had left by a one-horse buggy two days before he had arrived.

McCoy had slowly searched until he'd found their trail. It would have been more difficult but the man seemed unable to pass up a promising mark if he smelled a swindle.

So the pair had left signposts behind them as they made their way from Kansas City. One woman in Joplin, Missouri, had complained to the police of being robbed of $50. The description that she gave to Spur matched that off Teresa and Hanover. He'd known that he was following in their wake.

A man in Little Rock, Arkansas, had been bilked out of $300. Another sure indication that the thieves were still heading south.

Now he almost had them. Spur knew it wasn't wise to underestimate the man. Hanover had proved to be an adept woodsman, a smooth talker in town, and a man who seemed to be able to take care of himself and his woman under any conditions.

Until now. Unless something untoward occured, Spur knew that he'd capture them both after they went to sleep. He'd quiet the woman first by gagging and tying her, then go after the man. That would be best. He'd give them two more hours to settle down and be fast asleep.

As he waited, Spur watched the sky. The Big Dipper worked its way around the North Star in its nightly journey. An old cattle drive trailhand had told Spur how to use the Big Dipper constellation as a clock on a clear night.

The two pointer stars on the front of the lip of the dipper cup always pointed directly at the North Star. When they were in the position of nine on a watch, it would be ten P.M. By the time the pointer stars had dropped down until they were coming from the eight on the watch face, it would be midnight. When they lowered to the seven position, it would be two A.M. He pitied the poor city folks who had to rely on their Waterburys to tell the time.

Spur watched the Big Dipper slowly rotate in the sky. The glow from the unseen camp fire died down a little but still seemed to be burning well. It cast flickering shadows on the overhead trees even an hour after he had first noticed it. Were they still awake?

One A.M. Silence from the clearing in the brush ahead of him. But he still waited, wanting to be sure that the man and woman were sound asleep before he walked into their camp. The only sounds he could hear were occasional crackles from the fire. No voices, nothing.

When the pointer stars of the Big Dipper aimed at the North Star from what would be the seven position on a Waterbury clock, Spur drew his Colt .45 six-gun, pulled free the blue neckerchief from around his neck to have handy, and gently moved through the undergrowth toward the pair.

Long training had taught Spur to work through the trees and brush without a sound. Moving like an Indian, he never let a branch or bough snap back after passing. He never put his full weight on his foot for the next step until he was sure there was nothing under it that would make any kind of noise. He was as silent as a snake.

McCoy slowly moved to the back of the buggy, though he could barely see it. He still couldn't get a clear view of the camp site itself. It took him another ten minutes to work along the side of the buggy so that he could see the clearing in the flickering light of the fire.

First he noticed the fire, which had been banked against a foot-thick log that had been pulled into the fire. The log itself burned brightly but all other material had long since been consumed.

To the left he saw the two bedrolls. He silently moved that way. There was no sign of the horse that had dragged the buggy but the harness lay near it shafts. Strange, he thought. Maybe they hadn't tied it properly and the beast had wandered away in search of food.

Completely in the cleared area, Spur moved quickly, the six-gun in his right hand, the kerchief in his left. Which one was the woman's bedroll? The blankets were pulled up around their heads. He chose the smaller of the two and hesitated.

Something was wrong.

Spur bent and swept aside the blanket. It revealed a cleverly compacted mass of brush and dead branches. Angry, he checked the other one.

The couple had slipped away.

CHAPTER THREE

Exploding with fury, Spur McCoy kicked the empty bedrolls at his feet and ran to the buggy. Nothing of value remained. Lambert and Tessa had unharnessed the horse as he'd suspected. They had done it so that they could ride away right from under his nose.

He saw a carpetbag discarded to one side. It contained a torn dress, a ripped book and a newspaper from Kansas City with a front page story about the big swindle at the Kansas City Top Fashion Ball.

Spur spent little time in anger. He checked the area with a torch and soon found where the horse had been ridden away. The prints in the soft ground were deep, indicating that there were two riders and some luggage on board the beast. They wouldn't be able to make good time, but he had no idea of where they were heading. Spur ran past the buggy and thrashed through the brush to where he'd left his horse 200 yards away.

The tall sorrel heard him coming and whinneyed. Spur had been riding the animal for a fortnight and she was a fine mount, one of those sorrels with a reddish-brown body coat and an almost pure white mane and tail.

He stepped into the saddle and rode back to the small camp fire. Dismounting, he lit a larger torch made from a dry tree branch filled with sap and began the slow process of tracking the double-loaded horse, leading his own mount behind him as he moved.

Twenty minutes later the torch sputtered and went out. He couldn't find another branch that was dry enough to light in the damp land near the river. Spur slammed the dead torch onto the ground, mounted up and kept moving.

The trail had angled generally toward some faint lights ahead that he guessed must be back on the main road south. He couldn't be sure that the tracks would end up there, but it was the best bet he had. Perhaps if the couple wasn't there, or hadn't been past, he could still find a bed for the night. Even some soft hay in a barn would be a welcome sight right now.

Secret Service Agent Spur McCoy settled down to walking the horse to the lights.

McCoy was two inches over six feet tall, usually weighed in at an even 200 pounds and had reddish-brown hair that brushed his shirt collar and came low on the sideburns. He had shaved off his moustache a month ago but it was growing into its usual thickness above his upper lip.

He had a solid nose between green eyes. His lips were a little full. McCoy was a crack shot with any hand gun or rifle, had good hands and rode like an Apache. His face and arms were usually burned by the sun and wind, souvenirs from the countless months he spent in the outdoors. His often rough demeanor and quick gun seemed to be out of character for a rich man's son from New York who had a degree from Harvard University in Boston.

Ahead, McCoy saw the lights he'd noticed were from an inn on a country road. A lantern that had been left burning swung before the door. He assumed it was the customary signal that a bed was available for any weary traveller who happened upon the inn at night.

McCoy was about to pull the cord on the bell just outside the main door when a face stared at him through the small window in the panel. The door unlocked and swung open.

A man in his sixties held a kerosene lamp. He wore a nightshirt with a robe over it. His white hair was mussed and frizzled. The innkeeper stared at Spur with bloodshot eyes.

"Gory be!" he said. "You just fixing to go to bed? Damn near time for me to be getting up."

McCoy threw up his hands. "Sorry. Did a young couple in their thirties stop by here a few hours ago, maybe three hours past?"

"They be friends of yours?" the old man asked, squinting out of one eye and closing the other as he cocked his head to one side.

"Not necessarily friends, more like kin. We were supposed to meet here earlier. I got delayed."

The man shrugged. "Yep, they were here. Ate a mess of sausage, cheese and bread, bought my best horse and rode on toward Alexandria."

"Where's that?"

"About fifty miles down the road, then two or so west. Fair to middling wagon road now. Can take a buggy. They were asking about one. Not a chance to get one this side of Alexandria though. Not unless they buy one off somebody on the road, or at a farm along the way. This couple seemed to have enough money to buy whatever they wanted."

"They should have enough cash," Spur said, unconsciously looking over his shoulder. "They stole it. Fact is, I'm a lawman. Looking for them."

The innkeeper laughed. "You mean that pretty little thing? She's a thief?"

"Yep."

"Hell. She could steal my heart, but the guy with her kept her on a close rein."

"I better take that bed and breakfast and get a late start. How much for both me and my nag?"

The old man scratched the stubble on his jaw. "You being a lawman, a dollar for grub for you and your horse, a stall and bed. I'll throw in a pair of sandwiches to take with you tomorrow."

Spur handed the man a greenback and headed for the barn with the sorrel.

"Take the first stall inside," the man yelled after him. "Moonlight should be enough to see by. There's plenty of oats in the bin by the door."

"Thanks!"

When McCoy came back he found the old man sleeping in a chair just inside the door. The innkeeper woke at once and showed him up a flight of wooden steps to a room and shoved a straight backed chair under the knob. He sat on the side of the single bed, blew out the lamp that the man had left and eased onto the straw mattress. Wasn't as good as feathers, he thought as the coarse grass

scratched his back, but better than a wet log.
Spur was asleep before he could turn over.

Before noon the next day, Spur had found the
trail again. The couple had stayed ten miles farther
down the road at a small farm house. The woman
who came to the door told McCoy that the couple
had been drowsing in the saddle. They said they had
been lost in some woods for three hours and were
glad to be back on the road to New Orleans. The
man and woman had stayed the rest of the night and
left only two hours before Spur's arrival. McCoy
tipped his hat to the woman and hurried along.

New Orleans! It made sense. That was the perfect
destination for Lambert Hanover and Teresa. Lots
of old money in that place just waiting to be stolen.

Spur stopped for food at a crossroads store where
the man said he had seen the couple less than two
hours before. The store owner was about 30,
with a hole in his jaw where a tooth had been
knocked out. Spur figured he hadn't had a bath in
at least a month. His long johns top served as a
shirt. His blue jeans looked dirty enough to stand
in the corner by themselves. The store owner's right
eye was slightly closed, which gave the impression
that he was always winking.

"Oh, damn yes, I saw them. Asked directions.
Both mounted and looked to be riding a little fast.
Best dressed folks hereabouts. They got down for
a rest and the lady used our convenience out back."

"I see." Spur nodded. "Is there anything you can
tell me about them? How they looked?"

The storeman chuckled. "I don't know about him,
but that little filly had the biggest gazongas I ever
did see!" He smiled. "I mean big! A man could die

of suffocation between those two huge—"

"Sounds like the pair I'm looking for," Spur said, breaking into the man's sentence.

He guffawed. "She's got a pair alright! Hey, you a lawman or something?"

"Does it matter?"

The store owner stiffened. "Not one hell of a lot. Look, you gonna buy anything or you just rustling up free information?"

"I'll buy in a second. Any towns along the road?"

"Yeah. A little place called Wet Prong about ten miles along. Alexandria's near to forty miles from here due southwest. You heading for New Orleans?"

"Probably."

Spur bought half a dozen eggs, a loaf of bread and a slab of bacon. He paid the man 37¢ and got back on the trail as soon as he could.

As he rode, he thought about New Orleans. It would be an easy place for Hanover and Teresa to get lost. There must be 150,000 people in that seaport by now. From there they could book passage to England, France or half the ports in the world. They could even go back to New York in first class luxury.

He remembered from the telegram and the packet of information mailed to him that the woman was originally from the New York City area. And that Lambert G. Hanover was also a gambler.

Spur rode until dark. The sturdy sorrel had recovered her strength but McCoy decided against going on into the small town that glittered before him. It might not even have a hotel.

The Secret Service agent made a camp off the

road in some brush along a stream. He fried up a dozen strips and had a feast of bacon sandwiches with the fresh loaf of bread. He would eat the eggs for breakfast. When his pot of boiling coffee got down to grit and grinds, he threw it out and went to sleep with his head against his saddle.

Just after daylight, McCoy was on the move again. He had demolished all six of the eggs, soaking up the over-easy soft yolks with the sliced bread that he'd warmed to light brown over the coals of his fire.

A half hour into the new day the sorrel took him down the road. Three miles ahead he found the village of Wet Prong. Spur smiled as he saw the words written on a sign over the barber shop. It had to be the oddest name he'd ever heard. Might be best not to ask what it meant or where it had come from.

And as it turned out, Wet Prong did have a hotel. He let his sorrel drink her fill and walked into the two-story building. A $2.50 gold piece loosened the tongue of the hotel man. He was short and squat and owned the Wet Prong Inn. It sported eight rooms and his own apartment.

Torrey wore eyeglasses, had a large mole on the side of his nose and talked out of the corner of his mouth.

"Yeah, now I remember," he said, fingering the gold. "This fancy couple came in just about dark. They had been riding, even with her wearing a fancy skirt. Anyways, they registered as John and Joanna Ford, had supper across the street and went back up to their room. Haven't heard from them this morning."

"They still in their room?" Spur asked. Maybe at

last he was getting lucky.

"You deaf, boy?" Torrey said. "I ain't seen them come down!"

"What room they in?"

"I ain't supposed to say that." He stuffed the gold coin into his pants pocket and crossed his arms.

"I'm a U.S. lawman. You tell me quick or I'll run you into the county seat for obstructing justice. You'll be an old man before you see the outside of a jail cell again!"

Torrey rubbed his pocket. "Okay. Okay! All you had to do was ask! It's room eight. Top of the stairs, to the right, end of the hall."

Spur loosened the strap over his six-gun as it banged against his thigh in its holster. Going up the stairs, he hauled out his weapon and made sure that the hammer rested on the empty cylinder. He cocked the hammer on the landing and moved down the hall, staying to the left side so that the boards wouldn't squeak.

At the end of the hall, he stopped before number eight. The door was closed. He listened. Spur heard nothing from inside the room. He backed to the far side of the hallway, took a big step and slammed his right foot against the door beside the knob.

The door broke free of the lock and slammed inward, hitting the wall beside the hinges. The room was empty.

The window stood open. Light curtains blew around it. Spur charged to the opening and looked out. A blonde-haired woman sat on the sloping roof that extended from the floor of the second story over the porch. She looked at him, yelped and vanished over the side.

McCoy kicked through the window, slipped and

skidded down the rough shingles to the edge. He
saw no horses, no riders, no one. He hung his feet
over the edge, lifted his six-gun into the air and
jumped the eight feet to the hard ground of the
alley.

Spur rolled to absorb some of the force of his fall
and leaped to his feet. He ran for the street.

A bullet slammed close past him and he saw the
gush of gunpowder blue smoke at the far edge of
a second alley. He fired once at the area, splintering
off some of the wood, and rushed toward the spot.

No one stood beyond the near corner of the
building. It housed a ladies' millinery and clothing
store. It was the only place with a door. The thieves
must have gone inside it.

Spur ran to the store and went inside. A half-
dozen racks holding women's clothes, some
cabinets and hat racks greeted him. Just as he
walked into the store a woman stepped out from
behind a rack of dresses. She had a gown over her
head and was apparently trying to get it off. He
couldn't resist looking at her pretty chemise and
white petticoats.

An older woman came from behind the partly
undressed female. "Sir! Please leave! This is no
place for a gentleman! We're fitting this lady with
a new dress and she's—exposed!"

McCoy lowered his six-gun. "Ma'am, a man and
a woman just slipped in here. They're dangerous
criminals and it's my job to catch them. Did you see
them?"

She shook her head. "Out! Out of my shop or I'll
call the sheriff. He knows what to do with men who
burst into women's dressing rooms!"

"But ma'am, I'm—"

The full-bodied shopkeeper grabbed a feather duster and pushed it into Spur's face, making him sputter and gag. "Get yer hide out of my store!" she yelled.

Spur flung away the dusty weapon. "Did you see a man and a woman race in here just moments ago?"

"Of course not!"

The woman with the dress over her head remained rooted in place. McCoy couldn't see her face, but her chemise did tent forward over what had to be full breasts.

"That does it!" the rotund woman said. "I'm going to get the sheriff." She strode toward the door.

Spur sensed rather than heard movement behind him. A heavy object crashed onto his skull before he could whirl to face the danger. McCoy fell and groaned as his Colt six-gun slid from his hand. He momentarily blacked out but quickly returned to a hazy consciousness as his cheek hit the slick floorboards. He couldn't move.

"Gracious!" The shopkeeper screamed.

"Shut up and stand still!" a man yelled.

"Kill him and let's get out of here!" It was a younger, softer woman's voice.

"No, Tessa. We're not going to kill him. I've never killed a man in my life and I'm damn well not starting now!"

"Get some sense! If you don't finish him off he'll just come after us again, Lamb!"

McCoy blinked his eyes to clear them and gently tilted his head. He saw the woman drop her dress back into place and fasten some buttons. She was blonde and beautiful. In spite of the pain that threatened to split apart his skull, Spur figured he'd never forget Teresa's face.

"He won't come after us anymore. Instead of killing him, I'm going to break his leg. You know how hard it is to ride a horse with your leg in a plaster caste?"

McCoy gathered his strength. He pushed against the floor and futilely lunged toward his distant six-gun. Before he could close his fingers around the weapon something hard and cold banged against his skull again, jolting him into the black of total unconsciousness.

CHAPTER FOUR

As she stood in the Wet Prong dress shop, Teresa Salvare smoothed her dress, fluffed out her long blonde hair and stared at Lambert G. Hanover. He really was weak, she thought. Weaker than any man had the right to be.

"For God's sake, Lambert! Are you serious about not killing him? Just busting this man's leg is crazy. He'll still come after us."

Hanover laughed. "He just might at that, Tessa. Then I guess I better smash both of them. Hand me that footstool and I'll get it done right."

The gunshot from a .45 held firmly in both hands of the female shop owner sounded like a dozen sticks of dynamite as it echoed in the small store. Teresa put both hands to her ears, her face twisted in surprised pain.

"You ain't doing a goddamned thing!"

Lambert slowly turned, putting on his best smooth-talking smile. He looked at the woman who confidently held the six-gun in her hands, the muzzle aimed dead center on his chest. Her grip was sure and firm.

"Don't you try nothing!" the woman said. "I'm warning you, sir!"

"My good woman! Surely you realize that I was only jesting with the man here about breaking his legs."

"Oh sure, Yankee! With him out cold like that? Hell, I wasn't born yesterday! It ain't no joke to club a man in the head twice with a gun butt." She sighed. "Now you move slow like and walk over to the door. Take yer trashy blonde whore with you. You're lucky I ain't calling the sheriff; he'd make dog meat out of your kind."

"Now madam," he began.

"Lamb, we better get going," Teresa said.

"In a minute!" Hanover smoothed his voice. "You really wouldn't shoot me, would you?"

The woman smiled. "You willing to bet yer worthless life to find out? I've shot a .44 since I was ten. Killed more than a hundred rattlers, and I don't mind adding another one to the list. Move or make out your last will and testament!"

"Come now, woman! A wonderful lady like yourself, highborn and bred and—"

The .45 blazed again. The heavy slug tore into the top of Lambert's high crowned hat and ripped it off his head. The con man's hands shot toward the ceiling.

"That's better," the plump woman said. "Mister, I was born smelling gunpowder."

"Okay. Okay! Just don't shoot again!"

Teresa ran to the door and opened it. She disappeared outside and Lambert quickly followed her.

"Come back and you'll get more of my Southern hospitality!" she said, watching until they were out of sight.

"Trouble, Pamela," a balding man yelled as he stormed up to the woman's shop.

"No, Paul. Nothing I can't handle. Get back to your barber shop."

She waved him off, walked back into her store and locked the door. McCoy still sprawled on the floor where he'd fallen, all legs and arms. Pamela Crowley knelt beside him, pushed his Colt .45 into his holster and examined his head with a delicate touch. "Okay, mister, I'll take care of you." She stood with an effort, went into the rear of the store and returned moments later with a wet cloth.

McCoy softly groaned. A good sign, Pamela thought. It meant that he wasn't dead. The cold cloth on his head brought a quick response. Within a few minutes the big man turned onto his back, blinked a dozen times and stared up at her.

"What the . . ."

"Don't talk, mister," she firmly said. "You just rest now. The two you were after are gone."

"Good." Spur McCoy tried to raise his torso to look at his legs. "Are they broken?" He shook his head.

The woman snorted. "No. I wouldn't let them. I've done a bit of shooting in my time. That man seemed scared to death of my .45."

Pain rushed through his body as he tried to sit. Spur strangled back a cry and eased onto the hard floor.

"You won't be chasing that pair for a day or two. I want you to lie right still while I go fetch our

doctor." Pamela shook her head as she looked down
at him. "At least, he says he's a doctor. Don't have
no diploma on the wall, but who'd expect a real
doctor to hang up his shingle way out here in Wet
Prong."

Spur grinned at the words.

"I don't even want to know what you think about
my town's name." She stood and went to the front
door. "If any woman comes in wanting a corset
fitting, you tell her you'll do the job for me."
Pamele Crowley cackled high and long as she
hurried out the front door to the street.

Spur McCoy felt for his holster. His six-gun was
back in place. The woman must have returned it.
At least he could defend himself if the pair of
thieves came back. There he had been, enjoying the
sight of the half-undressed woman while her
partner had slipped up on him from behind. That
was damned dumb of him. Never again.

This pair had turned out to be slippier than a
freshly caught trout. Spur sighed. He'd better get
up and follow them right now. No sense in losing
more time. McCoy reached forward and started to
sit. A giant gong went off in his skull, pushing him
back to the floor. He shook his head to quiet the
ringing. That only started the bells clanging even
louder.

He knew he wasn't going anywhere for a while.

Spur found the wet cloth beside him and put it
back on the top of his head. It somewhat eased the
throbbing, pounding pain. Right now would be a
good time for a shot of laudanum, he thought.
That's what drugs like that were for. But if he got
one he'd want another one and then another and
he'd be drugged out and in bed for a week. Spur had

seen laudanum—that tincture of opium—ruin too many lives to mess with it himself.

Five minutes later he tried to sit again. This time he got almost upright before his eyes blacked out and he slowly eased down onto his back below all the fancy women's dresses.

As he forced himself to rest, all kinds of crazy thoughts jostled around in his brain. Head injuries could be nothing more than a bump. They could be bad too—permanent damage. He'd given them and he'd taken them more than once.

When he heard the front door open Spur hesitated opening his eyes. Was he blind? As the footsteps approached him he snapped open his eyes in a purely defensive reaction. To his relief, he saw a small man with a black case and a frown.

"Good, you're alive. Feared you was all dead and I'd wasted my trip out here."

"Come on, William Sykes!" Pamela said. "It was all of two blocks."

Ignoring her, the doctor knelt. "Head hurt a mite?" he asked. His eyes bugged out like those of a frog.

"All of a sudden I'm feeling much better," Spur smiled.

"You sure as hell don't look too good. Blood on your scalp. Hit twice on the head could be part of the cause of that." He smiled. "You're damned lucky you ain't dead."

Spur suddenly sat up. He wobbled a bit but didn't pass out. "Where did that couple go, the ones who were in here?"

The store owner moved over so that she could see Spur. "Last I saw of them they were heading into Limson's Livery Stable."

"Probably rented a buggy," he said. "Still heading toward New Orleans. That's the way I'll be moving."

"Not right now, young man!" Dr. Sykes said. "You'd better not try it for a day at least. A hit to the head can cause all sorts of problems. You may feel fine now but tomorrow, who knows? Dizziness, blackouts, loss of memory, even unconsciousness. One guy I knew got pistol whipped. He brushed it off, had another beer and walked home. That night he went to sleep and never woke up again."

Spur reached for the doctor's hand. "If I can stand, I can ride. Come on, Doc. Help me up."

"Don't reckon that's a smart idea," Sykes said. He put out a hand.

McCoy gripped it and stood with surprising ease. "See? Nothing to it!"

But his knees shook. A wave seemed to break inside his head. The room tilted as the solid floorboards beneath his feet buckled. Spur fell against the doctor, clutching at the air.

Spur McCoy lay on a bed. He groaned and opened his eyes. His feet hung over the far end and his tender head crowded the wall behind him. When his vision cleared he saw the small room in more detail—light pink roses stretched along the wallpaper that covered the ceiling as well.

"You finally awake?" a soft voice said beside him.

With what turned out to be some effort, Spur McCoy turned his head to see who had spoken. A young girl with long brown hair and brown eyes smiled at him. She leaned forward and adjusted the blankets beside him. The scooped neckline of her blouse fell open; he caught a glimpse of the tops of two white mounds.

"I'm awake now," he said as he unconsciously licked his lips. The girl's femininity and obvious charms lesened the dull ache in his scalp.

"Good. Mother told me to sit with you until you woke up," the young woman said. "She told me you saved her from a pair of robbers today. Is that true?"

His slight nod made Spur wince.

"How nice of you!"

The indirect light shining through the window illuminated her. She was slender, short like her mother, perhaps about 20. The girl pressed a delicate white hand onto his forehead, still smiling.

"Just checking with the family thermometer to see if you have a temperature."

"I'm not complaining." Her flesh against his felt so good, so healing.

"Not a trace of fever!" She retrieved her hand. "That's good. Doc Sykes said I should run over and tell him if you had a temperature."

He tried to nod again but the pain increased tenfold. Spur gave her a helpless grin.

"You poor dear man! Don't try to talk, or nod or anything! Mother says I chatter enough for at least two people, like a magpie or something. Of course, I've never seen a magpie so I guess I have to take her word for it."

"They don't, ah, look anything like you."

Spur enjoyed the sound of her laughter. "By the way, I'm Jessie. Jessie Crowley."

"Spur McCoy. Where am I, and why am I here?"

Jessie smiled broadly. "You're here behind the

store. This is where Ma and I live. You're here because Doc Sykes said you had to have a day's bed rest before you go riding off again.''

"Oh."

The young woman leaned closer to him. "So, how do you like my bed?"

Spur lifted his eyebrows. "This is your bed I'm in?"

She nodded.

"Then I guess I better get up."

Jessie grabbed the blankets from his hand. "Nothing doing! You're stark naked! Besides, Ma would skin me alive if I let you up. Like it or not, Mr. McCoy, I'm your nurse."

McCoy looked under the covers and saw that she was telling the truth. "Okay, little lady. You win. I don't make it a habit to pass up the opportunity to be naked in a woman's bed." He sighed and looked out the window. "You know the hour?"

"Oh, somewhere after three I'd say. The only clock we have is out in the store. I don't hold much with clocks." Jessie held her arms above her head and stretched. The action tightened the white blouse over her breasts.

"That's pretty, the way you stretch," Spur said with admiration. "It's so natural. Like a baby colt just after it wakes up."

Jessie smiled. "Even though you just called me a horse, I'll take that as a compliment."

Spur laughed. The woman lowered her head, her lips trembling.

"Could I—I mean, I know you're wounded, but couldn't I just kiss you once?"

Before he could answer, a speeding slug tore a

hole in the billowing curtains and slammed into a
kerosene lamp beside the bedroom door. Fire
burst into life as the liquid dripped down the
wall.

CHAPTER FIVE

"Shit!"

Spur McCoy's curse mixed with Jessie Crowley's scream as the exploding lamp sent flaming kerosene onto the girl's bedroom wall. She jumped and gave him the room to push himself from the bed.

He forgot that he was stark naked. McCoy's head pounded and his vision blurred as he grabbed a blanket from the bed and slapped the flames licking the rose wallpaper. "Stay down!" he shouted.

"Okay!"

He barely noticed the fact that no more shots were fired as he busily smothered the growing flames. Moving the thick woolen blanket so quickly that it couldn't be lit, Spur quickly contained the fire on the floor.

That left an orange-yellow stream of flames along the wall. He put them out within ten seconds, surveyed the area to make sure everything was extinguished and turned around.

Jessie stood trembling, holding her shoulders, her blonde hair veiling her face. Spur smiled and held up the blanket.

"Sorry. I guess it ruined it."

At his words the young woman caught his gaze, nodded and parted her lips. She looked below his waist. "Someone wants you dead!" she said, putting a hand to her breast. "They really do."

"I thought we'd established that earlier." His skull felt like it was going to explode, so he sat on the edge of the bed, kicking at scarred floorboards. "Oh, hell, I'm sorry, woman. Forgot that I didn't have a stitch on."

"Never mind about that. Nothing I ain't see before." She lifted her gaze from his crotch with an effort. "Aren't you scared?" Jessie asked.

"Naw. Are you?"

"Well, I—I mean, I—" She cautiously peered out the window. "No one's in sight."

"Good. They probably couldn't resist one last pot-shot at me. I'm sure those two are on their way out of town in that damned buggy of theirs. I should follow them but. . . ." He rubbed the back of his head and shook it to clear away a few stubborn cobwebs.

Jessie faced him and writhed as she stood on the floor. "Why Spur, I don't know what's coming over me! That fire lit more than the wallpaper!"

"Hmmmm?"

Delicate white hands travelled up and down the woman's torso and thighs. "I'm all excited. The danger! The blazing inferno! It's—it's—oh, Spur!"

Spur grinned as the woman panted before him, writhing like a cat.

"You want to do something about it?"

"Sure!"

"What about your mother?"

"It's no problem. She closed up the store early and went to fit Mabel Ledet for a wedding dress. Said she'll be there until all hours. And it's two miles south of town." Jessie turned around and bent to close the window. She shut what was left of the curtains.

The movement stretched her tight skirt, revealing the luscious rounds of her bottom. Spur stared at it, at her, and eased his naked body full length onto the bed.

"Come here!" he barked.

She caught her breath and turned to him. "What?"

"I said, come here! My brain's the only thing not working right now!"

Jessie Crowley fell onto the mattress beside him. Their bodies banged together. Spur enjoyed the softness of the woman. He took her head in his hands.

"Ma told me to get you something to eat. I should be going to the kitchen." She slowly blinked.

"You'll do just fine." He pushed his face between her breasts, nuzzling the fabric that vainly tried to cover the gap between them.

Jessie moaned softly and pushed him away. "Here. Supper's already ready." She opened the buttons on her white blouse, frantically ripping them until the garment fell from her shoulders, revealing her bare, upthrust breasts.

Spur sighed at the pink tips of her areolas. "Nothing I like better than Southern cookin'."

He took them in his hands and kissed Jessie's nipples. The young woman gasped at the contact of his wet mouth and tongue on her sensitive flesh. He sucked and gently teethed her.

"Mmmmm. I love a man who likes to eat and doesn't mind showing it!" she said.

"I could eat all day," he said as he switched from one soft mound to the other.

"But we better not let Ma find us like this. Just a moment, Love."

She sprang from the bed and lodged the top of a straight-backed chair under the doorknob. Spur smiled at the bounce of her breasts as she skipped back to the bed. "Now, where were we? Oh yes!"

A cool hand ruffled the fur on Spur's chest. His whole body tingled as her hand teasingly moved lower, hesitated at his navel, then scraped his thicker pubic hairs. The nearness of her fingers drove him crazy. Bloody poured to his groin to display his obvious arousal.

"You hungry too?" McCoy asked.

Jessie Crowley firmly gripped his hardening penis. "Famished! Absolutely starved!" The young woman slapped her tongue against Spur's organ and licked. "Mmmm."

Despite the dull throb in his skull, Spur knew he couldn't take much more of that. She tasted his spasming penis and took his testicles in her hand.

"Hey, little woman! Get on up here!"

"Why, sir, I'm just getting started!"

But she bent toward his face. As they kissed, trading tongues in a lashing, liquid exchange, Jessie grabbed his head. McCoy groaned and broke off the kiss.

"Oh! I'm sorry, Spur! I forgot!"

"It's okay."

Jessie lowered her brows. "Look, honey. Maybe

I better do all the work."

"I won't argue with you. But don't you think you're overdressed for this party?"

"Hmm? Oh, of course!" The woman slithered out of her skirt, and chemise and petticoats, flinging the feminine clothes onto the floor. "There! That's much better!"

Their bare bodies molded together. Jessie's fingernails scraped along Spur's biceps as they clenched. Another kiss. He thrust his groin against the woman on top of him. His passion grew.

She unsealed their lips and huffed. "Okay, lover boy. Just lie back and enjoy it!"

Jessie moved her hips over his crotch. Reaching down between her legs, she gripped the base of his erection and pointed it straight up. A quick repositioning was all that was necessary. She lowered her body, caught his hardness and sank onto it.

Spur kicked as their bodies connected. The angle was perfect and so was the woman. She hit home, rose and bucked, pushing her hips up and down and back and forth. Her moans and the sweet sensations made every nerve in Spur's frame burn.

"Oh yes!" Jessie said, obviously enjoying herself. Her juices lubricated them both, allowing the young woman to more fully impale herself. Her bottom slapped against his thighs.

Spur stared at the lovely face, at her breasts jogging before her, at the woman's unashamed expression of pure delight. He took her waist in his hands. Jessie's knees sank onto the bed on either side of him. She lifted up on her hands and rode him like a bucking bronco surging into an all-out gallop.

Heated flesh slapped together. The scent of her

perfume permeated the room. Spur thrust up into her, meeting her downward strokes, increasing her pleasure and his.

"Yes. Yes!" Jessie gasped. She stared at him for as long as she could, arched her back and yelled as pure sensation exploded through her beautiful body.

She continued to bang onto his erection as she rolled through her climax, heightening Spur's pleasure. Tears squeezed from the panting woman's eyes. She shook like an aspen in the wind, flinging her head back and forth, gasping and shrieking.

Spur McCoy felt the familiar tightening in his scrotum. He gritted his teeth and pushed harder into her. His hips came alive, spastically jabbing, thrusting, driving into her body.

"God. God!"

Jessie trembled through another orgasm. Her contractions around him pushed Spur over the edge. He went blind and roared as their pelvic bones crashed together, as he pumped out his seed into her willing body, as the woman fell onto him and clutched his sweating shoulders and rode him harder, milking him of every drop until he was a senseless mass of flesh on the soaked bedsheets.

In the timeless moments that followed, Spur felt Jessie's breath against his mouth. He pecked her lips but there didn't seem to be enough air in the room. Gasping, feeling the thousand explosions that had raged through him finally taper off, he pressed his cheek to hers and held the young woman until the room brightened and he had recovered.

Spur tried to speak but all he could produce were grunts and guttural words. He laughed and licked her neck.

"Mmmmmm," was all she could say.

A half hour later, when the sweat on his body had cooled to a chilling sheen, Spur felt the girl stirring on top of him. He removed his arms from her neck as Jessie pushed onto her hands and looked down at him.

"I do declare!" she said.

"You, ah, declare what?"

The blonde beauty smiled. "My late daddy said learning to ride a horse would never do me any good. He sure was wrong!"

Spur laughed.

"Oh heck! It's way past supper time. We better get some real food."

"Whatever you say, Jessie. I never argue with a woman who's still got me inside her."

"Spur McCoy, you nasty boy!"

She playfully slapped his shoulder and slipped off his softening penis. "I'll go see what I can find in the kitchen. Don't you run away now!"

"Yes ma'am."

Jessie grinned as she got up from the bed, removed the chair from under the door and disappeared into the hall.

He laced his fingers behind his head, carefully avoiding the damaged areas, and stared at the ceiling with a relaxed smile. He wasn't even going to think about Teresa and Hanover until tomorrow. They were in a buggy. It would be easy to track and they'd have to stick to the roads. Sure, tomorrow was soon enough to think about work.

Jessie rushed into the room carrying a basket. It pressed her breasts almost flat, but they quickly recovered their normal shapes as she set the box on the edge of the bed. Her eyes glistened with delight.

"Guess what I found?" she asked him.

"Ah, a foot-long sausage?"

She laughed. "No, that was before! I found some sliced ham. I didn't know we had it." She removed the top of the basket. "I also have some bread, mustard, horse radish and two bottles of beer. Also some brandy. She poked through the basket. "There are some peaches picked just two days ago—fresh and almost busting out with juice. And a big slab of cheese. Think that's enough?"

Spur licked his lips and rubbed his hands together. "For starters," he said. "You really worked up my appetite, little lady."

Jessie glanced at his crotch. "Me too." She pushed the basket toward the foot of the bed and kissed Spur's bristly cheek.

"What's that for?" he asked, staring at her.

"For coming into my life—even with a lump on your head. For giving a bored country girl a little fun!"

"You're welcome, but the pleasure was all mine. What about supper?"

Jessie laughed. "Who the hell cares about food?" The blonde woman kicked the basket onto the floor.

"Hey!" Spur protested. "There goes our supper!"

"Correction—*your* supper. I got what I wanna eat right here." She gripped his shrunken shaft.

"Now, Jessie!" Spur began. "I can't guarantee—ah—um—hell! How do you know I'm not too hungry to—ah—well—to go again so soon?"

"Why Spur McCoy!" She manipulated him, rubbing up and down with a delicately firm hand. "It would be against my Christian morals to force you into doing anything you don't want to do!" Jessie stroked harder.

He laughed. "It wouldn't exactly be force." He felt a tightening between his legs. "Uhhnh! Little lady, you do that good!"

"Do I?" She turned innocent eyes to him.

"Yes."

"Think you can put off supper for a while? Say, an hour or two?"

"I surely do." He grinned and leaned back. "You're pretty convincing, gal." Spur's mouth hung open as the young woman stroked him.

Within seconds she wrapped her fingers around his full-blown erection and smacked her lips. "What have we here?"

"You know darn well what that is!" Spur said as his left leg involuntarily flexed at the new surge of sexual arousal flowing through his body.

"Are you responsible for this?" She pressed his penis between her soft breasts and grinned as she saw it was too long to completely bury.

"No. You are."

"Oh. Should I kiss it?" She pulled back from him and turned her questioning eyes toward Spur's.

"If you want. I promise it won't bite you."

Jessie smiled, held her mouth over the engorged head and let out her breath. The warm air made Spur tingle and grab the sheets in exquisite pain.

"That ain't fair, girl! Teasing a wounded man like that! I'm going out of my head!"

"Not this one." She moved her hand to its base and slid his penis between her lips.

As the woman vigorously worked him over, as Spur propped his head on a pillow to watch, as he gently took her ears in his hands and guided her movements, McCoy knew why they called the small Louisiana town Wet Prong.

CHAPTER SIX

Spur rubbed the back of his head. Jessie had carefully washed the dried blood from his wounds last night before they'd gone to sleep. She'd also rubbed some ill-smelling herbal ointment onto them. His fingers discovered that the area was still tender. But in the ten minutes or so since he'd dragged himself from bed he'd noticed no dizziness or delayed side effects.

The Secret Service agent stepped over the shattered remains of the gunshot kerosene lamp in the darkened room. Outside, a few birds opened their throats. It was almost dawn.

As he put on his Stetson, Spur heard the girl whisper in her sleep. Jessie Crowley was a fine young woman, but he didn't want to give her any chance of talking him out of leaving immediately.

Fully dressed, he smiled at Jessie, blew her a kiss and walked out the door. Labored breathing told him where her mother had installed herself. He tiptoed past the door but it quickly opened.

"Mr. McCoy!"

He turned and smiled. Soft light spilled from Pamela Crowley's bedroom. "Mrs. Crowley." Spur removed his hat.

The middle-aged woman pulled a nightgown around her plump form. "You feeling well enough to go out travelling this morning?"

"I sure do."

"At least let me make you some breakfast." She brought a candle from her bedroom and started walking toward him down the hall. The dancing flame illuminated her soft, kind face.

Spur backed. "Thank you, no. I have to get back to my assignment. You've been a great help. Thanks for—"

"Oh, shush about that! I couldn't stand back and watch that man break your legs—or that hellion shoot you! After all, I'm a human being."

"I'm greatly obliged."

"Did my daughter take good care of you?" Pamela Crowley asked, beaming at him.

"Yes. She's a wonderful doctor. Ah, good morning, Mrs. Crowley."

"Good morning, Mr. McCoy."

He hurried from the house.

The morning air was unusually crisp. Fog hung over the streets and blotted out the two-story buildings on distant blocks. It smelled of dampness and rain and rotting vegetation. Spur replaced his Stetson and ampled down the uneven, dark street. His head felt fine. His legs worked well.

He was okay.

The sorrel he'd rented was still at the hitching post behind the hotel where he'd left it. She hadn't been fed or watered. The mare snorted, shook her head and danced. Spur rubbed her head and walked the beast to the livery stable. A weary-eye man, just rising to go to work, accepted McCoy's money and let him help himself to all the water and oats that the horse could take.

Fifteen minutes later she was ready to be off. So was he. As he stepped into the saddle, Spur did a mental check. His canteen was full, though water was never a problem in this rain-soaked country. He didn't have any food, but there should be plenty of places to grab some grub.

It was time to be moving on.

"Come on, old girl!"

Spur slapped the horses' flanks with his heels. The slight pressure was enough to send her charging south along Moss Avenue. To his left, Spur saw the sky lighten to a dull blue behind the towering trees. A new day, a new urgency to find Lambert G. Hanover and Teresa. He quickly left Wet Prong behind him, guiding his horse on the empty road.

They must still be heading for New Orleans. As the sun rose in the east Spur could finally see the trail. There were dozens of buggy tracks just outside of town, but as he continued to ride most of them turned down country lanes. Soon only one set moved down the old wagon road.

After ten minutes Spur stopped, stepped down and looked at the tracks. There didn't seem to be any sign of broken treads or loose wheels—nothing to help him identify them at a later time. He'd have to reply on his instincts.

McCoy lifted into the saddle and galloped the sorrel for half a mile more, eased off and let her follow the tracks at a walk. Because Lambert and his lady had left early yesterday afternoon, they would have been well ahead of him before they'd stopped to rest last night.

Knowing something of their background, Spur figured they'd likely choose a farmhouse or a country inn. The pair probably wouldn't be doing any more camping, he thought with a wry grin.

The trail continued due southeast along the wagon road. Here and there, farm wagons had obliterated the buggy tracks, but the same thin wheel marks always showed themselves again further along the road.

Two hours after dawn Spur let the sorrel rest and take a drink. He rubbed her down and surveyed the plant-rich land. Birds flew in unison overhead. A rabbit hopped by without a care for its safety. A thick-bodied snake slithered through the plaintains and coneflowers that dotted the ground near the stream.

Then he heard it. The unmistakable sound of a buggy approaching. The road went around a bend 50 yards from him so he heard it well before he saw it.

Spur drew his Colt and waited.

A minute later he holstered his weapon. It was a strange sight. Two Catholic nuns, dressed in black and white habits, waved at him as their broken-down buggy rattled behind their broken-down nag. He returned their greeting and got a good look at them as they passed by. Both must have been at least sixty.

"Come on, girl; let's do it."

The horse whinneyed.

By four o'clock he approached a farm house near

the road. The buggy tracks he'd been following had been wiped out again by farm traffic. Spur turned in at the house and reined up at the back door, knowing that only ministers and salesmen use the front door of a farm house.

He knocked. A worn woman in her thirties walked into sight, wiping her hands on a large blue apron. Her hair had been tied into a bun at the back of her neck. A three year-old boy ran for her and hugged his mother's leg.

"Afternoon, ma'am," Spur said, touching the brim of his hat.

"Menfolk are inside," she said, looking past him and noticing his holster. "What you want?"

Spur knew that the menfolk were out in the fields. She was alone and scared.

"Not wanting to bother you, ma'am, but I was wondering if a couple in a buggy stopped by here last night, wanting a place to sleep. She's rather tall and blonde. He's tall too with dark hair."

The woman nodded and even managed a smile. "They did indeed, sir! Said they was from New Orleans and was rushing back there. Paid me two dollars for a room and supper and breakfast. Land sakes, I ain't seen two dollars in two years!"

Spur nodded. "I suppose they left this morning, right?"

"Fact is, they did. Said they were going to Alexandria, then on to New Orleans." She smiled. "I haven't been there since my son ran off with—well, you probably don't want to hear about all that."

"I'll be moving on. You, ah, haven't noticed anything missing around your place, have you?"

"Missing?" She thought. "A sow ran off in the night a week back. That's about all. Why?"

"I'm a lawman. Both of those people are wanted. They're smooth-talking thieves. Con artists."

The farm woman knitted her brows. "Land sakes. They seemed so nice!"

"Yes, ma'am. That's their job." He reached into his pocket and sniffed the air. "Am I mistaken or is that peach pie I smell cooking?"

"Yes it is. Would—would you like to stay for a slice? I've got two of them bubbling in the oven right now. There'll be plenty for everyone."

"It's tempting, but no thanks." Spur held out his hand. "I appreciate your help, ma'am."

"Why, it isn't no trouble talking to a lawman!" She took his hand.

McCoy slipped her a silver dollar and turned before the woman could protest.

"Well, thank you, sir! Thank you so much! Lord, this is a fine day!"

He smiled as he mounted up and headed south on the road. Spur soon spotted the buggy tracks again. At least Lambert and Teresa hadn't changed their plans—or route. They'd probably figured that he'd given up and left them alone.

But then again, they didn't know Spur McCoy.

An hour later, still two hours before sunset, he rode into a thick forest. Huge, ancient trees bent over the wagon road from both sides. Their branches met overhead, plunging the area into flickering shadows. Yard-long strands of Spanish moss brushed Spur's Stetson. His sorrel balked and sniffed the air as they trotted into the secluded portion of the buggy road.

"Steady, girl," Spur said. "What's the matter? Smell something?"

As he rode, letting his protesting horse pick its

way as slowly as it wanted, McCoy tried to form images in his mind of Lambert G. Hanover and his lovely lady, Teresa. She should be easy to remember, but as he tried to recall her face he came up with a blank. All he could dredge from his mind was a dazzling image of a woman—blonde, tall, but no details.

Hanover's face was even murkier. Spur removed his hat and rubbed the bumps on his head. Maybe those blows had done more damage than he'd suspected.

But he remembered that he'd been reeling when he saw the con artists. His head had been aching, his vision wasn't perfectly clear. Would he recognize them again if he met them on the street, away from their buggy?

Putting on his hat, McCoy didn't know. To make matters worse, the woman was supposed to be expert at changing her appearance, mannerisms and forms of speech. An ex-actress from New York.

"Come on, girl, let's get a move on!" he said to the mare. He didn't want them to reach New Orleans. If they landed there before he caught them, they could blend right into the masses of people and drop out of sight forever.

The sorrel slowed its pace and finally stood still, despite Spur's urgent words and signals. It had decided it was time to stop. Frustrated at this new and irritating behavior, he dismounted. The horse wandered through the underbrush in search of the river that trickled beside the wagon road.

He wiped his forehead. The humidity had stuck his clothing to his body. Dragonflies droned and jerked to and from the shafts of light that penetrated the overhead leaves and branches.

Spur McCoy went to the side of the road, leaned against a tree and watched as a large spider casually walked right up its roughly barked trunk.

The slop-slop of the horse's drinking lulled him. Spur shook his head and yawned. He had to go. No time to waste.

"Come on, girl!" he called sharply.

The sorrel whinneyed.

"Now! Get over here!"

To his surprise, the horse pranced up to him, its eyes shining and the breath blasting from its huge nostrils.

Spur smiled. "You had me worried there for a minute," he said, and rubbed the beast's neck.

Something hit his shoulder as he stepped into the saddle. Spur looked up but quickly ducked as pebbles and rocks rained onto him from the towering trees above.

"Damn it!"

The sorrel went crazy. A stone hit Spur's head. He groaned and slumped in his saddle.

CHAPTER SEVEN

Spur McCoy regained consciousness just as he started to slip off his horse onto the ground. The stones that had fallen from the trees halted. In a moment of blinding pain, augmented by his sorrel's jostling, frenzied kicking, McCoy shook his head and looked up at the old pecan trees.

"Jesus Christ!" he said, trotting the horse in circles. "Who the hell's up there?" His head ached, pounded. Spur removed his Stetson and rubbed his bumpy scalp. Fortunately, he couldn't feel any fresh blood oozing from the wounds but he was still dizzy.

High-pitched laughter echoed from the trees.

But he could still talk. "Show yourselves," he said, swaying on the saddle before righting his body. *"Now!"*

The chuckles halted.

"I mean it! You've got ten seconds. If I don't see you I'll fire into the trees and hope I get lucky!" McCoy drew his Colt .45 six-gun and waved it above his head. Two densely foliaged pecans rustled and fell silent.

"Five seconds!"

Nothing happened.

"Four . . . three . . . two . . ."

A pair of dirty-faced boys dropped directly onto the dirt before him from the trees, rolled in the dust and sprang to their feet.

Spur smiled at the unexpected sight. They're just kids, he thought. Dirty-faced, rambunctious children. He holstered his weapon.

"Whaddya doin' here, Yankee?" a brown-haired lad asked as he rubbed his running nose.

His pal threw an arm around the other boy's shoulders. He was pudgy and dressed only in a ragged pair of denims. "We don't like your kind! Ain't that right, Lucius?"

Spur fought off a smile. "What does it look like? I'm travelling. That's what roads are for."

"Sure!" Lucius grabbed his mud-caked suspenders and turned to look at his friend. "He wuz spying on us, Matt. Just like I thought. Lookin' around for some innocent Southern boys so he could kidnap them." His eyes lit up. "Think that Yankee's gonna torture us now?"

Spur growled at them.

"Yeah. He looks mean enough."

"Shut your mouths, boys!" McCoy said. He rubbed the top of his head. One well-aimed rock had increased the pain in his old injuries.

They stuck out their tongues and pushed their thumbs into their ears.

He stifled a laugh. "You boys do this often?" McCoy said in a stern voice. "You could kill someone, throwing rocks onto their heads!"

"We don't care! We're just protecting ourselves!" Lucius said, shaking his head back and forth and wiggling his fingers.

"Against what?"

"Wicked Yankees who're coming to steal all our land!" Matt said.

"Boys, that was years ago. During and after the war between the states. That's been over for, oh, five or six years at least. No one's fighting any more."

"Still 'an all . . . ." Lucius said.

Spur smiled at them, tipped his hat and turned the sorrel south. "Ask your father if the war's still on. He'll set you straight."

Matt laughed. "Heck, Pa's the one who put us up in them there trees to watch the road!" He stepped closer to Spur. "If I yell my head off he'll come down here and shoot you until you're dead."

McCoy shrugged and kicked his mount's flanks. "Go!" he said in a strong voice.

The horse gladly followed the command. As he rode away McCoy turned back. The boys scooped up the rocks they'd just thrown and hurled them after him. He was soon out of range.

Just what he needed, he thought as the trees separated overhead and the late afternoon sunlight spilled onto him again. A pair of ragged Southern defenders.

Teresa Salvare frowned as they stood on the banks of the Mississippi River next to their buggy. "What a backwater town!" she said staring at Baton Rouge. A hot breeze ruffled the woman's pink bonnet. "Lamb, there's nothing to see here. How much longer until we get to New Orleans? Honestly,

I can smell all that money downstream!"

Lambert G. Hanover spread out his hands. "Patience, Tessa. Baton Rouge has many fine houses. Sure, it isn't New Orleans, but it's a rich field for our business."

Teresa tapped her booted foot. "I don't care. Let's get back on the road."

He turned to her. "We still have a few days until the race begins. Why shouldn't we do some business here? It won't take more than two days to get to New Orleans. We have plenty of time, my dear."

Teresa crossed her slender arms. "Lambert, we're going. I can't stand this place!"

"This isn't like you, Tessa. My good woman, you robbed a country church of its collection yesterday! Are you getting highbrow on me?"

She smiled and took his arm. "No. Just more selective. Come on!"

The thirty-year-old woman dragged Hanover to the buggy. He sighed and climbed onto the seat.

"Maybe you're right," he said as Tessa settled down beside him. "No sense in taking needless risks way up here when everything we've been waiting for is so close. Alright, my dear. We'll go."

Teresa threw back her head, took off her bonnet and ruffled her blonde hair. "Lamb, I still wish we were going to board the *Robert E. Lee*. The *Natchez* just isn't as good a sternwheeler."

He smirked at her. "When did you become expert in these matters?"

The woman affected a broad Southern accent. "Why suh, I was bohn and raised in New'ahlins! You know that!"

"You know why we have to take the *Natchez*," Hanover said, ignoring her. "Though both men swear they're not going to be running a race, Captain Cannon of the *Robt. E. Lee* won't take on any passengers, while for Captain Leathers of the *Natchez* it's business as usual. And the people sailing on his sternwheeler—statesmen, planters, bankers and such—will be burdened down with so much money that they'll welcome the opportunity to turn it over to us."

Teresa laughed. "Heck, Lamb. I think I'm falling in love with you."

Hanover smiled.

"Ah, darling, what about that man who was following us? The one we spotted in the woods, which must have been the one who later caught us in that dress shop in Wet Prong?"

He straighted his shoulders. "He's no gentleman. Allowing a woman to come to his aid."

"That's not what I mean, Lambert! Just suppose we didn't scare him off? What if he's on the road right now following us? And who is he anyway? He didn't look like a Kansas City policeman."

He sighed. "Tessa, there's no use in worrying about the impossible. I hit his head so hard he'll be flat on his back for a week. By that time we'll be on the *Natchez* steaming toward St. Louis. The boat won't stop for anything except to refuel, so we'll be safe and he'll be stuck down here. Don't fret your pretty little head, Tessa."

She frowned. "Maybe, but I still think you should have let me kill him." Teresa patted the derringer she'd stuck into her bodice. "Honestly, Lambert, I don't understand why you won't use firearms!"

Hanover closed his eyes. "My dear, we've discussed this time and again. I *am* a gentleman. Gentleman don't soil themselves with gunpowder or blood."

Teresa stared at the monotonous passing of thousands of green leaved trees. "But I like to do it. What does that make me?"

"A lady. A lady who's handy with weapons. And a very able partner who's saved my hide more than once." He smiled and drove on.

A half-hour before the sun set they came upon a small Cajun village. Teresa turned up her nose at such spartan lodgings so Lambert pushed the horse harder. They made it to a civilized farmhouse just as the western sky deepened into black and the stars popped out above their buggy.

"You must be all tuckered out," a friendly farmer said as he greeted them at his door.

"We are indeed. Could you put us up for the night?" Hanover draped an arm around Teresa's shoulders. "Me and my new bride?"

"Sure! Put the horse in the stable. I'll get your room ready." The man's face was lined and sunburned. "I—I haven't had much company since my wife passed on last year. All I got to remember her by is a gold locket."

Teresa beamed.

Two hours later, Spur was still riding. The buggy tracks had continued with no apparrent stops. For a while or so they'd been overlayed with three or four other sets made by different buggys, but Spur could pick out the narrower, better-made tracks that Hanover's rig had made. He stopped every now and then to ensure that he was still on the right road.

Spur McCoy had no idea where he was, and hadn't seen a town since early that morning. It was nearing dusk, so he figured he'd be sleeping under the stars again.

He found a likely spot and dismounted. The sorrel drank. As night fell around him an eerie fog rolled in. Some distance from him it seemed to glow with an internal light. Must be a big city out there in the distance, he thought, but the flatness of the land made it impossible to see.

He'd find out in the morning.

CHAPTER EIGHT

The old plantation house had seen better days, Teresa Salvare thought as her partner directed the buggy down its long, tree-lined avenue. The glorious pillars that supported the porch, which was level with the roof of the two-story structure, were pitted. One had completely collapsed and lay in massive blocks across the dead lawn.

But she hadn't argued when Lambert had suddenly wanted to stop. It was too tempting. Teresa knew that behind the house lay the fields which may or may not still be bursting with well tended crops. Their condition could indicate whether the owners of the plantation outside of Baton Rouge had held onto their riches, or had lost everything in the ravages of the Civil War.

Before the house, on the other side of the road, lay the wide, slow moving Mississippi River. White steam and black smoke trailed from the stacks of a huge paddleboat as it glided along the water. Not far from it, ten sweating men stood on a cotton laden raft.

Teresa shrieked at the sight of the dead dog lying beside the avenue. She grabbed Hanover's arm.

"Lamb, maybe this wasn't such a good idea."

He smiled. "Now, Tessa. Just because they can't keep up their house doesn't mean that they don't have anything worth stealing."

She sighed. The air was drenched with the spicy-sweetness of magnolia blossoms, and the thirty-year-old woman gazed at the ghostly flowers that festooned the trees.

"Well, if nothing else, I can enjoy the perfume." Teresa sighed and looked at the house. "It doesn't seem like anyone's still living there," she said. "No smoke's coming from any of the chimney's. Why, even the cookhouse stack is dead. Let's turn around, Lamb. No sense in wasting our time."

He turned to her. "Maybe you're right," he said. "Just a little further though. Might as well see."

"Oh, alright!" she huffed, and relaxed against the jiggling seatback.

Two minutes later they were much nearer. "Well, at least there're some horses. Someone must be here." Lambert G. Hanover pointed at the five magnificent steeds tied up at the hitching post.

The sound of gunfire within the plantation house made Hanover rein in their buggy's horse. More shots.

"Let's get out of here!" Teresa said.

"I believe you're right."

"Just go!" she shrieked.

The man coerced their tired beast back in the direction from which they'd come. He used his switch with just the right pressure to urge it to move faster, but Teresa grabbed it from his hands and brutally lashed the poor animal.

"Run, goddammit!" she wailed.

The roan took off. Though the avenue was fairly smooth they nearly bounced from their seats as their buggy tore down it. Additional gunshots sounded in the distance behind them. Teresa gripped Hanover's thigh with one hand and urged the horse to run as fast as it could with its heavy load.

The man bent and looked behind him. "No men in sight yet," he said. "Hurry!"

They cleared the avenue, left behind the magnolias and turned onto the main road headed for New Orleans. Teresa limply held up the switch and gasped.

"It's okay now," Hanover said as the complaining horse instantly settled into an easy gait.

"I told you it was a mistake," she said bitterly. "If we'd turned around when I mentioned it—"

"We'd have been on the road a few minutes earlier. You're right. I should have relied on your feminine intuition."

"Dern right you should have! Hasn't it gotten us out of trouble more than once?"

"Yes. Are we agreed? No more jobs until we reach New Orleans."

She nodded. "Fine, Lamb. Whatever you say."

Not long after they'd gotten to the wagon road five men flashed by them, riding hard, torsos bent toward their horse's pumping necks. Teresa shivered at the thought of what they'd left behind them.

But she had to fight off the urge to go back and see for herself. Teresa imagined the dying bodies oozing blood. The thought made her all warm inside.

Spur shook his head and walked out of the dilapidated plantation house. The whole family had been gunned down. He'd followed the buggy tracks up to the house but had been curious as to why the pair he'd been following had turned back without going in. Once there he saw the reason.

The hoof prints showed that five men had probably done the work. Some local trouble, he figured. Hanover and Teresa weren't involved.

Judging from the tracks, he was still at least a half-day behind them. He was a few miles out of Baton Rouge. They were well on their way to New Orleans. What were they after? Just more con artistry, more money to swell their already bursting collection of illegally gained earnings? Or something bigger?

Spur sighed and rode from the plantation. He had to find them, capture them, and take them into custody alive. That was the hardest part, though he didn't mind admiting that the last thing he wanted to do was to kill a woman.

What irritated him the most was that he couldn't quite picture Teresa's face. He did remember thinking that he'd never forget it—but he had.

He cursed, spat and pushed on beside the broad Mississippi River.

"At last!" Teresa Salvare said.

New Orleans spread before them like a jewel. The river glittered in the sunlight as it bent around the famous town. Steamers, barges, rafts and keelboats littered its surface. Everything from cotton to

merchants and their families were being carted up
and down the Mississippi River. The air was heavy
with the scents of thousands of flowers mixed with
the smell of rotting fish on the banks beside the road.

"Let's find the best hotel in town and get settled
in as soon as possible."

"I heartily agree, Lamb," Teresa said, her eyes
shining. "I thought we'd never get here."

"Try to think of it this way," Hanover twirled on
the tip of his black Van Dyke beard. "Since we've
arrived here a week later than we'd originally
planned, there are that many more rich people
who've come into town. That much more cash and
stocks ready for the taking. Many more easy targets
for our work. Does that cheer you up?"

"Of course! I wasn't complaining, Lamb."

"Of course. My mistake." He shot her a grin and
guided the buggy down the winding, narrow streets.

Hundreds of people littered the wrought-iron
porches of the homes. Faces of every color and
mixture of races stared out onto a gasping city as
the heat and humidity of the day increased to an
almost unbearable degree. They were blocked at an
intersection by the passing of a funeral procession.
Mournful music and the cries of the bereaved mixed
with the neighing of horses and the clanging of a
nearby church bell tower.

Once the way was clear again, Lambert G.
Hanover guided their exhausted horse down a few
more streets until one hostelry caught his eye.

"That's a likely place, isn't it?" he asked his
female companion.

When she didn't respond, Hanover glanced at her.
Teresa was staring at the eye-catching jewelry worn
by a well-fed dowager as she stepped from a

carriage.

"Tessa!" he said.

"What is it?" She didn't break her gaze.

"Haven't you learned yet? Jewelry is poison. It's too hard to be rid of. Money is simple, clean and neat. It can be spent anywhere with no questions asked. Diamonds and all that are for petty thieves."

She lowered her head and sighed. "Okay, Lamb. You're right. But I couldn't let her walk by without admiring her fine adornments."

"Fine adornments!" Hanover grunted. "My dear, you were thinking of bolting from the buggy, grabbing them from around her thick neck, jumping back in and switching our poor horses to death in a vain attempt to flee! Am I wrong?"

Teresa Salvare crookedly smiled. "You know me too well, Lamb. Far too well."

He laughed as he stepped down from the buggy and helped the woman onto the dusty street. "The Hollister seems like a fine hotel. But remember— we don't do anything here."

"I know. Too dangerous. I'm not a child, after all!"

"I guess I forget, sometimes," he said as he unloaded their considerable baggage and they stepped into the luxuriously appointed inn.

The sky was dark by the time Spur dragged into New Orleans. Exhausted, all he wanted to do was to bed down for the night, but the first five hotels he tried were full. As he walked into the sixth, the Hollister, and got the same answer from the well-dressed night clerk, Spur stomped on the ground.

"Aren't there any rooms available in town?" he asked.

The tight-lipped man shrugged. "I don't know. It's especially busy right now, 'cause of the race."

Spur shook his head, stormed out and rode to the next nearest hotel. It was fancy but he didn't mind that much. A woman in white linen smiled as he walked up to the counter.

"A room for the night, sir?" she asked, purposely taking in his face.

He couldn't hide his surprise. "You have rooms available?"

"Of course, sir! Frankly, we're the most expensive hotel in town. Even the well-to-do folks are staying in less costly lodgings. They're saving their money for the race, I suppose."

"Fine."

He signed the register. "What are the charges?"

"Ten dollars a night, sir?"

Spur didn't even react to the enormous sum that she'd mentioned. He simply fished out $30 and handed the gold pieces to the woman. "Might as well pay in advance," he said.

The lovely innkeeper laughed and stashed the money in her cash drawer. "Mighty obliged to you. Room 14." She handed him a key, dangling it from a slender, white hand.

He nodded, grabbed the key and walked up the stairs, ready for a night of doing nothing but sleeping and dreaming.

Though he didn't turn up the kerosene lamps, Spur saw that the room was outrageously luxurious. But the lawman was too tired to care. Moonlight flooded the room from the window, and all he could see as he walked in and locked the door behind him was the bed. It looked good. Real good. Even empty it was the prettiest thing he'd ever seen.

Spur chucked his clothes and dumped them on the Persian carpets that covered the floor, pulled off his boots and socks and flopped onto the pigeon feather mattress.

He worked a kink out of his neck and enjoyed the comparative coolness of the sheets. Soon, however, the humidity of the town beside the river crept into his room and made him sweat profusely. Cursing, Spur rose and went to the windows. He opened them, allowing a light breeze to filter in.

As he stretched out again the wind chilled him. It took him several minutes to drift off to sleep. As he laid there he heard a man and a woman in the room next door arguing.

Something about a race . . . .

CHAPTER NINE

Teresa Salvare slowly moved the boar bristle brush through her hair, lovingly caressing each blonde strand. Sitting before the window as the early morning breeze blew through the city of New Orleans, she gazed down at the street and smiled.

The town was bustling beneath her. Everyone in the city seemed to be out during the coolest part of the day. She lost count of the number of expensive carriages and well-dressed people who passed below her hotel window.

Teresa felt a warm hand press against her shoulder.

"Good morning."

"Lamb," she said. "You finally got up."

He yawned. "What are you looking at out there?" The man, wrapped in a brocade robe, bent and put his head near hers, peering through the window.

"What am I looking at? Why, the riches of New Orleans! What else would I—I—" She threw down the brush. "Lamb! I don't believe it!"

"What?"

"Look. There! That man!"

"Which one? Honey, there must be at least a hundred men in sight."

"You fool! The one in the brown Stetson! Right there! He's turning back. He's walking into our hotel!"

"I'll be damned. I'll be goddamned!"

Teresa blew out her breath. "Am I right?"

"It sure looks like it. That's him. The lawman who caught up with us in Wet Prong."

"What's he doing here?" Teresa demanded. "He doesn't belong here! He belongs six feet under!"

"Calm yourself, Tessa."

She watched him walk out of sight into the hotel, then stood and paced, clutching her elbows. "I told you we should have killed him!"

"That wouldn't have been too easy, with that pistol-packing woman around."

Teresa stopped. "I would have taken care of her too," she snapped. "Or I could have, if only you weren't so scared to use guns. Honestly, Lambert G. Hanover! If I didn't know better I'd think you were—"

He pounced on her, grabbed Teresa's arm and twisted it. "You'd think I was *what*?"

"Stop it! You're hurting me!"

His eyes glazed over. Hanover increased the pressure, staring the woman down. She yelped. The man suddenly released her and faced the wall, his body rigid, arms hanging tightly. "I'm sorry, Tessa."

She rubbed her developing bruises. "Sorry?"

His nostrils flared. "You have no right to talk like that. You know nothing about me—my background.

the reason I do things the way I do."

"You never talk about it." The woman retrieved her fallen brush, sat at the window and worked on her yellow hair again. "How could I know?"

"Do you consider me to be a gentleman?"

She smiled at her reflection in the silvered mirror. "Sure, I guess, Lamb. Usually. When you're not trying to twist off my arms."

He sighed. "I was born to a poory family. My father put food on our table by picking pockets. He wasn't above killing his victims after he'd robbed them. We lived in the dirtiest, most downtrodden part of Philadelphia. Mother never spoke of how my father earned his money. I only knew that we managed to get by."

Hanover looked at his partner. "One night I couldn't go to sleep. I'd broken my arm while playing with a friend and it ached and ached. So I heard them talking. We all slept in the same room, you understand." He closed his eyes. "My father was describing his day's activities. When he was through, he bragged that he must have killed fifty men and woman in the last few years. Fifty. He bragged about it, Tessa!"

She stopped brushing and shook her head.

"I hid under my dirty sheet and stayed awake until morning. After my father had left and my mother had walked to the street market, I stole as much money as I could find in the house and ran away. Two days later I was working for the Tompkins, a wealthy family. I did that for years as I grew to be a man. I watched my employers and learned how to act in high society. How to be a gentleman. Eventually, I saved up enough money to buy myself the finest suit that I could find and fell into gambling. From that it was a short trip to stealing—but I never, never used a firearm!"

Teresa sat silently, looking blank-faced at him. "Because you father—"

"Yes! Because my father had killed all those innocent people. Oh, you know that I'm no saint. I love my work, but I'm not about to continue the family tradition."

"Have you seen your family since?"

He shook his head and grabbed a cigar from a table. "No. My mother died from a fever a few years after I left. Later, I heard through friends that my father met his end in a grubby Philadelphia alley not far from Independence Hall, gunned down in cold blood by one of his victims. You see, my father had mistakenly tried to rob a policeman. It was the last thing he ever did."

Hanover bit off the end of the cigar, spat in into a gleaming spitton and lit its tip with a lucifer match. He puffed until it glowed. "So don't talk to me of guns, Teresa. I won't use them. Still, if it should become necessary, to protect our lives—you handle that."

She rose and went to him. Teresa's nostrils flared at the strong scent of cigar smoke. "So I have your permission to kill that man? The one we just saw outside? The one who's here to lock us up and, probably, to have us hanged?"

He puffed and nodded.

Teresa smiled.

That morning, as he stepped from the Hollister Hotel, Spur realized that he'd forgotten breakfast. He continued into the street for a few paces before his stomach grumbled. That settled it. He turned and walked back into the hotel to find the dining room.

This wasn't the rough eating establishment of some frontier town hotel. It was a real restaurant, with fresh flowers and linen on every table, crystal glasses and sterling silver flatware. He got a table near the windows.

The starched-collar waiter took his order and returned almost immediately with a cup of coffee and a small plate of strange round doughnuts. Spur took one bite. The delicious taste made him quickly consume every morsel.

During breakfast, Spur looked at the other diners and realized that he'd underdressed. He had put on a clean pair of riding clothes but still he was plainly out of place in this rich town. Because the pair of thieves he was following usually mixed with the rich folks, the highest class of society, he realized that he'd better change.

After his meal he started up the stairs. A blonde woman was just stepping down them. They met in the middle. She let out a yell and stumbled right into his arms.

Spur easily grabbed the woman's shoulders and held her until she'd righted herself. Fine peach-colored silk crackled beneath his fingers. She smelled of jasmine. The beautiful woman gave him a rueful smile.

"I declare!" she said in an accent that dripped honey. "I just can't get used to this new pair of boots."

"Are you alright, ma'am?" Spur asked as he removed his hat.

"I think I'm fine. Let me see."

She took a tentative step and immediately hurled

forward. "Oh!"

Once again catching the woman, Spur grinned as she raised her right foot behind her. "I knew it! The heel came right off. That cobbler cheated me out of good money!"

The Southern belle spun around her head. Their faces were inches apart. Her breath was laced with mint.

"Kind sir, do you think I could call upon you to help me back to my room? I could never do it alone."

"Of course. Back up stairs?"

"Yes. If it wouldn't be too much of burden on you."

"Not at all."

She placed an arm over his shoulders as they turned on the step. Spur firmly grabbed her waist and guided her back up the ten steps.

"It's room 23, down the hall," she said, and smiled sweetly at him.

Spur certainly didn't mind the distraction. Her body was warm and firm. It bulged beneath the woman's bodice, betraying the presence of her breasts. She felt so good, he thought, as she limped down the hall.

"Here we are! Just push the door open. I'm too trusting to use the lock, or to check new boots before I buy them." The woman gave him a rueful smile.

"Fine."

The door swung open. Spur helped the beautiful woman in her room. Expensive dresses lay in careful piles over virtually every part of it save for the bed, so he guided her to its edge. She lightly sat and smiled up at him.

"Thank you, sir. I never could have done it alone."

"It's no burden helping a pretty lady in distress."

She laughed and unbuttoned her boots. "These sorry things belong in a junk heap! Of all the nerve! That shifty-eyed Italian charged me eleven dollars."

"They'll charge whatever they can get away with." Spur backed to the door.

The woman flashed him a smile. "Why, wherever are you going?" she asked.

"Well, away."

She fluttered her eyelashes. "I thought you said you were going to help me."

Spur grinned. "And I thought you meant up the stairs. Is there something more I can do for you?"

The Southern belle kicked off her boots and stood. "Yes, there is, Yankee. If you'll be so kind as to close the door?"

He quickly did so. "I really should be getting to my work."

The woman smiled and pulled off her bonnet. Golden hair rained down around her face. "And what might that be?"

"Ah—er—"

She arched her back. "You couldn't take out just a few minutes more?"

He stared at the swells of her breasts, her slender waist and the curve of her hips. "Maybe I could." This woman was making the crotch of his pants uncomfortably tight. And she knew exactly how to do it.

"Good. I guess all Yankees aren't alike. My daddy always said they wouldn't lift a finger to help out a woman, especially one from the South."

He approached her. His excitement must have been obvious to her. "Things just aren't that simple.

We're all individuals."

"I see. Do you think you could help me again now?"

"Yes. Anything."

The woman turned around. "I can never reach those buttons on the top of my dress."

Spur McCoy smiled and pulled them free of the cloth flap. As he worked his way down her back, the peach material parted to reveal a cream-colored chemise.

"That's much better!"

He pulled his hands away.

"Oh no! Don't stop! My arm's hurting from that silly tumble I had on the stairs."

"Whatever you say, ma'am." He returned to his work.

"Call me Marie."

He unfastened the last button. "It's done."

"Good."

She turned around, reached into her now sagging bodice and pulled out a pearl-handled derringer.

CHAPTER TEN

Spur backed from her. Teresa Salvare looked down at the derringer she'd just produced, then up at the man. She smiled, laughed and placed the weapon onto the dresser drawer.

"A woman all alone in this city can't be too careful," she said. She watched the man's face unknit. "My daddy, the Colonel, taught me how to use one of those things, but I've never shot anything bigger than a tin can."

"I hope it stays like that." The man's face visibly relaxed. It had been a tense moment or two. "You had me worried there for a second, Marie."

"Really? How odd!" Teresa said, thickening her Southern accent.

"Well, you turned around and showed me a weapon. I'm out on the frontier a lot, not used to these comfortable cities. You meet all kinds of men and women out there. Tough ones. So I was naturally startled. I hope you don't take that as an insult. It was a natural reaction."

She smiled. "Oh, I see." She held her hand briefly over her lips. "I don't think of that pearl-handled beauty as a weapon, necessarily. Most times it's just a dadblamed nuisance, jabbed between my—you know. But I never got out on the street without it." Teresa played the role to the hilt. She called on every acting lesson she'd ever received.

"It pays to be careful. Especially in a town of this size." He took off his hat. "Where were we?"

"Oh yes, I remember." She slipped down the left shoulder of her dress. "You were about to do me another favor. What I hope will be a *big* favor."

He laughed. "I don't get many complaints. Marie, you're absolutely intoxicating."

"Really?" she asked as she slipped off the other side of her dress. Her stretched chemise popped into view.

"Your face, your lovely body, even your voice. It's getting me so excited that I can't be held account-able for my actions."

"So who's counting?"

Spur pulled off his boots. "Are you sure you're all alone? No one will come barging in here, will they?"

She laughed. "Of course not!"

As they undressed, Teresa kept smiling. The moment simply hadn't been right. She had surprised him, yes, but he still had his holster and his own weapon. If he was a professional lawman he could easily outdraw her. Even before she'd finished aiming and firing he would have shot her.

So she'd had to change her course of plans. Bedding him was one way to ensure that his Colt .45 was far out of reach. She thought about how

she'd prepared for this, concealing weapons of
various types around the room.

Of course, he wasn't bad looking, Teresa thought.
She was particularly attracted to his strong jaw,
piercing eyes, and, now that she saw it, his hairy
chest. The lawman grinned at her and dropped his
pants and underdrawers. The enormous proof of his
masculinity swung up between his legs and reached
for the sky.

She gasped and slapped her breast. "My!" Teresa
said. "I have a feeling you're going to be doing me
a very big favor!"

Spur laughed.

Lambert G. Hanover cursed as he paced Chartre
Street, dodging aged women, French-spouting
priests, quadroon children and a host of other
everyday folks. He'd walked there, some four blocks
distant from the hotel, because he didn't want to
be involved in Teresa's plan in any way—not even
to hear the deed being done.

He knew she was safe enough. The lawman hadn't
recognized her as they'd met on the stairs—
Hanover had stayed long enough to watch that
much of the proceedings—and she was a crack shot,
better than many men he'd known.

And despite his deep-seated distaste for violence,
he'd had to agree with her plan. Hanover was smart
enough to realize that with the lawman out of the
way their stay in New Orleans and the trip up the
Mississippi would be that much pleasanter.

"Bananas! Sweet yellow bananas!" a street
vendor called as she pushed a wooden wheeled cart
down Chartre. "Buy my sweet yellow bananas!"

"Hey!" he yelled.

The vendor hurried to him. "You want buy my banana?" she asked him.

"Yes, my good woman. How much?"

"Ten cents a finger." She licked her lips as he removed his money clip.

"How much for a whole bunch?" Hanover asked.

She widened her eyes and pulled at the scarf that covered her frizzy black hair. "Oh, sir, they come all the way from the Antilles. Captain just brought them into port. Sweet and eating-ready."

"Fine, fine!" he said as he studied the strange, exotic fruit. He caught a whiff of its odor. "Just tell me how much you want for a whole bunch!"

She picked one up. "You taste before?"

"Once, in Boston. Woman, give me your final price or be gone!"

"Okay, okay. Ten bananas, dollar-fifty."

He pulled two dollar bills from his money clip and handed them to the fruit vendor, took the bunch and walked stiffly from her. Before he turned the corner he heard her plaintive call:

"Bananas! Sweet yellow bananas! Buy my sweet yellow bananas!"

Lambert G. Hanover walked quickly down the winding streets until he came to Jackson Square. Across from the baroque St. Louis' Cathedral, he found a wrought-iron bench, tore off one of the costly fruits and examined it.

Now all he had to do was to remember how to get the fruit out.

Spur smiled as the woman stood stark naked before him.

"Do you still think I'm a lady?" she asked, perfectly comfortable in her exposed condition.

He took in her beautiful body and swallowed hard. "Marie, after seeing all of you I'd say you're definitely a lady. All lady."

"That's not what I mean," she said. Her breasts bounced as she walked toward him. "I mean a cultured, classy lady. One you'd accept into the finest homes."

"Sure! I guess. It's sort of hard to tell without any clothes on."

"I know. That's why I like it this way." She rubbed her right nipple.

Spur's erection throbbed even harder before him.

The woman smiled. "I don't believe I caught your name, Yankee."

"McCoy, Marie. Spur McCoy."

"Well, then, Spur, come to bed. You'll find out just how much of a lady I am!"

He laughed and sat on the velvet-covered mattresses.

"You coming too?"

"Of course. But I almost forgot to shut the drapes. Don't want anyone looking in from across the street."

The woman pulled them, blocking out the intense morning sunlight. The room darkened considerably, cutting off a clear view of her deliciously round bottom.

"Now we're all set." She went to the bed.

Spur edged over to give her room. The woman faced away from him, spread out her arms and fell directly onto the mattress on her back. "Take me!" she said.

Aroused by the woman's undisguised desire, at her bold willingness to reveal her true feelings, the Secret Service agent didn't think twice about it. He rolled on top of her and kissed her.

"No preliminaries? Just do it?" he asked.

"Yes. Now! Spur, I'm wet. And I'm on fire."

She reached between their bodies and gripped him. He moaned at the sensuous feeling of her hand. She lifted her knees and parted them, opening herself.

"You're the boss," he said. Spur positioned himself and thrust into the very willing woman.

She gasped and shivered. Spur pushed deeper. She arched her back and raked his flesh with her fingernails. He drove in full length and grabbed her shoulders as their bodies were fully connected.

"Jesus!" she said. "I mean, that's what I like!"

"Come on." Spur nuzzled her neck. "You can drop the act now."

She went stiff below him. "What ever do you mean?"

Spur laughed. "I know you're not a lady, though you act like one. But I don't like ladies. Just say whatever you feel like saying. I won't tell anyone. Okay?"

"Okay. I guess I don't have any choice."

"Tell me how this feels."

He reared back and plunged into her. The woman shivered and shook as their pubic bones crashed together. She was a mystery, Spur thought as he began the slow, rhythmic pumping that man and woman had enjoyed since the beginning of time.

But there was no mystery about her reaction to the hot sex. Marie bucked and writhed beneath him, crumpling the exquisitely expensive velvet comforter. She dug her fingernails into his back.

"Faster. Faster!" she said.

When his pace didn't satisfy her, she grabbed his

buttocks and pulled them back and forth, deeply impaling herself on his penis, furiously trying to bring her body to an intense explosion.

The woman dropped all pretenses, Spur thought, though he was barely capable of organizing his mind. Her blonde hair swirled like an unholy halo around her head. She constantly moistened her lips between low moans and urged him to go as hard and as fast as he could.

Guttural pants blasted from between Spur's lips. Their bodies banged together. He looked down at her furry mound and pounded into her with twice the strength as before.

"Oh heck. Oh hell! Goddamn it, Spur! Spur! SPUR!"

Her hands slapped against his sweating lower back. She locked her fingers and pulled him back and forth, shaking and spasming. The old cherrywood bed creaked and groaned under their shifting weight. Spur held onto the woman to maintain their connection as she kicked and fought her way through the blinding experience.

"Jesus, Marie!"

He didn't even think of holding back as his scrotum contracted. Her undisguised passion soon led to his own, and Spur drained himself in a series of animalistic thrusts mixed with grunts. Every muscle in his body flexed and tightened with each brain-numbing spurt.

Their trembling bodies swayed on the bed. The woman's passion subsided before Spur's. He maintained the heated contact as the last few tremors shot through his being.

The blonde woman relaxed and draped a hand over his back. Spur slumped onto her, putting his full weight on the delicate woman. He kissed her neck between his gasps.

The room was suddenly incredibly hot but Spur couldn't do anything about it. He was helpless, spent, his mind whirling with thoughts about this beautiful woman who'd brought him to the peak of the human experience.

She sighed and rubbed his shoulders, her fingers tracing the still tense muscles that she found there. Spur smiled as she hummed a tune.

"I'm sorry," he said. "I must be crushing you. Here, let me move off."

"No, you're not crushing me at all. Well, maybe you are, but I like it. Stay right there, Spur!"

He nodded. "Okay."

Their lips met. It was a sweet, lingering kiss, drained of all passion. Her soft mouth and cheeks, the way she darted her tongue against his, excited Spur all over again. He wasn't exactly surprised to feel new life returning to his still buried penis.

She broke the kiss and regarded him with raised eyebrows. "My word, sir. Again?"

He nodded. "Unless you're too much of a lady."

Marie laughed out loud.

The first banana had been delicious. Hanover found it to be slightly mushy, but that was to be expected. After all, the fruit had travelled by schooner for two weeks to reach the port of New Orleans.

The second was even better, and before he knew it Lambert G. Hanover had eaten three of the expensive fruits. He threw down the peel, dabbed at the corners of his mouth with a handkerchief and stood. Clutching the remaining fruit, he left the bench and leisurely strolled through New Orleans.

He realized that this wasn't Kansas City. It wasn't a raw city but one steeped in history that was written even before Jefferson's historic Louisiana Purchase. The French had been there in force. Several other nations had grappled for control of New Orleans and the prize that lay behind it—the Mississippi River and its avenue to riches.

As he walked by St. Louis Cathedral he passed a large dark-skinned woman. She held her chin proudly and her voluminous white cotton dress billowed in the breeze. Her lips moved with a soundless, continuous chanting.

He was about to dismiss her as a harmless crank when Hanover happened to look down. The man was shocked to see two snakes coiled comfortably around her arms.

He stumbled over a stone. The woman halted and slowly turned to face him. She took in his surprised face and fancy clothes.

"The blessings of St. John and Ellegua on you, my child," she said, and walked off.

Though Hanover had certainly heard of it in legends, he hadn't expected so see much of it during his short stay in the city. But there it was, plain as day.

Voodoo.

After the second time, Teresa Salvare was truly exhausted. She lay beside the panting man for several minutes until she'd regained her wits.

He stirred as she sat and put her feet on the floor.

"Going somewhere?" he asked.

She patted his hairy stomach. "Just to get a glass of water. You want anything?"

"Mmmmm."

She shook her head and walked to the pitcher that stood on an elaborately carved table. Once there, though, Teresa stared into the empty basin and sighed. It seemed such a terrible waste. He was so handsome, strong and intelligent. Such an incredible lover. To top it all off, he had the biggest one she'd ever seen—certainly far more impressive than Lambert's tool.

But she faced facts. He was the enemy, she told herself. And the enemy had to die. Teresa looked around the room. She saw the derringer where she'd placed it. She thought about the knife under the mattress and the packet of poison she'd placed beneath the whiskey bottle.

What should she use?

"Marie?"

His throaty voice broke into her thoughts. "Yes, my love?"

"I think you took off two inches."

She spontaneously laughed and realized it was no act. "Spur, it takes two people, remember? I certainly didn't do it all alone."

"Okay. I'm too tired to argue."

Teresa turned and saw him settle on the bed. His head flopped away from her.

He trusted her completely. He couldn't have recognized her. If he had, the lawman wouldn't have allowed himself to be placed in such a helpless position.

He was such an easy mark. Then why couldn't she kill him?

Teresa firmed her resolve. She went to the table where they kept the liquor.

"I'll never move again," he said from the bed.

"I know just what you need. A touch of whiskey."
She slipped the folded paper from beneath the
bottle and sprinkled its white contents into a glass.
Teresa's hands shook as she opened the whiskey
and poured it into the glass. The powder dissolved
and was soon invisible.

That done, she poured her own glass, replaced the
cork in the whiskey bottle and carefully took Spur's
glass in her right hand. Picking up her own, she
walked to the bed.

"Come on," she said. "Take a drink. It'll make you
feel better."

"I'm asleep," Spur said, yawning.

"It'll do you good, honey. Put some life back into
your veins." She tapped his shoulder.

Grumbling, he flipped over. His head comically
landed on the dented pillow. Spur extended a hand.

Teresa Salvare gave him the drink that contained
the poison. She raised her own glass. "To . . . sex!"
she said with forced brightness.

He nodded and raised the tumbler to his lips.

CHAPTER ELEVEN

Spur hesitated and looked into his glass of whiskey. Drinking hard liquor so early in the morning wasn't his idea of starting the day out right. But was it still early? The room was so dark with the curtains closed that he had no idea of the time.

Still, a bit would be a good bracer. The woman hadn't begun drinking yet either. Spur shrugged.

"Aren't you going to take a sip at least?" she said.

"What are you, a daughter of a whiskey manufacturer trying to increase your old pappy's profits?"

"Hardly!" Marie said. "I just think you might . . . you know, need it. After all the work you just did. I mean, that we both did."

He gazed into the amber-colored liquid. "I guess a little wouldn't kill me."

Marie's smile faded. She downed the contents of her drink and turned her tumbler upside down.

"My dear, you're trying to make me a drunkard."

He rested the rim of the glass against his lower lip.

The beautiful, naked woman suddenly bounced up and down on the bed. The movement made Spur's arm wobble wildly, which spilled his whiskey all over the mattress.

"Oh dear!" she said, quickly grabbing the now empty glass from his hand and spiriting it away to the table. "Look what I've done! I'm sorry." She returned to the bed. "I guess I was just so eager for you to take a drink, thinking it might put you in the mood again—"

"Again!" Spur said, dabbing at the two dribbles of whiskey that had landed on his chest.

"—that I was impatient. So I started jumping up and down like a little girl." She ruefully smiled. "That shows me that sometimes it's better to act like a cultured, genteel lady instead of the hot-blooded woman I am."

Spur grinned and looked down at the whiskey-soaked comforter. "If you were simply preparing me for another roll in the hay, Marie, you might have just saved my life."

Her gaze found his. "What?" The woman shook her head in confusion.

"One more with you would have been the death of me." He slapped at his limp organ.

She laughed and grabbed a towel. "I guess I better clean up that nasty spill," she said.

"And I probably should be getting dressed." He looked down at his chest. "Care to lick that liquor off my chest?" he asked with a leer.

The blonde haired woman held out a hand. "I—I—no, Spur. I don't think so. Not only would I get lost in that fur of yours, but I already had a full glass. That's enough to last me until December 25th!"

"Okay." He grabbed a corner of her towel and wiped himself dry as she rubbed the ruined velvet comforter.

Lambert G. Hanover looked up at his hotel window and frowned. She still hadn't opened the drapes, which meant that the man was still in their room and probably alive. A sudden thought bothered him, so he pulled out his money clip.

He had more than enough. Hanover walked across the street, dodging a speeding carriage and two men on horseback, and stepped into the barber shop.

"I need a shave," he said, fingering his Van Dyke beard as the squat barber looked up at him.

"Okay, okay. Hold your horses. So much damn work all the time," the barber said as he grabbed a pair of rusty scissors.

Perhaps the lawman hadn't remembered what Teresa looked like, but he couldn't count on that being true of himself. He could have described him to the local police. Might as well change his appearance.

"Cut too?"

Hanover shook his head. "Ah, what?"

"I asked if you wanted a cut too?"

He shook his head. Settling into the chair, half-listening to the barber's unintelligible banter, Hanover wondered what color his hair should be this month. Brown? Red?

He smiled. Red it would be.

"I'm awfully grateful for you help," Teresa Salvare said as she saw Spur to her hotel room door. "For everything."

He touched the brim of his hat. "Nothing any red-blooded American wouldn't do for a lady in distress. Sorry I have to leave, but business is waiting for me."

She smiled. "I understand. I have to look after some of my own affairs." She kissed his cheek, patted his behind and scooted him out the door. "See you around, Spur!"

She closed and locked the door. Teresa sighed and looked at the window. She should open the curtains to alert Lambert, but the last thing she wanted to do was to face him. She had no idea how he'd react. Would he be happy? Furious? It was too much to think about.

She turned up one of the kerosene lamps and tidied up the room, selected one of her good pairs of boots from the free-standing closet and put them on. Cutting off the heel of one of another pair had been a small sacrifice to lure the handsome lawman into her hotel room, but now it just seemed silly.

In the past, Teresa had killed men with firearms. She'd always done it quickly with little or no time for thought before pulling the trigger that released the hammer and the speeding death.

But this had been something different. Deliberately setting out to murder a man and then carrying out the plan had proved to be impossible, especially while she was still basking in the glow of their recent exertions on the stained bed.

The first time he'd hesitated to drink the poisoned whiskey Teresa was startled to realize that she didn't want him to down it, that she wanted him to live. By the time he'd finally relented and raised his glass again she'd had the uncontrollable urge to do something, anything to stop him from killing himself. So she'd bounced on the bed as hard as she could.

It had worked. He was still alive and now gone, lost somewhere in the city. The paddleboat race was still a day away. What would she and Lambert do until tomorrow?

Teresa wearily stood, went to the window and opened the drapes. Then she sat beside the dark-colored spot on the velvet comforter, waiting to give her partner in crime the bad news.

Frustrated at his lack of progress in tracking the thieving couple in bustling New Orleans, Spur leaned against the corner of a pastel pink building. Bored and hot, he turned and read the notices that had been plastered all over the flat surface. There were signs trumpeting the arrival of medicine men, of revival meetings to be held next Sunday beside the Mississippi, of an upcoming ball. But one notice caught Spur's full attention.

A CARD TO THE PUBLIC

Reports have been circulating through the city that the great steamer NATCHEZ is intending to engage in a race at 5:04 P.M. June 30th. Such reports are untrue. All passengers may leave with her on that day in the knowledge that the steamer NATCHEZ will be be racing any other craft on Thursday, June 30th, but will be making its regularly scheduled trip to St. Louis.

> *T. P. Leathers, Master*
> *Steamer Natchez*

Spur smiled as he read the public notice. Despite the captain's carefully worded announcement, it was obvious that a race was on. He realized that everywhere he'd gone that afternoon people had been talking about the race.

McCoy stopped at the nearest saloon and listened to several conversations. Men bragged of how much they were betting, and they weren't talking about the great wheel of fortune that stood in one corner of the dingy little saloon.

"The *Robert E. Lee* is the fastest steamer afloat!" one red-faced man yelled.

The man sitting at the table with him guffawed and scratched his bald head. "You're full of beans, Fletcher! The *Natchez* can beat old Cannon's leaky barge any day!"

"Ten bucks says it can't!"

"Twenty dollars says it can!"

"Boys, boys," a suited man said as he slapped the pair on their backs. "Why don't you start talking about real money? I have $1,000 on the *Natchez*."

"You hear that, George?" Fletcher asked his drinking partner. "Caron here's going to be dead broke in a few days."

"Now see here, Fletcher!" George began.

"Fuck you!"

They pushed back their chairs. A fistfight broke out. Spur had heard enough. He wandered outside into the intense heat.

The first man he passed was taking bets. So too were several others. New Orleans had gone crazy with the fever of a steamboat race up the great Mississippi River.

"You what?" Lambert G. Hanover roared.

Teresa lunged toward him from across the room at the Hollister Hotel. "You heard me, I couldn't do it! I thought you'd be happy, Lambert, since you'd probably rather wait for a chicken to die before you'd shoot it for your supper!"

"I never asked you to shoot him!"

Teresa pushed back her shoulders. "I did poison his whiskey but he didn't drink it. That's in the past. So what do we do now?"

He paced. "It's the 29th. If we can hide out somewhere tonight, and board the *Natchez* just before she leaves, he'll never find us again."

"That's just what I was thinking." Teresa poured herself another drink. "So where can we go?"

"I'm sure we can find a party to attend. I heard of a few happening tonight."

"Fine. Then go out there and do what you know how to do best! Give them some sweet talk and get an invitation! I'll start packing."

"No. First we move to another hotel, then we think about this evening. I'm not sure that this Spur McCoy is registered here, but he knows where you're staying. That's dangerous enough."

"Okay!" She exploded with activity, throwing dresses and hats into her leather luggage. "Let's pack!"

"You never should have let him go, Teresa," Lambert said as he quietly folded his best suit.

She flashed him a fast smile. "That's just what I was telling you the other day. I'll never hear the end of this, will I?"

Hanover exploded. "Damn you, woman!" he shouted. The veins popped out of his neck. "You say you're as tough as any man but when it comes right down to it you can't do the one thing that—that—" he paused and bent closer to the bed. "Teresa! What's this stain on the comforter?"

Her face colored. "That's the whiskey that he didn't drink," she said.

Lambert G. Hanover faced her. "On the bed? You were on the bed with him?"

She nodded.

"And he took you, didn't he? Didn't he?"

Teresa waved off his question. "Yes! I figured it would distract him!"

Hanover laughed. "It must have distracted you, too. Okay. I'll hate myself for this, but you've forced me to come to a decision. If we ever run into the man again, I'll cut him down myself before he can blink an eye."

"With what?"

"With the firearm I intend to buy as soon as we're out of this hotel," he said evenly.

She started to laugh but withheld the urge. Sweet, cultured Lamb kill a man? She couldn't picture it. "I'll believe that when I see it."

Teresa caught the long yellow object that Hanover threw at her. "What is it?"

"What does it remind you of?" He leered.

"Ah—well—"

"Never mind. It's a banana."

She turned it over in her hands. "It's food, right? Do you eat it?"

"Yes. But I don't suppose you'd want one right now. Not after that lawman's banana."

She huffed and returned to her packing.

CHAPTER TWELVE

Spur leaned against a lamp post. He ignored the fact that his clothes were hanging from his body, soaked with the sweat that New Orleans' impossible humidity had produced.

The dampness of the air wasn't the only thing impossible. Spur had no idea of how to find Lambert G. Hanover and Teresa, the thieves he'd been following for over three weeks now. He'd stopped in at 12 saloons. He'd gone to dozens of women's dress shops and millioners. And he'd found nothing.

Surely they were in New Orleans. Their trail had headed this way and it seemed the perfect place for the con artists to ply their trade, with all the conspicuous wealth of the rich port town waiting to be taken into their greedy, thieving hands.

But where were they? As he leaned against the kerosene lamp post down by the river and stared at the dozens of people who passed, Spur realized the enormity of his task. Finding the two among the 150,000 or so souls who inhabited New Orleans wasn't going to be easy.

All he had to go on were the cryptic descriptions that his boss, General Halleck, had sent him. Sure, he'd seen them briefly, but he couldn't remember their faces.

Spur removed his Stetson and rubbed the two lumps that sat on the top of his head. They were still tender but were obviously healing. The swelling had gone down. He had to admire Hanover's sense of placement—he'd hit him just where it would make his brain so disoriented that the whole incident was somewhat cloudy in his mind.

On the street before him, a short, stocky man lugged a huge basket on his back. Inside it, hundreds of crablike creatures flexed their pincers and wriggled around.

"Crawfish! Buy my live crawfish!" the street vendor said in a plaintive cry.

Spur sighed and slapped his wounds. The pain seemed to jolt something inside him. Encouraged, he tried to remember exactly what had happened in Wet Prong, to recreate the whole agonizing scene.

He remembered the shop. He remembered the woman with the dress pulled over her face, hiding it but showing off her underclothing. He remembered the store owner demanding that he leave. Then the crushing blow that had come from behind him and which had sent him reeling to the floor and momentarily blacked out!

Okay so far, he thought.

Spur recalled coming out of it, groggy but fairly conscious. The woman pulled down her dress. She'd argued with the man. Spur had still been on the floor, flat on his back, but he'd seen both Hanover and Teresa. *What did they look like?*

The woman had wanted to kill him, but the man stated that he'd simply break Spur's legs. His words came back to him.

"You know how hard it is to ride a horse with a broken leg?" Hanover had said.

Then the shopkeeper had threatened the con artists with a six-gun. The pair of thieves had made themselves scarce in a hurry.

What came after that wasn't important, at least not for his purposes, so he went back over the scene. Nothing more. No details of Hanover's and Teresa's appearance. All he could remember was that she had long blonde hair.

Frustrated, Spur slapped the top of his head again. The new pain firmed his resolve. He tried to picture her. The yellow hair . . . the soft chin . . . the blue eyes . . .

Spur panted. Was he doing it? Was he finally remembering her?

She was beautiful. A perfect, short nose, flawless skin, luscious lips and a body with curves in all the right places.

Confusion swirled in his mind. Was that Teresa, or was that the woman he'd spent a few hours with earlier that morning? The one who'd broken her heel on the stairs in the hotel?

Spur rubbed his forehead. Which woman was it? The more he thought about it, the simpler it was. It was both.

Teresa, the thief from Kansas City, was Marie, the woman he'd bedded.

The thought struck McCoy like lightning. It couldn't be. Could it? Yes it could. She'd lured him

to her hotel room with the story of the broken
heel—that was easy enough to prepare if she'd
known he was staying there too.

Once in her room, Marie/Teresa had showed him
her derringer. Had she meant to fire it, to kill him?
If so, why hadn't she just done it?

They'd made love twice. She was so willing, so
exciting, so totally involved that he couldn't believe
she knew he was the lawman who'd been following
her and her partner.

He shook his head. It didn't make sense. Teresa
would have simply killed him and been done with
it. Unless . . . unless she had been toying with him,
showing that she didn't consider him to be a real
threat.

"Fuck!" he said aloud, startling a flock of birds
and three small boys who were walking by with
popguns. They turned angry faces at him; he'd
alerted their potential prey.

Spur flew down the street. He dodged the endless
procession of buggies, carriages, riders and people
of every race walking the heated streets. He gasped
the liquid air, breathing in the aromas of sausage,
fresh fish, horse droppings and cheap perfume. His
boots pounded the dust.

A buggy was just pulling away from it as he
neared the Hollister Hotel. Spur surged in front of
it and stopped, forcing it to halt as well. When he
saw the driver—an aged black woman—Spur
smiled and waved her on.

Then into the hotel. He didn't bother with the
front desk but took the steps two at a time up the
stairs. On the landing he headed for room 23. The
door easily opened.

The room was empty. The piles of dresses were

gone. No personal articles were in sight. Spur cursed and took one last look around the room.

He found an ashtray on an inlaid table. The butt of a cigar was propped onto it. Lambert G. Hanover must have stayed out of sight while his lady was entertaining Spur.

McCoy huffed. He couldn't believe the woman had tricked him! How could he have been so blind, not to see that the very thief he'd been looking for had taken him to bed?

And why hadn't she killed him? If he was right—and everything pointed to it—Teresa/Marie should have blown him to bits. But she hadn't. Why not?

Spur stared down at the mattress and saw the amber-colored stain that marred the velvet comforter. He remembered that after they'd screwed two times she had urged him to drink some whiskey. It seemed strange that a woman would want her man to drink so early in the morning, but she'd been so insistent that he'd finally given in.

Then Teresa/Marie had bounced the bed so hard that he'd spilled the entire contents of his glass. He'd thought it was odd at the time but now it seemed even odder.

And she wouldn't lick off the few drops that had splattered on his chest.

Poison? It seemed likely. Teresa had almost tried to do him in with the derringer but had quickly decided against it. Perhaps the fact that he had still been armed had changed her mind. Then she'd slipped poison into his whiskey but had made it impossible for him to drink it.

Perhaps she wasn't the cold-blooded killer she'd made herself out to be in Wet Prong. Perhaps she had a sense of right and wrong.

Or maybe she'd simply lost her nerve.

Spur rubbed the stain.

"Lordy!" a woman said behind him.

He turned to watch a black maid walk in, her arms filled with fresh sheets.

"What are you doing in here? They told me this room needed to be made up."

"It does. Sorry."

He went down the stairs and banged on the bell at the front desk. This finally produced the manager, a thin, tall, white-haired man who slipped into his coat as he appeared from the office.

"Can I help you, sir?"

"I hope so. I'm registered in room twenty-four. My friends were staying in twenty-three. We were supposed to leave together today, but their room seems to be empty."

"Hrmph. Let me see." The manager opened a large ledger and ran a finger down the listings. "Ah yes. The Dodsons. They checked out about an hour ago. I can surely state that I was sorry to see them leave. Or at least, Mrs. Dodson. She was a most beautiful woman."

"Yeah. Thanks."

Spur walked out into the heavy, moist air. He couldn't believe that he'd spent an entire night in the room next to the thieves from Kansas City, and had spent the next morning in their bed.

"Really, Mr. Tompkins!" Clara Widdington said. "It was such a delight to meet you today." The aged woman fluttered her hands before her enormous bosom. "It's not often I get visitors from home. You could have sent me a telegram, after all."

"We left on such short notice," the gentleman

said.

"I see. I'm trying to remember when last I saw your parents. You hadn't been born then, of course; in fact, your mother and father had just met. When he came to me on that day in, oh when was it, 1840? 1845?"

"Something like that," he said, smiling.

Clara shook her head, sending her double chin bouncing. "Whenever it was. When your father called on me and told me that he was marrying some woman it broke my heart. Your father was always a ladies' man. I was so shocked to hear the news."

"People change."

The woman peered at him, nodded and smoothed her expensive silk dress over her knees. "Indeed they do. Would you care for some liquid refreshment, Edgar dear?"

"Yes. That would be lovely."

She smartly clapped her gloved hands. A black youth appeared.

"Yes, ma'am?"

"Jean, two mint juleps."

"Thank you, ma'am." The servant bowed and left.

As the elderly woman continued to talk of the "good old days," Lambert G. Hanover sat stiffly on the settee in Clara's parlor.

What a stroke of luck he'd had! Hanover had gone to a furniture store earlier that day, just to pass the time, and had fallen into talking with an obviously wealthy woman—his favorite kind. When he'd stated that he was from Philadelphia, she'd asked if he knew the Tompkins.

Indeed he did, Hanover had said, and told her that he was Edgar Tompkins, the couple's son. In fact, Hanover had worked for the Tompkins in their

home right after running away from his parents.
The woman had believed him and suddenly he was
an accepted part of New Orleans high society.

It had been only too easy.

The servant appeared holding a silver tray. After
Clara Widdington had selected her glass Hanover
took his.

"A toast. To Philadelphia!" she said with a
flourish.

They drank.

"Tell me. What is your new bride like?" she
asked, dabbing the corners of her mouth with a lace
handkerchief.

Hanover cleared his throat. "Well, she's beautiful, she's intelligent, a good dresser. She laughs at
my jokes . . . ."

"Yes, yes, my dear. That much is obvious. But
what about the really important things?" Clara's
left eye twitched.

He took another sip and smiled. "Of course. Trust
me. She comes from an impeccable background."

"Yes, yes. And?" The aged woman edged forward
on her seat.

"And her parents are quite wealthy."

Mrs. Widdington touched her left hand to her
bosom. "Thank goodness for that! I'd hate to think
that you were breaking the family tradition,
Edgar."

He smiled. "Are you sure it's no problem? Marie
and I staying the night here? The steamship doesn't
leave until five tomorrow afternoon."

"Of course it isn't any trouble!" Clara said,
fluttering her left hand in front of her face. "It's
kind of you to ask, but really, Edgar! Imagine you
and Marie languishing in some classless hotel.

Besides, there isn't a room available in town. Something about some nonsensical steamboat race. I don't know." She set down her drink and patted his knee. "Besides, you're practically family. If things had turned out differently, I could be your mother, my dear."

He looked into her eyes. "That would have been lovely, Clara."

She raised the handkerchief to her nose.

Upstairs in Mrs. Widdington's home in New Orleans, Teresa went on an expedition. Lambert was keeping the woman occupied as she staked out exactly what they should take on their departure the next day.

There was so much jewelry that it dazzled Teresa's eyes. She couldn't resist slipping an emerald ring onto her finger. It fit perfectly. The ring held a huge, rectangular, nearly flawless emerald. It was so massive and so beautiful.

She placed the ring in her purse. The old biddy would never notice it being gone, and she certainly didn't have to tell Lamb about it.

Moving pictures and checking behind books, the beautiful woman finally found the safe. That was his strength, breaking into the confounded things, so she returned everything to its original appearance and memorized exactly which books the safe had been hidden behind.

That done, she returned to the room that the woman had given to Lamb and his "bride." She had to admit that the man was fabulous. It was so easy with him that she almost hated to leave New Orleans and board that cumbersome steamship tomorrow.

But he had to have his recreation as well, Teresa thought. He'd been complaining for two weeks now that all he really wanted to do was get back to the gambling that he loved so much. Starting tomorrow he'd have his chance.

Not just any card game satisfied Lambert G. Hanover, she thought wistfully as she checked her appearance in a gilt-framed mirror. It had to be very high stakes. The other players had to be of the highest social standing. He had to have thousands of dollars riding on the game or Lamb simply wasn't interested.

Certain that she looked fine, Teresa went downstairs.

"There are you, my dear!"

Hanover instantly stood and greeted her with a gentle kiss on her cheek.

"I hope you've found everything you need, my dear," Clara Widdington said.

"Oh, yes." She swung her purse. "Everything."

CHAPTER THIRTEEN

New Orleans. Teresa and Lambert G. Hanover.
The three of them had gotten together, and the
city by the Mississippi River had gathered its arms
around them. Spur kicked over an empty milk can
as he walked along Burgundy.

"Hey! Watch your fine steppin', sir!" a voice
behind him said.

McCoy turned. A black woman stared at him from
behind a half-opened door.

"I'm sorry." He tipped his hat and pulled at his
sodden shirt. "This isn't the best day of my life."

She hooted. "You tellin' me?" The maid pushed
the door fully open, revealing an elaborate garden
in the courtyard and, behind it, a stately house.
"Lordy, I'm overworked as it is. And now the missus
invited some rich couple from out of town to stay
the night." The round-faced woman tugged on her
pristine uniform. "Midnight'll never come. That's
when I head home. Just this morning the missus

promised me I could leave early tonight and go bet on the Wheel of Fortune, instead of cookin' for three and lookin' after her unexpected guests."

Spur nodded and began to walk away, but he turned back to her. The maid adjusted the white scarf she'd tied around her hair.

What if Teresa and Hanover hadn't gone to a different hotel? It wasn't likely that they'd leave New Orleans. Maybe they were staying with friends, or had managed to finagle their way into some wealthy household. It was an interesting idea.

"What're you staring at?" she asked.

"I'm sorry. Just thinking. You say that a rich couple came to call?" he asked.

She nodded. "Uh huh. White folks by the name of—oh, I can't think straight."

McCoy smiled and sat beside her on the stoop. The maid immediately rose.

"Sir! You shouldn't sit beside me. I know my station, and you should know yours! Fine thing it would be if anyone saw me putting on such high-faluting airs! It's against the natural order, me sitting beside you."

He stood and took her arm. "My good woman, do you have a family?"

She nodded. "No husband, but yeah."

"What's your employer's name?"

"Miss Emily." She crossed her arms. "Why?"

A delivery cart rattled down the stone street.

"Could you tell me what Miss Emily's visitors look like?"

"And why should I do a thing like that?" she demanded.

Spur saw hope in her eyes. He reached into his coat pocket. "I could make it worth your time."

The maid licked her lips. "Yeah?"

"What do they look like? These visitors from Pennsylvania?"

"Oh sir, I haven't seen much of them. Been in the kitchen all day long. Just used the front door to put out the milk can."

"But you got a glimpse?" Spur smiled and patted his pocket.

The maid's eyes ignited. "I may have." She delicately ran a hand down her chin and held it before her.

Spur proffered a silver dollar. The woman quickly grabbed it.

"Yes sir! I saw them all right. The woman—oh, she's a fine thing! Fancy dresses, hats that must've come from France. One of them could feed my family for a week." The maid bit the coin she'd just been paid. "And the gentleman!" She rolled her eyes.

"Is he tall? How old would you say they are?"

"Jasmine!" a female voice shrieked from inside the house far behind the maid.

"Coming, missy! Sir, I must go."

Spur gently took her arms. "Well?"

She looked at the house and then back at Spur. "Let the old biddy wait for her tea!" She arched her eyebrows at the forbidden thought. "Okay, sir. The gentleman's way shorter than you and round. He's as wide as he's tall! And the woman—his wife— why, she must be approachin' seven feet. A tall, gangling thing. But her dresses are so purty you don't notice at first."

"JASMINE!"

"Oh, I'm sorry, sir. I must be going. Please?"

Spur released her arms. "Thank you."

She disappeared behind the door. They certainly weren't the two he'd confronted in Wet Prong. It had seemed promising when she spoke of a fancy couple, but Spur should have known that it wouldn't be that easy to find two needles in the haystack of New Orleans.

He discovered a nearly hidden alley extending behind the fine house and plain doors that clearly marked the servants' entrances. Maybe Jasmine couldn't help him, but someone else might just have the clue that he needed.

He knocked at the first door, but the butler said that the master was out at the moment, and no, he'd had no guests.

The servants at the next house were of no help; their employers had gone to Paris. They'd left only a small caretaking staff behind them.

Another door, another knock. A shining-faced young girl giggled and said that her mother was having a baby and she had to run and boil some water.

Spur tried again and again, always coming up with nothing but determined to keep trying until he'd called at every fine house in the city.

As he lifted his fist to yet another back-street door, Spur knew that the con artists may have indeed gone to another hotel. But he doubted it. Why waste their time there when so many people were willing to put their valuables in danger at their hands?

"How will you explain it to Mrs. Widdington?" Lambert asked as he stared out the window in the room that their hostess had given them.

"Oh, something about how my hair started falling

out. She'll never suspect. Sometimes it helps to be a woman—other girls expect you to be vain." Teresa tugged and primped and fussed over her appearance in the full-length oval mirror until she was satisfied at the effect. "Well? What do you think? Do you like the wig?"

Lambert G. Hanover couldn't hide his astonishment. The woman before him wasn't Teresa Salvare. At least, it didn't look like her. The blonde hair was gone, covered with a dull red wig. A beauty mark was perfectly centered on her left cheek. Her lips, usually painted the brightest red, had softened to a less intense shade.

Most startlingly, his partner had somehow or another reduced the apparent size of her bust. Opening her eyes as wide as they'd go, Teresa tied on a bonnet and straightened her back.

"How do I look?" she sweetly asked.

His mouth opened.

"Don't stand there like a man who can't talk. What do you think?"

"My God," Lambert said. "Jesus. Teresa that's the most amazing transformation you've ever done!"

She laughed and held up her arms to display herself. "It's nothing for a woman of my temperament and rare theatrical abilities."

Lambert frowned. "I'm not sure how we'll explain you to Mrs. Widdington. Vanity aside, you look so different from the woman who walked in here that she's bound to notice. The old biddy might even get suspicious, and that wouldn't do either of us any good."

"Don't worry, Lamb. Mrs. Widdington's so old she can't think straight. Why, she must have introduced herself to me at least three times. And how often did she mention her beloved, long-haired cat?"

He roared. "That's right. The invisible cat that never seems to be around. It must've died years ago but she forgets it. Perhaps you're right, Teresa. Maybe she won't notice. But what if she does?"

Teresa smiled and sat on the embroidered, gilt chair. "If she does, I'm sure Mrs. Widdington's too much of a lady to mention it."

"Fine." He kissed her cheek. "The party begins at eight. We have to have everything packed before then."

"As usual," Teresa said with a sigh.

"You haven't forgotten the location of Mrs. Widdington's safe?"

"Of course not!" she haughtily said. "I know my job."

"Good."

"Just remember to tear yourself away from the gambling tables long enough to break into the old bag's safe. While I sit there and chat and do absolutely nothing."

"Tessa—" Lambert began.

She held up her hands. "I know. I know! It's best that way."

"I realize how boring it can be, pretending to be interested in gossip about persons you don't even know. But just one more night, my dear. That's all I ask."

She looked up at him. "Okay. But Lamb, just don't go back on your promise. After we sail on the *Natchez* up to St. Louis we will stop for a while. For all the money we've stolen we sure haven't been able to enjoy it! Why, we must have over $200,000, and just think of what we've had to do. Ride on horseback. Stay at filthy farmhouses. The dirt! The horrid food! The smell of horses!"

Hanover grinned. "My, you've become quite a lady. You weren't too refined when I dragged you out of that saloon! I've made you into a lady. A lady can put up with anything if she can increase her wealth. Be patient, my dear," Hanover said. He rubbed her shoulders. "In three or four days—depending upon how long the paddleboat race lasts—you'll be able to do anything you want. Anything!"

"Okay."

"What's the first thing you want to do?" He knelt beside her.

Teresa smiled. "Marry you."

"Be serious!"

"Okay. Buy everything I've ever wanted. Not dresses but things! Sparkling things. Shiny things!" Teresa looked at Lambert. "You're, ah, not going to lose all our money gambling, are you?"

"No, my dear. That I will not do."

"Sure." She sighed. "Of course not."

The young black boy rose from where he'd been kneeling. He hadn't been able to see anything through the keyhole, but the couple's voices had been easy to understand. They were criminals? They had stolen their money?

He walked down the second-story hall, avoiding stepping on those spots where the floorboards creaked. Why weren't they calling each other by the names that they'd given to Mrs. Widdington?

Jean scratched his head and went to the stairs. He didn't know what to make of all that he'd heard, but it certainly sounded like the man who'd come to stay at Mrs. Widdington's home wasn't Edgar

Tompkins from Pennsylvania.

They were thieves. Or least it seemed that way.
Jean shook his head. Should he try to talk to the
old woman? Warn her? He didn't know.

The only time he'd ever spoken more than one
sentence to his employer had been when he'd shown
up with a letter from one of her society friends
pinned to his shirt saying that the son of one of her
servants needed a job. She'd looked him over, sat
him down in one of her fancy chairs and had a long
talk with him.

Back then, Jean had been too young to be
nervous. In the last two years Mrs. Widdington had
barely noticed him unless she wanted something,
such as one of her endless drinks. So they hadn't
spoken again.

His daddy would know what to do, Jean thought.
The boy rubbed his eyes and went downstairs. His
fourteen-year-old mind couldn't settle on an answer.

Tell her, he thought.

No, don't tell her. What's she to you?

She pays me good money.

No, not enough money.

Tell her right now.

Don't tell her!

Jean sighed and straightened his white coat. He
went into the parlor.

Mrs. Widdington glanced up at him.

"Oh, Jean, you startled me! I was just studying
the Psalms. What is it?" she pleasantly asked.

He couldn't talk.

"Now really, Jean?" Mrs. Widdington laughed
and twirled her reading glasses in her left hand.
"Don't be nervous. You know you can speak to me."

He violently wrung his hands before him. "Yes,

Mrs. Widdington. But. . . ."

The wealthy woman set down her Bible. "Just say it, my dear boy."

Jean swallowed. "Uh, your guests, miss."

"What about them?"

"I was going up to put the flowers in your room and I—I heard them—"

Mrs. Widdington leaned closer. Her eyes narrowed on either side of her hawklike nose. "Yes? What did you hear them doing?"

He blushed.

"I know you don't speak much. At least, you never have around me. Some folks might think you were afraid of me. But Jean, if you have something to say then simply tell me! What is it?"

"Are you sure he's who he says he is?"

She went blank. "Jean, whatever are you talking about? Of course he's Edgar Tompkins!"

"Yes ma'am. But—but they were talkin' about stealin' and thievery and all that."

Mrs. Widdington molded her face into a smile. "I believe I told you not to listen in at doors, Jean. You simply misunderstood them. Edgar and Marie were probably discussing some problem they had in the past with thieves. I'm afraid it's rather common among some servants."

"Ah—ah—"

"No need to worry." She propped the glasses on her nose and picked up her Bible.

"Yes ma'am. Thank you, ma'am."

Jean's knees shook as he walked from the parlor. He'd known she wouldn't believe him. But he had heard them—the woman saying they'd robbed a lot of money. Calling each other by different names. And her going on about some wig.

Jean stopped at the kitchen door. The young black boy turned around, searched the empty house behind him with his eyes and walked through the double doors. The fragrance of simmering soup lulled him into forgetting everything but getting a mouthful of supper before it was laid on the rustic table.

Dusk sank onto the city. Spur pushed into a dark alley. The feeble light from kerosene lanterns had already begun to shine in a few windows. Just a couple more houses and he'd stop that part of his investigation.

A cat cried out and shot past him. McCoy grinned and moved deeper into the alley. The houses weren't so fancy now. The neighborhood wasn't as good.

The alleyway turned inky. Somewhere in the distance he heard feet rustle. Probably some servant hurrying home with the master's whiskey, he thought.

There was no answer at the first door. He walked to the next. It was difficult to decide where to place his feet; he couldn't see the cobblestone surface of the alley in the darkness. Half by feel and half by insight, Spur made his way to the next house.

His knock brought a startled, elderly white woman who clutched a kerosene lamp to the door. Her lined face peered at him from behind the door.

"What are you doing out there? White folks call at the front!"

"I'm looking for a couple." Spur had said it so many times that the words flowed out. He was surprised to see the woman. She wasn't dressed as a servant.

"I don't know about any rich man and woman!"

she said. "But since you're out there, have you seen my wild-eyed slave—I mean, serving girl?"

Spur winced at the woman's slip. Apparently, she was one of the many who hadn't accepted the fact that, in the United States, human beings could no longer own other human beings. "Sorry, no ma'am."

She curled her upper lip. "It figures. That bitch snuck out around half-past six. Probably to see that good-for-nothing boyfriend of hers. Lord only knows what they're doing out there in the dark."

"No one out here but me," Spur said. "At least I haven't seen anyone."

The woman frowned. "I've got ten guests for a sit-down dinner and no one to serve them! I'm sure that boy's master'll track them down and beat his hide."

"Thanks for your help, ma'am." Spur sighed as the door closed, cutting off the slice of light.

Just two more houses, he told himself. Then he could quit and get a well-deserved drink.

Voices ahead. A man and a woman laughing. Someone else silenced them with a low "shush!" A drum softly sounded under an unseen player's hand.

The alley was so dark that he couldn't see a blessed thing. Curious, Spur walked deeper into it. Something glinted about ten yards ahead. Metal? A weapon?

He couldn't tell, but it sounded like a party was beginning right there in the alley. A woman began singing in a language which McCoy had never before heard. More laughter. Objects clinked together. Feet shuffled on the paved surface of the alley.

He fought the impulse to call out to them. This

might get interesting, he thought. If nothing else it would break the monotony of the day. Spur stealthily approached them, making no sound.

A circle of light blazed into existence. The match moved and created another flame. Then two more sprang from the darkness and danced. The three candles barely illuminated the wizened black woman's face. Spur saw chicken feathers fly in the breeze that had kicked up as the sun set.

"When we get through with this, old man Franklin'll never beat you again, Lyle!" a wizened old woman said. "Your master is done gonna have the gris-gris put on him."

Spur's fascination with the strange spectable before him didn't prevent him from hearing the footsteps rapidly approaching from behind.

Someone was coming.

The candles flared. The drumming went on. Wary of being attacked, Spur darted through the darkness across the broad alley. Just as he made it to the wall explosions shattered the nighttime air with light and thundering sounds.

CHAPTER FOURTEEN

A man screamed in the pitch-dark alley. The candle flames were quickly pinched out. Boots hit the cobblestones. Spur flattened against the far wall and jerked his head back and forth, trying to figure out what was going on without becoming too involved.

"I got you now, Lyle!" a man's voice said. "Git on up here and there'll be no trouble! You know you aren't supposed to leave without my permission!"

"No!"

A grunt. "I figured you'd be out tomcattin' with your woman. Then I find out you're voodooin'! Get your black ass back into the house, Forder. Now!"

Spur couldn't resist. "Slavery was abolished years ago," he said.

"Who was that? Who said that? Damn, it's so dark in here. Johnny, hand me that lantern."

Seconds later Spur heard liquid sloshing onto the ground. A match roared into life. It quickly lit the kerosene, transforming the inky alley into a brightly lit corner of New Orleans. McCoy drew his Colt.

A portly man in an expensive suit chomped on the end of his cigar and trained his pistol down the alley. Behind him stood a younger man with the same face. Probably his son, Spur thought. On the other side of him, up against the dead end of the alley, stood three blacks: a young couple and the elderly woman he'd seen earlier.

"Back away from here!" McCoy shouted as the kerosene flamed before him.

"You protecting my boy?" the fat man asked.

"You're treating him like a slave. He isn't your property. He's a human being."

The Southerner guffawed. "Says you. Forder, I'm giving you ten seconds to be by my side. If you don't move I'll shoot your girlfriend. Then I'll shoot your mother. If that doesn't convince you, well, boy, I'll shoot you. Come here!"

"Leave us alone!" the servant yelled. The two woman screamed.

"I'm warning you. Go home!" Spur shouted.

The man altered his aim. "I'm getting powerfully tired of your yakking," he said. "Maybe I'll just take care of you first!"

"Try it."

Spur drew and peeled off a shot. Before the man could react the bullet had sent his weapon spinning from his hand. McCoy smiled at the surprising accuracy of his aim, especially considering that he only had the dancing light of the fire in the street to work with.

"Sumbitch! You nearly shot my head off!" The obese Southerner turned to his son. "Johnny! Give me your—"

Spur fired again. The bullet passed between Johnny's legs and dug into a plaster wall just behind him.

"Drop it," McCoy said.

"Shit, boss!" The weapon fell to the ground.

"Thanks. Now, Johnny, I suggest you and that over-fed slaveowner get your butts out of this alley before I decide to start shooting at something else!"

"You can't do this, Yankee!"

Spur waved with his weapon. "Willing to bet your worthless life on that? Get moving!"

The well-dressed Southerner shook his head. "I'll be back for you, Fordor!" he yelled as he and Johnny disappeared around the corner.

"Everyone all right?" Spur yelled toward the rear of the alley before he looked away from the now deserted alley entrance.

Silence. He turned and saw that the three of them had gone. Disappeared.

A quick check of the area showed no blood. He hoped no one had been hurt. Spur sighed, waited until the kerosene had harmlessly burned itself out and chose a new alley. He had to find Teresa and Hanover.

Mrs. Widdington placed her Bible on her lap. She didn't believe Jean for an instant. The boy was becoming quite uncontrollable. First it had been his sudden interest in girls. And now this! Accusing her houseguests of being thieves!

She shook her head and climbed the stairs. Edgar and his bride were apparently still preparing for her party that evening. Light shone from under their door. Clara Widdington smiled as she thought of those far-off days in which she'd dreamed of marrying that other Tompkins, the man who'd swept into her life and breezed out almost as quickly as he'd come.

The woman turned up the kerosene lamp in her bedroom and sat before the mirror. Now, what to wear? Clara smiled and tapped her chin. Of course; the green silk that she'd already decided on. How silly of her to forget. But what to go with it?

She lifted the wooden lid of her jewelry box. Definitely not the rubies. Sapphires wouldn't do either, and she feared that the diamond pendant would seem too ostentatious. The emerald ring would be fine.

Clara Widdington searched through the box. When she couldn't find it, she sighed and went through a second tangled collection. As she rummaged through gold bracelets, strands of perfectly matched pearls and other mementoes of past suitors, Clara remembered how she'd happened to receive the emerald ring.

The fine English Duke had been so admiring of her charms that after—what was it, two or three nights together?—he'd gone out and purchased the ring for her. That was some time ago and she'd rarely worn it since.

But tonight she had to have it. After five minutes of searching Clark Widdington realized that it wasn't there.

She felt her heartbeat rise in her agitation. Calm yourself, she said, fanning her face. Jean had mentioned thieves. Clara smiled. Of course! The boy had taken a fancy to some new girl and had to have extra money to spend on her. He'd stolen her ring!

* * *

Teresa lowered her voice. "I just have a feeling, Lamb. We can't go to that party tonight."

Hanover allowed himself a grunt. "You just don't want me to have any fun. You're afraid I'll bankrupt us gambling."

"No, that's not it at all." She tugged at her wig. "Something's up. I can't be sure what it is, but all is not right here."

"That sounds like a line from one of your plays." Hanover lit a cigar and contentedly puffed. "My dear, the race doesn't start until 5:04 P.M. tomorrow. Why leave now before the party, before I can have the chance to legally earn some spending money?"

"Legally?" Teresa laughed. "You're the crookedest player I've ever seen. Shaving your cards. Weighting your dice. I know all about it, Lambert!"

He stood. "Tessa, that's a lie. I never cheat! Well, at least not at cards. Besides a—"

"A gentleman wouldn't cheat. Ha! Lamb, don't change the subject. I don't care. You can gamble somewhere else, anywhere else in town but here!"

"Lower your voice!" He stubbed out his cigar. "I don't understand why you're so nervous, Tessa. This isn't like you at all. Is it because of that lawman? The one you took into our bed? The one you made love to?"

She flung herself onto the bed. "Maybe it is. I don't know. Call it woman's intuition. I can distract her for five or ten minutes. You can get into the safe. Why, she might have more money than we can carry!"

"Unless she puts it in a bank." Hanover crossed his arms and studied the woman who sat on the bed and looked brightly at him.

"As soon as we're settled into a hotel, I promise you we'll be so busy in our room we won't have time to sleep."

Hanover began to speak.

"That is, after you've gambled as much as you want." She rushed through the soothing words.

"Well . . . ."

"It wouldn't do for you to be rusty on the steamer. What do you think?"

He sighed. "Okay. Fine! Gentlemen don't argue with women if they can possible avoid it. Get packed. I'll take a look. Then keep the woman and that nosy servant of hers out of the way for at least fifteen minutes. With my luck she's got a safe that's hard to break into."

Spur called at three more houses but the servants were too busy to talk to him for more than a few seconds. They shooed him away as soon as they saw that he wasn't a friend or a late deliveryman.

Frustrated and still angry at having allowed himself to be tricked by the beautiful criminal he'd been following, McCoy walked out onto Basin Street. Garish music blasted from the rows of saloons and gambling "palaces" that lined both sides of the narrow avenue. Glamorous women, unfettered by the conventions and dangers of the west, strolled unaccompanied, looking for customers.

"How about it, honey?" a delicious belle asked as he walked by.

"Sorry. I like horses."

Spur heard her laughing as drunks made their nightly rounds, prostitutes perched against walls and fistfights broke out around him. He had to get to just a few more houses.

McCoy had nowhere else to look.

An imposing, magnificent house came into view as he turned a corner. He checked the back of the building but there was no rear entrance. Spur straightened his hat and walked up to the front.

A very young black boy opened the door and gazed up at him.

"You here for the party?" he asked.

"What?"

"You here for the party?"

"Ah, no."

"Sorry." The uniformed servant started closing the door.

"Wait! I'm looking for a pair of thieves. Well-dressed, elegant white folks. In their thirties. The woman's tall and blonde."

The boy's mouth dropped. "That's them!"

"I'm a lawman. You won't get into any trouble. Know anything about them?"

He looked back into the house and nodded. "Mrs. Widdington didn't believe me! But it's true! They said they'd stolen all kinds of money."

"Jean! You little devil!" a woman said from inside the house. "Where's my emerald ring? If you stole it I'll forgive you, but not until you give it back to me."

Spur's gaze met the boy's eyes. The kid shook with fear.

No time to waste. McCoy pushed open the door and rushed into the well-furnished house.

A large woman was hurrying down the stairs. Her fleshy face was a mask of anger.

"What are you doing here?" she demanded as she

reached the floor. "And where's Jean? Have you seen my houseboy?"

Spur twisted around and saw the empty doorway. He didn't blame the kid for running away.

"No, ma'am." He tipped his hat. "You're missing an emerald ring?"

"Darn tooting!" she said. "I just checked. It isn't in the box I've kept it in for, oh, fifteen years."

"Who are you?"

"Mrs. Clara Widdington."

"And you have houseguests?"

She drew back. "Why yes."

"They stole it. I'm with the Secret Service. Name's Spur McCoy."

"Secret Service? Why, I knew a man once—"

"Where are they?"

"Who?"

"Your houseguests, Mrs. Widdington?" McCoy shouted.

"Why, upstairs, but—"

He ran to them and flew to the landing. Once there he checked every door along the hall. The first revealed an empty, long-disused room. The second was obviously a guest room. Luggage was piled in every corner. Fancy dresses laid in heaps.

And the window was open.

CHAPTER FIFTEEN

Spur ran to the opened window and leaned through the frame. The street below was deserted, but just below the window grew a massive gardenia bush. The seven-foot-tall shrub could have broken the thieves' fall as they escaped.

"Sir, I must ask you what you're doing in my house!" Clara Widdington said as she stepped into the room.

Spur turned back to her. "Your guests seem to have left."

"Really? Impossible! I've been in the parlor since early this afternoon. The front door is the only exit from this house. I would have seen them walk by."

He shook his head. "She was blonde? Beautiful? And he was a rich, thin, tall gentleman?"

"Yes, that's them," the dowager said.

"Great!" He pushed a foot through the windowsill.

"Sir, I don't know what's going on here! Things

are entirely out of control!"

"Your houseboy didn't steal your emerald ring," Spur said as he stuck his left foot outside as well. "It was Lambert G. Hanover and his lady."

"*The* thieves from Kansas City?" Mrs. Widdington said. "Friends told me about them!"

"Yeah. Nice meeting you."

He bent over double. When his torso was free of the window frame, Spur stared at a distant light and pushed off.

The gardenia bush cushioned his body as he fell the eight feet from the window. Spur jumped to the ground, brushed off his clothes and stooped to retrieve his hat. There, beside the fragrant tree, lay a ten dollar bill.

They had come that way! But where had they gone? No one was in sight, save for a few children and their weary mother who trotted after them down the street.

Spur lit a match. He clearly saw the impressions of a man's and woman's footwear in the moist, bare earth. They headed away from the house and out onto Duphine Street.

"At least I've been robbed by the best!" Mrs. Widdington yelled from the house as McCoy set off to follow the pair's tracks.

It was easy at first. He kept stopping and checking by the light of matches to ensure that he was still on their path. From the looks of the deep, somewhat abbreviated footprints, their boots hadn't lingered in their endless contacts with the ground. The pair had been running.

The piles of clothing in their room clearly indicated that Teresa and Hanover hadn't taken anything but money with them. If they hadn't left it at some location between New Orleans and Kansas City, that is. They were traveling light and on foot, but unless Teresa was a tougher woman than Spur thought she was, they'd have to rest. At least one of them would have to.

Where would they go? Spur wondered. To a hotel. That would be the obvious choice. Then, first thing tomorrow, they'd buy a brand-new set of belongings and clothing and go on with their dirty work.

He struck a lucifer on a stone and sneered at the sight. The footprints he'd been following were lost in the wake of a carriage that must have passed by only moments before. A few feet further and the unpaved street was covered with hundreds of footprints of every kind. Hanover and Teresa had effectively covered their trail.

McCoy cursed as the match burnt his thumb. He shook his head. Go to the first hotel, he told himself. They had to find a place to spend the night.

"It's all your fault!" Teresa said as she hung the bags containing their money on the wall of the horse stall.

"All my fault? Woman, I agree with you. I was just going down to the safe when we heard the old biddy yelling about her emerald ring. Five seconds later you've grabbed the cash and we're flying out the window! And I got a hole in my best suit."

"What does that matter? By morning your gentleman's clothes will be covered with horse shit!"

"Tessa!" Hanover said.

"I said shit and I meant shit! Not dung, not manure, but shit!"

Hanover sighed and leaned against the empty stable. "Honestly, Teresa! Such language!"

"Don't get so uppity with me!" she said, brushing away the soiled straw in search of the clean. "You've said it often enough."

"That's right, my sweet. And it's all I've been hearing from you lately."

They'd been lucky enough to find an empty livery stable and had walked right in.

"Just admit it," she asked.

"Admit what?"

"Oh come on, Lamb! I didn't exactly have to force you out of that window. You recognized his voice, too. That man who was talking to Mrs. Widdington." Teresa gave up on her guest and sat on the fragrant straw.

"Yes. It was that lawman from Wet Prong."

"His name's Spur McCoy. I told you that."

"I don't know how he did it, but he found us."

"He was just lucky. That's all." She leaned against the open boards that created the stall and wrinkled her nose.

"No. He's very good."

"Don't tell me you're worried about him? After all the lawman we've had chasing us?" Teresa softly laughed. "I'm worrying about you, Lamb."

He turned to her from across the stall. "Why couldn't you control yourself, Tessa? Taking that ring was the stupidest thing you've ever done."

She nodded. "I know. But it was pretty. I never thought she'd miss it."

"And because of it we're out an untold sum of money."

Teresa stood, unhooked her purse from the wall and rummaged inside it. Seconds later she sat again and held her hand toward Hanover.

Even in the darkness, he whistled at the sparkle

and flash of green fire within the stone.

"Isn't it a beauty?" she asked.

"I have to say that it is," Hanover rose to his knees and moved closer to her. He took Teresa's hand in his. "It's the largest emerald I've ever seen."

"But worthless for resale, right?"

"Yes. Too risky." He swiftly removed the ring from the woman's finger and threw it into the next stable.

"Hey! Lambert G. Hanover, are you out of your mind?" She scrambled to stand on the slippery straw.

"Stay right there, woman!"

In her anger and surprise, Teresa stumbled to her feet and stood.

The man grabbed her wrist and threw her onto the ground. Her body bounced on the lush straw. Standing over her, Hanover pointed at her lovely face.

"You will go to sleep. You will not look for that ring. You'll leave it behind here to remind yourself of how dangerous your frivolous ways can be."

"But—"

"No. Shut up. Good night."

Lambert laid beside her and placed an arm around her body. She sniffled and finally relaxed into the stinking but fairly comfortable straw.

"At least we still have the money, Lamb. At least we still have that."

"Yes. And each other."

Spur had followed a dozen false trails, trying to find one that led directly to one of the big hotels that were only a few streets away. But each time he'd soon realized that he'd been fooling himself.

Asking at the desks for them would be meaningless. They would never use their correct names. What could he do? Check every single room in every single hotel in the town of New Orleans?

Spur pounded his fist into his left hand. Might as well turn in for the night and start again in the morning. More out of habit than anything else, he lit his last match and bent down to inspect the ground.

Surprisingly, the area was fairly clear. He saw a familiar set of boot impressions that were remarkably similar to the ones that had led away from Mrs. Widdington's house. Dragging from exhaustion and an unsatisfied appetite, Spur wearily followed the tracks.

A man and a woman had walked this way recently. That was certain. But who was it? Hanover and Teresa, or some other couple?

He'd followed them for 50 feet before the match burned out. Spur got down on his hands and knees. He almost smiled as the tracks were lost in a sea of fresh horseshoe impressions. It made sense. He was near a livery stable.

He stretched, yawned and walked to the small barn that lay to the rear of the workshed. Peering in through a hole between two timbers, Spur saw nothing but a succession of empty stalls and dimly-lit heaps of straw.

No one was there.

The next morning, Spur rose, gave himself a whore's bath and shaved. Dressed in fresh clothing, he went down to the restaurant for some breakfast.

It was jammed. Men, women and children were practically dancing on their toes. Spur pushed through them and finally made it inside the restaurant, but no food was in sight on the tables. Instead, a bearded, black-coated man was addressing the crowd.

"And I, Captain Thomas Leathers of the steamer *Natchez*, can assure you fine folks that I and my vessel are not involved in any race with any other boat that may leave New Orleans this day."

Raucous laughter echoed throughout the restaurant.

"Sure, Leathers," a distinguished man said. "Neither am I."

An elderly man holding fistfuls of dollars strode up and stood between the two men. "Really?" he said. "Then tell me something, Captain Cannon. How come the *Robert E. Lee* is leaving today at 5:00 with no cargo? No passengers? And no earthly reason for sailing to St. Louis?"

"I already told you, Posner. I'm sailing the *Lee* to Louisville to pick up a shipment. It is Captain Leathers that is racing today—not I."

The laughter pounded in Spur's head.

"You mealy-mouthed, egg-sucking old fart!" Leathers said. "I'm doing no such thing!"

John Cannon fingered his long white beard and smiled. "And neither am I."

Uproarious laughter. Money changed hands all around Spur. A momentous race was about to begin —despite the men's assurances to the contrary— and everyone was betting on it.

He vaguely recalled hearing about it and seeing posters concerning the race when he got into town. Spur scratched his stomach and realized he'd get no food in that restaurant. When a fresh mass of people pushed against him, trying to squeeze into the already crowded room, Spur slipped through them and went outside.

He stopped as the sunlight hit him. A race. The couple in the hotel room next to his had mentioned a race two nights ago. That had been Teresa and Hanover.

He made a mental note. If he didn't catch up with them by 4:00 that afternoon, he'd be watching a race between two steamships—the *Natchez* and the *Robert E. Lee.*

CHAPTER SIXTEEN

Teresa Salvare dipped sparkling water into her hands and poured it over her body. Around her, the world awoke. Birds sang. Clouds passed far overhead. The stream trickled. And sunlight flooded the cottonwood and willow trees that hid her bath from prying eyes.

She could only smile as she cleansed her body of the effects of her night in a dirty horse stall. How ridiculous! They had more money than they could spend in a year and yet they couldn't do any better than an empty livery stable for lodgings. It was absurd, but true.

Enough of this bathing, she thought, and wriggled her perfectly formed nude body. The filtered sunlight and a gentle breeze both warmed and chilled her. As she looked up onto the bank of the nameless stream, Teresa realized that if Lamb didn't return soon she'd be trapped in the open, naked, with nowhere to go.

Footsteps crunched through the underbrush ahead. She instinctively bent and hid behind a stand of brilliant orange and black coneflowers.

"Tessa?" a man's voice softly said.

Lambert appeared with two sets of clothing over his arms.

She stood and ran to him. "I thought you'd never get here! Figured you might've run off with some woman."

He arched his eyebrows and laid the woman's clothing over a bush. "Aren't you forgetting, my dear? All the money's back here with you. I'm not that stupid. Now hurry and dress while I have my bath."

"Okay. Did you have any trouble getting the clothing?" Teresa said, bending to study the florid red silk dress.

Lambert G. Hanover undressed. "Not at all. I found a very accommodating woman who sympathized with our plight—being thrown from our carriage—and she was so glad to help out."

"How sweet! Get into that water, Lamb. You smell like you spent the night in horse dung!"

"Dung?"

Teresa struggled into the single petticoat her partner had managed to get. "Yes. This morning, it's dung."

After breakfast, Spur found the front page of a newspaper in the road. It had been ground into the dirt but was still readable. Dated Thursday, June 30, which was today's date, it wouldn't have caught his eye if it hadn't had a screaming headline:

THE STEAMERS WILL RACE!!
Despite their claims to the contrary, Captain

John W. Cannon of the *Robert E. Lee* and Captain Thomas P. Leathers of the *Natchez* will indeed launch their momentous race at exactly 5 o'clock this afternoon. Cannon has stripped his vessel of all cargo and even passengers to increase his speed, while Leathers is taking both on board as usual.

Enquiries have been coming in from San Francisco, New York, St. Louis, London, Lisbon, Paris and many other cities. The worldwide attention which has been drawn to the race has undoubtedly caused millions of dollars to be bet on the outcome. We'll know in three or four days who will come out ahead. The stakes are, of course, high: The captain who proves that his steamer is the fastest during the 1,200 mile race will undoubtedly enjoy the most cotton shipping business in the future.

This is the race of the century! The Mississippi will become a gigantic raceway for the two captains, well-known within town for their mutual dislike. The *Picayune* will produce a special race issue with all the results as soon as they're known.

McCoy reread the article. Millions of dollars have been bet? Hmmm. Were Hanover and Teresa planning on stealing that money, or perhaps the funds of the passengers which, according to the article, will only be riding on the *Natchez?*

Spur walked down to the wharf. Dozens of boats of every description bobbed gently on the slow-moving water. He saw the *Princess,* the *Dubuque,* *City of Chester* and several other before he finally spotted both the *Natchez* and the *Robert E. Lee.* The names of the last two had been proudly repainted over the sternwheels.

The *Robert E. Lee* was unusually quiet for a working steamer. No roustabouts were loading bales of cotton. No early arriving passengers were waiting to go on board. The ship was practically deserted. Even the boiler deck was empty of its usually boisterous hands.

The *Natchez*, however, gave the appearance of businss as usual. Spur watched the sturdy-boiled, black men hauling cotton on board. Off-duty deck hands crouched in circles, probably enjoying a round of that dice game they'd invented—craps.

The air filled with the smell of wood smoke. A riverboat slipped its moorings. White steam and smoke poured from the two sets of stacks. The *Dubuque* majestically moved upriver, joining the ragtag fleet of barges, rafts and keelboats that littered the surface of the Mississippi River.

As he watched the *Dubuque* head away from New Orleans, Spur felt all of his efforts toward capturing Hanover and Teresa flowing away as well.

But he still had at least one chance of finding them before the *Natchez* left on "the race of the century." The thieves had left Mrs. Widdington's house without their luggage. If they were going to pass themselves off as rich folks, they'd have to get new clothes.

Spur sighed and headed for the dress and fine men's wear stores. Every single one of them was closed, so he went to a saloon, stood at the bar and got a watered whiskey.

He drank, listened in on the local gossip, played one hand of poker and returned to his hotel. As he walked in the deskman called him over.

"Good morning, sir. A telegram came in for you just a few moments ago."

He took the wire and went up to his room. Sitting on his bed, Spur ripped open the envelope and read the message.

It was to the point. General Halleck wanted to know how he was doing on the case and when he'd be turning over Lambert G. Hanover and Teresa Salvare to the proper authorities—alive, if at all possible. He was also instructed to recover as much of the money, stocks and bonds as he could find.

Spur crumpled the telegram and threw it against the far wall of his hotel room. So her last name was Salvare. That was news to him, he thought, as he took off his hat and stretched out on the bed. McCoy crossed his legs and wedged his hands behind his head. This was the worst case he'd ever worked on.

Absolutely no leads. Nothing to go on. Spur closed his eyes, hoping it would help him think.

A vigorous knocking on the door roused him from his mental activity. He rose and went to it. The lovely face shocked and surprised him.

"Good, you're here, Mr. McCoy," the blonde-haired woman said. "May I come in?"

He smiled and stepped back to allow Teresa Salvare into his hotel room. He should march her to the police but she was only half the prize he was after. He'd play along for as long as possible.

"How've you been, Marie?"

Teresa twirled her white parasol. "As well as can be expected. I was, ah, staying at a friend's house but she up and died. I mean, the poor dear *dropped dead* before my very eyes!" She laid on a smooth Southern accent. "It was so horrifying that I didn't know what to do."

"And so you came to me for comfort?"

Teresa looked back into the hall. "Well, not exactly. You see, I didn't tell you much about myself yesterday, after we—well, you know." She smiled.

"No?"

"No. In fact, I didn't tell you anything."

Spur started to close the door. Teresa went to it.

"Ah, leave it open!" she cried.

"Open?" He sighed. "I guess you didn't come back here for round three."

"No." The parasol spun in an endless circle. "You see, I'm—I'm in trouble."

He nodded. Was she actually willing to confess? It didn't seem possible that this was the woman who'd threatened to kill him in Wet Prong, and had most probably tried to do so in her hotel room.

"What kind of trouble?"

Teresa closed her umbrella and rested its tip on the floor. "I—I don't know how to tell you this."

"Just go ahead. It's best to get things out in the open. Don't you think?"

She smiled. "That's just what my mother always used to say. Okay. The truth is, I find that I'm rather, ah, low on funds. When I saw the dress shops here I spent and spent. Then there were the hotel feels and dining and—well, Spur, I'm flat broke. I don't have a penny to my name."

He tried to look sympathetic. "Poor woman!" Spur had to admire her: she was an excellent actress. No wonder Teresa and Hanover had been such successful con artists. "What can I do for you?"

She paced and looked around the room. "Well, ah, if you would find it in your heart to make me a small loan, I would make it worth your while."

Teresa Salvare stopped and gazed at him. She parted her lips and smiled. "I truly would. And I'd repay you as soon as I could."

"Well, it won't do, a beautiful woman like you in this city short on funds." What was she getting at? Had she and Hanover left the money somewhere on the way to New Orleans? Or had she hardened herself and was about to kill him? But if the latter was the case, why hadn't she let him close the door? Nothing made any sense.

"Of course, Marie. All you had to do was to ask." He reached into his pockets, frowned and snapped his fingers. "Damn! I just deposited most of my money in a local bank. Can't be too careful with all the pickpockets around here."

She smiled. "Of course."

"I could write you a check—"

"I would appreciate it, but what I really need is cash. You see, I'm supposed to be leaving on a riverboat this afternoon and I can't pay for my passage."

"Hmmmm." Spur pretended to think it over. "Tell you what. Let's run down to the bank. I could withdraw as much as you need. Then, when you're back on your feet again, you could send the money to my uncle, General Halleck, in Washington, D.C."

"Your uncle is a general?" she asked, still playing the Southern belle.

"Now now, Marie. No sense in worrying over the war. Besides, he never went into the field."

"I'm sure. That would be absolutely wonderful, Spur!" She kissed his cheek. "That way I could leave New Orleans and get back home!" Her eyes shined.

He walked to the bed and picked up his hat.

"Where is home, Marie? Where do you live?"

"Well, I'm originally from Baton Rouge, but I'm rejoining my brother and his young ones in St. Louis. His wife left him just a few months ago and the poor dear simply can't take care of everything alone."

Time to get things moving. "I see." He straightened the wide-brim Stetson on his head and grunted. "Shall we go now, *Teresa*?"

"Yes. I can't thank you enough—" Her eyes widened. "My name's Marie."

"Sure it is. Where's Hanover?"

Their gazes met.

"I don't know what you're talking about."

"You can drop the Southern accent, Teresa. If you won't talk I guess I'll have to lock you up by yourself. He'll come after you." Spur pointed toward the hall. "Now walk!"

"Just like that?" Teresa asked.

"Yes. You came here to confess, didn't you?"

"No. That's not what I came here for at all." Teresa moved to the door.

Spur closely followed her. Just as she stepped out of the room, she dropped her parasol and put a hand to her mouth.

"Oh dear! I almost forgot something!"

"What's that?" Spur asked.

Teresa Salvare ripped the bodice of her dress and screamed as loud as she could.

"RAPE!"

CHAPTER SEVENTEEN

"What are you talking about?" Spur McCoy demanded as he stood outside his hotel room.

"Rape! Rape!"

Teresa Salvare grabbed Spur's hands and immediately pretended to wrestle herself from his grasp. Her dress and petticoats flailing around her, the woman pushed her way through the doorway and ran out into the hall, gasping, crying hysterically.

Two burly men at the end of the hall rushed up to her. Both wore uniforms.

"Hotel security, ma'am," one of them said, frowning below his thick red moustache. "What seems to be the problem?"

"He—he tried to rape me!" Teresa said. Catching her breath, she started to scream again. "He tried to pull my dress right off of me!"

Spur stood his ground. "This is outrageous! I did no such thing. She's lying!" Spur said.

One of the security guards raised an eyebrow. "Uh huh. And I suppose she ripped her dress all by herself, right? With no help from you?"

"Precisely."

Teresa increased the volume of her screams, stopping only to yell. "He said he'd kill me if I didn't—didn't—"

McCoy couldn't believe what was happening. The woman had set him up. She'd planned the whole thing. That was why she hadn't allowed him to close the door.

"Come with us, sir," the red-haired security guard said. "Help me out, Burroughs."

The two men warily advanced on Spur and quickly grabbed his arms. He was immobile. The woman's sudden actions had confused him to the point that he hadn't drawn his weapon.

"Take him away!" Teresa screeched. "Lock him up! Such vicious men shouldn't be allowed to walk the streets of New Orleans! I hate this city! I hate all men! The nerve of him thinking he could compromise my virtue!"

"Gentlemen!" Spur shouted above the woman's raucous voice. "I'm Spur McCoy, an agent of the United States Secret Service. This woman is wanted for robbery in Kansas city and right here in this town. She's trying to—"

The men tightened their grip.

"Unhand me!"

"Shut up!"

The pair of burly hotel security guards rustled Spur to the stairs and "helped" him down them. Heads turns as the three men walked across the lobby. Spur regained his senses and didn't struggle as they stepped into the sunshine.

"Sergeant Malbrough!" Burroughs said as a big-headed man barrelled down the street toward them.

"What is it, Don? Some trouble at the hotel again?"

"A woman complained that this man just tried to rape her. Right in the Hollister."

"Good work, men," the police sergeant said as he removed Spur's Colt .45 from his holster. "Would you be so kind as to escort him to the jail? He's a big 'un. I think I'll need your help."

"Be glad to, sir. Come on!"

"Sergeant Malbrough, this is uncalled for!" Spur yelled. "The woman who said I attacked her is wanted for robbery in at least two states, possibly more. If you'll send a telegram to General Halleck in Washington, at the Secret Service, I'm sure we can clear all this up."

"Oh, of course we can," he said, beaming. "Of course we can!" He went to speak with Teresa Salvare, who stood sobbing in the middle of the street.

Twenty minutes later, Spur was behind bars. He hadn't tried to resist because he was weaponless and outnumbered. Now, as he sat in the filthy, damp jail cell, Spur stared at the green fungus that grew along the walls and sighed.

The woman was absolute poison. She was so audacious, waltzing into his room and then charging him with rape just to get him out of the way for a while. Though the charges wouldn't stick, it could prevent him from stopping Teresa and Hanover from boarding the *Natchez* before its historic trip to St. Louis. If the racing boat was as fast as the paper had said, it would be there in record time and he'd be still rotting in a New

Orleans jail cell.

Even if he was suddenly released just moments after the *Natchez* sailed it would take him weeks to ride up to St. Louis. Hanover and Teresa would have vanished by then, with the money they'd stolen, and he would be suffering through the humiliation of his first failure at solving a case since he'd started working for the Secret Service.

The thought made him grunt. McCoy stood and paced the 8 foot by 7 foot room. He hadn't seen anyone since he'd been dumped into the cell. The sergeant had had to go off to do something and no one else was around. Even the other cells were empty, save for two snoring drunkards who shared one among them. They lay face down on the floor.

Spur grabbed a tin cup from the floor and banged it on the bars. He kept it up for five minutes until a harried Sergeant Malbrough finally reappeared.

"Cut down on that racket!" he yelled. "You'll wake up my other two guests!"

"Sergeant, believe me. I'm a Secret Service agent. I'm a federal law enforcement man. Two notorious artists, Lambert G. Hanover and Teresa Salvare, are in New Orleans. I've been tracking them for two weeks now, after I was called to the case by my boss. They stole something like two-hundred thousand dollars in cash and negotiable stocks and bonds in a protracted Kansas City spree. The—"

Malbrough planted his hands on his hips and laughed. "Do tell?"

"I'm trying to!" Spur said, but he soon quenched his anger. "I'm no common criminal and I never tried to rape that woman. Look, Malbrough. What would it hurt to send a telegram to Washington? What would it hurt to wire General Halleck at the

Secret Service?"

The sergeant scratched his chin. "It'd cut into my leisure time. Oh, I'll admit you're a very smooth talker. But you're up against a very serious charge, Yankee. We don't cotton to men who try to take women against their will. Shit, McCoy, there's plenty of them who'll do it. They're all over the place—and not just the ones who charge, neither. My boy, you're in a heap of trouble."

Spur nodded. "Granted. Granted! Just send the telegram."

"Why should I go out of my way to waste my time on the likes of you?" he asked, and spat on the floor.

"Here." Spur dug into his pocket until he found what he'd been looking for. "Catch!"

Sergeant Malbrough's hand came down around the twenty-dollar gold piece that Spur flipped to him.

"The telegram's on me," McCoy said. "Okay?"

The Southern policeman whistled. "That's a lot of money. You tryin' to bribe me, boy?"

"Just send the damn telegram!" Spur said. "And, if it isn't too much trouble, have one of your men go to my room at the Hollister Hotel. Room twenty-five. If my bag hasn't been stolen, he'll find a document hidden inside the bottom explaining who I am and what my ongoing mission is."

Malbrough raised his eyebrows, took off his hat, wiped his forehead and grunted.

"Washington won't be too happy to hear that you've locked up one of their special law enforcement agents. It's best that you release me as soon as possible. These things do happen," Spur admitted, "but how'd you feel if I mistook you for a murderer, threw you into a cell and had the gallows readied to snap your neck before I even found out who you were? Think about that, Malbrough!"

The sergeant rubbed the gleaming coin. "Yeah. Well, I should send a wire to my cousin in New York anyway." He nodded. "Okay, McCoy. I'll do it, since you paid me. But just don't go anywhere." Malbrough laughed. "You hear me? Stay put?" He walked out.

Spur sat on the rickety bed and shook his head. A few minutes before he'd been thinking that this was the most confounding case he'd ever been on. Now, incredibly, it had gotten that much worse.

General Halleck will clear things up. Spur knew he would. But how soon? If he didn't get out by four, he only hoped that the *Natchez* would be late in leaving the wharf and sailing for St. Louis. That wasn't too likely since it was involved in the biggest race the Mississippi had ever known.

Teresa slipped into the Rue Orleans Hotel and quickly went to her room. Once inside she closed and locked the door and started undressing as she stared triumphantly at her finely dressed partner.

"How'd it go?" Lambert G. Hanover asked as he puffed on his cigar.

"Like a charm. Spur invited me into his room even. He knew who I was, all right, but he played along like he didn't. Finally, he called me by my real name, so I yelled rape like we'd planned." Teresa smiled. "The sergeant was very understanding as he interviewed me afterwards. Hell, I soaked his shoulder with my tears!"

"And? And?" Hanover stood. "What happened?"

"My dear Lamb, Spur McCoy—our enemy—is

locked up. Behind bars. The poor dear can't possibly stop us from boarding the steamer!"

Hanover blew out his breath. "Good. That settles that. Within hours we'll be mixing with the elegant crowd. We'll do everything that we've planned to do. Get to know the merchants, the planters, the foreign dignitaries. I'll gamble. You'll gossip and make new friends. Then, just before we dock at St. Louis, we'll go through as many of their staterooms as possible. We'll pick pockets like mad. We'll be among the first ones off. After that, it's the train and we'll be heading for San Francisco."

Teresa Salvare slipped the dress from her shoulders and stood in her chemise and petticoats. "Won't that be a glorious day, Lamb! No more running. No more hiding. I'm so tired of all this!"

"So am I." Hanover crushed out his cigar. "You sure are beautiful, Tessa, standing there in your underthings, your round, firm tits jutting against your chemise." He grinned and went to her.

"Why Lambert G. Hanover!" she said, throwing her hands over her bosom. "I'm shocked at such an ungentlemanlike statement coming from your lips."

"That's not all that's going to come from me."

He grabbed her. Teresa laughed as the man gently pulled her to the floor.

Spur stood motionless in his cell. One of the drunks coughed and rolled over on his bunk. There were no windows and no clocks in sight, but he knew he'd been locked up for at least two hours. If it got any later . . . .

The sound of the boots approaching the rear of the jail cell announced the return of Sergeant Malbrough. Sure enough, he soon appeared in the doorway holding a piece of paper.

"I'll be damned! I can't believe it!"

"Believe what?" Spur asked.

"Well, I sent the telegram like you asked me and waited around for an answer. You could've blown me over when the answer came back an hour or two later." The policeman shrugged. "I guess you are who you say you are. I wired this here Halleck fella what happened along with a description of you. He told me to let you go, that I was 'obstructing justice.' So I had one of my boys go to your hotel room. Sure enough, we found this."

Malbrough pushed a familiar piece of paper through the bars. Signed by General Halleck, it was a concise declaration that McCoy did indeed work for the United States Government. It didn't mention the Secret Service but it had apparently convinced the sergeant of his innocence.

"Sorry, McCoy. I guess that wild woman really is a thief." He grabbed the keys.

"She sure as shit is. I don't blame you, Malbrough. Just don't let it happen again."

"I won't." The man unlocked the cell. "You can count on that!"

"Where's my piece?" McCoy asked as he finally walked from the iron-barred prison.

"Right here." The sergeant pulled Spur's Colt .45 revolver from where he'd stashed it under the waist of his pants. "If I can help you out, let me know."

"You can start by telling me the time." Spur checked the cylinders and holstered his weapon.

"Time? Uh, think it's about 3:30. Something like that. Why? You going somewhere?"

Spur slapped a hand onto the crown of his hat and dashed for the door. "Yeah, I have a boat to catch!"

CHAPTER EIGHTEEN

Spur McCoy bolted from the jail and shot into the street. It took him a second to get his bearings but he was soon off toward the distant wharves.

As he hurried through the streets of New Orleans, he had no idea if Sergeant Malbrough's guess at the time was correct. Two- and three-story buildings blocked a clear view of the two boats he was after. After a few minutes every street looked the same, the same hotels, the same wrought iron balconies, the same baskets filled with flowering plants.

McCoy slowed to let a buggy through the intersection and then took off again. His unfamiliarity with the city wasn't helping now that he had a deadline. Spur silently cursed Teresa Salvare until he finally got his bearings and headed straight for the wharves.

New steamboats had taken the places of the ones that had left since he'd been down by the river that morning. Spur smiled as he saw that both the *Robert*

E. Lee and the *Natchez* were both still in port.

Hundreds of people milled around before the grand steamers. It must be the wealthiest crowd ever assembled in New Orleans for any purpose. Between the gawkers and the men exchanging fistfuls of money for bets on the race's outcome, vendors hawked their wares and children cried. Spur saw at least two pickpockets at work but didn't give them any attention. He had bigger fish to catch.

He pushed his way through the people, patiently at first, excusing himself and tipping his hat to the ladies whom he squeezed by. Soon the crowd pressed toward the steamships, crushing him between a fetid fat man and an elderly woman barely able to hold herself up with her cane.

Then the shouting began. Shouts of jubilation, boasts of superior betting skill, challenges and counterchallenges between the opposing sides.

Applause broke out. Spur looked up to see the white-bearded captain of the *Robert E. Lee* walk up the gangplank to his steamboat. Though he couldn't be unaware of the crowd's presence he never acknowledged them, simply went onto his craft.

"The *Lee*'s taking off four minutes before the *Natchez,*" someone nearby yelled. "They'll make it into St. Louis before the Nuthatch slips its moors!"

"Oh yeah? Look, Knepher, I've told you again and again that leaving early don't mean they'll win. They'll have to take four minutes off their arrival time."

Passengers began boarding the *Natchez*. Spur felt his pulse quicken as he watched the procession of well-dressed women and men strolling onto the glistening steamer. He kept a close watch but didn't see anyone who resembled Hanover and Teresa. Still, they may already be on board.

Or they could be lost in the crowd. Spur angrily pushed through the people. As he tried to slip through the crowd, a large man banged him with his shoulders and knocked McCoy sideways. Only the sea of humanity kept him from tumbling from the ground.

Wisps of steam rose from the double lower stacks of both paddleboats. Sparks and thick black smoke belched out of the fluted tops of the larger chimneys, the remains of the firewood that the steamers were burning to heat its boilers. They were preparing to set sail.

He had to reach the *Natchez.*

The pockets hidden in Teresa Salvare's dress were bulging with the money she stolen from the crowd that had gathered to watch the start of the race. She was well pleased with the day's take but it was getting late.

The whistles from the *Natchez* warned her that it was time to find her partner and to board. But there were so many people and so little room that she bit her lower lip. Would she be able to meet him in time?

"All aboard!" a white-suited man called from the foot of the gangplank leading to the *Natchez.* "We leave in four minutes!"

Four men released her mooring lines and the *Robert E. Lee,* its stacks increasing their output by the second, nudged forward from the wharf. An American flag flapped proudly from her bow. The race was on.

Don't panic, Teresa told herself. You have four minutes. But what if she couldn't find Lamb? Should she get on without him?

No. He has the money. *He has the money!*

They'd agreed to meet by the gangplank just as the *Lee* left. Teresa realized that ladylike behavior wasn't called for here. She kicked and clawed her way through the crowd, getting through the people as fast as she could, forging her own trail through the human forest.

She made good progress, but her destination was still 50 feet away. Teresa bit her lip again. It hurt. She liked it.

"Miss Salvare!" a familiar voice called.

Teresa turned. Sergeant Malbrough waved his hat at her from several yards away. If the man knew her real name the game was over. She hurried twice as fast toward the safety of the steamboat.

"Come back here! You got me into a lot of trouble!" he yelled, as Teresa tried to melt into the crowd.

Spur kept an eye on the boarding passengers. No tall couple. No one who even remotely looked like them—so far. Unless he'd missed a face or two while dodging hundreds of sweating bodies.

He finally edged his way closer to the gangplank, nearly punched out a man to get past him and finally stood beside the uniformed officer.

"Good afternoon, sir," he said to Spur, beaming. "Get on board, please. We're about to embark. We have to maintain our schedule."

Spur waved him off and studied the men, women and the few children who stepped onto the *Natchez*. Behind him, the *Robert E. Lee* had pulled well into the water and was laboriously puffing its way up the Mississippi.

Half the crowd ran along the enbankment,

following the paddlewheel, while the *Natchez* supporters stayed put. The sudden thinning of the crowd gave Spur a better look at them. One face instantly stood out.

True, he'd shaved off his Van Dyke beard and lightly reddened his hair, but that was the man who'd knocked him out in Wet Prong. Spur was certain of it.

He was even more sure as the finely dressed man looked his way, recognized him and ran.

Spur dashed past three nuns and tackled the tall thief. Hanover dropped the two leather bags he'd been carrying and went down on the ground. Spur sat on his chest and slammed his fist into the man's jaw. His well-placed punches soon did their damage. The skin broke. Blood appeared beneath his knuckles.

"Lamb!" a woman's voice called.

"Miss Salvare!"

"Someone help that poor man!"

He punched Hanover twice more until the groggy man's head fell back. He was out cold.

Spur shot to his feet. Three yards behind him, Teresa Salvare stood frozen, her hands limp at her sides, her mouth open.

"Come here. The game's over," McCoy said, panting.

Teresa turned to run but stopped as she saw Sergeant Malbrough approaching her with his revolver out and ready for business. The woman screamed and bolted for the gangplank, which a pair of roustabouts were just removing from the *Natchez*.

"No. Wait!" she wailed.

Spur easily cut her off and caught the beautiful

woman in his arms. "Don't fight it," he said. "Malbrough!" he shouted as Teresa dissolved into tears.

"Yes sir!" came the prompt response.

"Get those two bags! Beside Hanover!"

"Already got them, McCoy."

Spur smiled down at Teresa. "You can stop acting," he said. "I'm not buying it."

"Good. Because I'm not selling it."

Malbrough appeared with the leather bags in one hand. In the other he held Hanover's belt and the back of his pants. He'd dragged the man there.

"Let's lock these two up. I've been this close to them so often that I don't doubt they'd try to slip away again. And remember, Malbrough, we have to deliver them alive!"

The police sergeant clicked together his heels. "Yes sir!"

"Bastard!" Teresa Salvare said. "You bastard! We could have gotten away with it!" She spat.

Spur smiled as the warm saliva ran down his cheek. "But you got cold feet. Why didn't you kill me yesterday morning in your room? You had the chance."

She turned her head.

McCoy pulled her closer. "Come on. Why didn't you?"

"I—" The lovely criminal faced him again. Tears splashed her face. "Because you were so goddamn handsome that I lost my mind."

He laughed. "Okay, Malbrough. Let's get this trash off the wharf."

"My feelings exactly, McCoy."

Spur released one of Teresa's arms. "Hand me the bags. You take Hanover."

The woman stamped McCoy's foot with her boot. He howled. At the height of his unexpected pain she wriggled out of his grasp and ran.

"Damn it, woman!" Spur shouted. He took two flying paces and grabbed her waist, halting the woman's flight. "Not again. Not this time, Teresa."

"Let me go! Leave me alone!" she screamed.

He took her back to where Sergeant Malbrough still stood, holding out the bags for Spur.

"You're absolutely sure these are the ones?" the policeman said.

"Here. Take this." He pushed Teresa into the man's arms and took the bags. They were well packed. Inside he didn't find any clothes. No petticoats or handkerchiefs or fancy dresses made the sides bulge.

Spur McCoy pulled out a wad of cash.

"Yes," he said.

CHAPTER NINETEEN

At seven that evening, Spur McCoy was in his hotel room packing his bags. He'd just been to see Sergeant Malbrough again to assure himself that Lambert G. Hanover and Teresa Salvare were still behind bars.

Fortunately, they were, and Malbrough said that while the man wasn't saying a word, the woman was spilling out all the details of their "work." She almost seemed proud of it, the policeman had told him.

Spur had suggested that Malbrough put on extra guards and he had instantly done so.

Now, as he bent over his leather bags, Spur sighed. His work in New Orleans was nearly finished. All he had to do was transport the pair back to Kansas City.

That wouldn't be an easy task, not with them. Hanover and Teresa were experts at slipping away from him, so Spur had decided to take precautions to make sure that he managed to get them safely back to the city where they'd started their more recent crimes.

Travelling by buggy or horseback was out. It was too unpredictable and unsafe, not to mention the distance and travel time involved. Spur had searched for another way and was glad to hear that the steamboat *City of Charles* was leaving for Kansas City in two days. He booked passage.

Sure, it might be humiliating for Teresa and Lambert to spend five or six days in chains, but it was the only way he could be certain that they wouldn't escape. Sergeant Malbrough had offered to send a policeman along with Spur to keep an eye on the couple. It was a good idea and he had readily agreed to bring the fresh-faced young man with them.

He'd gone through the single bag that the pair had planned to take with them (the others, he thought, had probably been loaded on board, but there was no stopping the *Natchez* during its cruise to history). He'd counted precisely $110,000 in both bills and gold coins. Apparently even fussy when it came to money, Hanover had either only taken $100 bills or he'd had it changed into the higher denominations along the way. The money was clean and neatly stacked.

There were hundreds of stocks and negotiable bonds as well. It didn't look like they'd spent too much on their two and a half week trip from Kansas City to New Orleans.

Spur had wired General Halleck his final report on the case. He could relax for the next day. There were no immediate problems, no criminals to capture.

He poured himself a drink, sipped the bitter liquid and put down his glass. He knew what he wanted, and he couldn't find it at the bottom of a whiskey bottle.

Spur changed into his best clothes and left his hotel room. The Gilded Garter Gambling Establishment beckoned to him, but he passed it by. The prostitutes called to him but he wasn't interested in them.

He was hungry.

What was the name of the restaurant? The one that Sergeant Malbrough had suggested to him? Spur searched the eating establishments. Finally he saw a familiar name on one of their signs: Pierre's.

He moved across the street and walked in. The air smelled of sizzling steaks and grilled seafood. Elegantly dressed men and women laughed, ate and danced to the music of a four-piece string quartet. Spur stood just inside.

"McCoy!" a voice yelled.

Spur turned and saw the burly policeman.

"Come on over here!" The cop said, broadly smiling as he sat at a table with his arms around two women. Both were dripping with jewels.

McCoy smiled and went to them. The girls smelled of perfume. Their gowns were lavish. They were strikingly beautiful and, from the way they resembled each other, probably sisters. Both had masses of raven hair and green eyes.

"Hello, sergeant," Spur said.

Malbrough cleared his throat. "Hi yerself. Found the place alright, I see."

"No problem."

"Spur McCoy, I'd like you to meet Violette and Helena Rosengarten. They're sisters. Can't you tell?

Just got in from Prussia. Isn't that right?"

"*Guten tag,*" they both said, then exploded into high pitched laughter.

The sergeant leaned over the table toward him. "They don't speak a word of English, but that's no problem. They speak everything else." He settled back in his velvet-cushioned chair and squeezed Helena's shoulder. "Isn't that right, doll?"

"Ladies," Spur said in greeting, touching the brim of his hat.

The younger of the two, Violette, fixed her gaze on Spur's face and played with the pearls that hung around her neck.

"So sit down!" Malbrough yelled. "Take a load off your feet and order a drink on me. We're just about to catch a bite to eat."

"Great. I'm starving."

Violette stared at him. She raised her glass and touched her tongue to its rim. Never taking her eyes off him, the beautiful woman licked back and forth.

Spur smiled and she returned the feeling. He knew—or hoped he knew—what would happen after dinner with the vivacious foreign woman.

But in two days he'd be back at work. Once he'd dropped off Teresa and Hanover in Kansas City, General Halleck would be sending him another assignment. It was times like this, between jobs, that he felt it was all worthwhile.

He sighed as Violette placed her glass on the table and boldly took his hand in hers. It sure was good to be back among the living again.

DIRK FLETCHER

In these Special Giant Editions, Secret Service Agent Spur McCoy comes up against more bullets and beauties than even he can handle.

Klondike Cutie. A boomtown full of the most ornery vermin ever to pan a river, Dawson is the perfect place for a killer to hide—until Spur McCoy arrives. Fresh from a steamboat and the steamiest woman he's ever staked a claim on, McCoy knows the chances of mining gold are very good in the Klondike. And to his delight, the prospects for golden gals are even better.
_3420-4 $4.99 US/$5.99 CAN

Soiled Dove. When train robbers make off with a fortune in federal money and the treasured daughter of Arkansas's governor, Spur McCoy is sent to recover the valuable booty and rescue the voluptuous body. Trouble is, the sultry hellion has plans of her own, and they don't include being saved by the Secret Service. But a hot-to-trot hussy will never get the better of Spur McCoy—not as long as there are bandits to round up and beauties to bed down.
_3801-3 $4.99 US/$5.99 CAN

Dorchester Publishing Co., Inc.
65 Commerce Road
Stamford, CT 06902

Please add $1.75 for shipping and handling for the first book and $.50 for each book thereafter. NY, NYC, PA and CT residents, please add appropriate sales tax. No cash, stamps, or C.O.D.s. All orders shipped within 6 weeks via postal service book rate. Canadian orders require $2.00 extra postage and must be paid in U.S. dollars through a U.S. banking facility.

Name _____
Address _____
City _____ State _____ Zip _____
I have enclosed $_____ in payment for the checked book(s).
Payment <u>must</u> accompany all orders.☐ Please send a free catalog.

BUCKSKIN

GIANT SPECIAL EDITION

Kit Dalton

TWICE THE FIGHTIN', TWICE THE FILLIES IN ONE GIANT SPECIAL EDITION!

Muzzle Blast. A vicious little hellcat with a heavenly body, Molly Niles is the kind of trouble Buckskin Lee Morgan likes, especially when she offers him cold cash to drive her horses from Niles City to Fort Buell. Lee takes the offer, and things heat up quick—on the trail and in his bedroll. By day, he has to keep the herd from stampeding; by night, he has to keep the busty blonde safe from her enemies. It's a tough job, but Morgan has grit enough to guide the ponies, and spunk enough to tame a wild filly like Molly.
_3564-2 $4.99 US/$5.99 CAN

Shotgun! Before Morgan can use his hot brand to claim the frontier fillies in Miles City, Montana, he has to stop a ruthless gang of owlhooters who are out to grab every head of steer in the state. Between shooting up the vicious rustlers, and bedding down the sultry hustlers, Morgan figures he's ready to be put out to pasture. But when the job is done, one thing i$ for sure: There won't be a cowgirl in the territory who Morgan can't corral.
_3730-0 $4.99

Dorchester Publishing Co., Inc.
65 Commerce Road
Stamford, CT 06902

Please add $1.75 for shipping and handling for the first book and $.50 for each book thereafter. NY, NYC, PA and CT residents, please add appropriate sales tax. No cash, stamps, or C.O.D.s. All orders shipped within 6 weeks via postal service book rate. Canadian orders require $2.00 extra postage and must be paid in U.S. dollars through a U.S. banking facility.

Name _____

Address _____

City _____ State _____ Zip _____

I have enclosed $_____ in payment for the checked book(s). Payment <u>must</u> accompany all orders.☐ Please send a free catalog.